MW00851635

The Scenturion Spy
Book One: Becoming a Spy

David M. Goldenberg

Last Writes, LLC
Delray Beach, Florida

Copyright 2022 by Last Writes, LLC *LW*

Hardcover ISBN: 978-1-959064-01-5
Paperback ISBN: 978-1-959064-02-2
Ebook ISBN: 978-1-959064-00-8

All rights reserved. No part of this book may be reproduced in any form or by any electronic means, including information storage and retrieval systems, without written permission from the author, except for the use of brief quotations in a book review.

Published by BookLocker.com, Inc., Trenton, Georgia.

Printed on acid-free paper.

This is a work of fiction. All incidents and dialogue, and all Characters, with the exception of some well-known historical figures, are products of the author's imagination and are not to be construed as real. Where real-life historical figures appear, the situations, incidents, and dialogues concerning those persons are entirely fictional and are not intended to depict actual events or to change the entirely fictional nature of the work. In all other respects, any resemblance to actual persons, living or dead, events, or locales is entirely coincidental.

BookLocker.com, Inc.
2022

First Edition

Library of Congress Cataloguing in Publication Data
Goldenberg, David M.
The Scenturion Spy: Book One: Becoming a Spy by David M. Goldenberg
Library of Congress Control Number: 2022915551

This book is dedicated to my late son,
Marc Daniel Goldenberg,
who gave us much pleasure during his short life;
to my parents,
Leo and Lille Goldenberg, who helped
make me who I am;
and to my deceased sister, Shirley,
who taught me how to read and guided my
early academic development.

1.

IT WAS NEARLY one o'clock on an ordinary Monday, and I was having lunch in the cafeteria of the medical center where I work. I had just finished my bowl of tomato soup — they have very good tomato soup there — when a tall man I didn't know walked up with a tray of food and asked if he could share my table.

Visitors to the hospital are always welcome in the cafeteria, so I didn't think much about it — though I did note that, with his blue double-breasted suit, crisp white shirt, and yellow tie, he didn't look like someone who'd come to visit a sick family member. I really wasn't in the mood for conversation — I wanted to enjoy my lunch while reflecting on the pathology lecture for second-year medical students that I'd just attended as a faculty member — but what else could I do?

"Be my guest," I said, gesturing to the chair opposite me. As he placed his tray on the table, I noticed that he'd ordered a grilled cheese sandwich, iced tea, and a light salad with ranch dressing.

"Thank you, Dr. Davidson," he said, taking his seat. I was surprised that he'd called me by name.

"Pardon me; I'm usually good at remembering faces, but have we met before?"

"No. My name is Bob Ehrlich. I spotted you from your description: 6 feet, 2 inches, physically trim – no extra weight but also not overtly muscular, short brown hair parted on his left side, an oval head with clear, clean facial features and thin lips, and large brown, penetrating eyes. And your ID badge confirmed it: *M. Davidson, MD, Ph.D., Pathology, Empire Medicine.*

"Nice to meet you," I said, trying not to be obvious about eyeing his tray.

"I'm glad we can sit together privately," he said, glancing about the room as he retrieved a small black leather case from his inside coat pocket. He opened it to show me a startling credential: *Robert Ehrlich, Special Agent, Central Intelligence Agency, United States of America.* The office address was in Lower Manhattan.

"What is this about?" I asked.

"You attended a conference on olfaction in Philadelphia recently, but we didn't recognize your name from other events involving this kind of research. After researching you, we found it surprising that a physician doing cancer research had an interest in the sense of smell. It was suggested that I make your acquaintance and find out more."

"There were at least two hundred and fifty attendees. Did you investigate every one of them?"

"We do have a list of all olfaction researchers in academia, government, and business, since olfaction is an area of special interest to us. And we like to know our resources — and your interest."

"Well," I said, "it's a pretty simple story, really. During my time in med school at Dartmouth, I also pursued a Ph.D. in sensory physiology, specifically olfaction. This stemmed from my undergraduate studies, including neuroscience — learning about behavior and the importance of the sense of smell in the animal kingdom, especially mammals and, of course, humans. So, when I read about this conference just a couple of hours away, in Philadelphia, I decided — impulsively, I guess — to sign up and see if the field has advanced since my day."

"And what was your conclusion?"

"I was very impressed with the progress made," I said, dabbing my mouth with a napkin. "The finding that changes in olfactory acuity occur with a number of neurological diseases, and even viral infections, was stimulating. I think this is very exciting from a scientific perspective, and lately, I've been thinking about it from a commercial perspective as well."

"Interesting," said Ehrlich, taking another quick look to see if anyone was observing us. "That is what we — as well as our adversaries — think, too," he said, lowering his voice.

"Really?" I said, "that's fascinating."

"Yes, it is. Listen, Dr. Davidson, do you have a few minutes to talk privately outside? I'd like to learn a little more about you and also to discuss how we might help each other."

"What do you mean?"

"Well, if you could help us with our olfaction research, perhaps we could reciprocate and be of assistance to you in your commercial interests."

I checked my watch and told him I could spare a half-hour if that would suffice. I had my teaching lab at three o'clock.

*

THE BLACK LINCOLN Town Car was parked at the curb about fifty feet away. When the driver saw us coming, he started the engine. Ehrlich opened the rear door, and I slid in first. "Jim, our driver, will take us for a short trip around the neighborhood while we chat," Ehrlich said, pulling the door shut. Jim nodded at me in the rear-view and slowly pulled away from the curb.

"Dr. Davidson, my colleagues at Langley asked me to confirm some information we have on you," said Ehrlich, "and to assess your ability and willingness to help your government in its security work. Your Ph.D. thesis involved the measurement of olfaction in humans, after developing an olfactometer. You also studied emotional or autonomic nervous system responses to an odor, and that's what we're interested in."

"You actually read my thesis?" I asked. "You're now a member of a very small club."

"We do our homework, Doctor. Permit me to summarize the main points and fill me in where needed."

How much do they know about me?

"Okay," I said tentatively. "Go ahead."

"You're the third and last child born to Libby and Larry Davidson. Your parents emigrated to the U.S. from the Soviet Union when they were twenty and twenty-two years old, respectively. Your parents had two other children — your brother, who was twelve years older than you, and your sister, who was ten years older. How am I doing?"

"Perfect. But continue."

"Your family lived in a modest apartment in Williamsburg, Brooklyn, where your mother kept a kosher home, and you and your siblings were raised as traditional Jews, going to Hebrew school, having Bar Mitzvahs, and so on. The youngest of three children, you're now forty-one years old."

"That's right," I said softly.

"Your parents and sister are deceased, and your brother is retired after a career in real estate…"

I nodded — all true.

"Tell me about your boyhood and your schooling," said Ehrlich. "Did you have hobbies? Who were your close friends?"

In spite of my reluctance, I complied. *Why, exactly, am I doing this?*

"Living in a crowded tenement in Williamsburg, I had to grow up quickly. I roamed the streets with neighborhood buddies at a very early age, playing on empty lots, stickball in the street, and later at the school yard or the basketball courts in the shadow of the Williamsburg bridge. I knew kids of all races and ethnicities, and as we got older, some of them became parts of rival gangs — African Americans, Latinos, or

Caucasians from a variety of backgrounds, mostly Irish, Italian, Jewish, and Polish.

"Most of us went on to John D. Wells Jr. High School. I really excelled there, getting involved in student government, first as the eighth-grade representative and then, in the ninth grade, as school president. This was basically a popularity contest, and I was lucky to be running against a Jewish girl from an affluent family. A lot of the kids voting were Puerto Rican girls, and they preferred me to the Jewish 'princess.' Anyway, the election was more important than the activities afterward, other than my being able to leave classes when there were student government meetings. But as I look back on that time, being elected president gave me confidence and a sense of being different."

"Different how?"

"Not defined by my upbringing. Destined for a bigger life. I remember thinking I would like to become a judge – not knowing why and having no appreciation that I would need to go to law school."

"My senior high years were uneventful," I continued, "except for commuting daily to Stuyvesant High School in Manhattan for the late-morning session, and being more challenged academically than ever before. Commuting home during the afternoon rush-hour was truly combat training.

"I tried out for the football team but soon retired with a dislocated thumb. I wasn't built to be a football player, but I was a very fast sprinter — critical to surviving on the streets of Williamsburg, by the way — and later on, at the University of Chicago, I played intramural football with the dormitory teams. In the first two years, I made second string on the basketball team, playing guard because I was fast and a good shooter. But this meant that I played, at most, two or three minutes per game. Whenever winning was hopeless, I got to play longer."

"Tell me about your summer jobs," said Ehrlich.

"One summer, I was a delivery boy in Manhattan, transporting boxes of costume jewelry between factories in the jewelry section with a hand truck. This got me into good physical shape and a tan, I recall – many days were in the 90's. Another two summers, I worked as a busboy and then waiter at hotels in the Catskill mountains. It was there that I learned about the anthropology of wives and their kids living in these hotels during the week, visited by their 'hardworking' husbands on weekends. Some of the waiters, myself excluded, provided other forms of service to the women guests during the week."

"Why not you?"

"Jewish guilt, I guess."

Ehrlich nodded and smiled. "Thanks for this summary, Dr. Davidson. I'll share it with my colleagues, and I expect that my supervisor, Dr. Brad Williams, will be in touch with you soon." He signaled the driver to take us back to the medical center.

"In the meantime, we expect you to keep our meeting today strictly confidential. No mention to your colleagues at Empire State University, or ESU — you're to tell no one. Is this understood?"

"I won't tell anybody," I said. "But I have to say, I really don't know what to think about all this."

"Brad Williams will clarify everything when he gets in touch. Good-bye, Dr. Davidson."

I got out of the car and watched it disappear into the New York traffic.

Why did I tell him so much about myself, and what will this lead to? I guess when you're questioned by a CIA officer, you drop your usual need for privacy.

2.

IT WAS A beautiful May morning when I removed my pre-owned 2009 Jaguar XKR convertible — my one major luxury — from its expensive garage a few blocks from my apartment. Dropping the top, I drove from Manhattan to Queens and across the Whitestone Bridge to the Hutchinson River Parkway, then north on I-95 toward Westport, Connecticut. It felt great to be out of the city with the breeze in my hair.

I was excited and nervous about being on my way to my very first meeting with a venture capital group. My lawyer and I hadn't yet applied for a patent, but I had been diligently gathering my thoughts in preparation for writing my business plan. My pitch to the venture capitalist community, involved saying:

The sense of smell, among the five major senses, is the least understood compared to taste, sight, touch, and hearing. It is basically a chemical sensing system whereby odorants bind to specific receptors in the two nostrils, and the resulting neuronal electrical signals are transmitted to the olfactory bulbs in the brain, from where the nerve signals are distributed to other parts of the brain. These cerebral functions are responsible for the identification of odors, memory, and emotion.

If one could make drugs into odors that can be delivered both to the blood and brain via the lining of the nose, a medical business opportunity of 'olfactory pharmacology' could be created. Just like perfumes and cosmetics influence behavior, olfactory drugs could be designed to more specifically affect moods, thinking, and even neurological diseases.

The almost twenty venture capital firms I contacted either gave me a polite decline, saying the project was too early for their consideration, or just failed to respond. But I had heard about this V.C.

group, Sequel Ventures, from a friend in product development at Bristol-Myers Squibb. Sequel had told Bristol about a new technology that Bristol invested in, a small gene therapy company in Cambridge, Massachusetts. Sequel planned to take this company public as part of the investment by 'big pharma' and reap big profits on their startup investment of only $10 million.

It was an exciting thought. But how much should I say in our meeting? How much to reveal? With no patent yet, could I trust the V.C.s not to steal my idea?

A silly question: of course not. Yet, I decided to provide them with more information, since the sense of smell was not something that venture capitalists usually hear about. But this would not provide anything confidential to my business prospect:

Unlike sight and hearing, the sensitivity of the nose in humans is not precisely known, although some studies suggest that we can discriminate many thousands of olfactory stimuli or scents. Therefore, with hundreds of different olfactory receptors, it is much more sensitive than sight and hearing in terms of the number of stimuli that can be discriminated. These stimuli are usually mixtures of various odor molecules in different ratios. Since olfactory receptors in the nose that connect directly to the brain have been discovered, defined odors could be used to stimulate the brain and some of its functions instead of using pills or injections. Synthetic odors represent a new drug delivery method, particularly affecting human behavior and certain neurological diseases.

*

WESTPORT IS ONE of the smaller of the many picturesque and affluent towns on the Connecticut coast. The town green is anchored by the typical statue of a Revolutionary War soldier with his rifle held high. At each end of the oval are the obligatory cannons, and quaint shops surround the green and spill over to the intersecting streets leading to Long Island Sound.

My original contact at Sequel Ventures was with Bill Rhodes, the senior partner. I had written him a letter explaining that I'd been referred by our mutual acquaintance at BMS, and then I had described my idea very superficially, telling him also that I was in the process of writing a patent covering this invention. I said that if the subject were of interest to him, I would be willing to tell him more under a confidentiality agreement. I emphasized the uniqueness of the olfactory sense, and that it has so far never been explored in terms of making pharmaceuticals.

"We generally don't enter into CDAs until we're further along in discussions," Rhodes had told me when I followed up with a call. "We get a lot of proposals and select only a very few to pursue, but your letter did intrigue me," he admitted.

I was of course pleased, but I wondered how I could interest him in my idea if I couldn't disclose it beyond a general description. "Let's worry about that when you get here," Rhodes said.

So now here I am, waiting for the senior partner of a billion-dollar life science fund at Sequel to come out to meet me in their reception area. All around me were framed announcements, or 'tombstones' of public offerings of their many investments displayed — Centercede, Immunoproton, Medattack, Therapy Seeds, and others, working with such prominent bankers as Lehman Brothers, Oppenheimer, Salomon, J.P. Morgan. If this were to impress visitors and potential clients, it worked.

Finally, Bill Rhodes came out to greet me in the reception area. "Dr. Davidson," he said. "Thanks for coming. I'm Bill Rhodes."

"Call me Milt," I said, standing to shake his hand.

He smiled and escorted me to a conference room, where he immediately took a seat at the middle of the widest part of the long table, motioning me to sit directly across from him. "Would you like coffee or a cold drink?"

"I'm fine," I answered. Bill Rhodes was a powerful presence, the walking epitome of a confident, hard-driving, and financially comfortable player in both the financial and social worlds of New York and Connecticut. His tan attested to his hours of sailing, tennis, or golf — probably all three — with the 'right' people who played along the Connecticut shore of the Long Island Sound.

"I'd like to have one of our analysts join us," he said and made a quick call. Soon 'Robert Selden, M.D., Ph.D.,' as it said on his card, came in, greeted me, and sat down next to Rhodes.

Selden explained that he'd been working at Sequel for about a year, after earning a Ph.D. in physiology from Rockefeller University, and then an M.D. at Cornell medical school across the street on Manhattan's Upper East Side. After doing an internship at a Cornell-affiliated hospital in New York, Selden decided to go into investment banking, he explained, saying:

"Medicine intrigued me from an academic perspective, but I was anxious and often uncomfortable on the ward managing patients. I got interested in the pharmaceutical side of medicine and took a summer course at Columbia on the business side of drug development and marketing, getting intrigued with the new sciences being pursued in biotechnology.

"I read the brief summary of your business idea," Selden continued, "and found it both intriguing and quite radical. The notion of developing scents to affect different behavior patterns on a more objective, scientific basis is interesting, but I'm wondering how it could be the basis of a business."

I could tell that Rhodes wasn't pleased with Selden's launching right into the matter — it tipped me off that there was real curiosity, maybe even interest, in my project. At this point, though, I wasn't sure what to say. My attorney had warned me that until I had a patent that was found to be valid by the patent and trademark office — which we might not know for at least a year or two after filing — it could be treacherous to reveal too much. If I discussed an aspect that the patent wouldn't gain patent protection, I could risk its being adopted by another party.

"I can't really get into more specifics until we have a CDA," I said.

"Oh yes," said Rhodes. "Bob has our standard form for you to sign."

With that, Selden opened a folder and took out two copies of an eight-page confidentiality agreement and slid it over the table to me. I read through it quickly.

It looks reasonable, but what do I know?

"Well," I said, "my attorney wants to review all agreements before I sign them, so maybe I can just take this along and get back to you in a couple days."

Selden was noticeably displeased, but not the very cool Bill Rhodes. He just nodded to me and sat back, waiting for my next move.

"Let me just give you an overview of my technology and business plan, and we can get into more specifics once the CDA is in place — and, of course, once you've decided if you have an interest."

Rhodes again nodded, so I went on.

"Although I'm a practicing and academic research pathologist, involved in studying genes that may code for certain products made by cancer cells, I did research on olfaction during my graduate training for a Ph.D., while also completing my M.D. training at Dartmouth. I was interested in how defined odors could be measured and how they affected one's emotions."

Rhodes seemed perplexed, but Selden became more inquisitive. "What kind of behavior modification are you referring to, and what odors, in particular, were involved?" Selden asked. "Have you identified any new chemical classes? And, more importantly, how do you envision this as a new method of treating disease?"

We're now treading on proprietary information being developed in my patent filing, so I need to be very careful here.

"Pheromones are well-known as chemical substances that can affect behavior," I said, "and are usually used in the context of arousing sexual behavior in animals by the odors which contain these chemicals. It's well known that odors affect hormone production, even in humans. But although humans have these, they haven't been chemically defined, at least not extensively. I believe I have the ability to do this and to incorporate those related to specific behavioral responses, in different classes of individuals, based on certain genetic classes found in different populations. But I really can't get more specific until we have the CDA in place."

"In my view," I continued, "this can revolutionize the perfume business, and provide all sorts of behavior-modifying odors, from those that influence eating patterns, shopping, moods, and, of course, sexual arousal. Olfaction is also being studied in relation to disease, both from a diagnostic as well as a pathophysiological perspective."

As soon as I said it, I regretted saying so much. Now Bill Rhodes's initial skepticism had changed to something resembling interest, at least based on the intense way he was looking at me. Bob Selden was taking down copious notes.

"What genetic patterns would you define?" Selden said.

"This is really part of the invention," I said.

"Can you elaborate more on therapeutic applications?" asked Rhodes. I hesitated to respond. "Well, Dr. Davidson," Rhodes said, sliding back his chair, "we do appreciate your visiting with us. Please have your counsel review our CDA while we give this further consideration. We'll give you a decision of our initial interest or declination in a week or so. Okay?"

"Fine," I said. I stood to shake hands and leave.

"By the way," said Rhodes, "are you showing this to any other venture capital firms?"

In fact, I wasn't, but I didn't want them to know that. "I have a couple of appointments set up through my patent attorney, and a friend of mine presented the general idea to his companion, who is involved in the perfume business."

"Well," said Rhodes, "I wouldn't spread it around too much. The venture capital community is very small and well connected."

3.

WHAT AM I doing? I thought, heading to my car. This was basically a good meeting, but, no doubt, it was premature. I didn't even have a business plan to show.

And when was I going to find the time to get that written, anyway? I had published some twenty-five journal articles already, but that would need to grow to at least forty in the next four to five years if I were to be promoted to full Professor within five years of my current appointment as Associate Professor of Pathology. And these articles had to be in respected, high-impact journals. I knew this was the most intense moment in my career, especially if I intended to remain in academic medicine:

I love the challenge and excitement of discovery.

I didn't want to think about what wrenches the CIA might throw into my so-far-successful and seriously busy work life if they were really interested in working with me. Yet, no one from the CIA had followed up with me so far.

It felt good to be driving the quaint streets of Westport. Heading toward the waterfront, I realized I hadn't eaten since 7 a.m. when I had coffee and a Danish at the small deli a couple of blocks from my apartment.

After a delicious lunch in a small, local restaurant, I headed back into the city.

*

THE NEXT MORNING at about seven-thirty, after having downed a half-bowl of Cheerios and a glass of orange juice, I was out my door and walking east on 33rd Street toward the East River. The sun was shining, and the day was relatively cool, about sixty-five degrees. New York is at its best for me in the early morning, when only a few shops are just opening, the streets are just starting to fill with people, and cars are hurrying to various destinations. Feeling rested from my long sleep, I was enjoying my walk.

Then I felt the presence of someone following a little too closely behind me. I sped up, and so did he, but he caught up and began walking beside me on the curb side. He was tall and well dressed, not, apparently, one of the random weirdos one sometimes crosses paths with in the city. "Dr. Davidson," he said. "Brad Williams, I think you've been expecting me. Would you have a few minutes for a cup of coffee?"

We ducked into a small mom-and-pop café and ordered coffees at the counter, then took seats at a back table. Williams reached into his coat pocket and took out a business card, which he slid across to me. "Brad Williams, Ph.D., Associate Research Director, National Institute of Environmental Health Sciences, National Institutes of Health," it read, with an address in Rockville, Maryland. It all looked authentic to me — *of course, the CIA would be involved with the NIH.* I was surprised that Williams had a doctorate but kept it private. I didn't know many Ph.D.'s like that, but maybe it wasn't real.

Brad appeared to be about fifty or so, was very tall — well over six feet — with light-brown hair but already about half bald. "Thanks for meeting with my colleague Bob Ehrlich," he said. "Bob was impressed with you and recommended that we take this to the next level, especially since I was staying in New York for a couple of days."

He went on to explain that the NIH's National Institute of Environmental Health Sciences was forming a special task force to study the current state of applying odors in the workplace and in daily activities, including how to identify and prevent toxic effects of current and new olfactory substances, including fragrances of all kinds. I thought this was really farsighted — and what a coincidence!

"This Blue-Ribbon Committee will be attached to the National Institutes of Health," said Williams, "and you'll receive a modest honorarium for your time, plus travel reimbursement at the usual government rates. You'll have to have this approved by ESU, and of course, we'll supply the proper 'institutional' invitation."

"How much of my time are you talking about?" I asked.

"Maybe a couple of days four times a year, with occasional travel to relevant conferences. In fact, there's a conference in Vienna in a few weeks. We'd like you to attend."

"Vienna? What'll I tell my Chairman at ESU?"

"We'll take care of that. Your involvement with this prestigious group will be a feather in Empire's cap."

"Okay," I said, smiling. I was starting to feel very impressed with myself for being selected for this service to our country.

"You'll have to do a couple of days' orientation at Langley prior to the Vienna trip."

"Langley," I said. "Wow. But that's the CIA headquarters, right?"

"Yes," he answered. "The National Institute of Environmental Health Sciences is merely the front we're using to deal with our collaborators and their employers, instead of identifying us as the CIA," he murmured. "So, for all others, you'll be dealing with the NIEHS of the NIH, not the CIA!"

Williams smiled. "I'll set that up and get back to you with some dates to choose from," he said. Then he reached across the table to shake my hand. "Welcome to the team, Dr. Davidson."

*

THE REST OF the day was a blur. I felt like I was a movie star — Robert Redford in *Three Days of the Condor*, Matt Damon in *The Bourne Identity*. I had to force myself to focus on the now seemingly mundane tasks at hand.

When I got to my office, the first thing I did was check my phone for text messages. I had an hour before I had to attend a faculty meeting on our biology of disease course for second-year medical students. We met every other week to assess the progress of the course — how the teaching material was being received, what we could do differently and better, and so on. Some of these meetings were productive, but once we were so far into the course, it was more boring than not and usually degenerated into one of the faculty members complaining about not having enough time to present his or her materials, or something like that. A clash usually resulted, with the rest of the time deteriorating into arguments and no real changes or solutions.

After about half an hour, my reading was interrupted by a phone call from my lawyer, John Sackler, asking how the meeting with Sequel had gone the day before. I summarized it for him quickly, always feeling the pressure of having a $10-a-minute charge accumulating whenever we spoke. He agreed that I couldn't provide serious information to Sequel as long as their CDA was so one-sided, and we decided that he would revise it for their consideration.

The faculty meeting went just as I expected. We spent a worthwhile thirty minutes covering the content of the last week's lectures and student labs, and then the pediatric gastroenterologist started complaining that his disease section didn't pay enough attention and time to developmental problems in newborns and children. This was the perennial problem in all such multidiscipline, disease-oriented courses, where each area and representative felt he or she needed more time and attention from the students.

Egos are really big among educators, especially M.D.s in academic medicine.

I'm sure we all were thinking, *here we go again* — from my perspective, the fewer student-contact hours I had, the more time I could devote to my first love: research.

Emerging into the soft spring evening at the end of the day, I could hardly believe it had been only twelve hours since my unexpected conversation with Brad Williams.

I'm going to Langley.

It was a strange but exhilarating feeling to have this secret from all my acquaintances. *I guess this is what it's like to be a spy,* I thought, and I practiced my best enigmatic smile as I joined the horde of pedestrians headed downtown.

4.

MY APARTMENT IS a tenth-floor flat in a century-old building that stands about forty feet from Madison Avenue on the north side of 16th Street. Entering the dim lobby, I nodded to the attendant sitting behind his large desk and then waited for one of the two elevators available. I had climbed the stairs on occasion when the elevators were inoperable, which happened too often. Though the building had been renovated within the last decade, there were still hot water radiators and no central air, only window units. But at $3,600 monthly rent and good security, what could I expect for a location off Madison Avenue and fairly close to ESU?

My mind was racing, and I couldn't sleep. I was thinking about my olfaction project. I had a long way to go. I understood some of the sensory and neural processes involved in the sense of smell, but I needed more education on the chemistry of odors and which neural centers would be activated. I also had to continue to organize and develop my thoughts for the business plan. Tossing and turning, I finally went to my computer and worked on the summary that I had started earlier:

A recent scientific interest is the relation of olfaction to genetics. We know that genetic differences among individuals result in differences in the sense of smell: which odors are detected, sensitivities, and presumably also emotional reactions, although only a few odor receptors have been linked to certain genes. We can explain the many different smells and functions due to the odor receptor genes comprising one of the largest gene families of the human genome.

Not only do odors influence behavior, which is the basis of the perfume industry, but odor functions are affected by genes of the immune system, which maintains differences between individuals and whether organs can be transplanted (involving the Major Histocompatibility Complex, MHC, also known as HLA genes).

Human females can smell some odors controlled by such 'transplant' genes of potential sex partners, preferring partners with MHC genes that are different from their own. Matching such genes to those of potential partners is a potential commercial area of interest, adding to partner selection and matchmaking if substantiated in epidemiological studies.

In support of this idea, genetically related individuals (mothers, fathers, and children) can detect one another; mothers can identify their biological children by body odor, and vice versa. This is certainly already known for other species, particularly in mammals. From the evolutionary standpoint, this function, under genetic control, enabled humans to avoid incest.

*

I DIDN'T FEEL rested when I got to work the next morning, and when I pushed open the door, I was nearly knocked off my feet: there, sitting in the chair in front of my desk, was Brad Williams.

"Dr. Davidson," he said, standing up and offering his hand, "I hope you don't mind. A nice young lady down the hall showed me in after I presented my NIH credentials. I perhaps exaggerated a bit when I told her you were expecting me."

"No, no, that's fine," I said. "I was expecting you — just not this soon."

"I didn't think I would be back to see you until next week, but things are heating up in anticipation of this upcoming Vienna conference. We need to get you down to Langley for a routine clearance and orientation right away. We're thinking this weekend."

"This weekend? Look, Dr. Williams, I don't know if I can get away on such short notice — really."

"Call me Brad — please. May I call you Milt?"

"Sure — Brad."

"We can also talk about helping with your olfaction venture. Very exciting stuff you're planning, and a partnership will be beneficial to both of us. Working with us, you'll have a top-secret clearance. You'll learn things that people on the outside could never imagine."

I know he's right. I'm floundering a bit now on my project. This is a once-in-a-lifetime opportunity.

"One other thing," said Brad, reaching into his coat pocket. He handed me a cell phone. "I want you to use this phone when you need to reach me. And I'll text you on this phone when we need to set up a meeting. It's encrypted and cyber-protected."

I felt a little silly, since this suggested that my own cell phone wasn't secure. Had they been listening in on my conversations?

"Okay, okay," I said. "What's the plan?"

He smiled. "Make your train reservation to D.C. for midafternoon Friday, and text me your arrival time. I'll meet you at Union Station, and we'll drive out to Virginia."

5.

WHEN THE DAY of traveling to Washington came, I left the office at about 12:30 and swung by my apartment to pick up the weekend bag I had packed for my trip. My place isn't very far from Penn Station, just crosstown, so I was there and, on the platform, well before my scheduled 2:00 p.m. departure.

I looked out the window and daydreamed most of the way to Washington. I needed to work on my business plan, but I guess I was nervous, wondering what this weekend would be like, especially visiting the infamous Central Intelligence Agency.

We arrived at Union Station on time, and I went out front to look for Brad's car. I spotted him immediately, standing by the back passenger-side door; he waved to catch my attention. We shook hands and got into the back seat together, and his driver pulled away. Before long, we were cruising through pretty countryside on our way to Langley. Brad made me feel comfortable, with no shop talk along the way.

Checking in at the security gate, we then drove around to a back entrance, where I had to present various forms of ID, including my driver's license and my ESU badge, before signing an agreement not to divulge anything I might see or hear during my interactions with the CIA.

"It's standard Agency boilerplate," Brad said, obviously trying to downplay the importance of this required document. He then led me to a third-floor office, where my face and my iris were photographed and my fingerprints taken. From there, we went up to the ninth floor, to a conference room where six people — four men and two women — were waiting. There was a side table with warm and cold drinks and even some light sandwiches. Brad introduced me to everyone, though I learned only their first names; no last names were given. Nor were any names on the badges they all wore, just their photos and ID numbers.

I poured a cup of coffee before taking my seat where Brad indicated, at one end of the long table. At that point, I began fielding questions from the participants about my research, my teaching, and, in particular, my interests, activities, and ideas regarding olfaction. The latter was, of course, a sensitive issue for me, since anything I planned to patent would have to be kept secret. So, I talked in generalities of goals and possible medical therapy strategies without naming specific odors or how I would be testing behavioral reactions or effects on the neural pathways in the brain.

I was relieved that no one pressed me for more details than I was prepared to disclose, so it seemed to me more of a meeting for them to evaluate me — how I thought, how I expressed myself, and maybe even how I could communicate with them without revealing more than I wanted to. After about an hour, when I discussed my olfaction research early in my career, showing how defined odors affect vegetative, or autonomic nervous system reactions, such as breathing, heart rate, perspiration, just like lie detector test, which stimulated me to want to develop similar methods to affect brain activity. The meeting ended and Brad escorted me to the top floor to meet 'the head of this project.'

On the door of John Crayton's somewhat palatial office, he was listed as 'Deputy Director, Directorate of Science and Technology (DS&T).' Crayton welcomed me and introduced me to Dr. James Calhoun, Director of the Sensory Science Department within DS&T. I found Dr. Calhoun very affable, with a thick white mustache and penetrating blue eyes. He looked to be in his mid-fifties, I thought. Crayton was much older, easily in his sixties, and looked like a typical bureaucrat in his lightweight tweed jacket, blue shirt, and yellow-striped bowtie. He had a habit of tugging on his suspenders.

Calhoun led the discussion. "Dr. Davidson — or may I call you Milton or Milt?"

"Milt, please," I said.

"Milt, we appreciate your taking the time to visit with us. You've been vetted carefully by our investigators, and we're pleased that you'll gain a very high security clearance, so we'll share our trust and confidences with you. But I want to caution you that this comes with a major responsibility, since lives and the security of this nation and our allies are at stake, and we, therefore, cannot tolerate any breach of these confidences or the practices we've established for our senior staff, as you'll be learning about over these two days and, of course, in the future. Any questions so far?"

"Well, actually, yes. At this point, I'm not sure I *want* this responsibility, and I wonder if I should even be coming into these areas of such high security and sensitivity, since I'm *not* a trained agent, nor do I aspire to be. I'm just a scientist with interests in cancer research and, now, olfaction."

I paused, and then continued: "I want to be helpful, but I really don't understand what's expected of me and how I can contribute. I also need to know how much time this will require, since I do have a full-time position at Empire Medical Center. Having to worry about what I say and whom I discuss my science with will be new and strange to me. I don't know if I can manage this."

Crayton then spoke for the first time. "Milt," he said, "the Agency has diverse departments — engineering, telecommunication, special devices, sensors and probes, as well as chemistry, toxicology, microbiology, and sensory perception, including the five senses: sight, hearing, touch, taste, and smell. We have more than fifty different disciplines represented in DS&T, including some outstanding talent both within the Agency as well as consulting with us like we're pursuing with you.

28

"In sum, we have the most modern and best-equipped labs and the most talented scientists, as well as many highly respected consultants from industry and academia working with us. Although we appreciate that your association with us will impact your lifestyle and your collegial relationships, we believe we can offer you unparalleled relationships and resources."

"But what does that mean?" I asked.

"It means we need an olfaction scientist who is recognized externally as being independent of us, but who could collaborate internally on some of our programs to define and apply odors that could influence behavior or could even be a poison or an antidote to a poison. This effort is not restricted to us, by the way, but is being pursued in varying degrees by many of our enemies, as well as our friends. Some of them are much further along, making us vulnerable."

'But I'm just returning to my earlier work on olfaction!" I said.

Dr. Calhoun smiled. "This actually makes you *more* effective," he said, very calmly, "because you'll be accepted as an authentic academic scientist who is uncompromised and who is seeking to advance his knowledge on the sense of smell, on different odors and their effects, and also on how odors may contribute to medicine. Your efforts to develop a company give you even more cover and flexibility to travel freely. In other words, it's the perfect cover and role to look authentic and be able to establish relationships with other olfaction scientists, some of whom we know are also working for their countries' security agencies."

My God!

*

BRAD ESCORTED ME to the living quarters provided to visitors, which was a small apartment on their campus. It had a living room with a TV, plus a bedroom and bathroom. He said I could use my CIA cell phone for all calls, but it would be best to make only essential ones, since every area was monitored both visually and for sound — excluding, of course, the bathroom, he said, chuckling. I didn't believe for a second that toilets would be off limits for their surveillance.

I slept fitfully, concerned that I was already over my head with these people. Yet, I didn't know how to extricate myself, since I'd signed a secrecy agreement that had no time limitation. The next morning, Brad showed up precisely at 9:00 a.m. He then walked me back to the main building, where we again went through security. This time, I wore my new badge as a Special Consultant, no name included, just a number. The computer identified me both by number and eye scan.

Soon, we met up with Dr. Calhoun. "Ready for your tour?" he asked jovially. During our stroll, I asked him what their budget was. "It is of course classified. However," he said, "in the late nineties, there was a public disclosure that the entire national security budget was over $65 billion annually. That was more than two decades ago." He looked me square in the eye as if to drive home his point:

It's a whole lot higher than that now.

Whatever the CIA portion of that number was, it clearly dwarfed what I knew to be the entire annual budget for the National Institutes of Health, our government's major source of medical research.

After a while, we took the elevator to the second-floor basement, B2, and then walked down the hall to another reception area where my badge and face were scanned again. In Room B2-37, Dr. Calhoun introduced me to 'Mark,' head of the olfaction lab group. Mark wore thick glasses, was overweight, and spoke fast like a typical New Yorker. He was to give me a quick tour of a few of the labs. It was clear that they suffered no budget limitations.

Mark explained, "We are still developing unique instruments for measuring different odor molecules and mixtures of odors. We have the advantage of bringing other scientific groups in the building into their projects, so that, for example, the infrared and optical imaging groups were collaborating on the olfactometry development."

I was impressed and said so. Mark was particularly proud of their chemistry laboratories, which were mostly across the hall and looked like a typical pharmaceutical company's chemical synthesis and analysis labs, with many staff wearing goggles and some with protective hoods moving about. I also noticed a lot of chemical and biological hoods against the walls so that toxic molecules could be isolated from those working with them, protecting the lab personnel.

"Most of the labs are under negative pressure," Mark said, "so that the lab air couldn't leave the room. We also have ultra-safe rooms of the quality required for working with highly dangerous viruses." He explained that they sometimes did get biological samples to study, and with these, they took the highest level of precautions, with staff being fully suited to deal with potentially dangerous, contagious viruses. "We also occasionally receive body fluid samples to analyze whenever someone had died under strange circumstances, and there was suspicion of foul play."

I had no idea that the CIA had such laboratory resources and activities.

*

AFTER THE LAB tour, we went to a conference room down the hall, where six members of Mark's team, three men and three women, were waiting. At this point, Brad and Dr. Calhoun excused themselves.

Mark introduced me to his team, but they weren't introduced to me. "You'll get to know them in time," Mark said. I helped myself to coffee and sat down in the chair prepared for me. Mark opened the discussion by saying that they had been given a bit of knowledge about my interests in olfaction but wanted to hear it directly from me. Once again, a challenge — and especially so because this was a group of olfaction specialists. They would want specifics.

I began by again describing the studies I had done for my Ph.D., but more briefly. As I spoke, one of the three women in the group nodded and said that they had read my thesis and were impressed with how much progress I'd made with so few resources in my graduate school lab. She also said that they were familiar with my professorial advisor and that I was fortunate to have his mentoring.

Then came the questions about how I envisioned finding odor molecules that could be used to affect behavior or modify disease activity. They particularly wanted to know what led me to this idea.

"I'm sure you're aware of the history of perfumery and also of aromatherapy," I said. "In fact, there are aroma societies and practitioners who make all sorts of claims with regard to the use of essential oils in holistic medicine — none of which is truly proven so far, yet is accepted as a form of herbal medicine, because the so-called essential oil is extracted from the herb or plant source. When used medicinally, such essential oils can be evaporated into the air by using a humidifier, such as the famous Vicks VapoRub containing the essential oils of peppermint, camphor, and eucalyptus, which also can be applied directly to the skin. They are called 'essential' because of being the key source of the odor."

I presumed they knew all of this. "Currently, inhaled aromatherapy is popular as a treatment to reduce anxiety, tension, breathing difficulties, nausea, menstrual pain, and headaches," I continued to lecture. "There also have been claims of treating the common cold, enhancing memory and mental functions, insomnia, stroke, and even aiding in smoking cessation. Unfortunately, there have been few well-controlled trials. Another problem is that many odors have an association bias with them already, based on cultural or other experiences. Lavender, for example, reminds some people of their grandmothers, so there are already expectations. The fact is, most studies so far on aromatherapy fail to achieve the level of scientific scrutiny necessary to gain acceptance by the scientific or medical community, and certainly not by FDA standards to prove a medical use."

One of the team members then spoke up. "But aromatherapy may be absorption directly into the lungs or nasal circulation without involving odor receptors and smelling. And if you use an aerosol inhaler, you're not really employing olfaction, or actively smelling, so any presentation of odors will be involved with other forms of uptake in addition to or instead of smell. So how do you truly engage smelling as the method of absorption and processing by the brain?"

"Exactly the problem," I answered, "as well as the opportunity. For example, there was an article published in 2009 on the potential treatment of memory impairment due to dementia. Elderly patients with dementia, including some with Alzheimer's disease, were exposed, for about a month, to lemon oil and rosemary in the morning and lavender and orange in the evening. Compared to the previous month when they *hadn't* received aromatherapy, the dementia assessment scores improved, suggesting that there was a lessening of their symptoms when they were given this aromatherapy.

"Of course, this wasn't a controlled trial with a placebo given to a similar group of patients with dementia. My interest is to provide objective means to validate such putative changes by using modern diagnostic technologies available to measure neural or brain activity, such as MRI and electroencephalography, or EEG waves. Lavender is claimed to enhance memory and mental function, as well as to help with insomnia. Both of these applications could be studied by objective diagnostic measures and controlled trials, which I believe I can undertake — focusing, of course, on a better assessment of the odor molecules and doses given, which has not been subjected to sufficient scientific evaluation and definition.

"In fact," I said, "as I already mentioned, during my Ph.D. thesis work, my mentor and I studied involuntary reactions to defined odors, showing changes in heart rate, respiration, and sweating. We published this as a short note in the scientific journal, *Experientia.* For the most part, that work seems to have been totally overlooked. But we proved that it's possible to make objective measures of changes in body functions caused by an aromatherapy without conscious behavior."

Mark said this was exactly the conclusion that they'd come to independently, though not from the perspective of a medical intervention. "We're of course concerned with chemical warfare, and we know from our sources that some of our enemies are developing toxic substances that will be delivered by olfaction to either control the mind or be even more neurotoxic than if given by other means, including through the skin by injection or otherwise. We're studying a class of odor molecules that was originally developed in China but is being made into weapons in Russia, Iran, and North Korea. These odor molecules can paralyze the recipients for about two hours, during which they'll talk without restraint or the ability to keep a secret — and after which they have no memory of the event.

"Also, North Korea may be developing odors for torture. It appears to be a new category of torture, like psychotic drugs or hypnosis, which is less physically painful yet more effective. This is what our agents in the field have learned, but we haven't been able to reproduce this yet. And of course, we, unlike our adversaries, have some limitations on testing such things on humans, so we're constrained for now to animal studies, using the same imaging methods you described.

"We also know," he continued, "that a new class of neurotoxic odor molecules that can kill the recipient almost instantaneously, yet not affect others in the immediate area, is being developed. This could put us and our allies at grave risk, since it may be difficult to prevent their application and even more difficult to prove the role of these odorants. This is now a high priority for us, and because of its potential risks, we've been working together with some of our allies.

"This is where we need your collaboration, Milt," Mark said. "We want you to interface with their intelligence agents — starting with the Israelis, who're monitoring activities in Iran and elsewhere. This is, of course, highly confidential.

"In fact," Mark continued, there was an interesting novel written years ago which focused on the powers of olfaction, which you may have heard of. It was a German book written by Patrick Sűskind in the mid-1980s, called *Das Parfum,* or *The Perfume,* when it was translated into English. It was a tale based on using perfumes to control crowd behavior. In this case, the protagonist became a serial killer. It sold about twenty million copies worldwide."

"Fascinating," I said. "I've never heard of this book."

"It's about an eighteenth-century orphan boy, born in Paris. He was unique in being able to identify hundreds of thousands of specific smells and to recall them at will. In fact, he not only could smell mixtures of odors but also had the keen ability to break them down into their individual components. This helped him become a perfumer. Strangely, he murdered young girls whose scent fascinated and obsessed him. He killed them to preserve their smell in his possession. One father, however, caught him when he used his daughter as a trap, but she was killed anyhow. The boy was tried and sentenced to death but saved himself by wearing a new scent he created, which made him adored by others, including the dead girl's father, who then wanted to adopt him."

"His ability to concoct a perfume that created a mass affection of him after being sentenced to death for murder reminds me of your idea of odors controlling human behavior, but now on a large scale," he said.

"Wow, how prescient!" I remarked.

Suddenly, everything is becoming clearer — including the possibility of losing control of my own ideas.

"I can see how my medical uses of olfaction are directly relevant to using olfaction for your trade of spying and killing," I said. "But how can I be sure this will not compromise or interfere with my medical efforts and odor therapy development?"

Mark said that the CIA's lawyers had been discussing that very question, and so far, they believed that as long as any of my discoveries didn't compromise the CIA mission or aid our adversaries, I could pursue my work and even develop a business. "This will have to be spelled out in writing," he said, "to protect all involved parties."

"Also," I asked, "how much involvement and assistance could I expect from you regarding my own studies of olfaction in medical therapy? Do you have clinical resources?"

"We do have both MRI and EEG labs for human studies here on campus," Mark said, "and we retain a radiological consultant from a medical center in Washington, where we could also conduct clinical trials once approved by their ethics committee, but not identifying the CIA as the sponsor. This is where you'll come in, Milt — being identified as a collaborator and sponsoring the trial under a grant you'll receive from the Department of Defense or some other government department."

This was not only acceptable to me but also intriguing. But I didn't want to appear anxious, so I told Mark that I appreciated this information and would need a few days to think it over. He didn't seem surprised.

"Of course," he said. "We appreciate your coming to meet with us, and I'll be available for any other questions you might have. Just tell Brad if you want to reach me."

6.

THE NEXT THREE weeks went by quickly. I completed the first draft of my patent and sent it to my attorney for review, and I even wrote up a concise version of my business plan and forwarded it to Sequel Ventures now that we had a CDA in place. With all that done, plus signing off on some upcoming procedures related to our research project, I felt good about going away for a few days.

When the day of departure for Vienna finally arrived, I went to Newark Liberty International Airport's United lounge at 5:00 p.m. for our seven o'clock flight. I wore jeans, loafers, and a wool turtleneck. Since the CIA had covered all costs, I had booked a Business Class flight departing Newark on Saturday, arriving in Vienna early Sunday morning. I planned to return on Thursday afternoon, keeping it a short trip away.

After we lifted off, I reviewed the literature about the trip that the CIA had prepared for me. The conference was being held at our hotel, the Vienna Hilton Plaza on Schottenring, downtown, and was sponsored by the World Fragrance Association (WFA), whose headquarters was in Zurich.

It was to be a two-and-a-half-day program, starting Monday morning and ending after lunch on Wednesday. A banquet dinner was scheduled for Tuesday night in the famous Schönbrunn Palace, preceded by a private grand tour of the palace and grounds from 6 to 7:30 p.m..

We landed at about 7:00 a.m. Vienna was dark and raining, with not much to see but the lights of the airport and the hulking shapes of the buildings.

The immense hotel lobby was furnished as it might have been a century ago, but, of course, everything was updated, with numerous salons off the lobby, comfortable seating areas throughout the lobby level, busy counters to help the guests, and beautiful chandeliers replicating or actually derived from the nineteenth century.

My suite on the twelfth floor was very spacious. It consisted of a large living/sitting room with a flat-screen TV and a double-size window that looked out on the main street of the hotel's entrance; a kitchen nook; a very large bedroom with two queen beds, dressers, a couch and chair, and a smaller wall TV. There was also a very large, older-style bathroom with a spacious tub, a large, enclosed shower, a separate cubicle with door for the toilet and bidet, as well as another smaller wall TV screen across from the bathtub. A window brought natural light into the bathroom while providing a good view to the busy street below.

These are great perks when traveling for the CIA, since my usual trips paid by Empire Medical Center are economy class all the way.

7.

EVEN BEFORE MY alarm sounded the next morning, I awoke to the sunshine pouring through the partially closed drapes. After dressing, I hurried down to the ballroom where the conference was taking place, and where a breakfast buffet was laid out for the participants.

The conference president opened the meeting by welcoming the more than 250 or so participants, then summarized the week's agenda. The first session was devoted to speakers presenting issues related to government regulations in their respective countries with regard to fragrances, perfumes in particular. I was interested in the countries' different requirements for disclosing ingredients and how Europe was more revealing in this regard than the United States.

The next session discussed new chemical substances being included in fragrances in general, not just perfumes, and what was known in terms of toxicities, especially allergies or effects on normal organ functions. With such a heterogeneous audience from industry, academia, and government, I was surprised at how scientifically technical these sessions were, and how much information was openly discussed.

The time went by quickly, and I found the frequent coffee breaks interesting not only for the fine selection of Viennese pastries but also because this gave the participants a chance to get acquainted. I met Stephanie Strong from a marketing company in the UK, who actually approached me with a greeting, and then also a Charles Le Font from a small Belgian chemical perfume supply company. At lunch, I sat at a table with participants from South America (two from Brazil) and one each from China, Canada, France, Morocco, and Russia.

I wondered if it were a coincidence that the Russian, who claimed to be a scientist from the Russian Academy of Sciences in Moscow, chose to sit next to me as one of the first joining the table. He introduced himself as Dr. Vladimir Borofskov and gave me his business card that showed he had a Ph.D. and worked in Environmental Sciences. We chatted during lunch about the meeting and the presentations we'd heard. He said in reasonably good British English that he had never visited the United States but had learned English in school and in extended visits to England as part of a joint program in environmental contamination.

On my other side sat the representative from France, a Marie Chalfont, who worked for a small perfume company in Paris. She was polite but not very conversant. I noticed she was wearing a strong perfume, somewhat like *Opium*, but different. I still wasn't an expert in differentiating very many odors within a class, an ability that was innate to certain individuals, but throughout my life I avoided strong perfumes or smell – but never focused much on this until now. She also had a good command of English but with a distinct French accent. I, of course, noticed how attractive she was in a very tight knee-high dress that displayed her curvaceous figure, accentuated by her high heels showing off her nice figure. Her large brown eyes with pink eye shadow were particularly stunning, I thought. But we didn't converse much, although I was sure she noted my staring at her occasionally.

When the afternoon break finally arrived at 3:30, I was ready to get out of my chair and move around. I decided to relax for a couple of hours in my comfortable suite, where I could also check my emails. Then, at about 5:30 p.m., I called down to the concierge to make a reservation at a local restaurant, selecting one nearby, just down the street, that specialized in Northern Italian food. My reservation was for 6:00 p.m., very early for Austria. For a brief moment, I considered calling Marie Chalfont's room and inviting her to dinner, but I decided this was too forward after only meeting at lunch and not having been engaged in much personal conversation.

When I got back to my hotel room, there was an envelope on the floor just inside the door. It was from Vladimir, the Russian scientist who'd sat next to me at lunch, saying he was sorry to miss me in the late afternoon sessions but would like to invite me for lunch tomorrow; he left his room number. He invited me to join him and his wife at the banquet dinner the following evening.

My first thought was that this was part of a Russian clandestine operation.

Why is he so interested in engaging with me?

Was this because I had a suite, which was probably unusual for a typical conference participant from an academic institution, or because of other information? In any case, my job was to get acquainted with the international olfaction community, especially as an American scientist, and it was a good sign that this Russian wanted to have further contact. I sent a text message on the CIA cell phone to the number Brad had given to me, providing Vladimir's name and the other information from his business card.

It was then I remembered that my CIA handlers had cautioned me that hotel rooms were often bugged, so I would need to be cautious. I hadn't given that any thought at all since checking into this large hotel. How and when would anyone know my room and plant a bug unless it was done while I attended the conference? But I did not have any unusual or revealing phone conversation, only calls to the concierge or dining room. Vienna was reputed to be a center for multinational clandestine activities, where East meets West, so nothing should really surprise me. I did need to be cautious, though.

*

WHEN I GOT down to the conference room the next morning, there were already a lot of participants at the buffet table selecting a continental breakfast to take to our places at the long tables in the ballroom. As we waited for the program to begin, I saw some of the people I'd met the day before, though my Russian acquaintance hadn't arrived yet.

Marie Chalfont, the French woman who'd sat near me at lunch on Monday, came over to sit next to me, and we discussed how the conference was going, how we were spending our time in Vienna, and other small talk.

It's surprising how more engaging she is with me now than she was yesterday.

Now she seemed always to be probing, and I couldn't decide if it were just her nature or if there might be another meaning. She told me again that she worked for a small French perfume company, but she didn't name the company or give me her business card.

I guessed she was in her late thirties. Today, she wore a tight-fitting, two-piece, woolen light green suit, ending just above her knees, again emphasizing her slim, attractive figure. She was quite confident in her composure, and certainly noticed my eyes focusing on her anatomy while we conversed. When she listened to me speak, her eyes were very penetrating, as if she were analyzing my every word and facial expression, just like I experienced at lunch yesterday.

While seated in the ballroom, Vladimir came over and greeted me, saying he and his wife were looking forward to the evening and sharing a table with me at the banquet. Now, he was sitting in the row in front of me, and I noted that Marie Chalfont was about three seats away; she smiled when our eyes met. This time, a Chinese participant was on my right and an Australian on my left, but there was no time for conversation before the conference resumed for the short period before lunch.

I stayed at the conference for another hour or so, then went out to the lobby because my CIA phone had pinged twice. After putting in the code and my thumbprint, I read a disturbing message: The CIA believed that Vladimir could be an FSB agent — formerly called KGB before the dissolution of the Soviet Union — and could be dangerous, so I needed to be ultra-careful with him. They also said that Charles Hughes, an American from Iowa, was one of their CIA agents at the conference. Finally, the French woman, Marie Chalfont, was, in fact, a member of the Mossad, also known as *The Office*, the Israeli spy agency. Within fifteen seconds, the message self-destructed, clearly timed for a couple of minutes. Vladimir, the Russian, did not appear during the buffet lunch I attended.

*

THE BUS RIDE to Schönbrunn Palace took about forty minutes, winding through different neighborhoods of Vienna and giving us a good view of some local streets and sites. A tour guide on the bus explained in English that the 300+-year-old Schönbrunn was the former imperial Baroque summer home, that it had over a thousand rooms, and was one of Austria's most important architectural, cultural, and historical sites. Schönbrunn meant 'beautiful spring' in German, I learned, and was built and remodeled, with a Rococo décor, during the mid-eighteenth-century under the reign of Empress Maria Theresa.

As I entered the banquet's elegantly appointed ballroom at 8:30 p.m., waiters in black tie and waitresses in black skirts and white blouses offered each arriving guest a choice of champagne, white wine, or red wine. There were no seating arrangements, except for a head table bearing 'reserved' cards. I proceeded to the middle of the room and took a seat at an outside table for eight with a view of the musical group. As I expected, Vladimir came to sit beside me, with his wife on his other side, then Charles Hughes, the CIA agent from Iowa, and then Marie Chalfont took the chair next to Charles.

I am in good company with American, Russian, and Israeli spies.

The conversation with, or – better – the continued interrogation by Vladimir from our first meeting continued as I expected: "What is your particular interest in olfaction; what do you teach at Empire Medical University; how long do you plan to stay in Vienna; are you touring elsewhere in Austria or Europe; and is this your first trip to the Continent?" I gave perfunctory answers.

Vladimir pretended to be curious, but I knew he was interested in how often and how widely I traveled. For his part, he said that at the Russian Academy of Sciences, he was in charge of a section that was interested in fostering research in the five senses, including an understanding of the sense of smell, how perfumes are developed and marketed, industry and public health problems, and so on. "My educational and work background are in chemistry," he said.

He made a point of saying that he had never visited the United States but was hoping to have the opportunity to participate in a similar conference there. He would also like to visit some perfume companies and even academic laboratories researching some of these topics.

"I learned English in school," he said again, "and as a young boy I spent some summer vacations in Finland, Sweden, and once in England."

I gathered that his mission was to gain me as a colleague and maybe even a friend. He clearly wanted to establish contacts outside of Russia, but I wasn't sure if this was on behalf of the FSB, as my CIA contacts warned, or for personal reasons.

His wife, Natasha, wasn't able to speak much English, so she hardly joined in the conversation. She could, however, communicate with Marie in French, so they chatted privately and seemed to be enjoying each other.

Dessert included apple strudel with vanilla ice cream. I relished this typical Austrian delicacy, together with strong coffee. About a half-hour later, at about 11:45 p.m., the buses started loading for the return trip, and I said my good-byes to the others and hurried off to make the first one. But before I got away, Vladimir made a point of saying he hoped we could talk again tomorrow.

"Can you meet me on the outside veranda off the main lobby at 1:00 p.m., after the closing ceremony?" he asked.

I agreed, and when I got back to the room, I sent a message to the CIA alerting them to this scheduled meeting. I was disappointed that Marie disappeared when we boarded the buses.

8.

ON THE LAST day of the conference, I said goodbye to the few attendees I knew and then proceeded to the veranda, where Vladimir was already sitting at a table with a drink. Surprisingly, Marie was nowhere to be seen. As Vladimir called the waiter over to order me one, I thought he seemed a little ill at ease, frequently looking around as if to see if anyone were watching us. After my drink arrived, and while continuing to talk at a normal pitch, Vladimir scratched out a few words on his napkin and showed it to me: "Need your help to U.S. Embassy. NB and I want to defect. I am under close surveillance."

He ripped up the napkin after I read it and asked me to advise the 'Americans' to have someone contact him when he strolled in the city park a few blocks away, either at 6:00 p.m. today or 9:00 a.m. tomorrow. Then he got up and, before leaving, said, very softly: "I am putting our lives in your hands." I stood and shook his hand and said it was a pleasure meeting him, and I hoped we could see each other again in the future.

I went straight to the suite and texted Brad Williams what Vladimir had said. Receipt of the message was acknowledged, then the text exchange was erased. I was perplexed: The original CIA message about Vladimir had warned that I could be in danger because of him; now it appeared that he was the one in danger. Could this whole thing have been a ploy to make me expose my CIA connection?

I waited for a specific response from Brad. I remembered Vladimir saying, "I have rarely left Russia with my wife, maybe twice in ten years, and always to a neighboring nation that was in the former Soviet Union or in Scandinavia. This trip to Vienna is our first visit to a truly neutral city." I remembered that he was concerned that they were probably 'being watched.' But, for some reason, I was unsure if the lady with him was truly his wife – she seemed too touchy and amorous when they were together. I will need to share my suspicion with Brad.

*

IT WAS GETTING late in the day, and I wasn't sure what my plans were. I still hadn't heard more from Brad. Maybe I should go to the Jewish quarter and visit The Jewish Museum Vienna. I wondered if I should try to find Marie, since she might also enjoy visiting the Jewish quarter, because my CIA handler said she was Jewish, but then decided against it. I wasn't even sure if she were still at the conference, or even in Vienna.

Vienna had been a major center of Judaism in the Middle Ages, especially in the 1400s, and soon our taxi let me off at the Museum Judenplatz, an annex of the main Jewish Museum. There I took my time touring the excavations of a medieval synagogue. After that, I walked over to the Palais Eskeles at Dorotheergasse, which housed the Jewish Museum Vienna, the country's major collection of Jewish history. Austria was truly a cultural center for Judaism until the Nazis murdered 65,000 of their citizens. In the late nineteenth century, Vienna was also the birthplace of Zionism, the dream of establishing a homeland in what was then Palestine. Teddy Kollek, one of the most famous mayors of Jerusalem, was born in Vienna.

It was an intense and sobering afternoon, and by the time I left the museum, it was too late to make it to another of the city's sites. I decided to stroll back toward the hotel and hopefully find a nice restaurant or café along the way. After about twenty minutes, I ran across Café Mozart, a charming place with old tables and a Baroque décor. Although the pastries looked sumptuous, I decided to have an early light supper instead. The meal was delicious.

If I stay here much longer, I'll return to the States with a few extra pounds.

During dinner, I checked my phone to see if I had a message about Vladimir: nothing.

Should I try to contact Charles Hughes?

But I knew that wasn't allowed.

*

THE NEXT MORNING, I got up to make coffee and to check for messages before I departed for the airport and my return flight. Surprisingly, there was one on my CIA phone: "Thank you. Enjoy your return trip." Nothing more from Brad. Then the message disappeared.

There were also a number of emails on my personal cell phone.

An important one was from Mike Peters in my lab. He wanted me to know about a problem he was having with one of the intestinal cancer cell lines he was growing in the laboratory. Evidently, the rounded cancer cells had begun to be overgrown with cells that looked different, having a more elongated, or spindle-like appearance, and which grew faster than the rounded cancer cells. I answered that he should try to separate and expand the two cell populations, growing each separately so we could study them further when I got back.

At about 9 a.m., I was ready to go downstairs, when I noticed the strangest thing: The business card that Vladimir had given me, and which I had placed in my carry-on briefcase, was now lying next to the bathroom sink. I checked my briefcase, and sure enough, it was gone. I was positive that this wasn't a mistake I had made, which meant it had been placed there by an intruder. But why? Was it intended to remind me about Vladimir and his plight?

Is this a warning of some kind?

*

THEN, AS I was ready to leave the room, someone knocked on the door. I looked through the peep-hole and saw two men with hats. I then responded, "Yes?", but kept the door locked.

"Guten Morgen, Herr Professor. Wir sind Polizei... We are from the police," they continued in English, and held their identification in front of the peep-hole.

I looked at their identification badges more carefully after opening the door, but blocking their entering. They looked authentic, but how would I know, I thought? "Come in," I said.

The older of the two, a stocky man about 5 feet, 9 inches, with a half-bald head showing after he removed his hat, wore a two-piece dark gray suit, somewhat wrinkled and baggy, while the second man was younger, taller, thinner, wearing thick eye-glasses and dressed in a more stylish brown suit with a solid-yellow wide tie.

The senior detective apologized for his poor English, which I assured him was fine. "What can I do for you?" I began.

"You are attending this conference on smelling, and another American – a Charles Hughes from Iowa – is also here, correct?"

"Yes," I answered.

"Dr. Hughes was found dead in his room this morning, and we are therefore trying to learn about him from others who may have known him, such as his countrymen. Did you know him, Professor Davidson?"

"Yes, I mean I met him at the conference and sat next to him during a meal. But he was otherwise a stranger to me," I explained.

"Do you know any reason he would be murdered?" the detective continued. The other officer did not say anything, but he began strolling around my room, appearing to be looking around innocently.

"Murdered?" I exclaimed. "How?"

"We are still investigating, but he was in a fight and stabbed to death in his throat and chest. What do you know about him?"

"He was a research professor at the University of Iowa, studying olfaction – I believe his background was chemistry – and had a wife and two children. My God, why would anyone want to kill him?"

I, of course, couldn't reveal that he was a CIA agent. I really wasn't given much information from Brad why he was here, except I thought he was assigned to watch me.

"We would of course prefer your remaining here in Vienna while we advance our investigation, since you may be able to remember something of use to us," the elder officer said.

"I'm sorry, but I have a plane to catch later today, since I'm due back in New York where I have duties as a pathologist at the Empire State University. Here is my card, so you can contact me if you have further questions, but I told you everything I know about Professor Hughes."

"We discussed Professor Hughes and you, as the two Americans who attended this conference, with the American Embassy, and fortunately they assured us of your good reputation, requesting that we allow you to leave the country."

"Then, can I go?"

"Yes, Professor, but we hope you are accessible if we have further questions. Since an American was murdered in Vienna under such strange circumstances, we are also inviting Interpol to join this investigation," he stated as he bowed slightly and put his hat back on. Then the other detective came up to the door also, and both wished me "Auf Wiedersehen."

Taking this literally, I really didn't want to see them again! But if Hughes had been assassinated, this has got to mean that I'm also in danger.

On the taxi ride to the airport, I sent an encrypted text to Brad, reporting about the police visit and the murder of Charles Hughes. The only response was, "Received," before the message disappeared.

9.

I FELT GUILTY about staying in Vienna only the days of the conference and now hurrying back to New York already on Thursday. I was anxious to get to my office early on Friday morning. I knew Mike Peters would be in the lab, so I went straight there and found him talking with Dr. Jhanella Brian, a post-doctoral scientist who was working in my lab under an NIH fellowship. She was from Nigeria and had done her undergraduate education in South Africa and her Ph.D. in cell biology at the University of London.

Mike and Jhanella were interested in hearing about my trip, but I was impatient to discuss the problem that Mike had emailed me about in Vienna. I asked how the separation of the two kinds of cells was going, and he said it was still too soon to confirm that we had two different cell types growing separately, so it was premature to conclude that the cloning had been successful. I speculated that taking the tumors out of the mice meant that some of the murine cells within the tumor mass could grow out when the tumors were propagated in the cell culture flasks. This wasn't unexpected, but what was strange was the continuous growth of the putative murine cells, probably connective tissue cells surrounding the human tumors, after many culture generations. Normal connective tissue cells surrounding tumors usually don't propagate continuously but die off in one or, at most, two subcultures.

When I finally got to my office, my assistant told me my attorney had called and wanted me to call him back right away. Fortunately, I connected with John on the first try. He said he had a banker with experience in company startups and funding who was interested in talking with me. His name was Robert Phillips, and he was with a company called Bio Advisors, LLC, located in midtown New York. I phoned Phillips and left a message with his assistant, who told me he would be free to return my call after 1:00 p.m.

This gave me ample time to write a summary report of the Vienna conference for the CIA. They wanted key points of the conference (especially what I thought might be used for military objectives), a description of prominent speakers, and any personal interactions I believed would be of interest. Coincidentally, as I was writing the report, I received a text on my CIA cell phone saying they wanted to meet with me in New York at the end of the week if I were available. "Yes," I texted back.

I'm hoping the CIA will have some answers about Charles Hughes's death.

When Robert Phillips called, he told me he was a scientist (Ph.D. in molecular biology from Yale) who got a business degree (MBA from Wharton School at the University of Pennsylvania) and had been in biotechnology investments and startups for about four years. I was impressed when he described some of the business deals that he'd structured and found investments for, and I described very generally my idea and the essence of the business plan that was now with the Sequel Ventures group in Westport. Fortunately, Sequel did not require me to keep our contact confidential, although they suggested I not shop this around.

Phillips said he knew them well, and they were a reputable group, but he felt that I was moving too fast and needed to include a financial component of the plan in order to provide a basis for a funding negotiation. "Sequel will easily recognize that you're inexperienced in this process, and that could be a bit disadvantageous for you."

It's clear that these venture capitalists, although closely connected, are very competitive.

We agreed to meet for lunch sometime next week.

*

AT ABOUT 6:00 p.m., on my way out of the office, I swung by to say hello to John Bickers. He was clearly absorbed in something on his computer screen but pushed away from the desk, stood, and offered his hand.

"Welcome back, world traveler," he said. "How was your trip?"

John and I had a good relationship, and not just professionally. He was very personable and cared for his faculty, which we all appreciated – at least, I thought so. He had recruited me to ESU and was proud that I had my own peer-reviewed NIH grant and some publications in high quality research journals. Regardless of someone's background and prior training, it's often a gamble as to who will succeed in terms of developing an independent research program that will be a credit to the institution, the department, as well as the investigator.

But there were also serious economic concerns, since those with grants not only helped reimburse the institution for a portion of their faculty salary but also provided an overhead component for the parent institution, which could be as high as 60 percent of the direct costs of the grant; these non-research funds went to the office of the Dean and the academic department involved. So, the more grant funds, the more money that can be distributed within the institution. I disliked this part of managing medical education and research, but I recognized its importance. And I was glad others were responsible, not me.

10.

ON TUESDAY, I met Robert Phillips for lunch at the Union Square Coffee Shoppe. Although it was crowded and loud, we found a quieter area in the rear so we could talk. Phillips was very young and fashionably dressed in a beige tweed jacket, green shirt with a solid brown tie, and khaki slacks. He shook my hand forcefully. After placing our orders, Bob, as he asked me to call him, summarized his role at his fund and generally the kind of work and deals his fund participated in. They liked early-stage companies to finance, and then they helped organize second rounds of financing whereby they could increase the value of their initial investment severalfold.

Not a bad business, capitalizing on other people's ideas and work, so long as they pick a few successes.

"At present, there are more deal opportunities than venture money, so we can be selective — and can dictate very good terms for their money," he began.

Clearly, he's already negotiating.

In any case, I was a little put off by that tack. I told him, "I'm just beginning the process of finding investors interested in my idea and business plan, and I still have a lot of basic work to do.

"Whereas scents comprise our environment and are known by various industries to influence behavior related to products," I continued, "this hasn't been put on a scientific basis, where we predict and explain how an odor or a mixture of odors will and does effect a specific response, or how — carrying this further — we could exploit a pharmaco-olfactory therapy modality."

This clearly wasn't familiar to him, so he tried to get even more details from me, which I rebutted as being premature. I wanted him to understand that it was *I* who had the wares, and it was *I* who would decide whom I wanted to share this with.

It occurred to me that if he and his fund were in such demand, he wouldn't have arranged to meet me for lunch so soon, and he would've found a graceful way to end our meeting once I indicated I wasn't anxious to move ahead until I learned more about him and his company.

My reticence must have worked, because by the time we finished our lunch, Bob was asking, "How do we proceed? Would you like to come by and meet our partners?" and so on. I told him I would have my attorney forward our CDA to him and then a summary of our business plan, which I cautioned was still in an early stage of development.

This was a worthwhile experience. I had never dealt with venture capitalists, so each encounter taught me something – giving a seductive peak under the dress is important to capture control of the discussion, so long as you enhance the other party's interest to learn more. But you can't be too evasive, of course.

I got back to my office by about 3:00 p.m., so I had some catching up to do. Then, shortly before five o'clock, my CIA cell phone pinged with a message. I was to remain in front of the main entrance of the hospital at 11:45 a.m. tomorrow, so I could be picked up for a lunch meeting. It would be my first meeting with Brad since I got back from Vienna, and I was nervous about what to expect. I wondered if I would hear more about Charles, and also if Vladimir ever connected with our consulate in Vienna. And I also wanted to learn more about Marie, who disappeared before the conference ended.

11.

THE NEXT MORNING, at precisely 11:45, I waited at the curb of the entrance to the hospital. Almost to the minute, a black Lincoln Town Car pulled up, and the driver opened the back door for me. I got in next to Brad Williams.

He smiled hello and shook my hand like he was glad to see me. As the car pulled away, Brad said, "We're going to have a quiet lunch crosstown." We drove to an office building on 35th Street off Sixth Avenue, where we took the elevator to the fourteenth floor and entered an office without any receptionist. It was just a series of rooms with tables and seating arrangements, as well as a few computers on desks. Brad showed me into what appeared to be an office dining room. On one table were salads and sandwiches and iced tea. We helped ourselves and went to sit at a larger conference table.

Brad said, "It seems you had a good trip to Vienna and that, according to your report, you benefitted from the conference and made some interesting acquaintances, except for the tragedy of our agent, Charles, being murdered. I agreed and thanked him for the opportunity and the Agency's generosity, but asked what really happened to Hughes.

"Our agents located his cell phone, which self-activated with sound. We heard that Charles surprised someone in his room when he returned at about 8:00 p.m. There was a scuffle, noise of furniture being broken and some groans, and then silence. The intruder evidently killed Charles and then left his room. We only heard some sounds from Charles before he expired."

Then I asked about Vladimir.

Brad mulled the question for a moment, then said, "The situation is under control… He didn't contact anyone at the embassy, and then after meeting with you, seemed to have disappeared."

"If you remember, Brad," I said, "Vladimir's business card was relocated in my room, which maybe indicates that someone, possibly even Borofskov, was in there in my absence. Maybe the same thing happened to Charles, but he surprised the intruder and died by doing so. What do you think?"

"You may be correct, Milt. Borofskov is a mystery and could be an FSB agent who was in Vienna to identify CIA or other enemy agents interested in military olfaction."

He then changed the subject to Marie Chalfont. "We know, of course, that she's a top Mossad agent with a Ph.D. in chemistry. She heads a counterintelligence unit of the Israeli secret service that keeps tabs on efforts by foreign groups to develop chemical warfare, particularly mood-control agents, as well as potent toxins used in assassinations. She evidently wanted to do a profile on you."

"Me? Why? Is Mossad working with the CIA?" I asked, but Brad ignored the question. Instead, he asked if I'd thought more about the arrangement Mark had outlined when I'd visited Langley a few weeks back.

"I have," I said. "What worries me is somehow becoming restricted in my own research due to this involvement."

He assured me that they would respect my commercial viability "as long as no Agency secrets are revealed through it."

"That's what I mean," I said. "We still have a lot of loose ends to tie up. A lot of questions to get answered."

"Okay," he said. "You think about it, and we will too. But we need to get you back down to Langley soon to wrap it up."

*

WHEN I GOT home after work, I made myself a sandwich of Hebrew National salami with mustard on almost stale rye bread, just like I enjoyed when growing up. I was still obsessed with thoughts about the

CIA, but it was still early, so I went to my computer and worked a little more on my patent specifications.

My patent attorney had told me that the cost of patenting my invention could run into hundreds of thousands of dollars by paying my U.S. and also foreign patent attorneys, plus all the filing and maintenance costs. Since I didn't have that kind of money, I needed to finance my new company in order to cover these costs, but I knew that having at least a patent filing was critical to financing the company – a chicken and egg dilemma.

The first patent filing in a new technology obviously is the most difficult, since there are common processes that are described and can be applied to all future patents.

This required refreshing my knowledge and researching recent progress on the neurobiology of olfaction — how odors are sensed and how odor signals are retained and processed in the brain.

I wrote what I felt were several good paragraphs for the patent before bed:

Indeed, it is believed that our sense of smell is 10,000 times more sensitive than our other senses and much faster, since the nerves in the nose are connected directly to the brain, whereas other senses, such as taste and touch, reach the brain via the body and spinal cord.

Since the sense of smell is so intimately related to memory, it is not surprising that loss of smell has been related to neurodegenerative diseases, such as Alzheimer's disease and Parkinson's disease, where fading of the sense of smell is one of the first symptoms that can appear years before the diseases' typical manifestations.

Having composed this, I thought that my challenge and, in turn, my invention, was how to use specific odor molecules to predict biological effects — particularly how to define specific odors and odor mixtures to manage disease, both in terms of diagnosis and treatment, as well as to affect memory and behavior by controlling brain functions through activating or inhibiting neural centers in the brain.

12.

ON MONDAY MORNING, I was in my office reading the latest results of our cultivating different cancer and normal cell populations in special flasks. When Mike and Jhanella had separated the two cell populations and analyzed them microscopically, biochemically, and genetically, we learned that the spindle-shaped cells, which presumably were originally normal connective tissue cells of the host mice, were now very malignant, growing rapidly when transplanted in mice.

The other isolated large round cells were confirmed to be the same malignant colon cancer cells originally implanted into mice from a patient's tumor, having exclusively human chromosomes, enzymes, and proteins. What fascinated us was that the population of spindle-sarcoma cells had both mouse and what we believed were either rearranged mouse or truly human chromosomes presumably derived from the patient's colon cancer.

This was my current exciting project, and I was clearly in new territory of cancer science. I decided to call Dr. John Bogner of the molecular genetics department at my university medical center and arranged for him to visit with us and review our results. I knew he could easily help characterize some of the different 'marker' chromosomes of the new malignant cells to identify different genes and if they were human or murine.

I was thrilled that John had an interest in collaborating with us and helping clarify how the new cell population developed and its genetic makeup.

I speculated that we were witnessing a biological phenomenon that could explain how early cancers in humans advance and spread, or how they evolve to become more malignant.

Suddenly my reading was interrupted by a call from my office assistant. "There's a Marie Chalfont holding for you on line one."

I was immediately flustered but also intrigued. I took a deep breath and answered the call.

"Why, hello, Marie. What a nice surprise."

"Ah, so you remember me!" she said in her charming French accent.

"Of course, I remember you. I'm glad to hear from you."

"Pardon my calling so unexpectedly, but I'm in New York, and I thought that if you had time, it would be nice to get together."

I remembered her penetrating and captivating eyes, as well as her beautiful figure.

This caught me by surprise, but I was too curious to be anything but enthusiastic. I responded, saying "It will be my pleasure to see you again."

She suggested we meet the next day for lunch at a restaurant she liked in the Union Square area. She gave me her phone number in case I ran into any last-minute problem.

After we hung up, I felt a little stunned. Marie Chalfont was mysterious, charming, and quite attractive — of medium height, quite slender, and always wearing a tight-fitting dress that definitely worked to her shapely body's advantage.

True to form, I sent a brief text to my CIA handler informing him of this call and meeting, without receiving any response.

*

MARIE WAS SITTING at a table toward the rear and waved to get my attention, greeting me with a warm smile. We exchanged continental cheek kisses while she held both my hands.

She looked stunning, even better than I remembered her in Vienna. She was wearing a cleavage-exposing V-neck pink cashmere sweater and a short, tight blue skirt. Her lips were deep red, and her brown hair was pulled back and knotted with a red band. Her eyes sparkled as she thanked me for meeting her on such short notice.

"I am in New York visiting a very large company specializing in perfumes and fragrances," she said. "In addition to selling directly, they also supply other, smaller companies. My company is one of their customers."

She wasted no time turning her charm on me. "I enjoyed meeting you at the Vienna conference, Milt. And I am curious how you became involved with perfumes and smell, since I know you are a pathologist at ESU involved in cancer research."

"How do you know that?" I asked, knowing of course of her Mossad position.

She smiled coyly. "I checked you out on the Internet, of course. I've read some of your articles. I even learned that you're not married."

I didn't know how to respond, but it made me think that the Mossad probably already had a file on me, since both intelligence services were cooperating on the 'Oryol' project, the secret research being performed on olfaction by the Russians.

After the waiter served our poached salmon and house salads, I returned to her initial question. "I think I briefly explained my interest in olfaction to you in Vienna. It began while I was a graduate student, while also attending medical school," I said. "But more recently, I've been thinking about how to use odor molecules as a basis of diagnosing and treating disease, developing methods to put a more scientific basis to determining the effects of odors on neurological and other functions."

She stopped eating and just stared at me. "Are you serious?" she asked. "I had no idea this could be a new medical therapy — although I, of course, have been involved in developing and using perfumes to affect behavior."

It's certain that the Mossad, and definitely Marie, knew I was spying for the CIA.

"Well," I said, baiting her, "I assume you're aware of the use of odors in covert or combat applications."

I'm sure this is an important part of her work with the Mossad.

This didn't escape her. "I knew you were more than just a research pathologist," she said with a smirk.

Marie had grown up in a small town south of Paris, had gotten her business degree at the Sorbonne, and had taken advanced courses in chemistry as part of her doctorate program, I learned.

She had never been married, she said, simply because she'd been so busy with school and career and also had not yet met the right person. She told me that she had a brother, a physician in private practice in Paris, and both her parents were alive and living in her birth town. Her mother focused on raising flowers, and her father still taught in the local gymnasium or high school. She also explained that her family practiced Judaism, but more like our reformed movement. She, of course, knew my Jewish heritage.

A lot of information was shared in this one-hour lunch, I thought. For some reason, I wasn't sure that she was being honest with me, especially since Brad had informed me that she was a top agent of the Israeli Mossad.

Now what?

I didn't have to wait long for the answer. When the waiter brought the check, Marie quickly took it and declared this was her treat. Then she just blurted out, "And do you think you can untangle yourself this Friday to escort me to the Metropolitan Opera? I would like to see *La Boheme* on Friday evening, before I return to Paris, and I would love your company."

I was more than surprised and probably showed it because her next move was to take my hand and say, "I hope you want to share this evening with me as much as I would like to be with you."

I had been totally seduced by her charm and interest. "Marie," I said, "I gather you bought a ticket for me knowing your powers of persuasion. I hope you don't expect us to get married before your return flight!"

"Well, you never know — and that's the fun in life," she said, paying the bill with her credit card.

Outside, I waited as she called a cab. She kissed me, this time quickly on the lips. "Come to my hotel, The Mandarin, at Columbus Circle, at six-thirty Friday evening. We'll have a drink before the opera, which is just a few blocks away."

Feeling almost incapacitated by this aggressive yet charming woman, I ignored Brad's warning about her, and could only nod in agreement as she jumped into the taxi. For a split second, I thought of jumping into the cab with her and canceling the rest of my day.

She must be great in business.

13.

THOUGH I WAS excited about my pending opera date with Marie, the rest of my week didn't allow much time for daydreaming. When I got back to the office after lunch, I had an email from Dr. Bob Phillips, telling me that he had returned the signed CDA to my attorney and would now like to step up our discussions. So that his group could decide whether to take on this project, he specifically wanted to understand my olfactory business strategy and any scientific results supporting it.

I was complimented by their interest, but I also felt a little pushed by it, since I still had many decisions to make. But after thinking more about it, I decided to meet with Phillips again to get his ideas on how to form and finance the biopharma company I envisioned. I sent him a text asking for his availability, preferably this week if possible. This would hopefully prepare me for a subsequent meeting with Sequel's Bill Rhodes, which I was trying to arrange for early Friday when he planned to be in the city.

In the meantime, I asked my attorney to incorporate my company so I would have a defined entity that would be the basis of any business deal. I wanted to incorporate the business as *Pharmascent Sciences, Inc.,* a name I liked because it identified the technology as involving the sense of smell without telling more. John asked me to send him a few sentences describing the company and to decide where we should incorporate. He suggested Delaware, and I agreed with his recommendation that this would be the most company-friendly venue. He also assured me that doing this wasn't yet a conflict with my employment at ESU because it was, so far, a 'paper' company, but if a patent were to be filed, I would have to clarify whether it would be assigned to Pharmascent Sciences, Inc., ESU, or both.

Since this work wasn't related to my research at the university and certainly not to my teaching responsibilities, I assumed that my company would own the patent, and if ESU thought it owned my extracurricular time, I could perhaps satisfy them with a royalty percentage. I also knew that the university had a venture capital fund to help faculty start companies that would also benefit both parties, so I planned to meet with their business development office once I had more details about the technology, business prospects, and some venture capital interest.

*

BOB PHILLIPS AND his partner, Tom Bernham, of Bio Advisors, met with me a few days later. At the end of my meeting, Tom thanked me for visiting with them but, as expected, said that the information I'd provided was as yet inadequate for them to give this further consideration. They would have to evaluate the patent I planned to file, and of course, a business plan that would — at a minimum — provide timetables, risks, market projections, competition, and investment needs. Bob Phillips emphasized "I could help you once you're ready to share more of the proprietary science, the projected products, and disease indications with us."

But I'm not.

On Friday morning, I met with Bill Rhodes of Sequel Ventures in his hotel suite. I basically advised him of the business plan I was developing, told him I'd made good progress with my patent application, and that my business attorney had been able to arrange for me to discuss this with other interested venture capitalists.

Bill seemed surprised that I would even mention other V.C.s, since it may have appeared that I was negotiating before we even got down to a serious discussion. He was right, although he knew I couldn't give any other party any more than I had shared with him, which wasn't enough for an evaluation.

We ended the meeting in a cordial manner, but I was concerned that he might have thought I wasted his time. I decided to suspend these discussions with venture capitalists until my patent was filed and I had produced a strong business plan.

Now I'm faced with the question of how to juggle all the parts of my life in order to get this important work done.

At times, I felt that the cords that held me together were fraying. Meanwhile, Brad Williams kept insisting that I visit Langley again to finalize our arrangement – or, I guess, to make me a full-fledged spy or informant for them. I kept postponing, saying "I still need to advance my own project, moving Pharmascent Sciences forward." He remained friendly, but I had started to notice signs of his impatience. Maybe I needed an attorney to advise me of my rights – *I'm still a private citizen*, I thought. But seeking legal advice, I feared, could become a problem in terms of violating my security oath with the CIA.

I knew I shouldn't have signed this without legal advice.

Realizing I was at an impasse without advancing my patent application and business plan for Pharmascent Sciences, I resolved to spend every available hour over the next week focusing on that work.

14.

THE SHOPPING CENTER in the same building as the Mandarin Hotel was large and impressive, with literally hundreds of people moving among the stores. I took the elevator to the hotel lobby and found a house phone to call Marie. She answered immediately, "Come up to the twenty-seventh floor, room 2712."

When I arrived, the door was ajar, so I just knocked and walked in. Marie was standing near the picture window at the far end of the large living room, working on popping the cork of the champagne she had on ice.

When she turned to face me, she took my breath away. She looked strikingly elegant in her very long black velvet dress with large V-shaped cutouts in front and back. She wore a prominent pearl necklace, and her hair was bundled on her head with a diamond clasp, exposing her long, thin neck. "You look beautiful," I said.

She didn't overreact, but I could tell she was pleased with my compliment. She brought me a glass of champagne, and we toasted to our evening and each other. We then sat on the small couch together, Marie carefully placing herself very close to me as she told me about her week here in the city.

"It's been a busy time for me here, visiting a perfume manufacturer to increase our order of perfume ingredients to us. I also visited the Israeli consulate in Manhattan; they always want to know when I am in town," she said.

"But the highlight when I come here is the shopping!" she exclaimed.

She emphasized she always enjoyed shopping in New York, where generally she could find a good selection of clothes and shoes, even from France, at more reasonable prices than in Paris.

She said, chuckling, exposing her very white set of large and orderly, attractive teeth, "I always bring an extra suitcase for taking my new purchases back home."

Shortly after seven, we headed over to the Met, about six blocks away, because Marie wanted to book a table for dinner at the intermission after Act 2, and we wanted to select our food.

"I love going to operas in the cities where I'm traveling," she said. "At home, I have a subscription to the Paris Opera. I try to go to every performance."

"I'm lucky to get to two operas a year," I said, "and here I am in New York just twenty minutes from the Met. I do find time to see a lot of Broadway shows, though."

We arrived at the Met just after they opened for the audience at 7:30 p.m. and went directly to the dining room reception on the upper main level to place our orders for mixed salads, salmon for Marie and filet of sole for me, and glasses of Pinot Grigio wine from California, for the first intermission. Then we proceeded to our seats in the Parterre, row B in the center, which I was impressed that Marie could get on such short notice. But I was learning that she knew how to maneuver and get whatever she wanted, wherever she was.

*

AT INTERMISSION, WE hurried to the dining room, where we were quickly seated. Our salads were already waiting, and the wine was poured as we took our places. We were impressed by how efficiently everything was handled in order to get us served and back in our opera seats within the forty-minute break.

"I'm really enjoying this performance," said Marie. "Especially the scenery in the first act." Also, the principal singers were outstanding, she thought, and I had no choice but to agree.

When our main courses were served, Marie asked what I had been busy with since our lunch earlier in the week. I told her about growing cancer cells and observing how they interact with neighboring normal cells, and why it's important to study this to learn how and why cancer cells spread to distant organs and sites, which is the major cause of death from cancer. Marie didn't say a word during my mini-lecture on what is known, or more accurately what we don't know about metastasis; she just stared at me with those penetrating eyes until I finished.

Then she said, "Milt, I had no idea that you were so engaged in this area of medicine. I remember how fascinated I was taking introductory genetics in high school and college, but no one spoke about how different cells, outside of fertilization, could unite. Frankly, it gives me goose pimples to sit here with you as your date tonight."

"Ah, Marie," I said, "you're both kind and an excellent psychologist. You know exactly how to disarm a male companion while building his ego."

"No," she said, "I am serious. I knew you were a physician and a member of the faculty of a prestigious medical school. I knew you were interested in olfaction, but nothing more professionally other than your publications in cancer research."

"Well, enough about me," I said. "Tell me more about what you do at your perfume company — and how I fit into your agenda."

"Now *that* is a discussion," she said, smiling. "I will begin, but we are running out of time, so I will save the important parts to when we return to my hotel after the opera, okay?"

Here she was again, controlling the conversation and even our date. I was now programmed to return to her hotel suite after the opera, which would be at about 11 p.m. But since it was Friday night, why not?

Actually, I was delighted at the prospect of spending more time with her. Her eyes were studying me keenly, and I presumed she was thinking just as I was.

Will there be a romantic relationship between us? Am I up to it? What's her ulterior motive?

Those thoughts were on my mind as we prepared to return to our seats. We were already acting as a couple, walking hand-in-hand.

The next two acts went slowly in my view, since I was thinking about being alone with Marie later. In the last act, during the famous scene when Mimi was dying of tuberculosis, Marie took my hand and held it tightly, sharing the emotion of the last scene. The audience thundered when the final curtain came down, and rose for five curtain calls to applaud the cast.

*

AS WE WALKED back to the Mandarin Hotel, again hand-in-hand, Marie was very quiet. I couldn't tell if she were thinking about the opera and the tragedy of Mimi and Rodolfo or the rest of this evening. In any case, we enjoyed the walk and the fresh air and were back in her suite in no time.

Marie threw off her heels and invited me to take off my jacket and tie and make myself comfortable, while she offered me more of the champagne that she'd left on ice. We sat on the couch and sipped the champagne for maybe one minute. Then Marie moved over to me, took my face in her hands, and gave me a long kiss, her tongue exploring my mouth. She then started unbuttoning my shirt. I put my arms on her shoulders and neck, and she let her dress drop to the floor, and in no more than two minutes, she had all my clothes off.

She was eager to kiss me from my mouth to my genitals while I caressed her body. Then she stood up, took my hand, and led me to her bed. She was lovely, lusty, and wanted me inside her without further conversation or foreplay.

I was surprised to have such an exciting and passionate partner who evidently knew what she wanted. It was clear that I would spend the night in this room and in this bed with her, and by 2 a.m., we were finally exhausted enough to fall into a slumber in each other's arms. I did not anticipate this, but there were no regrets. How am I going to relate this to my CIA handler, but maybe I'm underestimating their resources?

In any event, this is the best part of my new role as a spy: romancing other spies.

15.

IT WAS ABOUT 7:30 the next morning when I first opened my eyes and slowly realized where I was and how I had spent the night. Marie was lying facing me, apparently still asleep. The sight of her made me recall how wonderfully passionate she'd been — and now she looked so angelic. I wanted to lean over and kiss her but didn't want to interrupt her sleep. To my surprise, she opened her eyes and smiled at me, moving closer to fold into my arms. I kissed her forehead and wished her good morning.

She then sat up. "Why do you carry two cell phones?" she asked. I was still foggy and needed to think about this for a moment — then I realized she had found my special CIA cell phone in my jacket pocket. I didn't know what to say.

"I got up earlier this morning and went to hang up your clothes," she said. "That's when I discovered that you have two cell phones, which I found strange. I examined both. The one you have not talked to me on had a strange device to record conversations automatically. I disarmed it."

She looked piercingly at me, making me very uncomfortable. "It's just something I need for work," I said lamely. "I can't talk about it." I was secretly glad that she had disconnected the recording device, which I was unaware of.

I then asked where she got this technical knowledge and capability to disarm the auto-recording attachment. Marie ignored my question and got out of bed. "I'm going to make coffee," she said.

The passionate mood of the previous night seemed a distant memory now. I reflected on the fact that I had slept with a spy, an agent of the infamous Israeli secret service, the Mossad, also called 'The Office.'

Was last night's passion just part of her Mossad role? Can I trust Marie?

Marie brought our coffees into the bedroom and got back into bed, looking at me while she sipped from her mug.

Should I ask her if this was all part of her plan? What did she make of my question about her ability to check out and manipulate my cell phone?

But I didn't have to raise the issue. Evidently reading my thoughts, Marie blurted out, "I was focused on meeting you and gaining your trust. But then I lost control of my emotions. I became attracted to you romantically, Milt. I regret the circumstances leading to our meeting, but I do not regret the outcome."

She looked into her coffee for a moment, then faced me again. "There is more to you than just being a medical scientist, Milt. So, there is a lot we need to share now that we have slept together and, I presume, have begun a relationship.

"I work for this small perfume company in Paris because it gives me access to other organizations and companies dealing with odors. Like you, I believe odor molecules have many more applications than just affecting behavior as scents. I am Jewish and love the State of Israel, so I am helping them defend themselves from the illicit use of odors in espionage and assassinations, and that is how I became focused on your participation at the Vienna conference.

"The Mossad has relationships with many foreign governments and their spy organizations, including those of our allies, so it is not unexpected that I would learn from them that you are also helping your own country's spy organization, your CIA."

There it was, the revelation that I had been expecting and was totally unprepared for.

How should I answer? Should I respond?

I knew that *any* answer would be a violation of my oath to the CIA, and I was sufficiently inexperienced in the world of clandestine activities to venture any explanations. But I guessed Brad and my other CIA contacts knew that Marie would disarm me very quickly.

"I agree we do have a lot to talk about, Marie," I said. "But I'm not sure what I can say at this time — only that last night has confused me totally. Maybe this was the planned effect, right? I've never known or had sex with a spy, until now."

"Please don't be angry or disappointed in me, Milt," she said. "I am talking with you as someone who shared her most private emotions and feelings, not as a colleague in the spy business or in the area of olfaction. We need to be able to trust each other," she said — very convincingly, I thought. "But I think we've said enough about this for now. Let's order breakfast."

*

MARIE THEN WENT to take a shower while I stayed in bed thinking about how my life was getting more and more confusing and complicated.

We went to the living room when the breakfast cart was delivered and enjoyed assorted rolls, eggs with bacon, fruit, and a pot of coffee. After Marie finished her croissant and fruit bowl, she came over to me on the couch and snuggled onto my lap and opened her robe so our bodies could touch as she caressed me and moved her body so she could easily arouse me as she sat on me. "I don't know if I'm up to your energy and prowess," I said.

"You let me worry about that," she said.

After we finished our second lovemaking, we showered — Marie for the second time — and dressed. Marie packed her bags so we could walk in Central Park before she had to head to Kennedy Airport for her flight to Paris. She checked out and stored her luggage.

While Marie was chic and casual in a sweater and jeans, I felt uncomfortable in my suit from the night before. Nevertheless, it was nice to stroll casually over to the park and onto the west side walking path in sunny weather and a temperature of about seventy degrees. We figured we had until three o'clock before Marie had to collect her bags and get to the airport for her 6:00 p.m. flight.

There was a lot to say, but it was a tricky conversation. Marie wanted to know more about my business ideas with regard to olfaction, and I told her about Pharmascent Sciences and how I planned to establish a scientific basis to selecting odors for medical applications, especially neurodegenerative diseases. She showed a keen interest in the financing aspect and said it might well be something her current employer or other contacts she had would be interested in.

"In fact," she said, "the Israeli Defense Forces and the Mossad are concerned about the use of odors as weapons, and this brings me in contact with Mossad businessmen who have capabilities to get involved in a business venture such as you're proposing. Did your CIA handler mention this to you?"

I wasn't sure how to respond, since no one mentioned this to me before Marie, so I just smiled as if I knew about this possibility and just continued to listen.

Yet, she was very cautious, having probably already told me more than her bosses in Israel would have approved. She did, however, suggest that the Mossad was already collaborating with the CIA "because they both have a common strategic and defense mission." I wasn't sure if she were speaking sincerely or just probing. It was clear that she'd concluded that I was working with the CIA but didn't know specifically what my role was. Fortunately, she didn't probe further. She just held and squeezed my hand as we walked.

I decided to probe a bit myself. "How serious is the threat of using odors as a part of chemical warfare?" I asked.

Surprisingly, she didn't hesitate to answer. "Unfortunately, we don't know, which is why we are worried. We do know, as many spy agencies do, including your CIA, that Russia and a number of rogue nations, including North Korea and Iran, are researching chemical weapons presented as odors, in order to kill in a more restricted or subtle way than mass exposure to poisonous chemicals and gases, as mustard gas was used in the First World War.

"The other threat from North Korea, after their nuclear arsenal, is their chemical weapon stockpile. According to South Korean sources, Pyongyang has up to about five thousand metric tons of some twenty different chemical toxins stockpiled, and this includes *VX*, which is much more toxic than *sarin* that Syrian president Bashar al-Assad was accused of using against his people in 2013.

"A sarin attack against South Korea could kill as many as two to three million people in Seoul, not counting a multiple of those who would be injured. And we suspect that North Korea's president had his estranged half-brother, Kim Jong-nam, killed in the Malaysian airport by having VX rubbed in his face," she continued.

"Since this chemical doesn't spread by dispersement, it was selective in its killing. The same could be true using certain chemicals that could kill by being smelled and then transmitted to the central nervous system, as you are suggesting for medical uses. Imagine if we could deliver an odor to someone targeted for assassination, and only this person is killed after smelling a small quantity."

"But how do you limit the scent to one person?"

"Well, Milt, that is one of the challenges to be addressed, *n'est-ce pas*? And I would guess your CIA may be interested in your ideas in this regard."

Now this all was starting to come together for me. The CIA had become aware of my interests in developing a drug therapy using odor molecules, while they were interested in the opposite application —

both finding selective toxic odors and probably also antidotes. They learned, through the usual spy network, of work being done in this area by our adversaries, so of course, the United States and presumably its allies, such as Israel, also had such programs underway, and probably intensive intelligence gathering to learn of the progress of our enemies and maybe also our allies.

"Will you come visit me in Paris, Milt?" Marie asked, unexpectedly.

"Marie," I answered, "I really want to be with you again, but my life is crazy right now. I don't know how to fit a trip to Paris in."

"Well," she said, clearly prepared for that, "maybe I can arrange for you to meet some prospective investors — maybe we could even make a trip to Israel to call on potential backers."

"That sounds really good to me, Marie," I said, even as I remembered all the other things I wanted to accomplish in the next few weeks. "I promise to think about it."

In time, we collected her luggage from the hotel bellman, who loaded her bags into a taxi. Marie and I hugged, and she kissed me on both cheeks and on my lips. "I am already missing you," she whispered with that lovely accent.

I watched as the cab pulled away, waving until she was out of sight.

16.

AFTER CHANGING INTO jeans and a polo shirt, I opened my computer and reviewed emails, and eventually returned to working on my patent filing. At about 8:00 p.m., I turned on the flat-screen TV in my living room, but nothing held my attention. I was already thinking about how we were going to develop an article to report our findings, and we would, of course, need to cite important papers published earlier by others. So, I kept searching the Internet while the TV droned on in the background.

Fortunately, I found a few reviews on the related subjects of tumors and their microenvironment, on mechanisms of tumor progression, and even on cell-cell fusion *in vitro,* or outside the body, such as in cell culture systems. But evidence for the simultaneous presence and function of cancer and normal cell genes growing in a human, or experimentally as a transplant in an animal, was not clearly demonstrated in the literature I found.

By now, my tiredness had caught up with me. Marie and last night were challenging and troubling, I thought, and also unforgettable. I closed my eyes and soon fell asleep, only to be awakened by a ping on my cell phone about 11:00 p.m.: "Just landed, flight comfortable. Thank you for a wonderful date. Maybe another soon?"

I groggily texted her back, "Absolutely."

*

ON SUNDAY, I focused on revising my patent application. By mid-afternoon, I finished another extensive draft, but I knew I would need formatting help from my attorney. He would also assist in writing up the patent claims, which are vital to defining what the patent covers and protects. What I still needed was a device that allowed quantitation of the odor molecules delivered, as well as a method to determine their uptake in the blood. Since the nasal capillaries would also deliver these odor molecules to a subject's circulation, I had to learn how much and in what timeframe the blood concentration was achieved. This would affect many organs, including the brain, which also received the circulating molecules that entered the bloodstream via the blood vessels in the nose.

It was a great feeling to believe I was on the verge of creating an entirely new pharmacology. I sent John an email with my draft as an attachment. I was so excited that I had to force myself not to call him. I knew it was best to let him make his own impression without my explanation. Anyhow, it was Sunday, and not the time to call your attorney, even if he shared his private number with you.

*

ON MONDAY, WE got great news. Almost as soon as I arrived at my office, John Bogner, my genetics colleague, was bursting through my door with pictures of his results from our lab experiment to show me. John had performed a number of tests, including characterizing the chromosomes of the cells we provided to him and analyses of their presumptive human gene expression profiles.

The original and maintained human colon cancer cells, either taken from mice or growing in culture flasks, clearly showed only human chromosomes, with some extra 'marker' chromosomes that probably represent relocated pieces of some of the normal chromosomes represented. However, there was some duplication, since the chromosome number was larger than the normal number of forty-six for human cells.

In contrast, few human-appearing, bi-armed, or 'X'-appearing chromosomes were present in the more aggressive, spindle-shaped cancer cells that I speculated were more murine than human. In fact, John was able to use probes for murine DNA to show their rodent origin. Even further, John applied special gene expression assays that showed these same cells with clearly an abundance of mouse chromosomes had retained functional human genes in addition to those of a mouse, and he confirmed that at least twenty human genes were present and still functional in these murine-appearing cancer cells, because their respective proteins were produced.

John was as excited as I was, since neither of us had experienced this in cell culture experiments or in the serial growth of human cancer cells in suitable mice that were used for this purpose.

We also know that result hadn't been described so far in the scientific literature.

While researchers had postulated on the interchange of genetic information between cancer and adjacent normal cells for many years, such speculation wasn't in the context of viable, genetically hybrid cells of tumor and nontumor origin being maintained in these new, highly malignant cells.

"Our cells," John concluded, "had human *and* murine genetic information in the *same* cancer cells." In fact, our new hybrid tumor cells were surprisingly much more malignant in the mouse than the parental, strictly human, colon cancer cells.

John and I agreed that we needed to expand these studies and confirm these findings in other transplant generations of the new, putatively hybrid tumor line and to collect all of our results and information so we could start planning an article for publication.

Since these were all new scientific findings for us and possibly with major implications both for genetics and for understanding how cancer genes may work, we wanted to be careful about making sweeping conclusions beyond the actual evidence we had, and so thought that sharing our findings with some of our colleagues in cancer and genetics research would be useful.

But then the research scientists' usual paranoia took hold. We revised our thinking and decided to keep our findings as confidential as possible before presenting them publicly at a meeting or in a journal, which would then give us scientific priority. We also discussed whether there was anything patentable in our research findings and whether we needed to report this work to the intellectual property office at ESU. Again, we decided such sharing was premature.

*

THE NEXT MORNING, as I was shaving, my CIA phone pinged. The text said that if I could make myself available today, they would pick me up in front of the hospital at 1:00 p.m. I texted back that I would be there waiting.

17.

AT ONE O'CLOCK precisely, I was picked up by the usual black Lincoln Town Car with Brad Williams in the back seat. He told me we were going to a special safe house about twenty minutes away. "I need you to put on this blindfold," he said.

I didn't appreciate this over-the-top intrigue, but I assumed he had a good reason. So, for the next nearly half hour, I rode blindfolded. "Why was the auto-recording device on your CIA cell phone deactivated?" he asked in a perturbed voice.

"Why was this inserted in the first place, compromising my privacy?" He didn't answer, but I could tell he was waiting for me to do better. "Marie Chalfont found it and removed it," I then admitted matter-of-factly.

"Well," said Brad," it's surprising to us that a Mossad agent could discover your CIA affiliation so easily. Our meeting today is to determine where we are and the risks in continuing with you."

Is this my out?

While there were pluses to being connected with them, I saw nothing but problems with my Pharmascent Sciences plans, my patents, and my freedom to collaborate with other parties. I didn't believe these were nice guys when doing the government's spy business, and I suspected they couldn't care less about my research and business interests independent of their own needs.

In a while, we slowed down, and I could feel the car turning. Then we stopped. Brad helped me out of the car and guided me into a building, then onto an elevator. We went up for less than 20 seconds or so. Then, as the elevator doors opened and we stepped out, Brad said, "Okay, you can take the blindfold off now."

We walked down a corridor with what appeared to be various offices and stopped in front of a door marked 511. Brad used his key to let us into a room furnished as a sitting room, where two other men and a woman were waiting. One of the men was Robert Ehrlich, who started this whole thing months before by approaching me in the hospital cafeteria. He didn't look as friendly now.

I was asked to sit in a leather chair across from the others, like in a witness chair. On the coffee table in front of us was a recording machine. Brad reached over and turned it on. Then he introduced me to his grim-faced colleagues. "Dr. Davidson, this is Judy Reagan, who is a member of the chemical weapons team; Jim Rossi, who focuses on a number of areas, including counterespionage; and Bob Ehrlich, whom you've met. Bob manages some of our operations here in New York."

Jim Rossi started the questioning. "Milt, we informed you during the Vienna conference that Marie Chalfont was a Mossad agent. So why did you get involved with her and disclose your CIA relationship?"

What could I say that wasn't going to be embarrassing? "Well," I said, "she's clearly more experienced at this than I am."

Bob Ehrlich shook his head dismissively. "What did you do, hold up a sign saying the CIA is interested in chemical weapons using smells?"

I wasn't used to being talked to that way, and I shot back with a definite edge in my voice. "Look, Bob — in my line of work, we don't use aliases and play secrecy games. So maybe we ought to just agree to disagree, and I'll go my way and forget everything that's happened. Okay?" I could feel my face getting red.

"I'm afraid it's not that simple," said Brad. "First, we can't risk your walking away now — you may not know everything, but what you do know is too much. Second, we need to get this involvement with Marie and the Mossad under control. And third, you've established contacts, such as Dr. Borofskov in Vienna, who are important to us. You fell into a honey trap, and now you need to help us take advantage of that." Suddenly, everyone appeared to be stifling a smile.

"Finally, and most importantly," Brad again spoke, "we lost a CIA officer at the Vienna conference, which was clearly also related to his monitoring you and some of the other participants."

Then Judy Reagan looked at me seriously. "Dr. Davidson, your involvement with Marie Chalfont has come to the attention of the highest levels of both the U.S. and Israeli espionage and counterespionage groups. Our director and the head of the Mossad are in discussions about you and Marie and how this should be handled in the future."

Reagan continued. "Our order for today was to make it perfectly clear that you're not to continue in any Agency-oriented discussions with Marie Chalfont. On the other hand, you *are* to maintain your relationship with her until we can get more clarity and instructions. She is not to know of this meeting. She is not to know that we're in discussions with her bosses at the Mossad. She is not to know of *any* of our plans going forward unless you are so advised by us."

Now it was my turn to stifle a smile.

Apparently, Judy Reagan didn't like the expression on my face. "Dr. Davidson," she said, "we're talking about matters of national defense, in which many lives are at stake. We have already lost an agent, who now has a widow and fatherless children. We will not tolerate any disloyalty, intentional or not, by you. And we have fairly broad powers to do what is necessary to protect our nation."

Clearly, that's a threat.

"Are you blaming me for Charles Hughes's murder?" I confronted them.

Ms. Reagan ignored by question, and continued: "We know it's going to be difficult managing Ms. Chalfont, who's a very well-trained spy and active field agent. She, of course, knows or suspects a lot about you and your CIA affiliation, but you have to try to be less communicative, yet let her continue trusting you. Has she told you anything about her activities last Thursday?"

"No, is there something more I should know?"

"Her main reason for being in New York, my handsome spy," she chuckled, "was not you, but interrogating a Hezbollah agent who is part of an ISIS cell working in Brooklyn, and whom the Mossad was thinking of recruiting as a double-agent. Marie is fluent in Arabic, especially the dialects in Yemen, and knows enough of their various cells and leaders to determine whether this Arab was being sincere."

"So, she wasn't here to do perfume business, shop, or take me to the opera?" I asked disappointedly.

"No, but she knows how to manage her time and objectives. In an hour, she learned that the potential mole was a plant, brought to deceive and mislead us. Neither the Mossad nor we had anyone else who could have trapped him into revealing this."

"How did it end?" I asked naively.

"Let's just say that neither we nor the Hezbollah cell will have need of his services. He just never walked out of our consulate to return to Brooklyn," Judy ended this conversation.

"Okay," I said, "I understand now. But I really am a novice at this; you have to be patient until I get more experience, or you find someone else."

"We're going to help you with that," said Brad, sounding less hostile. "In addition to visiting Langley again, you'll need to get special training."

"Wait a minute," I said. "I have a full-time job. I can't just 'go off' to some spy school. What'll I tell my department chairman? My dean?"

"We'll take care of that," Brad said. "I'll be in touch soon once we've come to some decisions. In the meantime, here's a new cell phone with encryption capability. Use it to stay in regular contact with me, and try keeping it away from any of your future lovers." Even I had to smile at this.

*

RETURNING TO MY office, I checked for messages. One was from Dr. Bickers, asking me to drop by his office. He had left his message at 1:20 p.m., and it was now almost four o'clock, so I went immediately down the hall to see him. His office was open, so I just knocked softly and walked in.

"Milt," he said, looking up from his desk. "Come in and have a seat." Then he asked how I was and how the work was going, which sounded to me like he had something more serious on his mind — which he got to right away. "Some of the staff think you've been distracted lately, Milt, so I wanted to see if I could be of any help or maybe a sounding board."

So, my stress is showing. I didn't quite know what to say. "Oh, John, thanks — I've become a servant to the CIA, I may be involved in chemical and olfactory weaponry, I'm trying to start a business on the side, and I have a new girlfriend" couldn't be shared with my department chairman.

"Thanks for your concern, John," I said. "I have some exciting new findings with my lab project, which I hope to share with you soon, but I'm very engaged with these experiments while having some other personal things to take care of. So, I guess I'm a little pressured."

"Well," he said, patting me on the shoulder, "I'm here if you need any fatherly advice. But, of course, I don't want to pry."

I was glad to get out of his office and back to my own, since I knew he was a keen observer and probably knew I was giving him only a partial story.

*

PART OF THE stress that others were noticing was due to my concerns about protecting my intellectual property rights, which meant I needed to invest in another expensive phone call with John Sackler. Amazingly, I got through to him immediately, and he said he generally liked the most recent patent draft I'd sent him. "That's great, John," I said, "but this call is about a couple of issues that are troubling me. I need your advice."

"Sure thing," he said.

"First, I'm a full-time employee of ESU, and I recall that my contract states that all inventions have to be submitted to the patent committee for review — and that if a patent is pursued or awarded, the assignee is ESU. But this olfaction invention of mine is totally unrelated to my work at the university and was conceived after hours and on weekends. On top of that, it's mostly prophetic and not reduced to practice. So how do I handle this?"

"Well," he said, "first — as I explained when you first visited with me — we need to determine if indeed you do have an invention. And if you do, we need to figure out how it is or isn't governed by your employment agreement. You may have to discuss this with an employment attorney who'll need to review your contract. I can give you a couple of names."

Always another damn lawyer.

"Okay, thanks. My next question is a little more diffuse. I am a consultant to the government," I said, "and this required a confidentiality agreement that bars me from sharing with any other party any information on this — I'm not even supposed to reveal that this arrangement *exists*. I'm having serious concerns about this arrangement and would like legal advice on how I might end it. But if I talk to anyone about it — you, for example — am I violating my secrecy agreement?"

"Confidentiality agreements should not be consummated unless each side has separate legal advice," he said, "so I gather you did not, since you're asking what should have been addressed before you signed one. In any event, it's your right to have legal representation in any business or private transaction, even with a government agency. So, I don't understand your concern."

"John," I said, "this isn't just *any* government agency. This is one that's involved in secret and security issues."

"My comment still holds. If I understand you correctly, you'll need an attorney experienced in dealing with the government and some of its more clandestine agencies. Does this in some way involve your invention and business plans for the olfactory company?"

"Yes," I responded, "but it's more expansive than that. It includes other activities of a highly secret nature."

John sent me an email before the end of the day, with two names each for employment and government contract attorneys, all of whom he knew well and assured me would be capable of handling my problem.

I jotted John a quick thanks, adding, "They look expensive."

He wrote back: "Another reason to discuss doing this with your employer. If you delay, they could refuse to reimburse you for any initial bills you'd paid."

*

AT JUST BEFORE 6:00 p.m., I got a text from Brad Williams, thanking me for our meeting and saying that they now had plans to share with me. He would pick me up in his car tomorrow at 1:00 p.m.

if that worked for me. He wouldn't need more than an hour, at most. I acknowledged and agreed.

I was glad for the chance to meet with him again so soon before I consulted one of these attorneys. I needed to have a frank discussion with Brad regarding my involvement and their expectations. I planned to make it clear that I have another life and wouldn't simply jump every time they called.

Yet, here I am, jumping at every ping of my CIA phone.

18.

BRAD WAS ON time, as usual. I got into the Town Car beside him, took the bottle of water he offered, and we began the trip among busy traffic in the Lower East Side of New York.

"My colleagues and I have discussed this matter with the Deputy Director," said Brad. "He is personally involved and has confided with his counterparts at our allies' counterintelligence agencies."

"This matter?" I asked.

"You," said Brad. It's been decided that this will be a multinational effort, and we'll bring you on board on a need-to-know basis so as to protect the identity of many of these agents. We're concerned about your inexperience, which, of course, resulted in the problem with Marie Chalfont, so we'll be providing you with an expedited training. Because of your strong intellectual background and scientific experience, we believe this can be done while you collaborate with our scientists on our research to develop olfaction antidotes as well as toxic odors. Of course, everything you do with us is of the highest level of security, which means we plan to reclassify you once you've completed training."

I guess he could read the shock on my face because he then said, "We appreciate that this isn't your current professional objective, Milt. But we're committed to having you as part of our team, and we'll, of course, make the necessary arrangements with your current employer."

Brad then stopped talking and waited for me to respond. I hardly knew where to begin. "Well, Brad," I said, "I'm complimented, but as you say, this isn't my desire or interest. It's not what I went to years of medical school and subsequent training for. So, I have to respectfully decline. In fact, I was hoping to discuss how we can end this relationship when you requested this meeting."

Brad didn't seem overly surprised. Instead, he sat back, looking straight ahead and not at me. "We expected this, Milt, but the Deputy Director asked me to appeal to your patriotism. He asked me to explain that we're at a very critical juncture where we know that our enemies are advancing a program of chemical warfare involving odors. I can say without exaggeration that this has the potential to be as big a threat as atomic warfare or chemical and gas toxins of the past. Russia, we know, has active research and experimentation on animals proving the existence of toxic odors that are specific and limited in their activity, so they can be used to kill limited numbers of people in a direct way, unlike chemical or gas warfare. North Korea also has active research ongoing in this area, and we believe they will be less restrained to test these on humans than the Russians.

"This can be used to assassinate individuals, or broadened to kill select groups, either immediately or in a protracted manner, so the event is delayed to a specified time. This is a new kind of warfare, Milt, and we need all the help and resources we can muster to take protective and countermeasures. We need you as part of a team, probably international with our allies, to catch up to the Russians, Koreans, and possibly other hostile nations as well."

Quite a speech.

In comparison, I sounded like Johnny One Note: "Brad," I said, "I recognize your concern and the efforts needed by our government. But I don't feel qualified or capable of changing my career and current research to become a government scientist or intelligence officer, despite your confidence in me."

Brad looked at me almost with a smile. "Milt," he said, putting on his serious face again, "we faced the same problem when we formed the Manhattan Project to develop the first atomic bomb and recruited top scientists to leave academia and industry to join the nation's effort to win the Second World War. We're doing the same now, including some prominent scientists and professors from various institutions, some joining us full-time and others part-time in consultant capacities, and the same is occurring with our partner nations, like Israel, France, Germany, and Great Britain. We've given this multinational effort the code name 'Scenturion Venture.'

"In terms of your other activities, we agree that it will curtail some of them, especially you're teaching regularly and your laboratory cancer research, but we hope your involvement will be for at most a year, and likely less. And we will, in fact, assist you in advancing your medical goals for olfaction, even providing laboratory and clinical resources available to us."

"And if I did conduct this research," I asked, "would the medical applications in diagnosis and therapy be mine, without having to license these to the government?"

"As with all government-supported research, the inventor has complete ownership," said Brad, "but gives the U.S. government a reduced royalty rate for use in government facilities and programs — the same as when a government agency supports research at a university or another nonprofit organization. The costs for patenting and commercial development would be borne by the investigator so long as he is not a government employee. In this case, you would be a CIA advisor and not an employee, although the responsibilities and commitments would be virtually the same. We want to make it easy for you to return to your professional activities once you've completed your mission for us. However, if the invention is deemed to require complete secrecy, filing a patent would be denied, of course."

"But I'm known more for my cancer research. I'm sure there are others who are better versed in olfaction and could contribute more," I almost pleaded.

"It's because of your credentials in pathology and cancer research that you're attractive to us, since exploring your company for odors that can be used pharmacologically is a new path for you while continuing your academic research at ESU, and gives you a great cover and reason to interact with other scientists studying olfaction from a military perspective," Brad again emphasized to me.

This had some attractive aspects, especially as I didn't think my work would result in some invention critical to national security while allowing me to venture into pharmaceutical research with defined odors. But, of course, I couldn't predict that in advance. Brad thanked me and repeated that this discussion was of the utmost confidence and secrecy. "I'll get back to you soon with a contract for your services and dates for your training," he said. "And your dean will be hearing from NIH, requesting your service. I guarantee that your supervisors will be pleased and proud to lend your expertise to us."

*

I WAS THEN dropped off in front of the medical center. I stood out there for a long while, not sure if I should return to my office or just go for a long walk to think. There was a lot to consider. Would this mission prove to be more dangerous than Brad was telling me? How would this change my responsibilities at ESU's medical school? How would it affect my academic career, including publishing, lecturing at conferences, and qualifying for promotion to full professor?

And do I even have a choice?

Strangely, it occurred to me to wonder what role, if any, Marie had played in today's developments.

As if by telepathy, my CIA phone pinged with a message from Marie. "Need to talk with you on a safe cell phone when you can talk privately," she texted. I didn't think my office would be suitable, or even my apartment, because now I'd become paranoid that I was being watched — and listened to — by either the CIA or another espionage group. But, of course, Marie knew that by texting me on the CIA phone, they would be reading her message — and evidently, she wasn't concerned about it. So, I stayed on the street a little longer to speak to Marie while walking.

She answered her phone immediately. "Oh, Milt," she said, "how good to hear your voice. Where are you, and what are you doing?"

"I just left a meeting," I said. "I'm walking in New York."

She told me that her Mossad leadership — she referred to it as 'The Office' — had advised her of my role with the U.S. agency and that her colleagues would be collaborating with them, and in turn with me, in the 'S' Venture. "I am delighted that we will be working together," she said excitedly.

I was taken aback at that. "I'm still deliberating, Marie," I said. "I have no experience in this kind of work, and don't want to change from professor to spy."

She chuckled. "Oh, mon c*hérie*," she said, "I am confident you will agree to join this project. It is vital to the future of our two countries, as well as all democratic societies. Of course, I have my selfish reasons for wanting you to participate."

*

A COUPLE OF days later, the contractual arrangement with the CIA arrived via special messenger, with a copy to the attorney with CIA clearance whom I had retained. At first reading, it didn't seem as daunting as I had imagined, but appearances can be deceiving. Fortunately, my attorney attended to it quickly, making only a few changes related to my freedom to invent and publish with prior CIA review, which had to be done within thirty days. The attorney also amended the part about my being prohibited from patenting only if a secret that could compromise national security were disclosed. Now it read that if this were disputed by me, I could have a mediation by a mutually appointed counsel of government employees, approved by the Inspector General, other than from the CIA.

I had a few days before I had to sign and send the contract back, but the very presence of it in my desk seemed to paralyze me. This thing we'd been dancing around for months was now *tangible,* and I found myself unable to focus on my usual daily activities. I even avoided my lab staff, since I couldn't accept dropping some of the research that I was so excited about.

Could I find a way to continue with that even while working on the Scenturion Venture?

I knew I had a good lab team and a committed genetics collaborator, but doing research part-time isn't fair to the project or to my colleagues. I was still soul searching even as I held the piece of paper that was to change my life and career.

19.

SATURDAY WAS AN unusual day for me because I had no plans. I was looking forward to traveling abroad for a while, in spite of my misgivings about leaving my work at ESU to spy for the CIA.

And Marie was on my mind as well. How stimulating and exciting she was, and we clearly had a great joint adventure ahead of us. I was glad that she probably would call later this evening; the very thought of it lifted my spirits, and I made a conscious decision to enjoy this day, starting with my week's supermarket shopping.

Then I took a walk to Union Square Park and visited the booths of the outside market. By 6:00 p.m., I was tired and hungry, and that feeling always led me to Jimmy's bar and grill near my home, where I could have a burger, fries, and a beer at the bar while watching whatever was on TV. There were a number of regulars with whom I could have some meaningless conversation.

Jimmy's was the place to go when I wanted to be alone but not by myself. While there, I got a text from Marie saying she would call about midnight, which would be 6:00 a.m. in Paris if indeed that's where she was. In no rush for a change, I sat at the bar and had a couple more beers, finally getting home about 9:00 p.m.

At precisely midnight, Marie called and seemed quite jubilant, saying that she was impatient for me to come join her in Paris. For the first time, she also said she was making arrangements to take me to Israel to meet her colleagues and get briefed on our future plans. I hadn't been to Israel in about ten years, so this sounded not just interesting but important — how many U.S. academics get to work with the Israeli Mossad?

After my dressing down by Brad and his colleagues, I made it a point to say as little as possible to Marie. Mostly I just listened. She also said she was telling her coworkers at her perfume company about me and some of my ideas. I wasn't sure I wanted this so well-known before I protected my inventions, but Marie didn't know any crucial details anyway. I was perplexed by Brad discouraging my interaction with Marie, but evidently her bosses at the Mossad encouraged it.

Or, was this all created by Marie herself?

She ended the conversation, saying that she was busy rearranging her apartment on the Left Bank to accommodate me for as long as I wanted to stay with her. I smiled, feeling pleasantly overwhelmed.

20.

AFTER A QUIET, uneventful weekend, I texted Brad Williams first thing Monday morning, saying that my lawyer and I had looked over the contract he'd sent and that I was inclined to sign it. He responded within the hour. "Great news. Will pick you up in front of the hospital tomorrow morning at 9:00 a.m. Will explain all then."

John Bogner was busy identifying the specific human genes that were present in these 'hybrid' cancer cells. My lab staff already knew of some, and many were associated with the growth and invasion typical of cancer cells. Was there a population of genes or DNA in these new cells that could infect nonmalignant cells and make them cancerous? Jhanella, Mike, and I discussed how we would test to see if we could 'transfect' such normal-appearing mouse fibroblasts, or skin cells, with DNA from our hybrid cancer cells and, thus, transfer malignancy. By doing this, we could prove that cell-free DNA from our human-mouse hybrid cancer cells could induce cancer in presumed normal cells of the mouse.

I left the lab feeling euphoric, since these results were unexpected and could lead us to a better understanding of the process of cancer formation, or oncogenesis, which may even have therapeutic implications, such as identifying critical oncogenes that may be targets for a gene therapy or even a vaccine. I knew these had been areas of interest in the cancer research community for a number of years, but as yet, had not been successful except in isolated animal experiments. No trials in humans had so far shown any real promise. I was determined not to interrupt or abandon this important work, but I was also concerned that pursuing a business venture with olfaction and, certainly, spying for the CIA, would be counterproductive to my real professional interests, and would be getting me into imbroglios with some of my spy colleagues.

*

ON TUESDAY AT 9:00 a.m., the now-familiar black Lincoln Town Car pulled up in front of the hospital, and I got in. Brad said he had a lot to tell me, and I was ready to hear it.

"We had some high-level meetings yesterday and last night," he said. "Here's the plan: The Director of the NIH's National Institute for Environmental Health Sciences will call the Dean of your School of Medicine and request that Dr. Milton Davidson be given a special leave of absence to work for the United States government, with your full salary being reimbursed to ESU for about six months, and with an option to renew for another six months — without any of this affecting your role and future tenure at the university. That will be an integral part of the agreement."

"I like it so far," I said.

"The Director will explain that this is a special project on olfaction that the NIEHS is undertaking at the request of the Director of the NIH, and with input from other government agencies. He will underscore the point that they're assembling an *elite* team of scientists from several universities, as well as from business and government labs. The Director will emphasize to the Dean that this is important work in the national interest and that the goal is to try to learn how certain odors are involved with disease, especially neurological diseases. He will say that the urgency of this project is related to chemicals and odors are given off in certain industrial settings that are critical to our government and several other nations, and that, in fact, members of our armed forces, and their families abroad, are being exposed. They will emphasize imminent environmental hazards."

"Wow," I said. "I'm impressed."

Brad said that the senior staff at Langley thought this sounded reasonable, yet urgent, and with sufficiently high NIH input as to evoke a positive response from the Dean. They expected that the Dean would handle all administrative steps at ESU, including advising my department chairman, Dr. Bickers. "In this way," said Brad, "you'll learn of this from your chairman, who will encourage you to accept this invitation from the Director of the NIH's NIEHS. Once you accept, you can then begin working out arrangements with your department and colleagues, who will be given the same story."

I thought this was an excellent plan, starting at the level of the Dean and with a request from as high in the NIH as you can go, including the NIH Director himself. Brad emphasized that the NIH Director was prepared to intercede, if necessary.

But how is this going to be appreciated by my lab colleagues, who will wonder how I could distance myself from our important cancer research findings at this pivotal time?

*

I WAS BACK in the office just before 10:30 a.m. It was about four-thirty in the afternoon when I got a message from Dr. Bickers that he needed me to come to his office, just as Brad predicted.

John jumped up when he saw me. "Take a seat, Milt," he said, clearly excited, and I sat down on his couch while he closed his door for privacy. Then he sat opposite me. "Milt," he said, "The Dean just called me. He asked me to speak to you about a call he received from the Director of the NIH's National Institute for Environmental Health Sciences. They're requesting that you be allowed time off to join a 'blue ribbon' team of scientists to help the government come to grips with what seems like an international problem with toxic odors being emitted in industrial settings. The Director told Dean Grossinger that this project is *vital* to the nation's defense."

"Well," I said, "I don't know what to say, John. What a surprise. I didn't realize that my earlier studies in olfaction were known to others."

"Milt, for you to be chosen in this way is an honor not just for you, but for ESU as well. The government will work with us and our attorneys to make this happen quickly, and with full reimbursement of your salary to the university during your absence. Your important lab work will continue, and they'll provide other support needs while you're on this sabbatical."

"How long will this take?" I asked.

"Up to six months, with the possibility of renewing for another six months."

"Wow. I don't know. That's a long time to be away."

"You've got to do it, Milt. I'll arrange for other members of the pathology faculty to take over your teaching and service responsibilities. I'm sure you'll want to arrange for your lab supervision yourself."

He volunteered to personally help out if needed. He looked at me, and he was beaming, like a proud father. "Well?" he asked. "What do you say?"

"I'm overwhelmed," I said, "and, of course, flattered. I'll certainly give it some thought."

But John was too excited to accept such vagueness. "Milt, you *have to agree*," he said. "Speaking for the Dean *and* for this department, we think it's *critical* that you let us respond in the affirmative to the Dean. He wants to handle this himself and asked me to encourage you to give of yourself to this important cause — without hesitation. The Director of the NIEHS emphasized that this was in the *national interest* and had the blessings of the NIH, the Department of Defense, and even the National Security Council."

Even I had to show I was impressed. I told John that I would, of course, do what was best for our institution and for the nation. Greatly relieved, he shook my hand vigorously and thanked me, on behalf of the Dean and ESU, for making this sacrifice.

21.

AFTER MEETING WITH Dr. Bickers, I texted Brad and told him I'd had *the* talk with my department chairman. Brad called me right away, and we both chuckled at how smoothly it had gone. "I told you," Brad said. He also said they were making arrangements for me to get an abbreviated training session with them. "We're tailoring it especially for you."

That sounded exceptional to me, considering that I was a 'consultant.'

But what do I know about the spy business?

"Well, please give me as much advance notice as possible," I said. "By the way, my passport has just been renewed, so no problems there."

He laughed. "It wouldn't matter anyway," he said. "We have our own passport and documentations office."

On my way home, I found myself thinking of all that I needed to do before starting this next chapter of my life.

What arrangement should I make for my mail? Who should have keys to my apartment?

*

IN THE MORNING, I had intended to review the draft *Introduction* I was writing for our planned article on the transfer of malignancy studies and list a number of references I wanted to include. But now that I was definitely going to work with the CIA, I couldn't keep my mind off my olfaction project — and in particular, which odors I would select first to study in my commercial work and for which medical disease or problem.

I thought Parkinson's disease would be an easy entity to study, since patients who are refractory to current therapies would have well-defined symptoms and signs that could be measured. I knew of a study where it was found that patients with Parkinson's had a reduced sense of smell, especially in white participants more than in African Americans, and that this 'hyposmia' occurred years before the disease was actually diagnosed.

But, among Parkinson's patients, could those with a normal sense of smell be isolated and studied in comparison to those with a smelling deficiency — with regard to course of disease and response to therapy?

Further, patients with Parkinson's seem to produce a specific odor, it has been observed. I had read that a British woman claimed to be able to identify individuals with Parkinson's disease by smell alone. Years before her husband became a Parkinson's patient, she noticed that he evoked a smell similar to musk, and this was confirmed to her when she attended support groups for the disease. When scientists tested her by exposing her to the clothes of Parkinson's patients, as well as controls who were disease-free, she was correct in all but one case, where she diagnosed Parkinson's in a control, unaffected person.

Surprisingly, this patient developed the disease three years later. I also remembered that chemists at Manchester University in England were studying perspiration and oils from the skin and other body fluids in an attempt to identify and then isolate the chemical molecules that produce this specific odor. I thought that this purified odor could be used to train dogs to smell this and then determine how specific it was for Parkinson's. Or, maybe the odor could be identified by gas chromatography, as in the case of other chemical products.

Stop it, Milt! You need to quit thinking about olfaction and return to your cancer paper.

Then my CIA cell phone pinged. It was a text from Marie saying, "Congratulations on your new consulting job." She also said she had bought a new flat-screen TV for her bedroom wall, "so my apartment will be more inviting for you when you move in."

What chutzpah.

I wondered what my CIA brethren were thinking of this text. It occurred to me that Marie might have a double dose of Jewish genes linked to her X-chromosomes, if such a construction did exist. She could be even more domineering than my Jewish mother, who ran our household like a titan while letting my father believe he was in charge. I wasn't sure I could adjust to Marie as even a part-time companion, despite my respecting her knowledge and capabilities as a Mossad agent, not overlooking her lovemaking prowess.

*

In terms of my research staff and colleagues, I decided to wait until Friday, when we planned to have our meeting to discuss all the lab results, to inform them of my plans, and to discuss how we would operate in my absence. I knew I needed to have a clear outline for the publication on the current findings we needed to complete, which would demonstrate progress on my grant from the National Cancer Institute, but I also felt confident that the CIA, or NIEHS, folks would get the message to the NCI program officer that I was of special interest to them.

The next two days were spent reviewing my standing arrangement to have rent, utility, and other bills paid regularly from my checking account and discussing with the building superintendent how my mail should be handled. I had nowhere to forward it and was sure my next address would be either at a CIA training center or at a foreign address, probably, at first, with Marie in Paris. I could have the superintendent collect it and store it in my apartment, but I needed someone who could look through it to identify mail of importance, unless I returned regularly.

22.

BY FRIDAY, I felt good about the progress I'd made with background information and my review of prior published studies, as well as an outline of the manuscript, in preparation for my 11:00 a.m. lab meeting.

From the genetics viewpoint, John was confident that we had sufficient data and comparisons to normal or nonhybrid malignant cells to publish our findings, and I felt the same from a biological-pathological perspective. I suggested that we submit the article to the journal *Cancer Advances*, which was very prestigious.

I knew I had to tell my coworkers about my upcoming absence, but I wasn't prepared to do it today; after discussing such promising results, I didn't want to bring them down in case they interpreted my leaving as abandoning them. Also, I thought I should first tell John Bogner, because I wanted him to take over a supervisory role for my lab. I knew he had a lot of other projects, but I was hopeful that our recent results had captured his imagination and that, maybe, my department chairman could also support my request through John's department chairman, invoking the support of the Dean if necessary.

After John's role was settled, I would tell Mike and Jhanella, assuring them that their positions were secure, that my grant wasn't in jeopardy because of my absence, and that I would stay in constant contact. Finally, if possible, I would visit in person every month or two.

We ended our meeting agreeing to circulate our different sections of the proposed article by Wednesday of the following week, so we could have another research meeting next Friday. The others thought this was a tight schedule, but I encouraged them to try, since the results were too important to delay reporting.

*

USUALLY, BY FRIDAY, I was looking forward to the weekend, but now I found myself feeling particularly pressed. I was planning to work on the *Introduction* and part of the *Discussion* over the weekend, but I also worried about how long it would take for all the legal agreements between the NIH, ESU, and me to be consummated.

I worked on my article draft most of the day on Saturday, making good progress. Later in the afternoon, I received a text from Marie, asking if I could talk. I dialed her number, and she said she was delighted to hear my voice.

"I have received instructions to prepare for your visit to Paris within the next month," she said. "I have been asked to arrange an indoctrination program from my perspective."

She didn't explain what she meant by that, and I didn't ask. I was trying to stay out of trouble with my own Agency, and I thought it best that we not discuss too much on the telephone, although keeping Brad and his CIA brethren in the dark was impossible.

After a little non-spy chit-chat with Marie, I got undressed and went to bed, but I found it hard to fall asleep.

Paris, within the month!

23.

THE REST OF the weekend was taken with getting my manuscript into near-final form, so when I got to the office on Monday, I was able to turn it over to my co-authors to complete the references and figures for me to review before it was submitted for publication. I also had 'the talk' with John Bogner, Mike and Jhanella. John agreed to supervise the lab in my absence, and Mike and Jhanella, while shocked at my news, were nevertheless impressed that I'd been asked to undertake such a prestigious assignment. I told them I didn't know yet exactly when I was leaving but that it would be soon, and I expected to have access to email so we could stay in touch.

After meeting with my lab team, I huddled with John Bickers for a couple of hours. I told him that the people at NIEHS had asked me to be ready to travel soon, maybe as early as the coming weekend. John seemed a little taken aback but also kind of excited. So, we put our heads together and made the necessary arrangements for handing off the full array of my duties for a while. John said that if some things weren't figured out before I left, he would take it on himself to devise a solution. Occasionally, as I was talking, I noticed him looking at me with an expression of pure awe and pride on his face.

Following our meeting, I ate lunch at my desk with my door closed. When I got Brad on the line, I said, "My chairman and I agreed that this would be my final full week. I'm ready to go as early as this weekend." I realized, of course, that I would be unable to have my usual lab meeting on the following week.

*

BRAD WILLIAMS PICKED me up at Union Station in Washington on the following Monday to drive with me to CIA headquarters in Langley, which only gave me a few days to prepare for my departure, including packing clothes for a colder climate. He explained that I was now entering the learning-about-the-mission phase, which he estimated could take a week or more. He then took me through the Langley facility annex to a room marked 2173, which was to be my residence there.

"You'll be picked up and escorted from here whenever you go out," he said, "so don't venture out by yourself." He pointed me to a wall phone and gave me a number to dial if I needed assistance any time. He also cautioned that no contact outside headquarters was permitted generally, but he knew my need to have some external calls, which was being arranged.

He left me to unpack and relax for about an hour, when I would be picked up to go to my first meeting. The room was really a small apartment, with a bedroom and bathroom, a living room with a small kitchen nook and windows facing the countryside and distant hills. The furnishings were like a modest motel, with flat TVs on the walls of both rooms.

This'll work for a week or so.

Then I wondered if my room was under surveillance.

An hour later, a man named Ken picked me up and took me back to the main building, then to a second-level basement conference room. Large screens adorned all four walls and were controlled by video systems on the conference table. Ken stayed, and Brad introduced me to the five other men and two women present, including Dr. Jim Calhoun and John Crayton. Then Dr. Calhoun took over the meeting, with Crayton slipping out without further comment.

Calhoun explained, "Our job is to educate you about the mission and our expectations." He said this was the most sensitive and important part of my education, so he'd made sure some of their top field and lab people were in the room. He then recapped what I already knew: that the CIA, together with some of its allies in espionage, was exploring the use of odors in defense, including as a means of interrogation, and in a different form as a means of coercion.

They were also trying to develop antidotes to odor attacks or even undertake preventive measures, including vaccines to protect against attacks with odors or specific chemicals introduced into the nasal cavity. I nodded my head, showing that I was impressed with these plans.

"Our operatives in other countries are reporting that this is a high priority with certain adversaries, such as Russia, China, Iran, and North Korea, but also, to some extent, with smaller hostile nations, including Syria and Lebanon's Hezbollah" he added.

"Our assets report to us about the ongoing activities and have, in fact, identified, by code names, certain chemicals being used in odor weaponry," Calhoun said. "But this is half the equation. We need to identify the chemicals and what the status of their experimentation is. And that's where you come in, Dr. Davidson."

"Milt, please," I corrected him.

At that point, he paused dramatically as every head in the room turned toward me.

"We need a scientist who can communicate with our agents and draw up a chart of progress with defined chemicals and future goals, working with any sources we can identify or even turn. This is why we didn't extract Dr. Vladimir Borofskov, who made contact with you in Vienna. Instead, we decided to use him in this effort, either as our mole or as a double agent. Once you're in Russia —"

Wait a minute. Russia?

"— and possibly interact with him, you'll be able to determine if he can help us — or if he is perhaps a double-agent for the Russian military's GRU. We will advise you if, when, and how to deal with him. Remember, Charles Hughes was murdered when he interrupted someone searching his hotel room, and you were suspicious that

Borofskov may have been in your room when you were out, his business card being moved.

"We have to consider," he continued, "that Borofskov may be the culprit, assigned to the Vienna conference as an agent of the FSB to assess the other Western country participants interested in olfaction, including you and maybe also Marie. Hughes may have been an attendee whom he had to investigate."

By the time Calhoun finished, I felt like my head was spinning. *Russia? Double agent? The FSB?*

"Look," I said, "I'm not at all confident that I'm capable of doing this. Especially in hostile countries. What will prevent me from having the same fate as Hughes, especially if I'm in Moscow?"

Then Calhoun offered: "Once you're in Moscow, Milt, we'll need to find a reason to interrogate Borofskov to determine if he, in fact, killed our agent, and what his mission is. He made a contact to you under the story of wanting to defect, but this was clearly a ploy to gain your trust.

"You won't be working alone, Dr. Davidson," he continued. "You'll be part of a network of other agents and scientists, since this is now more or less a NATO effort but also including Israel."

"Will I be working with Marie Chalfont and her Israeli handlers?"

"Initially, yes," said Calhoun, "because she works for a French perfume company made up of retired Mossad agents who're already investigating this problem. Also, because she'll be your contact to Israelis who are very active in understanding the role of olfactory research in these other adversary countries. Later in the week, we'll brief you, in detail, about various activities we *know* are underway."

*

WE SPENT THE rest of the day in an open discussion on what information they did and didn't have with regard to experiments being conducted at the chemical warfare site in rural Russia, where, evidently, the CIA had a mole and could get some limited information. But from what John and Jim knew, I gathered that their source wasn't a chemist: no formulas or precise chemical entities were known, only general statements about the kinds of experiments being conducted in animals and also in some volunteers. But were they truly volunteers? We knew that the Russian FSB, the successor spy network to the KGB, used prisoners for experimentation, so we couldn't be sure.

Although the CIA could get some limited information from the Mossad about similar studies in Iran, here again, this was only general information on the effects being studied. John emphasized, "we need a plan, but as we expand the circle of advisors, we increase the risk of our adversaries learning of our efforts, and then tightening security at their own labs."

Jim projected a list of code names on the whiteboard in the front of the room: CE20, CN122, XR16, YD99, and YD122. "These," he said, "are olfactory substances or mixtures named in documents we've received from our agents or referred to on Oryol computers that we were able to hack occasionally, so they are the principal chemicals of immediate concern.

"CE20 and XR16 cause severe neurotoxicity, leading to coma and death within ten days of a short exposure to the odors, and there is little dispersion beyond a small area of release," he confided.

"On the other hand, CN122, YD99, and YD122 cause rapid convulsions, nausea, vomiting, and unconsciousness, but are not lethal. The subjects usually recuperate within two hours, not remembering much after the initial revolting smell but fearful of it being repeated. During the initial phase of reaction, the subject speaks rapidly and without inhibition, giving the interrogators a chance to ask questions that the subject had resisted earlier.

"It is a form of 'truth serum,' like sodium pentothal, as a first-level response to the odors. The Russian FSB and Iranian secret service," he confided, "are experimenting with this to get information out of their captives without the usual physical torture."

John explained that we needed to get more information and results and to identify the chemicals themselves or the classes of chemicals being synthesized and studied. "The key," he said, "is to retrieve more information from the Russian and Iranian labs, so it's necessary to intensify our espionage activities in these countries and have our scientists involved with our handlers there so that they can rapidly evaluate if credible information is being secured, and maybe even establish some relationship to one or more of their chemists. The Israelis will focus on Iran, while we will spy on Russia."

But John complained that the CIA was still at a loss as to how to achieve this when the scientists being engaged aren't trained agents and would be at risk in the field. Among them, John said, "you are one of the best candidates in terms of age, physical condition, unmarried status, education, and interest in the behavioral effects of odors."

I'm not sure if this is a compliment or if it reflected their desperation.

John said at the end of our session that Vladimir, the scientist I met in Vienna, might be a good initial resource and that they were thinking about how to get me in contact with him again once he'd been vetted.

"He is still on our list of dangerous Russian contacts, but since he contacted you, he may have a purpose to build a relationship once you're in Moscow. "

"Of course," he said, "you need a reason to visit or spend time in Moscow, a topic of current discussion between us and the Mossad."

My business interest, he thought, might be a good cover, as Brad and the Israelis thought all along.

I asked if they planned to have me visit Israel. John said that this was being discussed. "You'll also be meeting with the French counterespionage agency when you get to Paris."

So, Marie had been right. She was clearly more involved with the CIA, evidently through her own Mossad handlers, than I suspected.

Before we broke for the day, John mentioned that they'd discussed my need to contact my lab and would make a computer and phone available to me, under supervision, at a defined time. "But if you want to come to my office with me, you can send your emails now."

I sent one to Jhanella, asking that she provide me with the latest draft of our manuscript to this email address. John said he would check his computer regularly and let me know when she responded.

Dinner was simple, hot dogs and hamburgers, and afterward, we all assembled in an adjoining living room with a fire blazing in the large fireplace. We sat around together, mostly drinking beer or wine, and talking about current events or sports, no business or personal matters. This gave me a chance to learn a little more about each one there, but only on a very superficial level. I guess this was intended for us to socialize and build some camaraderie. By 10:00 p.m., everyone had left for bed, but John came over and said I had email responses.

Jhanella had sent me our manuscript, which John had printed out, along with a printout of her email regarding other experiments being done, and gave them to me.

24.

BACK IN MY room, I sat down to read our manuscript, entitled, *"Fusion of Human Cancer and Normal Murine Cells Transduces and Transcribes Human DNA."* I was pleased with how they had turned all our drafts into a final version totaling 2,000 words, since the journal had this strict word limit. After watching the 11:00 p.m. news, I fell asleep with the manuscript as my last waking thought.

The next morning, I was back to the conference room, where today there were two other men waiting for me. This morning's conversation was about my going to Russia to make contact with our case agents handling their moles or contacts within the scientific community. The question: what would my cover be? One of the two new men — Stuart — said he'd been thinking about this for several days and agreed with the idea that Brad had mentioned from the very beginning.

"We have an opportunity related to Dr. Davidson's desire to start a new olfaction business. As a startup, he would be looking for funding, and that would give him a reason to operate in Europe and possibly also in Russia, if foreign investors can be secured."

He said the CIA, with its allied foreign agencies, kept a list of venture capitalists abroad who liked to invest in new companies, and in Russia, this was very popular when new companies were formed as offshoots of government projects and agencies, and where their president and other senior government officials, including members of their legislature, the Duma, could benefit from these ventures by becoming equity participants. "This is how the oligarchs became so wealthy and politically important."

Stuart suggested that some of the venture capitalists involved with financing the Paris perfume company where Marie Chalfont worked be encouraged to become initial major investors in *Pharmascent Sciences*, my new company's name, and through them we would secure the involvement of at least one Russian investor, preferably someone close to Putin.

"The investors would suggest to Dr. Davidson that the company establish research offices in Paris and Moscow, with later distribution centers elsewhere," said Stuart.

This would give me a reason to work in Russia, he suggested, to interact with those in the perfume industry, and to come under the protection of a powerful Russian oligarch who was close to Putin. In fact, maybe Putin would be a 'silent' investor if the business looked lucrative enough.

Stuart said he would work on this if everyone thought it was a promising approach. "The Mossad has its own venture capital fund that invests in companies with technologies of interest to them, and I think we could explore this avenue too," he said.

Of course, I know that the Mossad had a similar view.

I showed that I was impressed with this suggestion despite having to work in Russia. John and the other agents nodded in agreement and said it was very plausible and would give me reasonably free rein and protection in Russia if the Russian investor was well placed and if he trusted me and liked my business plan. Of course, he and the others would have to get good business terms, and that was what concerned me.

What the hell have I now gotten myself into?

*

THE REST OF the week, I was fed as much information on the workings of the CIA in the field as I could consume quickly. I was also shown videos of large community locations in Moscow, such as railway stations, libraries, parks, and other meeting places, so I would know the layouts, locations of the bathrooms, restaurants nearby, and even the locations of different drops used, including remote park benches. They also provided me with a more intensive visitor's guide to sights and government buildings.

The use of electronics and how to sweep my work areas or living quarters was a major focus in my training. They also exposed me to the different kinds of handguns that spies use, and I learned quickly how to use a small revolver and actually shoot targets pretty good, but they didn't want me to have a gun in my possession.

I needed to have the confidence of secrecy, yet I also needed to allow some surveillance to continue, or else my counterespionage role would be suspected. I was also instructed how to avoid being trapped by a purported defector whose goal was to disclose any CIA or other U.S. government relationship. At the end of each day, I wondered if my personality was being changed so I would hardly trust anyone or any situation in the future.

A major issue was how I was to communicate with my handler, as yet unidentified, and how to avoid too much contact with the U.S. Embassy or any U.S. government office in Russia. I needed codes, first- and second-level contacts, use of a cell phone that could be hacked easily, and then another that we could try to make secure, having encryption, but that would be swept and modified regularly. I needed to grasp CIA vocabulary so I could communicate in their language.

This is all very strenuous to assimilate and memorize, even with Ph.D. and M.D. degrees.

My instructors didn't tell me how long I would be at Langley, but I surmised that it would be until they were satisfied with my readiness to leave, first for Paris and eventually for Moscow. I also learned that I would be spending some time in Tel Aviv with Marie, where the Mossad would also take me into training.

Toward the end of the week, I spent time with the CIA chemists and sensory biologists in their labs, learning about the odor molecules they were synthesizing or extracting from plants or other biological materials and evaluating for toxic properties, both in microbial and cell cultures and also in animal experiments. I was impressed with their capabilities and resources, and their access to the latest and best equipment.

We scheduled a wrap-up session on my last day, on a Friday a week later, to review my visit and activities – including weaknesses and proficiencies. They supplied codes for me to use in contacting specific handlers, and they described the disguises I would need in the field and which they would ship to me by diplomatic pouches to the U.S. Embassies in France, Israel, and Russia, when I was settled in Moscow.

They gave me a variety of electronic devices, such as surveillance detectors, miniature cameras, and two cell phones with different Internet and satellite connections.

Finally, I was given three new passports, from Germany, France, and Israel, each with my picture but with different names. Together with my own authentic one, I was now the proud owner of four passports, each with a somewhat different picture of me, coordinated to the disguises I was to use when taking on the new identities. And I had two days to return to New York to get ready and pack for extended travel.

25.

THREE DAYS LATER, I was on an Air France flight to Charles de Gaulle airport in Paris, scheduled to land at 10:00 p.m. the same day. Marie was to pick me up and be responsible for me in Paris, and then we would travel to Israel together.

It was a comfortable and smooth flight, landing about thirty minutes early. I now carried two medium-sized suitcases, which the airline had let me take on board in the overhead baggage rack. I presumed that some influence by the CIA or French spy service had been exercised. I also noticed that when I went through baggage control, I was waved to a fast line once my passport was reviewed and my name inserted into their computer.

I didn't see Marie or anyone with my name on a sign, so I just stood and waited at the exit to Customs. About five minutes later, Marie came hurrying down the hall, waving at me. I waved back, and she jumped into my arms and kissed my cheeks three times, in good French welcoming tradition. I of course noticed that she looked different than in Vienna and New York, with different hair coloring, hair style, probably a wig, and wearing a pants suit emphasizing a different, less-feminine look.

Marie apologized for keeping me waiting, saying she only learned of the early landing while she was *en route*. She then showed me to the exit closest to where her car was parked and we climbed into her dark blue Citroen sedan. I had not ridden in a Citroen for many years, remembering how unusually smooth its ride was.

Before starting the engine, she leaned over and pulled my head to her for a *real* kiss while also grabbing my inner thigh. "I have missed you, Milt," she said, "and I am impatient to have you stay with me."

I smiled. "We also have some work to do," I said.

This did not faze her. "No matter, *chérie*," she said. "We will find time to get to know each other again."

She then handed me a small linen bag and told me to open it.

"Do I really have to wear this wig and facial mask?" I asked.

"The French secret service, DGSE, and the Mossad, are concerned that I may be sought by the Hezbollah, since I was involved with an attack on their agents in France a couple of years ago, and our intelligence has confirmed that I'm one of their major targets. My appearance is now different, and I try to alter it frequently, but if I'm recognized, you'll be taken also as a spy, putting you also at risk. So as long as we are together in France, you need to wear this disguise. Try it on."

I put it on, looked in the mirror above my seat, and chuckled, "Well, even I can't identify myself. I never had a bushy head of gray hair and a thick black mustache and beard."

Marie responded: "I agree. You won't be recognized, especially since you're not catalogued anywhere as a spy, at least not yet." We then drove out of the garage.

It was a nostalgic pleasure to see the sights of Paris once more, my last visit having been to a conference there more than five years ago. Marie negotiated the traffic very well, and soon we were in the 4th Arrondissement, coincidentally the traditional Jewish sector, which was a less-expensive neighborhood. Marie had to drive around awhile before she found a parking spot two blocks from her building on Rue des Rosier.

We hiked up the four flights to her apartment, which was small by U.S. standards but probably large for Paris. Off the foyer were two bedrooms, and straight ahead the living room, with a small dining area between that and the even smaller kitchen. The apartment was somewhat luxurious by French standards because there was a half bathroom in the hallway as well as a full bathroom with a separate shower and tub, as well as bidet off the master bedroom.

Marie helped me get my bags into her bedroom and asked if I were hungry, and I told her that Air France did not let that happen. I said I was still on New York time, so I wasn't tired yet. "Let's have some wine or maybe even take a walk — I just sat for eight hours on the flight."

She opened a nice bottle of French white wine, and we toasted our reunion. But Marie had other intentions, so after two glasses of wine, I allowed myself to be pulled into her bed. This turned into another eventful night, with my finally getting some rest at about 4:00 a.m.

*

THE NEXT MORNING, she woke me up to serve coffee and croissants that she'd evidently sneaked out to get while I slept. We sat in the living room with our coffees for about an hour, and Marie had a lot of questions about my Langley meeting with the CIA. I was cautious in what I said, since I hadn't been briefed on how much she knew or could know. Noticing my discomfort, Marie didn't press on.

Feeling rested, I showered and dressed, and we decided to go for the walk I missed last night, maybe also having lunch along the Seine or on the *Champs Elysees*. I love sitting at an outdoor café on this broad, fashionable street facing the *Arch de Triumph*. We got there at about noon and found a nice table at an outdoor café that I remembered from my previous visit as a tourist. The service was quite fast, probably catering to tourists; we had salads and then spaghetti and meat sauce, with some carbonated water and house red wine. Whether it was truly the food or the ambiance and charm of Paris, the lunch was good, and I felt fortunate to be in Paris with a lovely and loving woman who had no inhibitions. But the mustache and beard disguise were annoying me, itching me profusely at different times.

And all of this in the interest of national security!

Since it was a little after 1:00 p.m., we decided to go over to the Picasso Museum, not far from Marie's apartment. Once again, I was impressed with Marie's knowledge. She explained that during Picasso's long and productive career, he painted some 20,000 works, representing cubism, abstraction, neoclassicism, surrealism, and expressionism, examples of which Marie enjoyed pointing out to me.

I thought I knew a lot about Picasso, but Marie is truly the expert.

We had dinner at a small local restaurant in her district, near some of the Jewish restaurants. But in Paris, I didn't need any culinary fare other than the local specialties, so I let Marie handle all ordering, consisting of the traditional onion soup, tournedos of veal with mushrooms and heavy garlic, and Creme Brulé for dessert. She also ordered a superb Bordeaux, remembering this was my favorite red wine.

We walked home hand-in-hand, planning to have only cheese and crackers, coffee and a liqueur at her place. But by the time we climbed the stairs to her apartment, she was removing my clothes, and I knew there would be no cheese, coffee, aperitif, or anything but rolling in bed together.

*

THE NEXT DAY, during afternoon coffee following a visit to the Pompidou Museum, I asked about our plans to go to Tel Aviv and the Mossad later in the week.

"We will discuss this in private at home," Marie said, turning very serious. She said she would pick up some fish on the way home and cook for us tonight. "We can talk then."

Over a surprising, lovely dinner that she prepared, we began talking about the next few days and how we would collaborate on the mission.

"About five years ago," Marie reminded me, "I was hired by a small French perfume company, Toilette, which was formed in Paris to be a distributor of perfumes and related toiletries, primarily in Europe and the Middle East. The founders were retired businessmen from various industries, but I know at least two were former Mossad members, and I suspect the funding for the company either came from them or their acquaintances, or possibly even from the venture capital arm of the Mossad."

Marie explained that *The Office*, as it is called, supported the development of technologies that would advance their clandestine missions. But I was not sure why a perfume distributor would qualify.

"I could speculate that they wanted a perfume developer, since odors have become of security and military interest, but why a distributor?" I asked.

Marie then revealed that she'd been recruited a number of years ago "to collaborate with the French spy agency, DGSE — the *Direction Générale de la Securite Exterieure* — and in particular, its *Division Action*, which is responsible for clandestine operations." She then said, "We need to visit DGSE headquarters, code-named CAT, located in the 20th Arrondissement in Paris."

"After joining the DGSE," she continued, "I was encouraged by my supervisors to collaborate in a joint mission they had with the Israeli Mossad. This then led to a more intimate relationship with the Mossad, who also trained me after spending four months at a DGSE facility, resulting, in fact, to my becoming responsible for some Europe-wide activities."

"That seems like a real conflict between two independent spy agencies," I said, "and I can imagine its leading to complications. There have been many political differences between the two countries."

"Yes, we do have problems," Marie admitted, "so I am only involved in joint efforts, and both organizations are very careful to limit my knowledge to common interests and not activities that would put me in a conflict."

To me, that didn't seem like a workable arrangement, since you can't have dual loyalties in espionage. But I decided not to press further, and to wait until I was with the Mossad to determine Marie's relationships.

"Since we are meeting with my company tomorrow and are going to the DGSE the day after, I wanted to give you some background on both," she said. "Then I expect we will travel to Israel early next week, but I am still working on the route and our identifications. It is preferable that we not travel together using our real names, from Paris to Tel Aviv. But it is possible we will travel to Marseille and then take a ship to Haifa, taking different identities."

She then said it was still being discussed between the Mossad and CIA, both of which were concerned that our association could put me at risk. "It is possible that my counterespionage work is known to our enemies," said Marie, "especially Islamic extremists."

26.

WE ARRIVED AT Toilette's offices in the 10th Arrondissement at about eight-thirty the next morning. The location was on the fourth floor of an older building with the architecture of the early 1930s, with large windows and high ceilings. I didn't see a lot of employees.

After we registered at the reception desk, the General Manager, Simon Fass, came out to meet us. He escorted us to their conference room, where Financial Officer Jacques Corbet was waiting. Once there, I removed my facial disguise in front of them, causing them to smile and laugh. Marie said, "It was determined that Milt should not be recognized if I am identified by the Hezbollah." Evidently, Simon and Jacques were aware of her activities with the DGSE and Mossad.

Simon explained that their company was formed to fill a gap in the perfume industry, where some small manufacturers needed a distribution partner for certain territories. The company had 210 employees, mostly in sales and distribution roles in Europe and the Middle East, and a small staff in the Paris office. They didn't share sales revenues or other business details with me, since they were a private company, but their location and their furnishings suggested to me that they were doing well.

"Dr. Davidson," said Simon, "we learned of your medical interests in odors from Marie, which is why we suggested this visit. Do you have a business plan?"

Strange, I thought, since they were probably aware of my mission because of their relationship to the Mossad. But I decided to go along with them.

"Yes," I said, "but it's not in any final form, since I'm still identifying candidate products and the first clinical trials needed. I'm in discussions with potential partners and investors."

Jacques then said that they would be interested in being included in the investment discussions, since they were building distribution channels and could consider other applications — although they have no regulatory expertise, should there be medical indications requiring approval by the European Medicines Agency, like the FDA, and its equivalent in individual countries. I said that the final products would need regulatory approvals from health authorities, but I wasn't sure whether the first-generation agents could be sold as health supplements not making medical claims, so not requiring approvals.

"This would be an exciting opportunity if there were a differentiation from current aroma therapies," said Simon.

I agreed and said the key to my approach would be to develop these applications on a strong scientific basis, with neurological data and patient results, even if medical claims weren't being sought initially.

We spent the next hour learning more about each other's pasts, both businesswise and personally. Finally, Simon suggested we go across town to the Goldenberg delicatessen, an important Jewish landmark where we could get an early kosher-style lunch. I thought this was an unusual offer to a New York Jew in Paris, but concluded they wanted an excuse to get lunch there. Evidently, it was a favorite spot for the local Jewish population.

I replaced my disguise, and joined them in a large, black Peugeot waiting at the curb of a side exit. Jacques waved to a car parked, with the engine running, about 50 feet away, which I interpreted as their security coverage.

Interesting that even Toilette's management needs protection in Paris.

The restaurant was certainly not elegant, looking a little less well furnished than most delis in New York, but it was already about three-quarters full even this early. I noticed some guests dressed like orthodox East-European Jews, with their black garments, black hats, beards with sideburns (payis), and fringes down from the prayer shawls worn under their garments. We all ordered different specialties so we could share: stuffed peppers, matzoh ball and red cabbage soups, stuffed derma, potato pancakes, pastrami, flanken (boiled beef), and roast chicken, just like the delicacies I would have at a New York deli. It was a lot of food for just four of us, fit for a banquet, but Simon and Jacques really enjoyed eating, as their corpulent figures attested, and they evidently planned to take a lot of leftovers back to the office.

We departed from the Toilette offices at about 1:30, and Marie and I took a long walk and discussed the morning, Marie orienting me about our upcoming visit with the DGSE.

"It will be brief and merely for courtesy," she said. Since Marie was part of their organization and now on a joint mission with the CIA and Mossad, she felt obliged to brief them and to bring me by to meet her supervisors.

27.

THE FRENCH SECRET Service headquarters was always under surveillance, Marie explained, so it would not be possible to just walk in or be dropped off by a taxi. At 9:50 a.m., as prearranged, we got into a black van and a few minutes later were dropped off inside the covered archway of a side entrance. I removed my disguise in the lavatory before registering with the reception and passing through security. Marie showed me up to the seventh floor and to the office of the head of the Action Department, Charles Massigney.

Mssr. Massigney was tall, about six feet-four inches, with bushy orange-red hair and a light complexion. He was dressed impeccably in a light brown corduroy suit, yellow shirt, and checkered blue bowtie. After we entered, he moved quickly from his desk to extend his hand to me and give the usual trio of cheek kisses to Marie. For a fleeting moment, I wondered if the business of alcohol tissue swabs did well in France, since everyone was always kissing cheeks and spreading all sorts of germs that I didn't even want to think about.

But maybe this improves their immunity to infections, increasing the lifespan of the French – and not their consumption of red wine, as was often speculated about their diet.

Marie brought Charles up-to-date on our olfaction mission, my training with the CIA, our plans to go to Tel Aviv, and my going on to Moscow if we could devise a good cover for an olfaction pharma business. Charles thought for a few seconds, then asked if Marie had contacted their agents in Russia, especially Moscow.

Marie said she didn't want to do that before having further discussions with the Mossad — "since they have their own plans regarding Dr. Davidson." This was the first I'd heard of that.

Marie is very careful with her pillow talk.

I gave Charles the same summary of my company plans as I had the day before with the Toilette executives but provided a little more detail as to how I was going to get involved with learning the chemical composition of the odor substances our adversaries were developing and testing. Charles said he was fully informed of these activities, and this was all of grave concern, not only to French intelligence and their army but also in many quarters of medicine, since this appears to be a new class of neurotoxic agents.

When we were leaving, Marie emphasized that Charles was very capable and highly respected both in France and throughout NATO's intelligence and clandestine services, as well as Interpol. She cautioned that I should not be fooled by his modest demeanor.

"He is someone that no one wants to cross."

We discussed spending the rest of the day visiting Notre Dame Cathedral and, if possible, the d'Orsay Museum on the Left Bank. But Marie already had a text from the Mossad about our planned journey to Israel.

They suggested we take a night train to Marseille this very evening and then board an Israeli cargo ship, *Haifa*, which should embark tomorrow afternoon for Haifa, with a few stops on the way. Although this would require us to be on board for at least four days, we would get to Israel without registering with any immigration service. The ship had a limited number of private quarters for passengers, and if we agreed, they would reserve a cabin for us immediately.

Marie asked what I thought. "Could we leave tonight?" I asked

Marie's face lit up. "We could take an express train from the main station to Marseille, arriving tomorrow morning. From there, we could board the ship, and rest up before we depart. It would be terribly romantic, don't you think?" She almost shrieked with enthusiasm.

"I guess it would be the most secret option," I said, "but being on a cargo ship for several days doesn't exactly appeal to me." Marie looked disappointed. "But," I added quickly, "if we have nice weather and comfortable quarters, it could work out well."

She smiled. "Then I will accept Mossad's itinerary, and we will reserve train tickets to Marseille for late tonight, maybe around two or three in the morning," she said. "But in order to pack and get ready, let's just go to Notre Dame and then straight home." I nodded in agreement.

*

SHORTLY BEFORE MIDNIGHT that night, we were able to get a cab to the main railway station, where Marie picked up the tickets we'd reserved for the express train to Marseille, scheduled to depart at 2:10 a.m. We were in first class, so we could get some sleep before we arrived very early in the morning at Marseille's main train station. The seats were comfortable and the train only about half full, so we relaxed in our private cabin, both wearing our disguises, as the train headed south toward the Mediterranean.

After about 40 minutes, Marie got a text message on her cell phone and then jumped up and pulled me up also and shoved me into a corner of the cabin. She seemed quite upset, and I noticed, for the first time, that she carried a small revolver, which was now in her right hand. She faced the door and waited. About two minutes later, we heard some noise outside of our compartment's door and a loud pop. Marie then opened our door, took a step into the corridor and then released a shot, hesitated, and then returned to close the door quickly. Then, there was a knock on the door.

Marie called out in French, and evidently relieved at the response, she opened it – still having her revolver raised and motioning me to remain behind the door. One of our agents reassured her everything was under control, and Marie and I could see them hovering over two bodies and plenty of blood under their torsos. After a brief exchange, Marie shut the door and motioned me to return to my seat.

"Please try to relax, Milt. The DGSE agents identified two Middle-East-looking men following us into the train and taking a cabin in the next car. When they saw them come out and proceed down to our compartment, they followed and confronted them, just as they were going to knock and had their guns out. Our agents had the advantage of surprise, shooting one of them, but the second had a knife and was fighting with the other DGSE agent when I opened our door and was able to place a bullet to his head, killing him instantly. The conductor is helping them remove the bodies to their cabin."

"I can't believe how fast you reacted, Marie, and how efficient you were in taking down one of the assailants," I commented.

She didn't respond, but reloaded her revolver and placed it in her belt, exposed.

I had no idea that my partner in spying and lovemaking was trained to kill. I trembled and then remarked, "So, we've been identified and followed. Who are they?"

"Probably Hezbollah. As I already indicated, they are searching for me."

"But do you think I've also been identified? We were recognized despite our disguises."

"Probably just me," she said. "But if there is a picture of you in their system, it's probably not your face in the current disguise. So, in France, we will need a different disguise for you," she said.

"My pulse must be at 120," I announced. "I can't believe how fast this all transpired."

I need to inform Brad of this ASAP.

28.

MARSEILLE'S MAIN STATION was already bustling when we arrived just after 5:00 a.m. Since we were so early and didn't want to go to the wharf for several more hours, we found a café and ordered breakfast and bought a couple of newspapers to read. Marie assured me that we were still being followed by the DGSE agents. Later, it was no problem finding a taxi to take us to the Old Port and the berth for the Haifa vessel, which we knew was a large cargo ship. There would be a lot of activity in preparation for its early afternoon departure, and we wanted to get on board and stay out of everyone's way and view.

We identified ourselves as we boarded and were then led to our cabin by a young seaman who carried two of our bags. He began telling us in accented French, until Marie spoke Hebrew to him, that the captain would come visit with us after we were underway.

Our cabin was surprisingly spacious, with portholes on two sides, giving us a nice view from our upper level. We had a living room, a bedroom, and a bathroom with shower, plus a small outside patio. We showered and changed to more comfortable clothes and then took seats on the patio to watch the final preparations to depart.

Marie said she was excited to see the Israeli flag displayed high above the deck, giving her the comfort and security of being in Israel, or at least on an Israeli ship. About an hour after settling in, another seaman brought us some cakes and a bottle of dry French champagne, compliments of the captain. We toasted to our voyage and our soon being in Israel.

Captain David Spivak joined us at noon, apologizing for not welcoming us sooner, but he said he'd had some administrative issues to resolve. After checking our passports, he explained their route, taking about four days to Haifa.

Spivak was in his mid-forties, very muscular, with dark hair and a graying mustache. His uniform seemed a little lax to me, but I'd never been on a freighter before. The captain said in a thick Israeli accent, "Please join me and my senior officers for dinner, or you could have your meals brought to your cabin." We said we didn't want to be a burden, but he insisted that he would enjoy having guests beyond his own immediate staff. We agreed to come to his cabin at 6:00 p.m.

Shortly before our dinner engagement, a sailor came to escort us to the captain's dining room. It was a handsomely furnished room with wood paneling and a large table set for seven. The captain introduced his executive officer, Zev ben Levi (Zev Klingman), his chief engineer, Shmuel ben Yitzchak (Shmuel Rabin), and also two civilian passengers, Robert Klitzman and Benjamin Aharon.

Captain Spivak explained that Klitzman and Aharon were businessmen from Tel Aviv who were returning from Europe via Marseille. Both seemed to be multilingual, since they greeted me in English and Marie in French, and of course spoke Hebrew to the sailors. Marie introduced herself as working for the French perfume company, Toilette, and I explained that I was a medical scientist visiting some colleagues at the Weizmann Institute in Rehovot. That was the story that had been prepared for me because I, in fact, did know that institute from a prior visit to Rehovot.

Soon after we were all seated, the door to the kitchen opened, and the cook and his assistant pushed out a cart with several dishes prepared for us. The first course was mushroom and barley soup, warm bread, followed by boiled beef with boiled potatoes and carrots, accompanied by lettuce with tomatoes as a side salad. Both white and red wines also were offered.

Most of the conversation was trivial, like the weather expected, the projected arrival time in Haifa, some unexpected travel delays in Europe, mostly for Robert and Shmuel. They indicated that they were in the "import/export business," which suggested to Marie that they weren't going to share information about their occupations, at least on our first meeting. We kept our story vague, as well. Marie explained that we'd met at a conference on perfumes in Vienna, avoiding any further information about our relationship, but, of course, they knew we shared a cabin.

After dinner, Marie and I took a stroll on the upper deck, returning to our cabin about a half-hour later. The captain said that we probably still had an Internet connection, so I was happy to get my emails from the last two days. Before locking our door, we filled out the breakfast order, indicating that we would be up at 8:00 a.m. for service. This was unexpected and made us feel like we were truly traveling first class.

Jhanella had sent me a copy of the cover letter and the manuscript submitted for publication, which I read quickly. I felt a sense of accomplishment and completion of the first stage of this work, and immediately sent an email congratulating all the coauthors on the quality submission and asked that they let me know as soon as the editorial office replied.

I looked up to see Marie staring at me, wondering what I was busy with. I smiled and told her I was just cleaning up some emails, including a review of the article we'd just submitted for publication. She came over to kiss and congratulate me. She said she'd also contacted her case officer at the Mossad, informing him of the two civilian passengers traveling with us and our anticipated arrival.

It was strange to think how fast all this had happened with Marie. I'd been with her in New York for a day and a half and in Paris for three days, and we were already like long-term lovers. She was very comfortable to be with, almost always knowing my thoughts and needs, even before I did. Maybe that's why she was a dual Mossad and DGSE agent.

I wonder if she had been chosen to travel and protect me or if she has some other mission.

29.

THE MOSSAD DRIVER who picked us up at the dock immediately began talking with Marie in Hebrew. Then, in accented English, he introduced himself as Gabai and said he would be glad to tell us about the sites. Marie knew Gabai and told me that "he was a graduate of Tel Aviv University with a degree in archeology." With that introduction, Gabai launched into what must have been a canned but interesting spiel, which Marie translated.

The car drove us to Tel Aviv along the Tel Aviv-Haifa Highway bordering the Mediterranean. Gabai often glanced in the rear-view mirror, so Marie asked him if he were worried about something. He answered, and she explained that we had a Mossad escort car two cars back. Gabai also told Marie that they had intercepted some Internet chatter from Hezbollah that made them worry about Marie being tracked.

We saw several other small towns and cities on the way, and at Netanya, Marie said it was one of her favorite Israeli cities and that some of her relatives from France and the former Soviet Union had emigrated there. This was the first I'd heard of her having ancestors in the Soviet Union.

"It is one of the most beautiful and important cities of Israel," she said. "It has about half the population of Tel Aviv, or over 200,000 people, making it the seventh-largest city in Israel.

"And I bet you don't know it was named after an American philanthropist, Nathan, or Natan, Strauss, who was co-owner of Macy's Department Store, New York City Parks Commissioner, and also president of the New York City Board of Health. He donated about two-thirds of his personal fortune to the benefit of Jews and Arabs in Palestine in the late 1920s," she explained.

*

AFTER DRIVING ABOUT forty-five minutes, we came to a residential area in Tel Aviv with many apartment buildings. Gabai stopped in front of a six-story, older building on Zeitlin Street, and we took the very slow elevator to the fourth floor, then entered a large, three-bedroom apartment, where we would live during our stay in Israel. Marie, who had stayed here before, removed a suitcase from a locked closet and transferred her clothes to various drawers of the chest in one of the bedrooms. I did the same with my clothes, but in another bedroom.

"We will settle in and visit with the Mossad first thing Sunday morning, since it is now Friday, a half-workday due to the Sabbath. Let's take a walk; I want to smell the air and ocean," she said as she changed into sandals and shorts. It was obvious she could not delay experiencing the joy of being back in Israel. I understood, since this was the land of my forefathers, and I had visited here several times. But before we could go, Marie said she needed to pick up some food for the weekend because most shopping would close for the Sabbath by this afternoon. I used this time to change for a long, casual walk and to bring a bathing suit and towel for our visit to the beach. I remembered swimming at the beach in Tel Aviv during my last trip some years back, and how refreshing and clear the blue sea was.

Marie returned with two woven baskets carrying bread, juice, butter, milk, eggs, and most essentials for our weekend needs, as well as a bottle of red wine and one of white.

While walking, Marie said The Office had recommended that we spend as much time as possible just being tourists, in case Hezbollah or one of the other terrorist groups were watching us, and we should try to wear disguises. We knew this would be a challenge if we were to swim in the Mediterranean.

"I think The Office will have us followed while we're here, just to be certain that we're safe," she said. Then she told me she'd learned there was Internet chatter about a Mossad agent and a CIA agent traveling together. I felt a sudden tightness in my chest, and then turned around to see if we were being followed.

Marie laughed, "That's not what you do to check things out, *mon chérie*. I thought that the CIA gave you some training."

I was of course embarrassed, but just shrugged my shoulders and kept up with her brisk walking pace.

We walked about ten minutes from our apartment building to Rothschild Boulevard, one of the main Tel Aviv thoroughfares. It was flanked by trees and gardens on both sides and had walking and bicycling lanes in the middle. Marie talked almost continuously during our stroll, pointing out important stores, buildings, and talking about historical events of Tel Aviv. But I noticed that she often made a nonchalant effort to check behind us.

Once, without changing her facial expression, she said there was a car with two men in it trailing us about a half-street behind us. "But don't look around," she said, smiling, as though we were talking about nothing but the beautiful weather. After a couple of streets, the car was no longer visible.

Marie spoke so enthusiastically, as if this were the city and country of her birth and pride that it confused me. Originally, she'd told me that she had grown up in France. Yet when she spoke Hebrew, she sounded like a Sabra, an Israeli by birth.

"You may remember, Milt, that Tel Aviv is only rivaled by Jerusalem as the most important and second-largest city in Israel. It is clearly the financial center and also the focal point of high-tech, known as *Silicon Wadi*. It has the reputation of being "The City that Never Sleeps.""

"I thought that's *New York's* claim to fame," I said. She didn't even pay attention to my little joke. At the corner of Frishman and Dizengoff Streets, we stopped at a shop to buy a *sabich*, which is a pita filled with vegetables, including fried eggplant, plus a hardboiled egg and many local spices. I needed this sustenance for the rest of our excursion. I found it challenging to keep up with her.

We walked to Allenby Street, a long and busy thoroughfare known for having many bakeries selling freshly baked breads and cakes. This was also the location of the Great Synagogue, and Marie insisted that we go inside. I was impressed by the huge dome and lighting and the stained-glass windows that were replicas of the windows of different European synagogues destroyed during the Holocaust. Marie insisted that we leave by a side exit that opened to a small side street. Evidently, she had planned to try to lose any tail, but she did speak into her phone in Hebrew, probably for the Mossad agents tailing us but out of sight.

We also went to Dizengoff House, which was the "Independence Hall" of Israel. This was where the proclamation and signing of Israel's Declaration of Independence occurred in 1948 in the presence of about 350 people, led by David Ben-Gurion, chairman of the Provisional Government and the World Zionist Organization.

This neighborhood backed onto the famous Carmel Market, the largest one in the city. As soon as we went inside the market, it was obvious that we were in the Middle East, in contrast to the other places we'd just viewed. Pretty much anything you wanted could be found in this market, from food and fruits, juices, clothes, music, electronics, and some of the best local food delicacies in Tel Aviv. And following us would be more difficult in this crowded market than elsewhere. Marie escorted me, so we moved quickly through the market and exited on a side street.

By now, it was late in the morning, so Marie led me to the highlight of the city, the beach, which imparts its lifestyle to the city itself. There were different sections for different groups: families with children, surfers, joggers, volleyball players, nude, and gay beach areas. We changed into our bathing suits at the beach toilets, removing some of our disguises, and enjoyed cooling off in the water, which was calm and invited our swimming for about twenty minutes. I noticed that Marie often checked the beach occupants. If the Hezbollah were following us, they would have to wear bathing suits on the beach in order to not be recognized. But we didn't see any men like this – mostly youngsters or families. Then we dried off and wandered over to the Gordo Beach Café, where we ordered cocktails and watched a spectacular sunset over the Mediterranean Sea.

"What an unexpected pleasure today was," I said, lifting my glass to Marie. "Here's to your real home."

30.

THE NEXT MORNING, while Marie was showering, I received a text from Brad Williams on my CIA cell phone, evidently to confirm my whereabouts. They wanted to arrange a meeting with me before I visited with The Office the following day. I wrote back that we would be out sightseeing today, mostly visiting museums, and that Marie had made plans for us tonight, but I didn't know any details yet.

Brad asked me to be at the Tel Aviv Museum of Art in the late morning, sending him a text about thirty minutes before I got there. He said that after being at the museum for about a half-hour, I should go to the men's room on the ground floor, where I would be approached by a tall man with blonde hair and an open brown shirt. He would identify himself by saying, "Are you here with Brad?"

"If you say *yes*, he will leave and not approach you again. If you say *no*, then find a urinal where you can stand next to him so you can talk briefly unless the room is crowded. If there are others of concern present, our agent will say, 'Shalom' and leave, and we will try to arrange another meeting."

I deleted the messages before Marie came out of the bathroom, still wrapped in her large towel. She had such a beautiful smile when she looked at me, making her irresistible. But my mind quickly turned to wondering how I could influence our visiting the Tel Aviv Museum in the late morning, since I had no idea what Marie's plans for us were.

Once Marie was dressed, we walked over a few streets to Rabin Square, which Marie told me had been formerly called Kings of Israel Square. A traditional site of political rallies and parades, the square was renamed to honor former Prime Minister Yitzhak Rabin, who'd been assassinated there in November of 1995. A memorial marked the spot where Rabin was killed, at the northeast corner of the square, below the city hall.

Fortunately, our next stop was the Tel Aviv Museum of Art on Shaul Hamelech (King Saul) Boulevard, which was about fifteen minutes away by foot. We were there earlier than Brad had suggested, so while Marie was using the restroom, I texted Brad that I was there and that I would visit the men's room in about an hour.

When Marie came out, we rented earphones and an audio guide to the artworks and painters displayed in the various galleries. It was a huge art museum, Israel's largest, with a collection that included works by Chagall, Cezanne, Picasso, Klimt, Jackson Pollock, van Gogh, Pissarro, Rothko, Soutine, and de Vlaminck, as I read in the brochure. In the entrance foyer was a large two-panel mural made by the American artist Roy Lichtenstein. I felt comfortable playing tour guide for Marie.

Once inside, I steered Marie to the artworks of greatest interest to me, such as Pissarro's *The Vieux-Moulin in Knokke,* painted in 1894, Pierre-Auguste Renoir's *Nude Seen from the Back*, from 1880-1881, van Gogh's 1889 painting *The Shepherdess*, Marc Chagall's *Solitude,* from 1933, and de Vlaminck's *View of Bougival,* from 1906. For once, I could explain something to Marie, since these were among my favorite artists, and I had studied their works and lives for many years, including visits to the Metropolitan Museum of Art and the Museum of Modern Art in New York.

Even so, the recorded tour was very incisive about the painters and their works, and I was so transfixed that I nearly forgot my appointment in the men's room. "I need to use the restroom," I said to Marie. "I'll meet you back here in a few minutes."

The only person in the restroom besides me was a short bald man washing his hands, so I went to another sink and washed my hands, too. As this man left, a tall blonde man in a brown shirt came in and went to a urinal. I then went to the urinal next to him.

He looked over and said, "Are you here with Brad?"

"No," I said.

The blonde man looked around the room to confirm that we were alone. "I'm Jacob," he then said, "and I'll be your contact, or handler, while you're in Israel. Just text Brad if you need to talk or meet me, and I'll make the arrangements. But you'll need to find a way to free yourself from Marie if we're to connect, since we need to keep our activities confidential from her and from the others you'll meet tomorrow."

"I thought you were collaborating with them and with Marie," I said.

"Yes," he answered, "we are. Yet we have some independent needs, and we want you to remain able to differentiate your various involvements with the parties in France, Israel, and us, which we know can become complicated, especially if Marie is with you almost all of the time. You need to be cautious here, and she shouldn't suspect that we've expressed our concern. Although we're close, Israel and the U.S. have some divergent interests in the Middle East, including our relationships to Islamic groups, including Hezbollah. Speak with Brad about our concerns about the DGSE and possible leaks about your mission. I now have to leave, since this meeting is already longer than planned."

He then went to the sink, rinsed his hands superficially, and left quickly.

The comment about leaks within the DGSE worries me. I have to talk with Brad asap!

*

AFTER LEAVING THE museum, Marie took me over to Leonard Bernstein Plaza, where we sat in a café and ordered coffee and a very sweet honey cake that Marie said was a specialty of the house.

Then she excused herself for about fifteen minutes, and I wondered what she was hiding from me, since she hadn't walked toward the ladies' room. She returned smiling, saying she'd gone to make reservations for our dinner. But that didn't sound quite plausible — she could've done that on her cell phone sitting at the table with me. So, she clearly had some clandestine call to make.

Maybe the CIA is right about Marie and her Mossad colleagues.

We were both so tired that we decided to forgo other sightseeing and just rest at the café for an hour. For a while, we just watched the hordes of people passing by this way and that. "Fascinating," I said, "all these people who look so different, so many nationalities and different racial features. Yet they're likely all Israelis, don't you think?"

"They probably are," Marie said.

"You know, it makes me wonder," I said. "You told me you grew up in France. But you know Tel Aviv and Israel — and the Hebrew language — like a Sabra."

Marie hesitated, then said, "You are correct, Milt. But I do not like to talk about my early years. I prefer simply saying I am French and grew up in France.

"My parents emigrated with me to Israel when I was about two years old, from what is now Belarus, formerly of the Soviet Union. My father was a chemical engineer and had difficulty keeping his position because of anti-Semitism in Belarus.

"They never fully explained why we moved to France, but I think my father had some problems with the local bureaucrats in Netanya, which affected his work and integration into Israeli society. But after five years in France, my father died unexpectedly, and my mother had to support us. My parents never spoke much of the reasons for these moves and avoided explanations to me when I asked.

"So, how did you get involved with both the French and Israeli spy agencies?"

"After graduating from the university, I needed to find work because my mother was ill and needed financial assistance. My first job was with an import-export company that was an agent for shipping lines, contracting cargo between ports. They specialized in large container vessels or shipping oil between ports, mostly in Europe and the Middle East. It was a small operation involving two partners, two additional salespersons, and then me as the general administrative assistant. They hired me because of my knowledge of several languages and because, I guess, I made a good impression.

"After a few months, I was asked to travel to many of the shipping lines we used, so I spent more than half my time traveling to all the major cities with commercial ports, such as along the Baltic Sea, the Mediterranean, North Sea, and Atlantic. I visited the major ports and shipping lines in Europe, Scandinavia, and all the way to the Middle East."

"How did you manage as a young woman in a male-dominated, aggressive, usually crude shipping business? It must have been hard."

"I did run into some bad situations at first, but I soon learned how to present myself so that I could avoid risky interactions. In fact, after a time, most of the shipping businessmen I met became very cordial and protective of me, and I believe I had an advantage over competitors because I was a young woman. I think my bosses realized this after my first couple of trips, so they promoted me and gave me a small incentive percentage for new business that I recruited. So, except for the long trips away and neglecting my mother, and having virtually no social life, I thought my career was off to a good start.

"Then, about two years later, at one of my visits to Haifa, I was approached by a Mossad agent who told me that he worked for the Israeli government and wanted to discuss how I might return to a relationship with Israel, evidently knowing of the years our family lived in Netanya. Later I learned that this meeting was instigated by one of the owners of my company, who was Jewish and retained some relationships with Israel.

"And so, I was gradually conscripted into the Mossad because of their interest in my visits to all major ports in Europe and the Middle East, my innocent demeanor and cover, and my being multilingual. They surmised evidently that I was also a Zionist at heart because of my parents and many relatives emigrating from the former Soviet Union."

"How did you also become part of the French intelligence organization?"

"It came about because the Mossad learned of a planned terrorist attack in France, outside of Paris, and shared this information with their counterparts. It became clear that the French national police and counterterrorist authorities desired participation by the Mossad, since there was a cell outside of Paris that was active in Islamic terrorist activities that the Mossad uncovered. My superiors in Tel Aviv brought me together with them, and this cooperation just continued."

I found this most interesting but still had questions about how much was shared between the French and Israeli agencies, her loyalties, and how she managed to please what, with the perfume company, appeared to be three bosses. It seems the CIA thinks that there may be a leak within the French DGSE with regard to Marie, resulting in her being at risk with Hezbollah.

"Both the French and Israeli intelligence agencies arranged for me to receive an offer to join a French perfume company," she continued, "where I would be involved in their business and also learn this technology. I thought this would be an interesting change, so I gave notice to my employer. They were not surprised and were, in fact, quite supportive, so I suspect that they also had a hand in this, especially since one of the partners still had ties to Israel, and probably the Mossad."

I still have a lot of questions, but this is the most information that Marie has shared with me about herself so far. A call with Brad is overdue!

*

WE GOT BACK to the apartment a little before 4:00 p.m. Marie said we had dinner reservations for six o'clock, then an event thereafter, so we needed to be ready to leave shortly before six. I asked how we were to dress.

"Wear your best suit," she said. "But a tie, as in all of Israel, is optional."

Marie went to take a shower so she could begin dressing before me. Meanwhile, I sat on the couch trying to understand a TV program in Hebrew. I had studied the language as a young boy, but that had been a long time ago, and it involved mostly reading from the prayer book.

We walked slowly to Dizengoff Street again in our disguises, where we were welcomed at Keton Restaurant. Marie explained that they had been "serving Ashkenazi food since 1945, even before the State of Israel was founded.

"I thought it would be nostalgic to eat Kosher-style food delicacies from Eastern Europe, like our parents enjoyed," she said.

We were seated at a quiet table in the rear, where we sipped flutes of champagne to toast the evening. I ordered chicken soup with kreplach, while Marie had mushroom barley soup. We also enjoyed a heavy, Israeli red wine. We both shared cholent, which is a pot roast with lima beans and other vegetables cooked overnight. The meal was way too filling for me. I needed some coffee.

The restaurant became very full and loud by the time we were ready to leave, at about seven-thirty. We agreed the dinner was enjoyable more for its atmosphere than for the quality of the food and service.

"Even so," said Marie, "everyone needs to experience Keton when they come to Tel Aviv."

The surprise of the evening came as she escorted me over to Leonard Bernstein Plaza, where we'd been earlier in the day for coffee and cake, and into the Charles R. Bronfman Auditorium. To my surprise, Marie had secured us seats for an Israel Philharmonic Orchestra performance this evening that apparently had attracted the 'who's who' of Israeli society, based on the heavy security outside and within. I couldn't believe how many members of the Israel Defense Forces, or IDF, were stationed everywhere, carrying Uzi submachine guns.

This was a special evening with Maestro Zubin Mehta conducting, Itzhak Perlman on the violin and Pinchas Zukerman on the viola, in an all-Mozart program. The evening was honoring Mehta's long career as the orchestra's Music Director for Life. The Bronfman Auditorium was spacious and elegantly decorated, and it appeared that it was a capacity attendance with most people being very well dressed. Marie even pointed out some prominent Israeli political figures to me, including the Prime Minister and some cabinet members; she even recognized some plain-clothes security agents. The security was clearly very high. And we wore our usual disguises.

The program began with the overture to *The Marriage of Figaro*, and in the next two hours, with a twenty-minute intermission, presented Mozart's *Symphony No. 36, "Linz"* and *Sinfonia Concertante in E-flat Major, K. 364*. The audience was more enthusiastic than I could remember at any concert I ever attended, showing their love of their own famous musicians performing in Israel, even Austrian music.

31.

AT EIGHT-THIRTY THE next morning, I was picked up and driven to the Midrasha training center near Herzliya. Marie surprisingly decided instead to take a bus to Mossad headquarters, where she had some meetings.

Zvi ben Levi, the head of field agents in Eastern Europe, welcomed me, "Shalom, Milt. Welcome to the land of your ancestors."

We were in a conference room with two others, a man and a woman. The woman, Naomi Rutman, looked to be about sixty years old. She was slightly overweight but carried herself very well. Yitzhak ben Moshe (Cohen), also about sixty, had a mostly bald head, large brown eyes, bushy eyebrows, and a bushy mustache. He was slim and muscular and dressed in jeans and a blue tee-shirt, as well as brown open sandals.

Zvi began: "We're going to show you busy areas of Moscow where contacts could be made and how to lose someone following you."

They had a series of films actually made in Moscow at various crowded places, such as railway stations, underground Metro stations, airports, and cultural centers like museums, concert halls, and theaters. Government buildings, they said, were also opportunities, including courthouses. There were university campuses and medical centers that were also used for clandestine meetings and drop-offs, as well as frequented shops and department stores.

"The use of parks is discouraged unless close to major downtown buildings, where many people seek benches for lunch or snacks during workdays or also for weekend excursions, especially with family or pets," he advised.

I learned that they hadn't decided if I should have a small dog in my Moscow apartment or if they should give me access to someone else's dog when needed. They often used such dogs for drop-offs, especially if a message could be attached to a small case on the dog's collar, so anyone petting the dog and knowing where to look could take a message without notice. Caring for a dog, even part-time, wasn't something I wanted to do.

There was a lot to learn, and I realized I needed the years that were required to train Israeli agents. But Zvi said, "You shouldn't be polished, since that would be a giveaway of your being trained. Your trip to Moscow is only for business purposes and limited to a few months."

That was the first I'd heard of a duration for my visit to Moscow, and I hadn't expected to be there so long. Yet, the intrigue of being in Russia for the CIA while developing my own biopharma company with a totally new technology involving the use of odors as drugs was compelling, certainly original.

After lunch, I was oriented to codes and how to make and encrypt messages, and how to hide or retrieve them in a suitable drop-off. I was confused very soon, which Zvi said was expected and that by the time they 'graduated' me, I would be sufficiently competent. I was shown different paper sheets and ink and how to make messages temporarily invisible or reduced in size so that a magnifying glass was needed to read them.

Yitzhak had me for the rest of the afternoon in his laboratory, where he showed me a collection of cameras, films, and electronics and taught me how to use these for different purposes, and how we needed to transmit either the cameras or films shot. Some were so small as to fit easily into the palm of my hand yet had tremendous storage, magnification, and picture capacity.

I was also shown how to either corrupt a computer or download any program, including tips on how to try to override passwords. This took about five hours because Yitzhak wanted me to practice, so I had a rudimentary knowledge of all of this before I went to Moscow, but I knew that I was still an amateur in cybernetics.

We were supposed to end our day early because it was Friday, and everything, including the Mossad general operations, shut down early in the afternoon for the Sabbath. But the program I participated in was so long that I was driven back to the apartment at around 6:00 p.m., interfering with the onset of the Sabbath.

*

MARIE WAS ALREADY there when I got back. We had a glass of wine and discussed our plans for the evening. It was clear that I needed to return to the Mossad training on Sunday, but it wasn't certain what my next plans would be beyond that.

Marie suggested we make it an early night by getting dinner at a local restaurant downtown and then coming back to our apartment. I also had a lot of material that Zvi had given me to read about Moscow, including a primer on basic Russian phrases and tourist sites.

*

ON SUNDAY MORNING, Marie and I were driven to Mossad headquarters, not to the training center. Today, we were to discuss what the Mossad knew about the development of odorous weapons by adversary countries, the extent of animal and human testing, any production capacities developed, and what specific missing information was needed.

This involved the intelligence heads of the former Soviet and the Eastern Europe blocks, but another analyst, Shlomo Einhorn, also joined us. Shlomo had spent many years as an intelligence agent in South America, the Middle East, and Europe. He was asked to come back for this project because of his undergraduate degree in chemistry from Tel Aviv University. He was well over sixty-five, bald, about 200 pounds, and short. He wore thick eyeglasses and very casual clothes, and around his neck was a heavy gold necklace with a star of David.

"We have been studying several chemical groups that, given as odors, caused rapid neurotoxicity while others affected anxiety, attention, sleep, and uncontrolled movements, similar to Parkinson's disease," he explained. I concluded that they weren't sure if any were rapid toxins and whether they functioned via the olfactory system as compared to intranasal uptake by the rich vascular system. It was clear that their information was sketchy.

Then, something strange happened. Shlomo switched into Hebrew suddenly and spoke to his colleagues very quickly, so I wouldn't understand. But I did catch the word 'Aleksai,' which I presumed was Russian. I decided to ask Brad about this and not Shlomo.

Their problem, Shlomo admitted, was "the difficulty of focusing on ongoing research in Russia, or in any of its former Soviet bloc allies, or even North Korea, because of limited contacts and resources in most of these countries, except Iran." Since they had to seek intelligence from other areas, Moscow was chosen because the research facility in Oryol was identified; the CIA had a mole there. But maybe the mole was operating through the French or Israeli secret service. That information would eventually be shared with me, I was told, but I wondered why I never heard anything about this from Marie.

We spent the rest of the day with the Mossad business group, describing some of the investors they planned for me to meet in Paris, including one or two Russian industrialists. This was still in development, they said, so no arrangements for me to return to Paris had yet been made. They also showed me my revised business plan, with *pro forma* projections of sales, regulatory and research timelines, costs, and return on investment for a typical odor therapeutic that could be used to treat Parkinson's disease. I was glad they'd worked on this;

it would've taken me days to complete the necessary information and graphs, if at all.

Then they turned the tables on me, challenging me to defend the numbers and timelines in preparation for my presentation to prospective investors. They said they were preparing power point slides summarizing everything, making it a very professional presentation. I was to defend the business plan to upper Mossad management the following day. Surprisingly, Marie stated that she "would work on this with Milt before our next meeting." Evidently, she was more involved in this prospect and with helping me with Pharmascent than I had appreciated.

So, it's clearly also a Mossad project – not just of interest to the CIA.

*

WE WERE RETURNED to our apartment earlier than usual. I had my business plan to study that evening. Getting investors and being able to explain and defend the business was essential to the success of the venture, so I needed to become knowledgeable about each section. I had to be able to explain it to savvy and experienced businessmen who probably wouldn't have a background in odors and olfaction. But I was assured that they would be expert at reading profit and loss statements and would focus very diligently on the financial numbers. I was curious to see how Marie would critique everything. Marie also offered to help by peppering me with questions about the business plan.

Should I ask her who Aleksai is? No, I shouldn't reveal I noticed this.

After ordering dinner in from a local restaurant, we settled down to a question-and-answer session on my business plan. Surprisingly, Marie was really sophisticated in her understanding of business, which

I gathered she had acquired in her former and current jobs. But where did she learn how to challenge cost, marketing, and sales numbers?

The more I get to know her, the more enigmatic she becomes.

32.

THE NEXT DAY, I finally received an encrypted text message from Brad, announcing that he wanted to arrange a secure phone call with me. Although Marie thought it strange, I told her that I needed to take a short walk after breakfast. She, of course, knew I wanted privacy but didn't say anything.

Brad said that it was agreed by all that Marie would help me find an apartment and office for Pharmascent in Moscow, but the CIA and Mossad business offices were already working together to advance a plan to get me established in Moscow. I was glad to know my company was making such progress, even without my direct involvement, which was fine with me. I concluded that Simon Fass had arranged this, and was advancing, with Mossad, the identification of investors.

Brad's main reason for the call was to advise me that the key to getting the information out of the Russian research facility was to have me try to establish a communication with the chemistry group in Oryol, maybe via our mole, '*A*,' there. He said that *A* (meaning *Aleksai*) might have such a chemist in mind. Brad hoped this would be our source, since this chemist should be accessible to me via the Jewish community in Moscow, "which I know you were connecting to, Milt," he said. The CIA and Mossad were hoping that I could get some insight into the work and odors being studied by the Russians.

Brad again emphasized the secrecy of this mission, saying that even our agents and those of the French and Israelis were only able to get limited information beyond learning that they are doing this defensive research.

Brad made it clear to me that "although you'll be working with the Israelis and the French, your first and only true loyalty is to the U.S." For that reason, I need to keep my CIA controller fully informed. Brad said he would remain my primary contact even when I travel to or outside of Russia.

"But why have you kept your Russian mole, 'Aleksai,' so secret from me?" I asked. "Afterall, it seems that this was known to the Mossad, because I heard Shlomo say it."

"We couldn't risk talking about this too early in your engagement, especially since Marie became so attached to you. But it's now clear that since the Mossad knew, Marie likely also knew," Brad advised.

Now I felt even more anxious and inexperienced about which information I should keep from Marie and from the Mossad officers who were engaged in training and grooming me to spy in Russia.

It's clear they also have limited trust in me.

The best Brad could say, then was, "I wish you good luck, Milt."

I laughed, though without humor. "That's the least you can do," I said. "I hope I prove useful and can survive this."

He tried giving me assurances that they were well-organized, experienced, and knew how to protect me or remove me quickly from Russia, if necessary. I didn't believe much of it but thanked him anyhow.

Most importantly, Brad advised that I needed to end my visit with the Mossad in Tel Aviv and return with Marie to Paris as soon as possible, since Simon Fass was organizing a meeting with potential investors for Pharmascent. This was also relayed to me by those in The Office.

"But what about your concern of leaks within the DGSE? Has this compromised our mission and put both Marie and me at risk?" I finally asked.

"We have, with the Mossad, wondered how the Hezbollah knew so much about Marie and her whereabouts, despite her always traveling in a disguise and being one of many involved in the Hezbollah assassination in Paris a couple of years ago. When they made an attempt against you both on the train, which only a small number at the DGSE and The Office knew about, we concluded that there could be a mole or double agent in the DGSE. Even Charles Massigney, their head of operations, has been concerned since the Hezbollah has been able to track Marie despite high precautions being made to keep her role and location secret. This is another reason why the Mossad and we want to separate her from you as soon as possible," he advised.

"Does Marie know this? She hasn't mentioned this to me."

"Yes, but she hasn't taken this as seriously as either the Mossad or we have, thinking her DGSE activities are known only to a small number of the French intelligence. But better overly cautious than sorry, since we know this happens regularly in the spy business," he said as we ended the call.

*

TWO DAYS LATER, we were back in Paris, each taking different flights from Tel Aviv. When I left the immigration checkpoint, I went into the men's room and again put on my 'French' disguise, and planned to use my French passport, since I didn't want to enter Russia with a passport showing my trips between France and Israel. Once in her apartment, Marie told me that we were going to see Charles Massigney at DGSE headquarters again, so that I could present the business slides developed with the Mossad to him and his team before the meeting with prospective investors later in the week.

After my conversation with Brad about a possible double-agent in the DGSE, this worries me.

33.

AT ABOUT TEN the next morning, we took the Metro to the 20th Arrondissement and proceeded to DGSE headquarters, entering through a side-door in an alley behind the building. Inside, I removed my disguise, and proceeded with Marie to the office of Charles Massigney. He had three staff members with him and introduced them only by their first names. Charles led off the meeting by inquiring about my activities since my last visit with them, and I updated him superficially, since I wasn't sure if he were probing or just being polite, and one intelligence agency always wanted, it seemed, information on what another was doing.

They had a projector and screen set up, so I loaded my thumb drive into their computer, which they screened in advance for viruses or other contaminants, and began the PowerPoint slide presentation developed at The Office, which lasted about thirty minutes. It summarized the science and business objectives, potential initial products and development timelines, and the costs and projected revenues and profits.

The group waited until I concluded before offering their comments and questions, which indicated to me that they had given this some thought and were concerned that it not be too scientific or technical. "The business parts are weak, yet the attendees are businessmen and not scientists," Charles criticized. They wanted me to tailor it more to the interests of the investment group.

Charles cautioned me that one of the attendees was French and very detail-oriented in terms of financial projections but wouldn't pretend to understand the science. Instead, he would rely on the others for that. They didn't know the other three — a Dutchman, a German, and a Russian. The Frenchman, Marie said, had ties to the Toilette founders, so she expected he would be supportive. "I don't know if he does business with Israel or Israeli companies, but I suspect a relationship."

After Charles's colleagues left, he told us, "I've been discussing the venue for incorporation with a French attorney, who had identified a Russian attorney to take care of business registration and other legal matters in Moscow." Charles summarized these tasks for Marie and me, and I was encouraged that they seemed so confident that my meeting tomorrow would be successful.

At lunch in a quiet café a few streets away, Marie shared her own thoughts about my presentation.

"You'll be presenting to businessmen of four different nationalities," she said, "so I think you need to make it much simpler, speak much slower, and pause after each topic to solicit questions."

She was correct.

Finally, I raised the concern about how secure we are with the DGSE, since any leak of the mission of the Scenturion Venture and the real mission of Pharmascent and me in Moscow would be devastating.

Marie pondered and did not respond immediately. But then said, "We always worry about such leaks and even traitors in our organizations, but so far it is mere speculation based on certain unexpected events, and without firm evidence. But this is also a concern of Charles about his organization, and both your CIA and my Mossad are fully aware of this."

"Yes, I recall the prominent double agents in Britain's MI6, working for the Russian KGB, such as Kim Philby, Guy Burgess, and Anthony Blunt," I added.

"Don't forget the prominent scandals of those Americans who spied for Russia, such as Julius and Ethel Rosenberg, Aldrich Ames, and Robert Hanssen. Whether for money or political views, spying has always been a two-way street," Marie surprised me.

This is interesting to hear from Marie, who evidently accepts double agents as part of the espionage system

*

CHECKING MY EMAILS after returning to the apartment, I saw that the editor of *Cancer Advances* had responded to our submission, and indicated that after making some minor changes, it would be basically acceptable for publication. The other authors were also copied in, so I responded to them all that I was quite pleased that we'd been given a chance to revise and resubmit.

I told Marie the good news and said how excited I was by the prospect of having our article published in such a prestigious and widely read journal. She poured some white wine from the fridge.

"To your success," she toasted, "in every aspect."

34.

WE ARRIVED AT Toilette at 9:30 a.m., an hour before the scheduled meeting. Simon Fass and Jacques Corbet greeted us in the conference room, where a nice spread of light food had been set out. Marie and I took coffee, and I selected a croissant, which was delicious.

The investors were ushered in, and we all introduced ourselves, conducting the conversation in English, which they knew better than I could converse in their languages. Before they sat down, they handed me their signed confidentiality agreements, which were sent in advance.

The four were well-dressed, distinguished-looking gentlemen, ranging, I thought, between about fifty-five and over seventy years of age. The eldest, Otto Pinedo of Amsterdam, spoke first, saying that he was retired except for sitting on three boards of directors and making an occasional investment, and that he last served as the Chief Executive of a mid-size Dutch bank. For a someone over seventy, I thought he was in great shape — tall and slim, with a slight gray beard and a full head of gray hair. He had penetrating brown eyes.

Jacques Corbet then introduced the French investor, René Marseult. He was a short, stocky man with a well-groomed long, thin mustache, which he liked to twist at the ends. He wore a brown plaid suit with a green vest and a yellow bow tie with butterflies. He was engaging and told me that most of his career was in insurance, where he was in the investment department of a large European insurance company headquartered here in Paris.

The third participant was Yuri Grobstein from Moscow, who was a little over six feet, slightly overweight, in his mid-fifties, and dressed in a dark brown corduroy suit with a solid green tie. He gave me a very firm handshake and explained that he was in the energy business, specifically a principal in a publicly owned Russian oil company, one of the new enterprises created by Putin about ten years ago. I was sure he was Jewish but didn't want to approach that unless we were alone.

The fourth and final person was Hans Becker, from Munich, who wore a three-piece dark blue suit, with a solid red tie, was of average height and clearly on the corpulent side, and with thinning light brown hair and what seemed to be blue eyes. He explained that his major professional activity was investing and serving on boards of directors. He had a financial background, having earned the equivalent of a Masters, or *Diplom*, in Business Administration from the University of Munich.

My slide presentation went smoothly, with interruptions only when I needed to better define a term or explain how olfaction works. Once they understood the process and my plans to expose specific synthetic odors to patients with neurological diseases, their curiosity grew.

Hans Becker asked if I could expand somewhat on risk factors or what could happen at each phase to derail the project, while Otto Pinedo wanted a better understanding of the cost projections and also how I derived the sales and profit/loss projections when the company's product plans were still so early and premature.

I very honestly conceded what was speculative and what the basis of the costs and sales projections were. It was clear that the projections were made very hypothetically, based on my current thoughts of product candidates.

Pinedo, the Dutchman, didn't say anything, just looked at me, so I wasn't sure I had allayed his concerns. The others seemed receptive, and thanked me for the presentation, and congratulated me for making it all understandable to them.

The conversation then progressed to initial financial needs and the use of proceeds. Although I had a slide on this, they wanted more discussion. I decided to give out a printed copy of my presentation, all marked CONFIDENTIAL, and asked them to turn to the table I provided on Capital Needs.

"I think I can set up the operation and contract out a lot of the chemistry and medical testing at an initial budget for one year of five million dollars. However, I think a two-year budget should be provided, and this, as shown in the table, would total about $11.5 million. I would not take a salary, but this would be carried on the books as a financial obligation."

I couldn't since I had a full-time job with ESU.

None of the participants raised any questions. But they all wanted to know how we would derive a valuation of Pharmascent Sciences and what equity percentage the $11.5 million would be for them. I said that this was, of course, a soft number, but we had derived a current valuation of forty million dollars, although I recognized that the patent that I was working on had neither been submitted nor validated, so there was a real risk there.

"These numbers compute to roughly a twenty-eight percent equity," said René Marseult.

Both the German and Dutch investors quickly asserted that that was too low a percentage for the current risk of the venture. The Russian said he would be more comfortable if there could be a Russian subsidiary, preferably in Moscow, so that the clinical trials and research could be done there.

"Actually, Mr. Grobstein," I said, "we have thought of the company residing in two countries — France as the home base, but possibly elsewhere for either research or manufacturing. I would support Moscow for a second office and operation if my budget could afford this."

I noted that Marie and the Toilette executives smiled at that exchange: the Russian had taken our bait. We could proceed with our plans to have an office in Moscow, giving me a basis to work there. Pharmascent would be my cover for living and working in Russia.

Grobstein continued: "Would there be a strategic or other reason for disallowing participation of other investors, including the Russian government?" he asked.

I said that those were ultimately questions for the board but that I hadn't intended to solicit any government investment, since that could bring restrictions and entanglements. "But setting the company up in Moscow could work out," I said to the group, "because Marie Chalfont of Toilette and Mr. Grobstein could assist me with the Russian language and making arrangements, while perhaps Monsieur Marseult and Simon Fass or Jacques Corbet could assist with also establishing us in France, at least legally."

Yuri Grobstein was delighted and said that he would personally help me get established and would introduce me to key business and government people, whom he thought would be critical to my doing business in Russia.

This is going even better than we'd dared to hope for.

I thanked him for his offer and future involvement.

I then asked the group what they needed in order to consider making a financial commitment. The Dutch and German investors simply said they needed a higher equity stake. The French and Russian businessmen said they agreed with them.

"Do you have a number in mind?" I asked. "It's critical to me not to dilute the shares too much too early, since the company will eventually need mezzanine financing. And, of course, when all of this is over, I still want to have a respectable share because of my seminal contributions."

The Dutchman said he would participate if the $11.5 million represented a thirty-three percent equity share, and the others nodded.

I didn't want to respond too quickly, so I just said I would have to give the matter further thought.

We ended the meeting with an agreement to have a telephonic conference call tomorrow at 1:00 p.m. to discuss if we had a compromise number. I wanted them to know that I was not yet saying yes to a thirty-three percent equity for $11.5 million. I also wanted some time to confer with others, including the two venture capital groups in the United States. The amount of money I was requesting was very small and could compromise the deal because of any party not getting much equity.

After they left, I sat with the three from Toilette, and we discussed the interaction and the investment impasse. Simon Fass thought that compromising at thirty percent equity might do it, while Jacques Corbet suggested that giving them another advantage might also be effective — for example, if I agreed to give them first refusal rights to the next financing, which would mean I couldn't give others better terms. Jacques said, "this addition is very valuable and could satisfy them without increasing the equity to thirty-three percent." Marie agreed with Jacques. I explained I would see what my American venture capital groups thought of this prospect and would try to communicate with them before our call tomorrow.

*

ALTHOUGH I DIDN'T express it to the Toilette group, I was actually elated that these investors were prepared to discuss and start negotiating investment amounts and equity ownership. I gathered that being brought together by the Toilette group, particularly Simon Fass, with probable involvement of the Mossad, the investors were already primed for this opportunity.

But could they even have a relationship with the Russian oligarch?

Simon recommended that I meet with the French attorney later today, so we could move the process forward, and I could have the attorney review the structure and terms being discussed from the standpoint of French laws and business practice. I agreed, and Simon said he would work on getting us an appointment immediately.

Marie stayed back with me after Simon and Jacques had left, and I told her I needed some time to try to reach the U.S. venture groups and didn't want to take up her time if she had something else to do. She got the point that I wanted privacy.

The first person I contacted was Brad. I told him we needed to talk, since I had investors interested, but the terms weren't yet finalized. I also sent emails to the Sequel Ventures people in Westport and to Bio Advisors in New York. I wrote that I was in advanced discussions with a European investment group and was attaching my current confidential business plan so they could let me know — promptly, I hoped — if they had an interest in joining the discussion. I said that my plan was to have corporate headquarters in France with a subsidiary in Moscow.

I knew that would probably deter the potential American investors from involvement because of not wanting foreign travel for each board meeting, if not telephonic, should they participate. On the other hand, my bargaining powers with the Europeans would be strengthened if I told them their contribution could possibly be reduced because of more investors, specifically sophisticated U.S. venture capitalists.

Although I knew they couldn't decide in a positive way so quickly, they *could* reject this out of hand. That would, at least, give me a better appreciation of how dependent I was on the European financing group.

With time to sit and think, I wished I knew what role Marie was playing with both the French and Israeli intelligence services and just who was instructing her about helping me get established in Moscow.

Is she an asset or a liability to me? Since she's a foreign agent and may be known as such by the Russians, wouldn't that immediately compromise me?

I needed to get some guidance on all of that from Brad.

Marie came back and said Simon would call her about the appointment with counsel soon, and in the meantime, we would have lunch at a restaurant about three streets away.

"But we should take a more circuitous route to assess if we're being watched," she said — a slightly shocking reminder of my new normal.

It was a nice day, so we walked around, again in our disguises, for about fifteen minutes before entering the small restaurant that was quite full with lunch guests. Marie got a call during lunch, telling us that we were to meet the lawyer, Francois Gullet, at 3 p.m. in his office off the Champs Elysees.

Still wondering about Marie, I decided to toss out the question of Dr. Vladimir Borofskov, whom we'd both met in Vienna.

"Since we're going to be in Moscow, I wonder if our paths will cross again," I said. "If he's even still there."

"What makes you wonder about him?" Marie asked.

"Well, we're going to be in Moscow, and he was a member of their National Academy of Sciences located in Moscow. Maybe it would be helpful to reconnect with him."

I didn't tell her that Borofskov asked me to intervene with the U.S. State Department to enable him to defect, but then disappeared from Vienna, and that the CIA suspected he may have had a hand in the murder of their agent, Charles Hughes.

"I really know nothing more about him," she said, "since he totally disappeared. But you're right, maybe he is someone we should try to talk with, since he should be well connected with the olfactory research community in Russia."

Watching her eyes as she talked, I felt that she was holding something back. It was just that she didn't look directly at me when she said this.

Why would the CIA know about this and not the Mossad, when they sent Marie to the Vienna conference to establish a relationship with me and perhaps for other reasons? Does the CIA know more about Hughes's murder and Vladimir Borofskov than they shared with me?

I knew by now that my handlers carefully measured what they told me.

35.

FRANCOIS GULLET'S OFFICE was easy to find from the Metro station, so we arrived about fifteen minutes early for our appointment. He was a bit under six feet tall, overweight with a wide abdomen and double chin, receding brown hair with gray sprinkles, a large nose and lips, and teeth yellowed from his smoking. Either pipes or cigars, I guessed.

Mssr. Gullet said he would need to get my input on Incorporating Articles, Bylaws, and other documents needed to establish the business in France and that his Russian colleague, Jolanda Terofskia, would do the same according to Russian laws. Gullet had some sample Incorporating Articles and Bylaws in English, so we could simply review and modify these to comply with the mission and future activities of our company.

"Is having a company name in English a problem?" I asked.

"*Mais non*," said Gullet, "this has become quite common in Europe and actually gives the company a better appearance as more international in scope."

His explanation of taxes and registration costs in France got me to thinking that my projections for startup costs might have been too low. But if I had to increase them, wouldn't it reveal my naiveté to the current investors? Then again, this might have been why they showed some skepticism with regard to my cash flow needs for the first two years.

After signing the papers and getting Mssr. Gullet's contact information for the attorney in Moscow, I said I would engage the Russian attorney myself, as well as a real estate agent to help me find offices in a reputable business area, as well as an apartment for me in a reasonable and safe area of Moscow.

"This is not where you should be frugal," said Marie. "Appearances and safety are paramount in Moscow." She said she thought that once Yuri Grobstein became an investor, he would help guide us. She also cautioned that we might be moving too fast with an attorney or others in Russia, since Yuri would likely have his own ideas on how we should proceed with establishing the Russian subsidiary.

"Yes," I said, "we can wait a little longer — until we get Yuri Grobstein's decision on becoming a founding investor."

36.

IT WAS ALREADY four-thirty when we left to return to the apartment. Although it was rush hour, Marie and I got back to our street in about thirty minutes, agreeing that we'd had a big day and needed to relax before going out to dinner. Kicking off our shoes and getting comfortable with a chardonnay, we stretched out on the comfortable chair and sofa.

"Well," I said, "I'm very pleased with everything we've gotten done so far. Thank you for all your help and support."

She laughed and said it was her pleasure to learn from me, since she'd never set up a business.

"I assure you, this is my first such effort," I said.

"I think you' re just being modest," she answered. "I suspect you have a double-dose of Jewish business genes."

I laughed and thought back to some of my earlier views, albeit often tongue-in-cheek. "It's true that we don't appreciate how genes affect behavior," I said. "If I could identify the X-chromosome, or a woman-related 'shopping' gene or genes, I could possibly develop a gene therapy or antidote to its messages to overcome the need to shop, which husbands and male partners could slip into their companions' coffee in the morning."

She found that hilarious. But then said, "What would happen to the fashion industry and other commercial enterprises? You would be executed! And how would women manage with their partners if they couldn't find a shopping alternative for their sanity? This is an important addiction in our modern society."

"True, but if we can increase sexual libido and other behavior activities," I said, on my soapbox now, "why not affect other innate desires? I once thought this was a worthy scientific project but then got redirected to olfaction.

"I believe selection and application of defined odor molecules and combinations could not only affect disease but likely also behavior. Isn't this the very basis of the perfume industry and the practice of ancient tribes since the beginning of human civilization? In fact, pheromones are *critical* to the sexual behavior and reproduction in most animal species."

With that, I shut up and became deep in thought. Marie's response was to join me on the sofa and begin to focus her attention below my belt.

This woman certainly doesn't need an aphrodisiac for her sex drive.

So, in the interest of keeping the peace and good international relations, I smiled and complied.

By 7:00 p.m., it was time to go to dinner, so we dressed and went for a walk in the neighborhood, eventually finding a café on Rue des Archives where we could sit outdoors. All the time, Marie assured me there was a Mossad car trailing us.

We ordered plain salads followed by a pepperoni pizza and a *pichet* of the house wine specialty, chianti. It was nice just sitting outside and watching the people. Most of the tables had guests doing the same – enjoying being outdoors and people watching.

"I am anxious about moving to Moscow, since I don't speak the language and know nothing of the local life and business mores. I feel a little insecure," I said.

"This is why I will be with you until everything becomes more routine, and you feel some confidence," Marie said. "I still remember Russian from my early childhood, although I am sure I need some refreshing."

"Besides," said Marie, "if you had too much Russian knowledge, it could raise suspicions."

We returned to the apartment at about ten-thirty and turned on the news. After about fifteen minutes, Marie left to take her shower, and I used this opportunity to call Brad.

He answered immediately and asked how the business development was proceeding. I told him that the four investors would be on the phone with me tomorrow afternoon, that we had met with the French attorney, and that I was waiting for responses from the two U.S. venture capital groups. I again emphasized that I was worried that I would screw this up and also put myself in jeopardy.

"I understand your concerns," Brad said, "and we're doing everything we can to keep your exposure and risks limited."

"Well," I said, "having Marie to protect my back while you caution me to limit what I share with her — except for my body — is a new and challenging requirement."

"I know you'll manage it well," he said. "She's a beautiful and stimulating woman. We have been assured by the Mossad that Marie is an asset and will be helpful to you."

"Yes, I'll manage through this. You know I'm quite patriotic." Brad chuckled at that.

He then told me they were checking out Yuri Grobstein. He confirmed he was indeed Jewish and had done or was doing business with high government officials, probably including Vladimir Putin.

"So, you should tread cautiously with him until we understand his motives and role within the Russian business and political worlds."

Other than that, Brad said the CIA contingent attached to the embassy in Moscow was preparing for me.

I then went to bed, falling asleep quickly.

*

WHEN I AWOKE at about 7:00 a.m., Marie was still asleep, so I went into the kitchen and checked my cell phone. As I'd hoped, the two venture capital firms I contacted had responded to my emails.

Jack Sperling of Bio Advisors thanked me for the update but said they would have to pass, since they needed much more time for due diligence. Besides, he said, they normally make a more significant investment, usually as lead investor.

Bill Rhodes of Sequel Ventures also said they needed more time to evaluate the opportunity, but if I had most of the funding needed and I wanted him as a minority investor, he would consider this once he knew who the other investors were, especially the lead investor.

I couldn't answer Bill's last question yet, so I decided to delay getting back to him until the afternoon conference call with the other four potential investors. I would need to settle the valuation, and if one stood out as lead investor, who would represent the investors on the board, I was sure Bill Rhodes would need to know that too. In any event, I was cautiously optimistic that Sequel Ventures could join the investor group, or at least I could lend credibility to the venture by mentioning their *potential* involvement.

Shortly before 8:00 a.m., Marie wandered into the living room and asked how I slept and when I got up. I told her to relax, and I would make us breakfast, first bringing her a cup of coffee. She smiled sleepily and then disappeared into the bathroom while I made eggs and toast.

Everything was ready about twenty minutes later when Marie appeared in her robe and joined me at the table. She seemed to enjoy the food and having breakfast served, and I was glad to reciprocate to all the care and hosting she had extended to me during the last few weeks, in Paris and in Tel Aviv. Although I may have been her assignment, it was obvious that she enjoyed caring for me.

After breakfast, I shaved and dressed while Marie took care of our laundry. She took extra time to dress and surprised me once again by having her hair, now black, in a ponytail. She was wearing dark blue silk slacks, a front-buttoned light blue cashmere sweater, and small-heeled open sandal shoes. Her face was tan with a tinge of rouge on her cheeks and pink lipstick. I complimented her on her appearance and asked if there was a special occasion today.

"No, Milt," she said. "I just felt like getting a little more dressed than usual when I go to the office. After all, I have a handsome, intelligent, physician-scientist who will soon become a business entrepreneur." At this moment, she spontaneously put her arms around me and gave me a long kiss, after which she whispered that she'd missed making love to me last night. Then, hand-in-hand, we left for the offices of her employer.

Simon Fass had his secretary in the conference room getting the call with the other four parties connected. At 1:05 p.m., I greeted everyone and thanked them for again giving us their time and attention. I explained that I'd made progress in establishing the French headquarters by engaging a business attorney yesterday, and that he expected to be able to submit the necessary papers for incorporation by the end of the week. However, "he anticipated that it would take at least ten business days to get approval from the various government agencies, including the revenue and taxation departments." Most on the call chuckled, saying that no European country, especially France, could move that fast, and "he was probably just being polite."

I explained that we had a very basic set of Incorporating Articles and Bylaws, which would, of course, be subject to modification by the board once it was appointed. The prospect of a subsidiary office in Moscow also was discussed, I explained further, but I would need to decide that once I was physically there.

"I'm now looking into the visa and other legal papers needed to develop this business in Russia," I added, since this was our goal, and I knew the Russian oligarch was keen on this.

"No problem, Dr. Davidson," said Yuri Grobstein. "Once we settle the business details today, I can help you through the complex business requirements in Russia. In fact, the Minister of Commerce and the Minister of Finance are acquaintances of mine."

At this point, I opened the meeting to questions by the prospective investors. But before anyone could speak, I thought I would share my recent accomplishment, so I could control the valuation discussion that I knew was foremost on their mind.

"As I mentioned yesterday, before coming to Paris and meeting with all of you, I met preliminarily with two venture capital groups in the U.S. Following our meeting yesterday, I contacted them and updated them on the business plan and our establishing offices in Paris and, probably, Moscow.

"One of the two, Sequel Ventures, whom you may have heard about as a leading investor in biotechnology and healthcare companies, expressed an interest in becoming an investor."

There was silence on the line, so I continued.

"I promised that I would give them these details after this conference call, assuming we can reach some understanding. Which, of course, would be subject to your legal review once we have the proposed arrangements written by our attorney."

"My congratulations on so much progress in this short time," the French businessman, René Marseult, remarked.

The Dutch investor, Otto Pinedo, then opened the discussion about valuation, which he thought needed to be settled before any investments were offered. Hans Becker, the German, said he had given this a lot of thought and believed even thirty million was too high for this startup.

"Well," I said, "after talking with the Sequel Ventures group, I understand that this is a function of who is the lead investor and how much he will invest and at what valuation. At a valuation of thirty million dollars, I think the U.S. venture capital group would definitely want to take the lead with an investment of up to ten million dollars, which would cover most of our needs for the first two years."

Of course, I'm exaggerating.

Yuri Grobstein appeared concerned that the European investors might negotiate themselves out of any reasonable stake, so he quickly jumped in.

"I do not think the initial valuation of thirty or forty million should be so critical," he said, "since we know there will be additional financing needed thereafter, and we could accept the higher valuation if we were to get a preferred position in future investments. I, for one, would invest five million if I could be the lead investor and a board member."

This was exactly what I'd hoped would transpire. As soon as Grobstein finished, the French and Dutch investors agreed and said they would each contribute three million at the forty-million-dollar valuation.

In contrast, the German investor said he wasn't comfortable with those terms, since the short time for this transaction and review of documents inadequate for his gaining input from his own business partners.

"Thank you, Herr Becker," I said, "but as much as I would like your involvement, we need to move forward if we have the oral commitments for the money needed as the first-tier financing, and I'm anxious to get Pharmascent Sciences started."

I exaggerated further, saying "I'm confident that the U.S. group will make up the difference needed, with my only concern being that they were speaking of a larger investment. And from the offers made by you all, they probably can't invest more than two million dollars unless one of you wants to reduce your amount."

No one responded, so I simply said, "Okay, then let's work on these terms, and if you all agree, have Yuri join the board representing the others as lead investor. Is this agreeable to all?"

I heard a yes from all but could not discern any response from the German. "Herr Becker," I asked, "should I conclude that you're not investing?"

"As of this moment, yes, I am not. But perhaps we could stay in touch, and if there is a change in numbers or investment level, you could contact me so I could reconsider, certainly for any future financing."

"Of course," I said. This meant that Becker didn't want to close the door completely.

So, with three investors committing eleven million dollars, I could respond to Bill Rhodes that we could accept his investment of up to two million, since the other investors had 'filled the book,' as they say in the investment game's lingo. I thought this would make him hungry for more if he knew and respected the other investors.

This meant I would need Simon Fass to compose a short biography of each of the three investors, so I could share this with Rhodes. If Rhodes wanted to invest more for his fund, I would be agreeable.

"Thank you all. If there are no other immediate concerns, I will conclude the meeting and ask you to patiently wait for our attorney to provide you with the necessary papers, which I hope will take only a few days." Then I said goodbye and ended the call.

37.

"THAT WAS SUPERB!" said Simon. "I was impressed by how you handled the valuation, how you used the U.S. venture group to strengthen your position, and how you graciously let the German exit although he was having second thoughts. Congratulations!"

"Thank you, Simon," I said. "But this would never have succeeded without your contacts and support. I have to get back to the Sequel Ventures group today, so can you get me short biographies on the Dutch, French, and Russian investors? And please include your own."

"Of course," Simon said. "I'll do it right now."

It's clear that Simon, involved with the Mossad, had orchestrated this, and knows the investors well. But I'm not sure if they're in any way connected with The Office, especially Yuri Grobstein.

After he left, Marie got up and kissed me on the cheeks and lips.

"I am so proud of you, *chérie*," she said. "You proved a better businessman than any of the others, because you controlled the conversation and negotiation, if you could call it that."

Marie and I just sat for a while, feeling pretty good about the way things were going. Soon I received an email from Simon with the biographies, so I could just forward them to Bill Rhodes. I sent him a long email clarifying the status of our financing and provided the bios of the investors, emphasizing that the Russian oligarch would join the board and that he was the lead investor at five million dollars. I then said I really wanted Sequel's involvement, and if Bill Rhodes was in agreement, I could accept up to two million from him in this first funding round. I also suggested that since there was only a small group of investors, maybe they can all constitute the initial board until the company becomes more advanced, such as when a secondary investment was made.

Marie and I went down the hall to Simon's office, and he waved us to sit down.

"Thanks for the biographies," I said. "Could you join us for lunch so we can celebrate a little?"

Simon came around the desk to shake my hand and said that he, unfortunately, had back-to-back meetings.

"We would love to have dinner with you tomorrow night," I said. "But we've already taken so much advantage of you that I must insist that we invite *you* to dinner. And please, bring your wife."

I'm not sure he has a wife, but I said it anyway.

Simon apologized, saying his wife and he had another social event. "But maybe when you return to Paris, we can get together," he offered. We then left to find a restaurant for a late lunch.

We took the Metro to a stop near the Tuileries and walked to Rue Saint-Roch, where Marie knew a small, romantic restaurant that served continuously, since we were late for lunch and early for dinner. *La Cordonnerie*, it was called.

At a comfortable table in the rear, we ordered red wine and savored its great body and taste.

"This is really a great selection at a reasonable price," I said.

"Since this is on the CIA, why are you worried about a few Euros?" laughed Marie, showing she knew very well of my spy activities.

"I can't change my habits even if I have an expense account," I said, "so I guess I'll always be a boring date."

"You're just the bore I need," she said. "I am already anxious as to when we will be separated."

"Yes, I've been thinking about my plans. We have a few days for the business paperwork to be completed, and I feel guilty playing a tourist in Paris while I have research back home to attend to, as well as beginning to collaborate with the CIA chemists on my ideas for therapeutic odors."

As soon as I said it, I realized I had said too much. My working with CIA chemists had not been disclosed to others, only the spies in the field, and now I had just handed the secret to Marie. She didn't show any facial change, so I wasn't sure what she thought about it, if anything.

But I need to be more careful.

"I think I should leave Friday for New York," I said to Marie. "I need to catch up at work for a few days before coming back to Paris or flying directly to Moscow."

She looked shocked for a fleeting moment, then caught herself. "I have become accustomed to having you in my bed at night," she whispered. "So do not push me off so early in our relationship."

"You *know* I have other responsibilities," I said. "I should be spending more than a few hours a day working and less time relaxing. Here, it seems in reverse."

"Look how much has been done in just a few days," Marie said. "I bet this is because of our good relationship."

"You may be right, but I need to get back to my lab during this important period of work. I definitely need to return home for a few days." I hoped that would end the discussion. I didn't expect her to be so surprised, since Brad had already agreed to this, which made it likely that the Mossad knew of my plans also.

"I'm sure you also have a lot to do in preparation for our move to Moscow, including making sure we have the visas needed," said Marie. "I could also get mine in New York if necessary."

Fortunately, our main courses arrived at that moment, distracting us from the troubling topic. After paying the bill, we strolled for a while, mostly in silence, before returning to the apartment.

*

THE NEXT MORNING, when I checked my phone for messages, there was an email from Bill Rhodes of Sequel Ventures, responding to mine summarizing the status of the financing and investors. He had sent it the previous evening after Marie and I had gone to sleep.

"We have reviewed your plan and the initial investors," he wrote, "and while it is not what we typically invest in, we believe your investment group will be helpful, and your Russian oligarch may be able to raise more funds that you will definitely need later. This is important, because we think you are underfunding this project, but there will be enough funds to get you established and to make some progress.

"However, we would require that Pharmascent Sciences also be incorporated in the U.S., preferably Delaware, with clear responsibilities and legal relationships between the French and Russian affiliates. Finally, if the documentation is acceptable in detail by our attorneys, we are prepared to invest two million dollars at the forty-million-dollar valuation, and we want to receive certain future options to invest under the most favorable terms, which will be defined and is common language for the initial investment group. We would also require a board seat."

Wow! I actually got them to invest only two million, which I know, and they emphasized, is below the minimum they usually do.

I guessed that they had confidence in this venture, or else it was just play money for them. Either way, their name as an investor would give us credibility while giving me a bit of leverage with my European investors. I couldn't wait for Marie to wake up so I could tell her the news.

I made coffee for us, then went out to the bakery down the street and bought an assortment of pastries for a celebratory breakfast. When I returned, Marie was setting the table in her robe and jumped up to kiss me good morning. I couldn't wait to tell her about the email from

Bill Rhodes, including his request that we also incorporate in Delaware.

"I do not know what this means in terms of a Delaware registration," Marie said, "but this is good news. Our European investors will be delighted, since this is a validation of their own assessment."

"Yes, sit down, and let's enjoy breakfast and not rush. Today, I plan to stay here and work on the olfaction research plan, so we can get the project started. I'm excited about getting the resources to begin, so please understand why I need to get back to the States soon."

Marie nodded and smiled. "I'll be back here by 6:00 p.m. at the latest. Is it alright for me to bring home some simple food, like cheese and sardines, for dinner?" I agreed that after our work, we should eat in and spend our last night together.

After she left, I finally could actually sit alone quietly at my computer, think, and write. I had said in the business plan that Pharmascent Sciences would advance two or three chemicals as odor formulations and would first determine blood and urine levels and then therapeutic effects. The chemicals were different flavonoids that had been used for centuries as part of alternative medicines in China and India. They were known to affect brain function as well as a number of diverse diseases, including cardiovascular, diabetes, autoimmune, and cancer. The literature was vast, but I was able to scrutinize and identify those with solid results.

*

MARIE ARRIVED AT about five-thirty and found me in a jovial mood.

"What makes you so happy?" she asked.

"I got a good deal of work done and then enjoyed a couple of glasses of your good Scotch whiskey."

"Wonderful," Marie said. "Maybe you need to be left alone more often."

"How was your day?"

"Not very interesting — just a lot of meetings. I'm tired."

"I like being home for the evening," said Marie, throwing off her shoes. "But I don't like the thought of your leaving so soon." She came and put her arms around me, and I gave her a long, deep kiss. Within minutes, we were in the bedroom, getting out of our clothes as fast as we could. It was only a couple of hours later that we decided to finally have dinner. The cheese and sardines on crackers, together with a chardonnay, were a perfect end to a wonderful day.

38.

AFTER A RESTFUL flight home, I was up early the next day and out on the very empty and quiet New York streets by 7:00 a.m.; it was Sunday. I sensed that I was already missing New York even before I had left it for Moscow. Today, I just wanted to walk and walk, to soak up the ambiance, to imprint the city's essence in my heart and mind.

I kept walking down Fifth Avenue and soon found a bench in Washington Square Park, where I observed the youngsters doing circles and jumps on roller skates, and just watched people walking by, especially a lot of what appeared to be college kids. The Park is surrounded by New York University buildings, dormitories, and many student hangouts.

Meanwhile, I received an email text on my cell phone from Bob Ehrlich of the NY office of the CIA, responding to my inquiry about securing a visa for travel and residing in Russia.

"We can either do this with you in New York at their consulate or at their consulate in Washington. We think you should do this in Washington, since they could use your presence when applying to conduct an interview if this is arranged in advance.

"To get a three-year, multi-visit business visa, you need a sponsor, such as a business, verifying the purpose and anticipated duration of your business activity, a photo, and your valid passport.

"I suggest, since Pharmascent Sciences is not yet incorporated in Russia, you get your investor, Yuri Grobstein, to write the letter, explaining that you are establishing a business venture with him in Russia. Since he has political connections and is a prominent oligarch, this should expedite the visa."

I texted back: "Thanks, Bob. I'll contact Yuri immediately and also download the visa application from the Russian website. Please let Brad know that we should schedule time together when I'm in

Washington to apply at the Russian consulate before it closes on Tuesday afternoon, since I'll arrive in the early morning at Union Station."

I then wrote to Yuri, asking for his assistance and saying that, hopefully, he could make this urgent, since I was planning to travel to Moscow by the end of the coming week, if possible. I told him I was also going to ask the attorney he recommended to begin the registration of the company and to get a tax number as soon as he could.

This will be a test of Yuri's political contacts and stature.

*

ON THE TAXI ride home, my cell phone rang; it was Marie. She wanted to know what I was doing and when I planned to return to Paris.

"I'm in a taxi, so I can't really talk right now," I said. "I've been busy catching up with seeing New York again. I've walked a lot since getting back."

"Well, good. Anyway, don't stay away long. I am calling because Yuri contacted us at Toilette and said he'd arranged for the Moscow attorney, Jolanda Terofskia, to reach out to you. Let me know when she emails or calls you."

When I got to my apartment, I decided to relax and watch some TV. I hadn't watched the CBS evening news for quite some time, so I relaxed catching up with a little national and mostly local news: typical accidents, murders, and New York political fights. Having recently watched the news in both Paris and Tel Aviv, I noticed how restricted the U.S. broadcast was to domestic issues, ignoring most developments or events abroad. I was about to step out of American life in a big way.

*

ON MONDAY MORNING, I awoke very early, making it to my office by eight-thirty by bicycle. I noticed a light on in John Bickers' office, so I poked my head in to see if he were there. He was surprised and welcomed me in, and we chatted for a few minutes, during which I told him how busy I was working with the European collaborating scientists for the National Institute of Environmental Health Sciences, but that it had also given me some time to play tourist.

John confided that he was having problems with certain members of the pathology faculty, mostly difficulties with regard to teaching assignments and the imposed reduction of time for research. I apologized that my sudden absence might have contributed to this, but he explained that he thought it was more related to two or three objecting to how he was running the department.

When I finally returned and sat down at my desk, several of the office and department staff, noticing that my door was open, dropped in to say hello. After twenty minutes, I shut the door, so I could have some privacy to review the manuscript that we would soon be discussing. But I found myself thinking about John's problems in the department.

I finally made it over to my lab, where they had coffee and donuts set out. I had missed the sweet donuts from the neighborhood Dunkin Donuts shop, although I certainly appreciated the superior quality of the pastry and croissants that I'd become accustomed to in Paris and Tel Aviv. Yet, when you grow up with the overly sweetened U.S. donuts, some addiction sets in, and you occasionally crave all that sugar. As a physician, I should know better. But what would one chocolate donut mean in the grand scheme? Likewise, although coffee was stronger and tastier abroad, I did enjoy a cappuccino from Dunkin and expressed my appreciation to Jhanella for thinking of me when she picked up some coffees for us.

After John joined us, we reviewed the plan for revising the manuscript. John volunteered to make the first draft of the responses to the reviewers, and I agreed to make some revisions to the list of references cited and to continue making revisions to the text, while Jhanella took responsibility for finalizing the figures and adding a new table listing the human genes present in the original patient's tumor and the mouse transplants.

39.

I RODE MY bike home in heavy traffic.

Good practice for being a spy. You have to keep an eye on your forward progress while remaining totally aware of everything happening around you. It's a life-or-death business.

I was back at my building in about twenty minutes. When I got upstairs, I checked my text messages and emails and found the response I was waiting for from Yuri in Moscow.

Dear Milt,

I have spoken with my contacts at the Politburo, who in turn spoke to the visa and immigration office here. They have noted your name, and I provided the attached letter for your use at the Russian Embassy in Washington. However, you may have to wait until Tuesday or Wednesday because it could take a few days for the Moscow staff to communicate with the visa staff in Washington to expedite your application. I, of course, vouched for you, as you will read. I addressed my letter to Comrade Sergeii V. Pukalov, head of the visa section of the embassy, so when you visit the embassy, try to introduce yourself to him. I am sure he will expedite your application and give you a visa within a couple of days. I trust this will be accomplished by Friday, but you must remember, as I was advised, for you to have passport photos, your passport and application, and the fee for a rush process, since it would otherwise take a couple of weeks. Let me know if you have any problems. I look forward to welcoming you to our wonderful Motherland.

Sincerely,
Yuri Grobstein
Member of the Order of the Russian Business Forum

The attached letter to the Russian Embassy's visa section head said everything needed to get me special attention as a distinguished scientist and entrepreneur who was coming to Russia to start an innovative pharmaceutical business, in which Yuri would be involved as a board member and investor. He added that he would personally take responsibility for my activities and work during my time in Russia.

I thought this was very nice and generous of Yuri, since we had only met in person once. Clearly, though, he had decided that he wanted the business and me in his country. This was exactly what my spy agencies had desired and predicted, so everything was on plan except for a delay while I waited for the visa. Even more important, Brad had intimated to me that Yuri was well connected with political figures, including high Kremlin officials.

I sent an email thanking Yuri, saying that I would follow his advice and visit the embassy in Washington this week. I immediately sent an encrypted text to Brad at the CIA, telling him about Yuri's email and my plan to visit the Russian Embassy on Tuesday or Wednesday, whenever I could get an appointment. This meant I should probably plan to stay in Washington until I received my visa.

Next, I texted Marie that my new plan was to be back in Paris Saturday morning, assuming I could get a flight for Friday night. I said this wasn't firm yet. She responded at once, although it was 2 a.m. in Paris: "I am eagerly awaiting your return and kissing your lips."

I spent the next half-hour completing the visa application, then sending it to Brad and Yuri so they would have copies, including my explanation of the business activity I was going to pursue in Moscow.

After packing my small bag for Washington, I was finally able to relax and think of what would be happening over the next few days. I really needed to make an outline of the research I wanted the CIA-contracted chemists to assist me with, and I was worried that I didn't have a nondisclosure agreement for them to sign.

*

ON TUESDAY, I left for Penn Station in time for the early Acela to Washington. The usual black Lincoln Town Car with a sign showing my initials as "MD" was waiting for me at the front curb at Union Station, behind where the taxis lined up. Dr. James Calhoun was in the back seat.

"I hope you had a nice trip," Jim said. "Today, we're not going to Virginia or anywhere near CIA headquarters, but to a commercial contractor in Silver Spring, Maryland, who works with us."

"Do we have time for me to stop at a post office for a money order that I need for the visa for Russia?" I asked. "I'll also need to get passport photos and was hoping we could do that on our way."

Jim told the driver to stop off at the post office downtown and to go to the photo shop on the side street of the post office, where they make instant passport photos. I took care of it all in about twenty minutes.

When we were back on the road, I asked Jim to tell me more about the contractors I would be meeting with.

"They're called Argus Laboratories, which was established by a group of government chemists when they retired. They support themselves mostly through government contracts, spanning many branches, from the Department of Defense, the NIH, and even some work for the FBI and our agency. They have very high security clearance, so they can be trusted with secret projects. Your key contact will be Scott Haber."

We arrived at a sprawling two-story building without windows. There was only one modest sign over the entrance saying Argus Laboratories. A guard-controlled visitor flow and identified all visitors by phone to someone in the building. He didn't open the gate until he'd received permission. Although a private company, the security seemed like a high-security government facility.

After being checked in, photographed and fingerprinted, Dr. Scott Haber came out, greeted Jim, and introduced himself to me. Scott was in his late sixties, with thin gray hair covering most of his head and a thin dark mustache. He was dressed very casually, with a brown shirt open at the neck, gray woolen slacks, and brown loafers.

He escorted us to a conference room at the end of the ground floor. Seated inside were two men and a woman whom I had met before: Judy Reagan, Scott's associate on the chemical weapons task force of the CIA. I certainly remembered her from the meeting in which I was criticized for becoming involved with Marie Chalfont.

Scott introduced the two men, both in white lab coats, as Drs. Ken Ming and Robert Samuels, members of his senior staff. Dr. Ming was in his fifties, short in stature with a large face and forehead, black straight hair combed up, and searching dark brown eyes. He spoke with a pronounced Chinese accent.

Dr. Samuels, in contrast, sounded like a Midwesterner. He had bushy, light brown hair and a face with a thin, dark beard. He seemed younger to me, maybe early forties, and notably casually dressed under his lab coat, with jeans and a gray shirt with an open collar. I noted he wore loafers without socks.

Scott said he thought we should first meet as a group before I took a tour of the labs and then sat down with his two chemists to discuss the project in detail. The idea was for me to give an overview of my ideas and plans to produce a series of chemical compounds that were to be my first candidates for pharmacological study.

I wasn't a hundred percent sure what to test or how this would work, but I didn't want them to sense my uncertainty. "My initial goal is to develop an aromatherapy for anxiety and hyperactivity states, possibly also aiding in sleep therapy. From there, I am interested in affecting a number of neurological diseases once I worked out the details of changing simpler emotional states where affected individuals consume many different kinds of medications as pills," I explained.

After answering a few basic questions, we then broke up, and I went off with Drs. Ming and Samuels to their lab after a short tour of the facilities conducted by Scott. Ming and Samuels had adjoining offices, so we just pulled a couple of extra chairs together in Samuels's, and I went to the wall writing board to be more explicit regarding the first structures I wanted synthesized.

The formula I drew was that of melatonin, which is commonly taken for jet lag or to aid in sleeping. "This, as you know, is a hormone made by the pineal gland, which is a small gland in the brain that's affected by light and controls sleep and wake cycles. Melatonin can also be found in small amounts in various foods, such as grains, fruits, vegetables, and meats." I explained, although I hoped my being so basic wasn't insulting... "and that our body clock determines how much melatonin we make.

"As the day becomes darker, melatonin begins to rise and stays elevated for most of the night, then dropping in the early morning. Clearly, light received by the pineal gland determines how much melatonin is made by the body. During the shorter days of winter, we produce melatonin earlier or later in the day, which can lead to feelings of winter depression."

This explanation is very basic, but I'm assuming they need to refresh their knowledge.

"Since natural levels of melatonin decrease slowly with age, I think it would be a simple goal to make an aromatherapy with melatonin for those individuals with winter depression and older individuals with sleep disorder. This would be a good beginning to my developing olfactory therapy for more serious diseases."

Once the basic formula of melatonin was reviewed, I began to show how simple modifications of the basic chemical structure could make it more volatile and available as odor molecules. Drs. Ming and Samuels caught on quickly and began to make their own suggested modifications, which then led us to a series of chemical variants that totaled about twelve new forms. I told them we needed to choose three or four structures as prototypes, so I could develop some methods to test their biological effects before testing them on human volunteers.

"This is really interesting," said Samuels. "But why is this novel when individuals can simply take melatonin pills that they can buy in any pharmacy or supermarket?"

"Agreed," I said. "But my goal is to develop methods to deliver medications, new and old, by a smell therapy, and to develop methods to measure the uptake in comparison to oral or intravenous administrations. Melatonin is an easy first example to work out these methods."

"So, is this going to be a first product or just a research exercise?" Ming asked.

"I'm not sure until we develop and test the olfactory form," I answered. "We may need to investigate sleep periods affected by melatonin odor in mice, and also to develop measurement criteria using brain waves or possibly even nuclear medicine scans of the brain. My challenge is to work out these methods so I can implement them in human subjects. I'm hoping that a collaborative lab, either in the government or in some association, can assist me."

It was already 2:30 p.m., and we had accomplished a lot for a first meeting. The chemists knew what we needed and said they would spend the next couple of weeks making these melatonin derivatives to determine their stability as odors. We had sandwiches brought in during our meeting, so I was ready to go.

*

AFTERWARDS, I TOOK a taxi to the Holiday Inn on Wisconsin Avenue in Georgetown, which wasn't far from the Russian embassy and its consulate nearby. After checking in, I took a walk in chic Georgetown. Along the way, I texted Brad, asking when we were to meet for dinner and if I should select a restaurant.

"Will meet you at 6:30 p.m.," he texted back. "Will let you know later re: restaurant." I smiled at that — he wanted to provide that information at the last minute, a cautious ploy for a CIA agent arranging a rendezvous.

On Wisconsin Avenue before M Street, I found a bookstore where I enjoyed roaming the shelves. I found an introductory book to conversational Russian, as well a tourist guide to Russia, and even a book on sites and neighborhoods in Moscow. I bought all three, which I planned to review in the next few days before leaving for Moscow. I also had the guide that the Mossad supplied to me. Later, I strolled up and down M Street, visiting some of the newer art galleries.

I received a text from Brad saying he'd made reservations for us at *The Sovereign*, a restaurant on Wisconsin Avenue just off of M Street, a block or so away from where I was. It was six-fifteen already, so I made my way there to get a table and wait for him to show.

The Sovereign was a quaint restaurant specializing in Belgian fare. I studied the menu displayed outside and was surprised at the variety of Belgian and even some Bavarian dishes.

I selected a table in the back and ordered a large glass of Belgian ale while I waited for Brad.

I was almost finished with my drink when he arrived. He was very casual, wearing a sports jacket, no tie, an open-collar white shirt, and dark blue slacks. He smiled broadly as he approached with his arm extended to shake my hand.

"Glad to see you, world traveler. Looks like you're ahead of me," he said, nodding at my ale. We ordered a couple more beers and then wine and dinner.

"How was your day in Silver Spring?" asked Brad once the waiter had left. "Where are you with the lawyers incorporating the company?"

"I should hear from all three lawyers by next Monday, I expect. As to the meeting at '*A*,' I think it went well for a first interaction. I'm impressed with the chemists and their facilities."

"We're pleased with them," said Brad. "They keep deadlines and seem to be otherwise efficient and reasonable in costs. Most of all, they're very discreet and respect our confidentiality needs. I'm not sure how long they've been engaged with us, but most are former colleagues or government employees."

The salads then arrived with the wine, so we interrupted our conversation to enjoy the food and the excellent wine.

"To your success," said Brad, holding up his glass.

"I'll drink to that," I said.

Then Brad got to the point. "You should be able to leave for '*M*' by the end of next week, so I need to give you some important information. But I have to avoid names and places, since we're in a public place."

I nodded and waited for him to continue.

"We prefer your flying directly to '*R*' without first meeting '*M*' in '*P*.' She can fly separately and meet you there, but we're trying to limit her stay in '*R*' to two weeks, which is what we think is needed to get you settled and ready to operate on your own. '*M*' will want to stay, and although we understand your intimate relationship, she needs to return to '*P*' because you need to operate on your own and without confiding in anyone but your other handler at our embassy in '*M*.' Her presence also increases your risk, since the Hezbollah has a relationship to the Russian secret services, and will clearly inform them that Marie is traveling with a man of the description you had in France, if she is in their list of foreign agents. It is good that the French DGSE had their agents following you, and also on the train. If the Hezbollah agents had succeeded, it would have been the end of your mission."

And of me, he forgot to mention!

"Well," I said, "I don't think '*M*' is the kind who'll just pack her bag and go home if she has other plans."

"Yes, we know that. That's why we're negotiating with her bosses to make this their decision. But you need to understand that she can't find a reason to object. And you need to stay neutral and not interfere with this plan.

"The second issue is your relationship to the oligarch, '*Y*.' He's key to your getting established and accepted as an entrepreneur by the business and political communities, and he could also be there to get you introduced to the scientists who'll be important for you to know. '*Y*' is, we believe, well respected by some members of the political leadership, including '*VP*,' so he'll be able to vouch for you and give you access to the right people."

"Is he a true party member or just a businessman staying close to the politicians and may be involved in their usual enrichment?" I asked. "Also, he's Jewish, but can he practice Judaism and be successful there?"

"We're not sure, but we do know he's participated in events and even prayer services at the synagogue near his home. There are a few Jews who are successful running companies that have close connections with bureaucrats and where they are welcomed by the social and political sets. But he's still an enigma to us, so we're very pleased that he's interested in you and your business venture. This could help us get to know him better. He could prove to be key to your operation. But in this regard, your involvement with him should be kept confidential from everyone, except your handler, and I do mean *everybody*." He paused to watch my response.

"Do you still have concerns about '*M*'? She, of course, knows that '*Y*' is assisting me.

"I'm not sure how to respond, because I don't know her that well. She clearly works for two agencies, and she has attached herself to you so that she's quite well informed about what we're doing and may present a risk to the operation if she's acting without supervision or on the periphery of this operation. As a field agent, she seems quite respected and was involved in an attack on Hezbollah agents in France. Our information is that she was one of the assassins of the Hezbollah team. And she demonstrated her self-defensive abilities on the train."

"I'm also a little uncertain about her early years in '*R*' before emigrating to '*I*,' and from there to '*F*.' We also know too little about her parents, particularly her father, and why he left '*I*' for '*F*'," Brad continued.

I understood the CIA's caution and concern about an associate in this Scenturion Venture being somewhat of a lone wolf whose role and mission were unclear, and someone who was involved in killings. But it made me wonder how they could've allowed the French and Israeli services to get so involved, drawing Marie into it before the CIA had more trust in her.

Somehow, that doesn't seem smart.

"Another point I want to raise," said Brad, "is our need to monitor your whereabouts at all times. We've lost some field officers in '*R*' in the past, so we want to put a mini sensor on your watch for tracking, in addition to that on your phone. I want you to be okay with that."

"You think I'll be in danger?"

"It's just an extra precaution and has been reliable in the past, although a good counterespionage group can discover this easily. If the sensor in the watch is uncovered, you may avoid a more thorough search of your body. We do have rescue units and methods to transfer assets out of the country very quickly, if necessary, so it's best for us to monitor you continuously. Just make sure you wear the watch at all times, even in the shower."

"This wasn't something I anticipated," I said. "It's scary what new science you spies are developing."

By this time, our main dishes were served, and I could turn my attention to trying to enjoy the rest of the meal.

But I'm clearly unsettled.

"I didn't intend to scare you with these concerns and precautions," said Brad, acknowledging my silence, "but I want to fully inform you and protect you, since you'll be in a strange country where the society is run differently than here. Remember, to everyone else, you'll just be a scientist expanding a business into their country, as requested by one of your investors. So long as you can fill that role, there should be no problem."

"I'll do my best not to disappoint you or put myself in danger," I said.

"We can't ask for anything more," Brad continued. "And I want you to know that we're grateful to you and are depending on you to help us complete this mission successfully. The highest officials of our government are aware of this and respect and appreciate your undertaking this mission, I can assure you. We also appreciate that 'Y' was brought in as an investor by 'M's commercial boss, 'SF,' who is clearly involved with the 'M'."

Then, with much fanfare, the waiter brought out our chocolate souffle, which we were sharing. We also ordered cups of cappuccino.

By the time I finished the dessert and coffee, I had forgotten the conversation and just felt happily full.

"I have two final matters to cover," said Brad. "If it's not inconvenient, I would like to pick up the passports we gave you before your last trip to '*F*' and '*I*,' since it would be risky for inspectors in '*R*' to find these if they search your belongings. We'll be providing you with other sets of passports when you get to '*R*.'"

"Also, you need to return the cell phone we supplied to you, and I'll want to borrow your own cell phone for about two hours."

I looked at him somewhat perplexed, and he immediately clarified.

"We want to revamp your phone to give you the capability of transmitting conversations real-time without anyone noticing. You'll simply press the number three, three times, and the phone will transmit sound received to another number, and we'll program this for your handler at the U.S. embassy in '*R*.' Also, if you press star * and then the hash key #, it'll signal that you're in trouble and we need to rescue you. These are just precautions that we like to make. I can have it delivered back to you this evening. There will also be an App for encrypting messages, just as you have in your current phone supplied by us."

I agreed. And for the passports and their phone, I said he should send someone around to my apartment at 8:30 a.m. on Friday. "If they call my phone, I'll come downstairs with everything."

We then shook hands and parted ways at the front door, me heading back to the hotel and Brad getting into the black Lincoln Town Car waiting for him. We knew we wouldn't be seeing each other for quite some time.

40.

THE TAXI RIDE to the Russian consulate, and not the Embassy, where the Internet indicated was the place to apply for a visa, took no more than fifteen minutes. There was heavy security in the lobby and a line of some twenty people at the visa section, but it was moving quickly. When I finally got my turn, I handed the woman my application materials, and she gave me a number to be called when they were ready for me.

About forty-five minutes later, my number was called, and I was shown to a small room where a consulate official sat with my application folder. A young woman about thirty years old, dressed in a white, long-sleeved blouse and with long black hair and glasses with black frames, sat across the table and greeted me in English with a heavy Russian accent. She asked the usual questions — what the purpose of my visit to Russia was, what kind of business would I conduct, did I have living arrangements, did I have relatives or friends there, and how I knew my Russian sponsor?

I explained that I'd met Yuri Grobstein through common business contacts and that he was becoming an investor and owner in my business. I also told her that our Russian attorney was in the process of incorporating the business in Russia and assisting me in renting office space and finding living quarters.

She seemed comfortable with my explanation, then turned to the letter in the file from Yuri. She asked why he wrote directly to the head of the Visa section, trying to determine if they had a relationship. I told her, "I don't know, but he had said he wanted to expedite the process, since he thought that I should travel to Moscow as soon as possible."

The visa clerk thought about this for a while, then again asked if I had any relatives or other friends in Russia. I said no, and she signed her name at the bottom of the form. She said she would hold my passport and asked if I wanted it sent to the New York address given. I responded that I was hoping it could be sent by overnight courier mail, since I would like to travel to Moscow by the weekend, if possible.

"As long as you provide the proper fee and forms, this should not be a problem," she advised.

*

ON THE TRAIN, I thought about a lot of things that needed to be taken care of. I had to confer with Marie regarding her travel plans and what living arrangements we would make while we searched for office space and an apartment. I sent an email to Yuri, telling him I had successfully completed the visa interview at the Russian consulate in Washington.

Jhanella had sent the final revised manuscript for my approval, which I had gladly given, so she could resubmit it to the journal's editor.

Marie wrote back that she would book a flight to Moscow once she knew my schedule, and that she had already contacted a real estate agent with some knowledge of English through our attorney in Moscow. She also confirmed that the papers for Pharmascent to do business in Russia had been filed with the business registration office in Moscow, and we were now waiting for their review and approval. "Without this," Marie emphasized, "we can't rent space, hire anyone, or otherwise conduct business." She had copied Yuri on this email in the hope that he could help expedite this.

I agreed that we stick to our plan to fly to Moscow as soon as I had the visa and my passport in hand. Marie already had a travel visa, she said, and I wondered when and why she'd traveled to Russia in the past.

This is probably better discussed in person.

With the pressing business out of the way, I dug into my bag and started exploring my books on Russia and Moscow, as well as conversational Russian. The words in my 'Russian for Dummies' book were written in English, which enabled me to read and translate them, but the pronunciation seemed challenging even when they were written phonetically. I wasn't optimistic that reading this book would prepare me for simple daily conversations. Once again, I felt a pang of insecurity.

How would I fare in Russia without someone like Marie at my side?

Putting aside the Russian language book, I turned to the books on Moscow and on Russian history. But I must have soon fallen asleep because I was shocked awake with the announcement that we were arriving in Philadelphia. I continued to read for the remainder of the trip and arrived at Penn Station on time. By 6:00 p.m., I was relaxing in my living room, watching the local evening news, and having a beer.

*

AN ISSUE THAT was on my mind was Bill Rhodes's concern about where the company was being incorporated and what my plans were to compose the board of directors.

"We could get tied up in socialist employment restrictions in France," he'd said, "so that we could never terminate an employee, at least not at a reasonable cost."

I did decide to turn to Simon Fass of Toilette, since he seemed so knowledgeable and had been so helpful to me. I sent him a text asking if there was a good time for us to have a conversation tomorrow. I also texted Brad Williams that I thought we should meet once again before I left, since I still had some questions.

I was concerned that everything was moving too fast. I was still anxious about getting settled in Moscow, as well as about the CIA's plans for Marie. Whenever I brought her up, Brad was either cautious about her involvement or avoided any clear statements as to her impending role during my stay in Moscow, other than babysitting me. Marie was apparently still an enigma to all of us, although she was a respected operative for both the French DGSE and the Israeli Mossad.

41.

I WAS HAVING coffee and a slice of toast when I received a text saying that the CIA car sent to pick up my package was downstairs. I dropped it off with the driver, whom I recognized from previous CIA meetings.

It seemed only about an hour-and-a-half later when my door bell rang from the lobby, and the CIA driver asked if I could come downstairs for the package.

As I was heading back upstairs with the cell phones, I got a text from Brad on the CIA one saying that I wasn't likely to receive my visa until early next week, which, of course, meant I would have to delay my departure a few days. Instead of being disappointed, I felt a strange sense of relief.

The CIA knows so much about the workings of the Russian consulate.

I still needed to shop for clothes suitable for a much colder climate. And I needed to slow down and get my mind prepared for the challenges ahead. Brad said we could meet on Monday or Tuesday, my call. Fine, I said, and he said he would confirm the time with me over the weekend.

Instead of going straight to the office, I decided to go to the local gym where, in more normal times, I often worked out before going to work. I had ignored that part of my life lately, and I missed it. Thirty or so minutes of swimming was just what I needed, and there was no rush for me to be in my office at any specific time today.

I was surprised by how many people were busy on the exercise machines or lifting weights at this time in the late morning. The near-Olympic-size pool was almost empty, with maybe ten people in it. Only four swimmers were taking laps in the designated lanes, so, after changing, I joined them in swimming at a good pace for the length of the pool.

I decided to swim in the lane alongside the most outer one, which was being used by the only woman swimmer, who looked to be a very strong and serious athlete. I thought it would be a good challenge to try to keep pace with her, so I dived in and began a crawl with an effort to match her speed. After three laps, I was no longer able to maintain the pace, but it did feel very good to unwind and stretch my muscles and increase my heart and breathing rates.

I rested after the fifth lap, and, surprisingly, my neighbor in the next lane stopped too.

"You did quite well," she said, smiling as she removed her cap and let her long blonde hair fall over her broad, strong shoulders. She spoke with an accent, which I guessed to be either Polish or Russian.

"Thanks for the compliment," I said. "But I'm obviously not in the same shape you are. Do you come here often?"

"I moved to New York recently and began swimming here a few weeks ago. It is really a great pool and exercise place in the middle of this large city."

"Pardon my curiosity, but are you Polish or Russian?"

"Russian. I moved to the U.S. with my husband about two years ago, to Chicago. But I am now a New Yorker."

"Where was your home in Russia, and what brought you to the States?"

She then climbed out of the pool to get her towel and dry off. She wore a one-piece bathing suit that exposed her very nice, long figure, very muscular shoulders, arms and legs, yet slim and quite attractive. She caught me admiring her and responded with a nice smile, with large, white teeth. I also got out of the pool and walked toward the chair where I'd left my towel, and she followed me to continue the conversation.

"I am Tania Kudnoska," she said, extending her hand to shake mine.

"I'm Milt Davidson," I said. "Nice to meet you. Care to get a cup of coffee in the refreshment area?"

"Good, yes," she said. "I am quite thirsty and hungry after working out for more than an hour."

We found two adjacent stools at the serving bar, ordered coffees, and Tania ordered a piece of marble sponge cake.

"Do you come in the mornings?" she began.

"I usually do, but earlier. However, I've been traveling for the past few weeks, so this is my first time back in a while."

"Yes, I did not see you here before. I come here almost daily, since I used to be on a swimming team before I emigrated, and I miss the exercise and joy of swimming."

"Where did you swim?"

"I was on a swimming team in Moscow, not at the Olympic swimming level, but in national competitions. But I gave this up when I moved here. My husband took a job at a pharmaceutical company outside of Chicago. I liked Chicago, but I was just learning English and had few American friends. I was mostly alone at home or exploring Chicago. My husband and I spoke only our mother language at home, but he was always traveling because of being in international sales."

This was more information than I needed, but I guessed that Tania wanted me to know she was lonely in Chicago and probably split with her husband and moved to New York. "Is it better for you here?" I asked. "Are you working?"

"I found a nice small apartment nearby, which is very comfortable in comparison to being in Moscow. There are some nice neighbors, and I am thinking of starting to look for a job. I did pharmaceutical research in Russia, and it was in the same company where my husband worked and where we met and eventually married.

"My husband and I separated, and he agreed to continue supporting me during our separation," she offered. "I also have an aunt, my father's sister, who emigrated to America about ten years ago. She lives in Brighton Beach, Brooklyn, and I get to visit often."

So, she got it all out: marital status, background and occupation, local relative, and having been a competitive swimmer.

"This is all quite a coincidence," I said, and reminded myself that coincidences don't exist in the spy world. "I plan to move to Moscow very soon, where I will start a business."

Tania looked astonished and almost shrieked with surprise, so much so that others in the lounge area turned toward us. I wasn't sure where this was going, but I checked my watch, and it read 12 noon. She noticed and asked if I had an appointment.

"I work at ESU Medical Center, and I really need to get going. I am there usually be 9 a.m.," I said, "but it's such a coincidence talking with a Russian just before I travel there. Maybe I can ask you some questions."

"Was it difficult for your aunt to emigrate here?" I asked.

"Yes and no. First, she and her husband had to wait four years to get immigration visas, even with sponsorship by her cousin in Minneapolis. They could not take much more than their luggage with clothes and some pictures and personal belongings, and at the ages of almost sixty, it was hard for them to cut ties to friends and relatives in Moscow."

Tania continued: "America is a dreamland of opportunity and freedom for many of us, particularly the Jews who lived in the former Soviet Union, except I guess for many who gave up their Jewish identity. It was a hardship being Jewish in Russia. We suffered during the Stalin era and for many years later, until Gorbachev came to power."

"Really?" I commented. "I didn't know he was supportive of the Jews and their practicing Judaism in their mostly anti-Semitic society."

"There has been a drastic decrease in the Russian Jewish community over the past fifty years," Tania explained, "from over two million in about 1960 to less than two-hundred thousand estimated to be living now in the Russian Federation. Yet, there has been a resurgence of open Jewish life in Russia since Gorbachev and Putin became president.

"According to Rabbi Berel Lazar, Russia's chief rabbi," she explained, "Putin, who grew up in a poor family, had Hasidic Jewish neighbors who were kind to him. The father of the family was Anatoly Rakhlin, Putin's high school wrestling coach, who was a mentor for him. It is said that Putin cried at his funeral."

Then Tania added: "When Putin was a Deputy Mayor of Leningrad, now St. Petersburg, he allowed the opening of the first Jewish school, and when the Jewish Museum in Moscow was being built, it is said that he donated a month's salary to its support. His name is listed on the wall as a donor.

"Nevertheless," said Tania, "there has been a resurgence of anti-Semitism in Russia despite Putin's being helpful to the Jews. Russian Jews still feel persecuted and continue to emigrate. While Israel is the first choice, America is a close second."

"This is fascinating," I said. "Is there anyone I should get to know there, and what about the Jewish community in Moscow?"

"You must visit the Moscow Jewish Community Center, located in Natasha Roscha," said Tania. "It is a beehive of activity, with two kosher restaurants, one dairy and one meat, many educational and social programs, and it has many daily prayer services for both religious and non-orthodox Jews, including Israelis and even some English-speaking Jews."

"Thank you so much," I said. "It's obvious you still have many good memories of your years living in Moscow."

I thanked her for sharing all of this with me. We exchanged cards and our addresses and contact numbers, and I had to then leave, being late to my intended arrival at work.

*

IN MY OFFICE at ESU, I received a call from Simon Fass in Paris. I told him that my trip to Moscow would be delayed a few days, but maybe this was good because I had so much to do. I wanted to bring him up-to-date, but also to ask him to continue helping me by joining the Pharmascent Board.

"Thank you, Milt," he said. "I would be honored. As you've noticed, I have a real interest in this enterprise and your work. Depending on the terms, I think my firm could be an investor."

I asked him to give some thought to other prospective investors for later financing. Ending the call, I gathered my laboratory notebook and went to meet with my lab staff, who had expected me in the late morning. Unfortunately, I had let myself be sidetracked by the lovely Tania.

When I finally got to the lab, Jhanella and Mike were sitting in Jhanella's small office with their lab notebooks and data graphs open. I asked if Dr. Bogner would be joining us, and Jhanella said she was to let him know when I arrived.

When John arrived, we got down to business. Jhanella then quickly summarized where we were experimentally since completing the manuscript. It all sounded promising, and I felt better about soon being out of daily touch. Before we ended the meeting, I told them I would still be around the first part of the coming week, and I would make sure we met again before I resumed my travels.

By the time I got home, I had a message from Brad that we should meet on Monday. I agreed.

42.

EARLY MONDAY MORNING, I spotted Tania immediately upon entering the pool area. She was hard to miss. She saw me too and waved energetically. When I reached her, she gave me a little hug. "Ready to swim?" she said and dived in.

I followed her and began swimming in the adjoining lane, but after a short while, I couldn't keep up with her. So, I just swam at a slower pace for about twenty minutes until I needed a rest.

After another fifteen minutes, Tania came out of the pool, removed her head cap, and dried herself. We then went to the snack area to get coffee. I told her that I thought I would be leaving for Moscow by the end of the week and was anxious because I knew nothing about the Russian language.

"I can help you with some basic words and phrases," she offered. "Let's try now. It would be fun for me to help you learn my mother language."

"Okay," I said.

The two of us were sitting at a remote corner table, and for the next half hour, she practiced with me as you would with small children learning a new language.

"Now, repeat after me until you get the pronunciation correct: **da!** (dah) — yes; **nyet!** (n'eht) — no; **spasibo** (spuh-SEE-bh) — thank you; **on** (ohn) — he; **ona** (ah-nah) — she; **my** (mih) — we; **oni** (ah-nee) — they; **vy** (vih) — you [formal singular and plural]."

Some of these took me a few times to pronounce before Tania thought it was right, and although I felt silly, I was getting the feel of the language. Tania then began with some simple phrases:

Izvinitye, ya nye ponyyal (eez-vee-NEE-t'eh ya nee POHH-n'uhl) — sorry, I didn't understand; **Izvinite, ya plokho ponimayu po-russki** (eez-vee-NEE-t'eh ya PLOH-khuh pu-nee-MAH-yu pah-

ROOS-kee) — sorry, I don't understand Russian very well; **Vy govorite po-angliyski?** (Vih guh-vah-REE-t'eh uhn-GLEEY-skee?) — Do you speak English?

These proved to be my limit for today, and it would be a challenge remembering them tomorrow. They were in my book, *Russian for DUMMIES*, however, so I could practice at home.

"You were good for a first try," said Tania. "Let's continue when you have time."

"Of course, but I don't think I will have much free time before I depart for Moscow, since I have a lot to get done in the next few days," I responded.

She was delightful, beautiful, and anxious for companionship – all reasons, I thought, not to continue this relationship when I have Marie on my mind, plans to relocate to Moscow, and my new profession as a spy-scientist. I no longer suspected her as a Russian agent in the U.S.

We left separately, since I showered in the gym and then went back home. I was getting nervous about my visa and wanted to be there in case it arrived.

43.

I WAITED AT home expecting my visa by overnight courier, and it actually arrived at about 10:30 a.m. The visa from Russia was impressive, taking two complete pages in my passport. One more step toward leaving for Moscow. The very thought made me uneasy.

The black Lincoln Town Car arrived punctually at 1:00 p.m. This time, Brad was driving, which was a surprise. I asked if he always came up from Washington for our meetings, wondering why Bob Ehrlich of the New York office was never present.

"Bob focuses more on activities in New York for the agency, but since you're involved in what will soon be a foreign assignment, it falls under my purview," said Brad. "I'm leading the effort of this Scenturion Venture involving Russia and our informant there, *Aleksei*, so it's important for me to meet with you personally. I took a CIA plane to a commercial airport in White Plains, which was an easy drive down here. I expect to be back at CIA headquarters in the late afternoon."

"Sounds almost easy," I said.

"I'm glad you finally got your visa," he said. "When you arrive in Moscow, do check in with the U.S. Embassy there. You'll be welcomed by the Vice-Consul, James Bradshaw, a career state department officer who will link you to our CIA head at the Embassy, Marcia Dubrovnik. Marcia has run our eastern Europe desk for about ten years. She's fluent in Russian and some other Slavic languages and has been posted abroad for most of her career.

"When you meet with Jim Bradshaw, he'll find a pretense to take you to meet Ambassador John Eldridge, if they deem it appropriate and if Eldridge is available. This will allow them to take you on the Ambassador's private elevator to the basement and the secure debriefing room. You'll only be able to talk for about a half-hour so as to not raise suspicions among the Russian staff there as to your activities. We're always concerned about the infiltration of our local staff by Russian intelligence, so your visit to the Embassy to register as a recent arrival should appear to be routine. Marcia will inform you how she wants to manage your activities and interactions with her, and of course, set up a system of communication."

"I don't understand," I said.

"We have to monitor you very carefully, Milt, since a lot depends on you. We're concerned that the Russians may already know more about Scenturion than we would like."

"What about Marie?" I asked.

"We need to get Marie to exit this project before much more happens," Brad said. "Since she has been involved in many other spy activities with the DGSE and Mossad, we have some concerns. I know you've been informed already."

"But she already knows everything about the Scenturion Venture and about me, so if she is already fully knowledgeable about me and my spy activities, it's too late to extricate her."

"True, but if I were the FSB, I would try to feed you with false information instead of exposing and terminating the Scenturion Venture. And someone in the role of Marie, connecting all our agencies, would be in a perfect position to orchestrate this, especially when having your trust and confidence. I'm concerned she'll learn too much about all of the Mossad's contacts in the Jewish community, which could be disastrous if it becomes known to the FSB. And if she is kidnapped by a hostile group, her information would be a prize and certainly she will have to eventually cooperate. They are usually successful at torturing enemy spies."

"This is very unnerving to me, Brad. Do you really believe she could be turned? Won't Marie figure this out if she's just dropped precipitously?"

"I agree," Brad said. "We need to give this more thought, and I need to talk with my colleagues at the Mossad, since they're her employers. But your demeanor with her will be critical. I may be totally wrong about Marie, but I have to be cautious and weigh all possibilities. Let's not do anything further until I can discuss this with my colleagues at the Mossad."

"Are you sure the Mossad's interests are aligned with ours? And you already have reasons to suspect a traitor working at the DGSE."

"We hope that both the Mossad and DGSE are partners, but all intelligence agencies have experienced double-agents, some getting major public attention, such as in Great Britain's MI6, our own FBI, etc." Brad said. "But we're also realistic that our countries have somewhat different long-term missions and pressures on the international scene."

Then Brad brought up another issue. "We know from our mole at the military research facility in Oryol that it was established less than ten years ago. We focused on determining which scientists were relocated there and surveyed moves made by scientists from the major cities, St. Petersburg and Moscow. We were surprised to find one chemist from Moscow who was listed in their information as Jewish, and further data they had revealed that he has a son who is twelve years old and whom he sends back to Moscow once a month to prepare for his Bar Mitzvah when he reaches thirteen. The synagogue he attends, and which gives his child instruction, usually on Sunday, is the Natasha Roscha Synagogue and Jewish Community Center. His name is Daniel Breslau, son of Dr. Joshua Breslau. The boy stays at his aunt's apartment when he comes to Moscow from Friday to Sunday afternoon, often attending Sabbath services on Saturday. Daniel is accompanied by this aunt, Dr. Breslau's sister, Katarina. Occasionally, his mother travels with him to be in Moscow. Evidently, she has some friends at the Jewish Community Center in addition to her sister-in-law and mother-in-law, who live together."

"And I gather you want me to get to know them and learn about Dr. Breslau's research activities in Oryol? Coincidentally, I heard about this synagogue and the Jewish community in Moscow from someone I met recently at my gym."

"Yes, we need to link you in some way to the activities at Oryol and Dr. Breslau. "We don't know if this is a valuable lead or not, but since we know his mother and sister have been trying to emigrate to Israel, Dr. Breslau may be accessible and may be a sympathizer to Israel and the West, so maybe it's worth your effort. But you need to be very, very careful, since he's closely watched by the FSB.

"But they allow his wife to make occasional trips to Moscow with her son?" I asked.

"Yes," Brad answered. "I guess the FSB are not worried so long as they have her husband in their control at the research facility."

"I'm sure the CIA group in Moscow can help, since they gathered all this information about Breslau. Interestingly, we also know that the Russian scientist you met in Vienna, and who we suspect may have been involved in the killing of our agent, Charles, Dr. Vladimir Borofskov, has been working as a senior administrator in Oryol. Is he truly interested in defecting, or is he an FSB or GRU agent? You may want to contact him when you're in Moscow, but you need to check with our staff at the embassy in Moscow first."

Also, Brad disclosed: "The woman at the Jewish Community Center who gives instruction in Russian to emigrants is someone who interacts with our Mossad colleagues, so I suggest you establish a relationship, certainly by learning some Russian from her. I think she is one of Mrs. Breslau's acquaintances, and her name was even mentioned by our mole in Oryol."

"But tell me more about the Russian you met at the gym," Brad inquired.

I told him about Tania and our conversation, and that I planned to see her when I go to my morning workouts. He just smiled.

*

SITTING IN MY living room with a glass of Merlot and some crackers and blue cheese, I reflected on my conversation with Brad, all the intrigues, and what had attracted me to both Marie and Tania. Marie was certainly more sophisticated and worldly, yet Tania had an innocence and sincerity that gave her a special charm. In the final analysis, I knew I had to continue with Marie.

I made reservations to fly from JFK to Moscow on Thursday afternoon, departing with Aeroflot Russian Airlines at 2:25 p.m. and arriving at Moscow's Sheremetyevo International Airport (SVO) at 6:25 a.m. I texted this information to Brad and also to Marie. She responded that she was thrilled that we were finally on our way and would meet me in the arrival area. She also said she'd booked us in a one-bedroom suite at the PR Myasnitskaya Boutique Hotel, which she had stayed at before.

"It is a charming hotel close to everything and with only ten rooms on three floors," she wrote. I immediately Googled it and read that on Myasnitskaya Street, we would be surrounded by cafés, bars, and restaurants, and would be within walking distance to major downtown sites. I was certain that Marie had arranged for a king-size bed and a nice view of the area.

At 7:00 p.m., Tania surprised me with a call.

"How was your day?" she asked.

"Very busy, but I finally made my flight arrangements to Moscow," I said.

Tania sounded startled. "I guess I had put this thought off. When do you leave?"

"Thursday afternoon, with the direct Aeroflot flight from JFK to Sheremetyevo Airport."

"That is only a day after tomorrow!"

"I was due in Moscow a week ago," I said, "so I'm really behind in my plans."

"Can we spend some time together before you leave?" she asked suddenly.

"I'm sorry, but all my time is occupied already."

'Then, can I accompany you to the airport?' she asked.

I thought for a moment and then said, 'No, Tania, I prefer going to the airport alone."

"Departing from friends is always a problem for me," I tried to explain.

"We've known each other for less than a week, Tania," I said. We can't start a relationship, but we should stay in touch and get together again when I return to New York, if possible," I suggested.

"I know that we are only just newly acquainted, but I miss you already. Just my luck! Why is moving to Moscow so important to you? You have a good job here," she asked.

I explained my interest in starting a company with a new pharmaceutical technology, and the support and resources being made available are best in Moscow at present.

Tania then responded: "I am sorry to be so selfish, coming into your life so soon and trying to change things for my own benefit."

"I understand," I said. "And I care about you."

Why did I have to say this and encourage her?

*

I AWOKE EARLY the next day and made coffee. I waited until later in the morning to visit my local Citibank branch to arrange an account for me to use in Moscow, where I knew they had several branches.

When I got home, I sent a text message to Yuri telling him that I'd received my visa, thanking him for his help and that I planned to arrive from JFK on Friday morning. Yuri responded right away, saying he was glad everything worked out and that he was looking forward to welcoming me to Russia. He said we should meet for lunch on Monday and that he would text information to me.

44.

THE AEROFLOT FLIGHT was on time, comfortable, and gave me an opportunity to think about the last few weeks and what I needed to do in the coming days. I was also able to doze for an hour or so.

After I picked up my large suitcase from the luggage area and went through immigration and customs without delay, I saw Marie waiting outside the International Arrivals' doors. She looked different, with a different hair cut or maybe a wig, and her face also looking different but I couldn't explain why.

She waved to me, then hugged me, kissed my cheeks, and gave me a strong kiss on the lips. I thought this probably wasn't wise in such a public area, especially, since I still didn't know how we were going to present our relationship to others.

"You look so different that I didn't recognize you at first," I said. "You've cut and darkened your hair."

"You mean it is so easy for you to forget me if I change a little?"

"No, no, of course not," I said. "The new hairdo is very attractive. I also like the pink silk scarf matching your pink lips. But your face also looks different. Did you do something different with your makeup, or perhaps it's your cheeks and eyes that are different."

This immediately changed her mood. "Yes, I needed to look different than the Marie in Paris," she chuckled and hugged me again. I hope our adversaries are as naïve as you are!" she exclaimed, adding: "I can't wait to get you alone."

"I missed you too," I said. "But I need some time to overcome my jetlag."

"I'll give you a *few minutes* rest, my darling," said Marie with a coquettish smile.

We walked over to the large outside parking area and got into the dark green 2010 Lala sedan that Marie had evidently rented. She said she knew her way around Moscow, so having a private auto would be more convenient to pick me up, since she wanted some privacy. She said she planned to return the car very soon, since public transportation is so good.

It took us about fifty minutes to get through light traffic to the PR Myasnitskaya Boutique Hotel, where Marie had checked us in and also provided my passport information to the reception desk in advance, since the desk was closed on Friday and weekends.

While driving, she explained that she'd been here for almost two days, viewing potential apartment rentals after contacting a realtor who spoke English. She had three apartments for me to see, she said, and the realtor would pick us up this afternoon at two o'clock.

"This gives us some time to get reacquainted," Marie said with a wink.

Where does she get this romantic energy?

The hotel was small but charming and nicely decorated, and, as Marie pointed out, it was conveniently located in downtown Moscow. Our suite had two bedrooms, one meant to also serve as a study/living room, and one bathroom with a tub and shower combination. It had a nice view of the street below.

I dropped my luggage in the larger bedroom and sat down on the couch in the living room while Marie hurried to open a bottle of champagne. She toasted to welcome me to Moscow and moved close to me to rub the back of my head. Before I lost all control, I said I felt sweaty from traveling and needed to relax in the bath for a while.

Marie then jumped up and began filling the massive tub for me, adding some soothing bubble bath that she'd bought in anticipation of my arrival. In the meantime, I undressed and put on the terry cloth robe supplied by the hotel. Soon after settling in the hot bathwater, I closed my eyes and began to doze off.

I didn't notice how much time expired, but I jolted awake when Marie inserted first her foot, followed by her naked body into an open space in the tub, between my legs and facing me. Her face and hair were as I knew her from the past, so I concluded it was a temporary disguise. I liked her better this way.

She then proceeded to put soap on the washcloth and rub the soap all over me, starting at my feet and then moving upwards quite deliberately.

It was both relaxing and stimulating, and I quickly forgot how tired I was and let myself enjoy her beautiful body, not to mention her talented hands. It took only ten minutes for us to attach our bodies in the tub, which did lose some water during our peak excitement.

"Thank you, Milt, I missed making love to you, and now you are back," Marie whispered.

My eyes were closed, and I just wanted to stay relaxed with her in my arms in the warm water and felt that I could doze off again. Brad's worries about her were the furthest from my mind.

Then Marie was climbing out and getting a towel to dry off. "Rest for a while," she said, "but we need to be ready for the realtor in about an hour."

"No problem — just call me when I need to get out and dress," I said, my eyes still closed as I sunk further down into the soapy water.

45.

VIKTOR BLOKHIN, THE real estate agent from Gorky Realtor Company, arrived in his small sedan at 2:00 p.m., as arranged. Marie introduced him to me as he climbed out to shake my hand.

He looked to be about thirty or so, with long hair tied back in a ponytail and a few days' growth of beard. He was dark in complexion, wore wide corduroy slacks and a gray wool sweater. He seemed cheerful, friendly and eager to make this tour with us.

Viktor explained that we were going to see apartments in the Arbat-Kropotkinskaya, Tverskaya-Kremlin, and Smolenska areas.

The last one Viktor showed us was our favorite. It was located in a renovated high-rise on Smolenska Str. It was a four-room, 1000 square-meter apartment with a balcony, two bedrooms, one bath, a small kitchen, and a living room. It was fully furnished with clean, modern furniture.

The price was the equivalent to $2,625 per month, and with a security deposit of one month's rent; that was relatively expensive for Russia, obviously catering to foreign visitors or businessmen. It also provided an underground parking space with the apartment for an extra fee. Brad had advised during our meeting that it was important for me to have such a space even if I didn't have a car.

Our search with Viktor took almost three hours. When he dropped us off, we asked him to email us a typical lease for foreigners so we could evaluate the terms and market for such rentals, and especially the minimal rental periods required.

It had been a very long day for me. Back in our hotel room, I turned on the TV and stretched out on the couch. Marie brought me some vodka mixed with carbonated water and some lime juice, which quickly relaxed me. She decided we shouldn't go out for dinner — she would pick up some takeout food instead.

While Marie was gone to get dinner, I checked out our rooms for any hidden recording devices or cameras, although I was sure that Marie did this already.

Marie returned in her disguise, carrying two large bags of food and some plastic plates and utensils. She laid everything out on the coffee table in the living room, and I realized just how hungry I was when I smelled the aromas from the containers. She had bought potato pancakes, mixed salad, and goulash with potatoes as the main dish. She also picked up a bottle of French Bordeaux of a winery unknown to me, but a good year.

While eating, I asked what our plans were for the next few days, and Marie said it depended a lot on what still needed to be done in regard to Pharmascent Sciences. "You really haven't shared with me what you've done since leaving me in Paris," she said, in a not-so-veiled reprimand.

"Well," I said, "the corporation is set up, and I hope it's already under registration to do business here. I've begun some chemistry research in the States, but it's too early to make any decisions regarding further development. I'm supposed to have lunch with Yuri on Monday, but that hasn't been finalized. We also need to find office space for Pharmascent, and I don't know where to begin regarding how much space, the staff needed, or where we should be located.

"I also need to visit the U.S. Embassy to register my being here and pursuing a business venture with an international board."

This is enough information to share with Marie at the moment.

"This means we could spend some time over the weekend sightseeing," said Marie, "and we can go by some areas and possible office buildings. We could also continue with the realtor or a colleague who knows commercial real estate, once you know your needs."

"I think I should wait to speak with Yuri and then the other board members before finalizing any plans for offices and staff in Moscow. What do you think?"

Marie nodded yes. Since I didn't know how private and secure our rooms were, although I checked them out and didn't discover any bugs, I put my finger up to my lips to let her know we shouldn't discuss anything more sensitive here. I could tell she got the message.

"We can also go to dinner at some of the better Moscow restaurants over the weekend," she said. "And, of course, we should walk around Red Square and explore some of the shopping areas."

"How are you so familiar with Moscow?" I asked. "I thought you were in Belarus as a child before emigrating to Israel."

"That's true, but I've been here many times doing business for Toilette, so I've gotten to know Moscow as a grownup too," she said. "In fact, if you are not too tired, we can take a walk later. We are very near many of the downtown shops and sights."

"I'd like that," I said.

*

RED SQUARE WAS only a couple of kilometers away, and the air was brisk at about forty-five degrees Fahrenheit, so we dressed in jeans and sneakers with light jackets to walk in the early evening. I was glad to get some fresh air and looked forward to exploring 'my' new city.

It was good to be able to talk without worrying about listening devices in our rooms. I figured that Marie, a French citizen who traveled here frequently, would be a good candidate for Russian police surveillance, which would, of course, implicate me, since we are together. This was probably why she was disguised, not knowing if the Hezbollah had shared her photo with the Russian authorities.

"I checked the rooms for hidden devices," she said. "I did not find any. But there are more sophisticated instruments that I may not be able to detect, so we should continue to be cautious."

"I also failed to uncover any bugs or cameras," I advised.

"How about surveillance of us walking?" I asked.

"I am taking precautions," she said, "but it may take some time during this stroll to identify any agents following us."

After walking about a mile and a half, we arrived at Red Square. I was in awe of this massive plaza with cobblestones, surrounded by architectural edifices from different historical periods. Marie explained the general misconception that Red Square is named for the red bricks that surround the area and a link to communism.

"Not so," she said. "The name was derived from the Russian word *krasnaya*, which means 'something beautiful,' but in contemporary Russian means *red*."

Soon Marie guided me away from the Kremlin, down Varvarka Street, where we descended some steps to a path that runs alongside a file of churches and mansions. After gawking at various imposing structures, we headed back up the steps to Varvarka proper, paused to confirm we weren't being followed, then walked down the hill past a busy intersection and eventually emerged in front of the Cyril and Methodius Monument, which portrayed the two ninth-century monks who invented the Cyrillic alphabet still used in Russia and many Slavic countries.

After that, we were ready to make our way back to the hotel. I felt invigorated and more relaxed as we ambled back slowly with Marie close to me and holding my arm. In the suite, we relaxed on the couch in front of the TV after Marie removed her disguise. She had bought a bottle of white wine from the Czech Republic that we opened and found surprisingly nice. Soon, though, I felt a deep weariness washing over me and couldn't stop yawning.

"Let's go to bed," said Marie. "We have a big day tomorrow."
I wonder where she gets her double dose of libido genes.

46.

WHEN I AWOKE at 7:30 a.m., Marie was already up, dressed and with her disguise on, but I wore mine infrequently. I suppose I was getting exhausted of all this clock-and-dagger routine. Both the CIA and the Mossad emphasized that I needed to become familiar with the major sites, Metro train stations, and parks downtown, so this was our plan for today.

We began our sightseeing by first buying some pastries to eat on our walk to the nearest Metro station. Marie had insisted that we 'tour' the Moscow Metro, which, she said, "is one of the busiest train systems in the world. It opened in 1935 with a single line serving just thirteen stations but has been expanded extensively since then."

As a New Yorker who avoided the subway whenever possible, I was dubious about their subway. But Marie was, as expected, an expert on the history of the Metro and managed to make it fascinating.

"At the beginning," she said, "it was one of the most extravagant projects of the Soviet Union, with stations made as luxurious palaces with rich artwork and murals. Stalin ordered artists and architects to design it to be both brilliant and radiant, so that passengers would admire it and consider him a patriarch."

The decorated stations had reflective marble walls, high ceilings, marble and bronze statues, grand chandeliers, stained glass windows, and rich mosaics. This ended with De-Stalinization in 1955, when new stations devoid of this art came on stream. But the architecture and art of the early stations were not altered.

We purchased all-day tickets so we could tour all of the original palatial stations. We started with the Komsomolskaya Metro Station, which, as Marie related, had tall pillars with pink limestone and bluish-grey marble and a Baroque yellow ceiling with eight mosaic panels of precious stones. The theme was the Russian historical fight for freedom and independence. Then in 1952, the Novoslobodskaya Metro Station was built with thirty-two stained glass panels surrounded by a brass border and illuminated from within. The theme of the Mayakovskaya Metro Station was based on the poet Mayakovsky's vision of the future. It had elegant columns made with stainless steel and pink rhodonite, white and grey marble walls, white and pink marble floors, and thirty-five niches. The ceiling comprised thirty-five mosaics.

We viewed about six more stations, all very majestic and impressive — and, surprisingly, clean.

"Is this not a treasure?" Marie said as we returned to the station nearest Red Square.

"I'm delightfully impressed," I said. "Quite different and cleaner than what I'm used to back home."

"It's the babushkas," said Marie, "the army of elderly retired women who are all over Moscow, cleaning the streets and public places. Also, the Moscow Metro is much younger than your New York subway.

"As you can appreciate, these artistic stations have many areas where a secret message or envelope can be hidden, but there is a risk that the babushkas could discover this during their extensive cleaning, so we need to be very careful," she said.

We decided to take the train to Gorky Park, getting off at the Park Kultury station so we could enter the park near the massive marble arch resembling Berlin's Potsdam Gate. The weather was nice and comfortably chilly. We strolled along the river for a while, looking at many older buildings dating from the eighteenth and early nineteenth centuries, including summer houses and the first city hospital.

Taking the long path gave us many opportunities to gaze behind us and on other paths to identify any familiar pedestrians who could be tailing us, but neither Marie nor I became suspicious. The paths were busy with people, including a large number of children. I steered Marie to a bench in a quiet path, and we sat and relaxed after walking for about an hour.

"It's really nice here," I said. "Reminds me of walking in Central Park."

"Yes, this is a treasure in Moscow and for all of Russia. Truly an oasis," she said.

"Marie," I said, changing the subject to my real concern, "how do we handle — and explain — our relationship as I establish the business and contacts here? Are you my companion who also works with me and helps me with Russian and getting established?"

"I thought this would be my role," she said. "Of course, I am really representing the Mossad and the French DGSE in the Scenturion Venture, but early this morning, I received a text message from Mossad's Mordechai Abramowitz that I should return to Tel Aviv for new instructions as soon as I have helped you get established here."

Brad has talked to the Mossad.

"This is surprising," I said. "Is there a new development? Do you think you've been recognized as a French agent by the Russians or by any Hezbollah agents?" I asked.

"If there is, I don't know it," Marie answered. "But I do know it is unusual for me to be called back so precipitously. Maybe there is Internet chatter about me and my being in Moscow. I will need to check with my Mossad colleagues. Have you heard anything from your CIA handlers that could explain this?"

"No," I lied and hoped I didn't look guilty. Marie was very good at reading my emotions.

"Well," she said, "I think we should stop sightseeing and spend much of tomorrow evaluating business office rentals."

"I agree, especially since I'm holding our first board meeting at the end of the week and will need to discuss planned expenditures. I know we need to hire an administrator to manage our accounting books as well as general business activities. Maybe you can help in the interview process before you leave for Israel."

"Yes, of course," she said. Then she moved closer and kissed me. "Most of all, I will miss you if they recall me from this assignment. And I was so excited about our living together here while you develop Pharmascent Sciences."

"I was too."

I hope she didn't notice I was concerned lying like this.

"I will call our real estate agent to see if their commercial group can start working on this. Maybe we could have some options by Monday or Tuesday," she advised.

"Good. And by the way, I want to visit the Jewish Community Center in Moscow, maybe tomorrow morning. I heard that they're a good place for Jewish immigrants and travelers to meet and establish contacts with Russian Jews. They also have some instruction in conversational Russian for foreigners."

I didn't tell her that Brad instructed me to meet the Russian language instructor at the Jewish center.

"That is a good idea," said Marie. "I will look up their address so we can visit in the morning."

Marie then said she needed to make a call to reserve a table for dinner tonight and wanted to surprise me with typical Russian cuisine. While she was on the phone, I texted Tania that I was planning to visit the Jewish Community Center tomorrow and would appreciate her sending me names of former contacts who might remember her and be helpful to me. I told her I was well and would write again soon.

*

AT FIVE O'CLOCK we returned to our hotel. I was surprised at how quickly the time had passed and how tired we both were from our Gorky Park excursion.

After entering our rooms, Marie again swept the area for hidden bugs or video devices and concluded there were none. I was impressed on how fast and efficient she did this. But we had agreed never to talk business there, since Marie wasn't confident of her detection device.

Marie took a long hot bath while I contacted Brad as well as Yuri with regard to our meeting on Monday early afternoon. Not wanting to limit my available time with Yuri, I asked Brad to see if Tuesday morning for my visit to the U.S. Embassy would work better.

Yuri answered immediately, saying he was anxious to meet with me and would have his car pick me up at the hotel at 11:00 a.m. to take me to his home, where we could talk comfortably and securely. He said he lived in a village west of Moscow, about forty minutes away.

I also heard back from Tania, suggesting that I contact Rabbi David Gordon at the Natasha Roscha Synagogue and Jewish Community Center, also giving me his email address. Tania explained that Rabbi Gordon was an American who had also grown up in Brooklyn and had been sent by the Chabad Jewish network to work in Moscow for two years.

After emailing the rabbi and hearing that Marie had turned off the water, I joined her in the bathroom and offered to rub her back and elsewhere. She closed her eyes and seemed to totally relax, with a big smile on her face. After about ten minutes, she actually fell into a light sleep.

I dressed for dinner in tan slacks with a light blue shirt and a light blue silk tie, and a navy blazer. Marie appeared about thirty minutes later, her hair up, dark red lips and rouge on her cheeks, wearing a black silk sleeveless mini dress with a plunging neckline that captured my full attention. She wore a single strand of small pearls. My eyes were also drawn to her strappy red high-heeled sandals.

"You look gorgeous, and, of course, different again," I said.

"Thank you," she said. "This is our first night out after a long separation, so I wanted it to be special."

The Moscow taxi looked like taxis in most places, and again the driver was unshaven and smoking a cigarette. Marie gave him the address of the restaurant and asked him to please stop smoking because it irritated us. He growled quietly, extinguished it, and tossed it out the window. He then bore down heavily on the accelerator.

In fifteen minutes, we arrived at Lavkalavka restaurant, located in the center of Moscow near Tverskaya street. It was a rustic room with brick walls and lots of wood. The lighting was perfect for a romantic date. Besides its Russian specialties, the restaurant was noted for organic food direct from the farm, Marie informed me.

The menus were in both Russian and English, and I quickly noticed that the waiters could speak several languages. Good to know. The guests at other tables also spoke a variety of languages.

After studying the menu, we ordered a 2013 bottle of Rosé wine from Crimea. Marie warned that this would be a rich and filling meal, so we should dine slowly. As appetizers, we ordered dumplings and duck and also warm carrot hummus. Then we selected borscht with beef brisket and a serving of cabbage soup. For our main entrees, we chose lamb shank with beetroot bulger and basil sauce for me and pike perch with creamy coriander sauce and spinach for Marie. I knew we would be dining here for at least a couple of hours.

Later, over coffees, I asked Marie to tell me more about her usual work and travel for Toilette — as well as for the '*M*,' as I abbreviated the Mossad, just as Brad did in our conversations in public.

I noticed that she was very careful and deliberate in her responses, quite different from our usual, more superficial conversations.

"Most of my work for Toilette involves visiting and gaining customers to buy our chemicals that are used to make perfumes and other fragrances," she said. "We are a supplier but do not make or market finished products. I do a lot of traveling for the company. We are international in our territory, mostly Europe and some customers in the mid-East."

"What do you do when you're not traveling?" I asked.

"I have assignments from the '*D*' (DGSE) or from the *M* while working for Toilette, and after I return to Paris," she said. "Although, to be honest, I sometimes need to take a few weeks off to readjust to Paris or to vacation somewhere where I can relax, doing almost nothing, but this is rare. I need all the interim times after returning to Paris to update my management and handlers, and to visit with friends and acquaintances in and near Paris. I do have some extended family there."

"So, this provided you a basis for contributing to your Zionist loyalties, I assume."

"Yes," she whispered. "Toilette was visited by some *M* members, since our head, '*SF*,' was connected with them probably even before he came to the company, but I, of course, was never given details. '*SF*' introduced me, and they then recruited me to make some contacts for them during my extensive travels, especially in eastern Europe. It was very innocent and simple at the beginning, but with time it expanded to my spending more time with them being trained and then given specific missions. I have been doing this for about eight years."

"And how did I fit into all this?" I asked.

"When we learned there was a military project involving olfaction by some of our enemies, we formed a task force — including the French, Americans, and Israelis — to try to learn the extent of this operation, which you know as the '*S* Venture.' You fell into our laps when your American colleagues learned of your interests in olfaction as a therapy and thought this would be a good cover for a clandestine operation to investigate this further. And to have a full-time physician-scientist above suspicion was a gift to the project."

Of course, I had learned of the Scenturion Venture from Brad already, but didn't realize that the Mossad was also prominently involved.

"Yes, I was sent to Vienna to make contact with you once your own group recruited you to attend the conference," she whispered. "The Office wanted one of their own to evaluate and connect to you," she whispered.

I felt a little embarrassed to have been such an international patsy.

"Thank you for being so honest," I said.

Not that I really thought Marie's explanation was totally on the up and up.

"And now that we have confided in one another," she said, "it is time to get back to our hotel so I can have you as my second and best dessert of the night."

What could I say to that?

"You look so luscious," I whispered. "I need to have you in my arms for as long as I can stay awake tonight."

47.

I DIDN'T OPEN my eyes until about 8:30 a.m., and Marie was still fast asleep. We were to be picked up by the commercial real estate agent at about eleven, so I just rested in bed until she woke up at about nine.

When I checked my email, I found that Rabbi Gordon had responded that he would be delighted if I came by this morning. I was hoping the language instructor also would be there for me to meet. I suggested to Marie that the real estate agent pick us up at the JCC at 1:00 p.m., and we could look at offices until 5 or 6 p.m. This worked out, so we dressed casually for the day and soon went down to find a taxi. Although the Metro was convenient and comfortable, I had enough of it yesterday, I advised Marie.

It was a short ride to the JCC, which appeared as a line of low-level buildings on a sprawling property. The furnishings were modest, and the layout was a large entrance leading to many corridors that seemed to have classrooms and other rooms of various sizes. The directory, in Russian and Hebrew, indicated that they had a gym, a mikvah for ritual baths, two synagogues for services, a library, music room, two kitchens, and two dining rooms, as well as studies and offices for the staff.

Soon after the receptionist informed Rabbi Gordon of our arrival, he came out to welcome us and shook our hands heartily. He spoke English with a New York-New Jersey accent, was dressed in black silk slacks and a long black jacket, with his prayer phylacteries hanging down, and wearing a black hat with fur. He looked like the Hasidic Jews I had often seen in Brooklyn. I estimated him to be at least forty years old, not as overweight as many of his peers, and about five-feet, ten-inches. Maybe he was younger, I also thought, because his beard and garb may contribute several years. He had an amiable smile, and his large, dark-brown eyes sparkled as he spoke, especially to another American Jew, even though I was clearly not religious and certainly not as orthodox as a Chasid.

David took us back to his tiny office, cleared off two chairs of the many books they held and asked if he could bring us some tea. We accepted, and after he returned, I told him why I was in Moscow and that I was being helped by Marie, a French Israeli who had roots as a child in Belarus.

"I want to have a relationship with the Jewish community in Moscow," I said.

He was obviously pleased by that. When he learned, later in the conversation, that we had about an hour-and-a-half to spend at the JCC, Rabbi Gordon immediately jumped up and said he would give us a short tour to meet some of the other staff members, many of whom came here from other countries in the former Soviet Union.

"Jewish life and religious practices are returning to the big cities, like Moscow and St. Petersburg," he said, "and these communities are now very organized and supportive, especially in bringing Jewish education and religious observance back after such long periods of anti-Semitism during the Stalin era and various periods of the past."

Unfortunately, the chief rabbi of the JCC, Rabbi Moshe Zedek, was not there, but Rabbi Gordon did introduce us to the head of youth activities, the chorus director, another rabbi responsible for Bar Mitzvah training, and the woman in charge of social events.

This woman, Laya Springer, who looked to be about forty-five, spent considerable time inquiring about us, especially Marie, and wanted our cell phone numbers, home address, and email addresses so she could apprise us of forthcoming social activities. We couldn't give her the apartment, since it was temporary and we had no Russian email, so I just provided my regular email address.

I was amused at how obvious Ms. Springer was with regard to learning what Marie's relationship was with me.

That's a Jewish woman for you. No, maybe just being a woman.

Rabbi Gordon said, "I have been getting instruction in Russian at the JCC and wonder if you might be interested."

"Yes," I answered. "I would definitely like to at least become conversational."

He gave me the contact information of the person tutoring Russian for foreigners, Miriam Keslov.

She's the contact that Brad wanted me to make.

David and Laya invited us to have lunch, so we joined them in one of the smaller dining rooms, the kosher nondairy one. I noticed there was a small kitchen staff and one woman serving the tables.

Laya told us there was usually left-over cholent from Saturday, "which is a stew that simmers from Friday night to Saturday with vegetables, lima beans, and flanken or boiled beef."

"I remember having that at home and would enjoy this nostalgic surprise," I confided. It was delicious, with the heavy loaf of rye bread that was freshly baked in their kitchen.

We drank a glass of kosher red wine and enjoyed being in this home-away-from-home atmosphere. Marie and I were like celebrities, since we were new arrivals for them.

During lunch, I asked if there were any physicians or scientists in the Jewish community. Laya Springer jumped in and said: "Indeed, there were two medical doctors, one a neurologist and the other a pathologist, but they come to the JCC very rarely. "I will locate their email addresses if you want to meet with them." I agreed very enthusiastically.

Rabbi Gordon said that the aunt of a boy from a city outside of Moscow, who comes in monthly for lessons for his Bar Mitzvah, is a pharmacist at a local hospital. "I think her name is Katarina Breslau," he said.

"I would also like to get in touch with her," I said, not showing that I had a keen interest in communicating with her.

"Some of my work involves pharmaceutical development, and it would be good to have such a contact," I said.

"Laya or I will email you all addresses," Rabbi Gordon replied. "Let us also know your home address when you've moved."

Getting introduced to the sister of the government chemist in Oryol via the JCC was clearly an advantage in terms of avoiding any appearance of my interest in her brother and the activities in Oryol.

*

AT ONE O'CLOCK, we thanked them for their time and hospitality and went outside to meet the real estate agent. He was waiting in a small black car, and when he saw us approaching, he got out and introduced himself.

"I have selected six commercial offices to show you, based on the information you provided," he said in fairly good English. We moved through the various options very quickly, since all were similar in amenities. They all provided twenty-four-hour security, reception and call answering, photocopying, accounting, and secretarial support, plus there were kitchens and various small dining areas and conference rooms. This meant we could lease a minimum of actual office space, using the other facilities as needed.

Marie and I agreed that Building 1 at 16 Tverskaya Street would serve our purpose. It didn't require a long-term lease and had two rooms and supportive office services. The larger room would be for the receptionist and a seating area, and the smaller room would be my private office. It had a nice view of the city and space for a couch and small seating area. There was also an optional car space in the basement.

The agent provided us with forms to complete for submission to the building management. We could move in immediately, he said, since there were several vacancies. Another advantage was that there were three Metro stations nearby.

*

WE WERE BACK at our hotel at about 6:00 p.m., tired from a full day. Marie suggested we rest until about eight o'clock and then go out for a light dinner. As soon as I hit the comfortable lounge chair in our living room, I fell off to sleep until I heard Marie moving around about an hour later.

"How was your nap?" she asked.

"Good, but I still feel tired. Maybe jetlag is still with me. What have you been doing?"

"Oh, just catching up on emails and scanning for local restaurants for tonight. Sunday is usually quiet, and not all restaurants are open. But I found one about three streets away."

It was a family-run restaurant noted for food typical of Georgia, having specialties from the Caucasus Mountains. Although we had intended to have a small, simple dinner, that was not this restaurant's fare, and we were hardly able to finish the rich portions. Everything was very tasty, the service good, and the ambiance perfect for a quiet Sunday evening. I wondered how much weight I gained since arriving here. I needed to get back to exercising and resolved to use the JCC's facilities for working out and swimming.

I stared at Marie sitting across from me.

How beautiful she is, and how mysterious.

"What are you thinking?" she asked, interrupting my thoughts.

"Oh, how good we are together and how easy it is for me to be with you in all aspects."

"That is so nice of you to say. I feel the same way. I do not become intimate with men so easily, although you would not think so from how fast our relationship developed. This is different with you, Milt, and I am a little sad that I might not be able to be with you as long as I had hoped."

We sat for another half-hour drinking coffee and the heavy red wine.

"What are tomorrow's plans?" she asked.

"I'm being picked up by Yuri's driver at 11:00 a.m." I explained. "He'll take me to Yuri's residence outside Moscow. He said he prefers talking with me at his home and not at the office — it's private, and we won't be rushed. I need to make a list of topics to cover. Do you have suggestions?"

"We really know little about him," Marie answered. "Other than he invests in companies, seems to be well-connected in Russian industry and politics, is a prominent businessman who does not deny being Jewish, and seems to want you to advance Pharmascent Sciences in Russia."

"You're right. I'll try to get more info, including why he seems to be so focused on this venture. Is it me, his connections to Toilette, or some other aspect of Pharmascent?"

48.

MARIE'S PLAN FOR Monday was to visit the French Embassy to register her presence here, then to a Russian customer of Toilette, and finally to the Moscow office of Toilette.

We were both dressed by 10:00 a.m. and enjoying our coffee. While waiting for Marie to finish putting on her makeup and latest disguise, I checked my emails. To my surprise, I had one from the editorial office of *Cancer Advances* — our revision had been reviewed and deemed acceptable for publication once all authors completed the attached copyright assignment and authors' forms and agreed to pay publication costs. I was beside myself and let out a yell.

"What is happening?" asked Marie, popping her head out of the bathroom.

"They accepted our article!" I almost screeched. "I am delighted!" I immediately forwarded the email and attachments to my coauthors, congratulating everyone for their participation and contribution.

This was great news indeed and a perfect way to begin a week that promised to be busy with setting up Pharmascent in Russia. That thought gave me a pang of guilt, since I knew that this diversion would delay much of the cancer research that I'd been pursuing at ESU. NCI grants are very competitive, and I was worried that although this article would be well-received and a credit to my grant, there were many more avenues that needed to be pursued, and it wasn't right for me to delegate those to my lab support staff.

When Marie finished getting ready, she came out and asked me to tell her more about the article.

"We worked on this for almost a year," I said.

"A whole year?"

"Well, even longer. In fact, I started to develop this project about three or more years ago. It took about a half-year to develop a grant application submitted for funding to the National Cancer Institute. I failed to get funding on the first try, but the comments by the review committee were helpful, so I reapplied and was successful the second time. I then had to set up a lab, buy equipment, and recruit two experienced staff members, one with a Ph.D. and research experience as a junior investigator, and the second being an advanced technologist with an M.S. degree and a lot of experience managing cancer cells growing in culture flasks. So, after more than two to three years of conception, writing a grant twice, and finally getting funding, we were operational, and after almost another year, we had the first promising results.

"I'm pleased that our first article emanating from this grant support is being published so soon after we began this research — and in a prominent journal at that. But I do feel a little guilty at abandoning my colleagues."

"Don't be that way," said Marie. "Enjoy this moment. I had no idea you were so involved in this project. You're full of surprises! Let's go downstairs for breakfast."

*

AT ELEVEN O'CLOCK, after having a croissant and coffee at the restaurant adjoining the hotel, I went out and noted the impressive, large, black Mercedes sedan parked in front of the hotel. I opened the door and gave my name. The driver introduced himself in broken English, said the name Yuri Grobstein to identify his boss, and motioned that I should take a seat in the back after rushing to open the back door.

Although I had learned some conversational phrases, they didn't get me far with this driver, who knew even less English than I did Russian. I thanked him in Russian and just sat back and watched the sights as he drove away from Moscow, due west, for about thirty minutes.

In a while, I noticed that we were coming into what appeared to be a more affluent area, with fancier houses and businesses than I had seen earlier. Most of the trip was along a highway adjacent to farms and small communities of dozens of smaller houses. The town we just went by was Barvika, I read, which was a riverside village with some elegant shops and clearly some large, expensive homes. We then passed a large, doughnut-shaped, granite facade of a modern-looking building with, to my surprise, a Star of David and the name Zhukovka Jewish Community Center in both Russian and Hebrew. I remembered Yuri saying that he lived in Zhukovka, so I was sure we were almost at our destination.

About ten minutes later, we went through large gates that the driver opened remotely and pulled into a long driveway leading to a very large and impressive home built from stone and lots of wood, with some round glass steeples and a massive front door. This reminded me of mansions on Long Island that were at least $15 million and higher. I had no idea what such a house would cost in Russia.

When we stopped, the entrance door immediately opened, and Yuri emerged, dressed casually in a brown suede jacket and black slacks and a black silk scarf around his neck above a light blue shirt.

"Yuri," I said, "what a beautiful home and neighborhood!"

"Thank you," he said. "We have been living here for about three years, as Zhukovka expanded and added interesting shops and, of course, the Jewish Community Center, which was built recently at a cost of 200 million rubles and was opened with a ceremony that included President Putin, because of his friendship with the chief rabbi, Borel Lazar, as well as being my acquaintance. Some of the wealthiest Muscovites live here, such as the Rotenbergs, who are in construction."

I smiled as I noticed the mezuzah on the right side of the entrance, required for Jewish homes. Yuri talked as he showed me into the house, which was massive and quite impressive. The foyer was long, with large, traditional, mostly Romantic-period paintings on the walls and what appeared to be Persian carpets on the floor. He led me through this area to his beautiful library with cherry wood, comfortable large couch chairs, and a fireplace burning real logs, with a large original abstract painting hanging on the only wall free of bookshelves.

Finally, we entered the dining room, where two places were set for us to have lunch.

Just before we sat down, the door to the kitchen opened, and his wife, Katarina Grobstein, and the housekeeper, Jolla, appeared, with the housekeeper holding our bowls of pea soup and salads. Katarina was a very attractive woman, tall and thin with short brown hair, dark brown eyes, and a long oval face. She was dressed casually but elegantly, in a silk cream blouse and long woolen gray skirt and black heels. She spoke good English with only a slight Slavic accent, welcoming me to their home.

"Please enjoy your lunch. It was nice meeting you. I have to leave for an appointment," she said as she withdrew.

Yuri explained that Katarina had been waiting for the car to return because she was going to the Prada store in the town. I showed my surprise that this small town could have this luxurious store, and Yuri explained that their shopping mall also had a Gucci store as well as Mercedes Benz and Bentley dealerships.

After lunch with French Sancerre, Yuri escorted me down a narrow staircase off the living room, first to the recreation room with a pool table and then past his wine cellar to a closed, heavy door that we entered for our meeting. He explained this was the most private and surveillance- and sound-proof area in his house, where he conducts most of his private business meetings and calls.

"Relax on any of these sofa chairs, and I will order tea, coffee, wine, or whiskey, as you may desire," he said.

"I'm fine after the nice lunch and superb wine."

During lunch, I had explained where I found an apartment and also a potential office, and Yuri thought both were good locations and with reasonable rents, especially if long-term leases were not required. He said having a car garage in the basement of both buildings was convenient, but I wasn't sure what he meant by that.

Before I went to the discussion about Pharmascent, I told him about my visit to the Natasha Roscha Synagogue and Jewish Community Center, where I had met a U.S. Chabad rabbi in residence there for a couple of years. I said I thought the rabbi would be helpful to orient me, and I had also learned they gave instruction in conversational Russian for immigrants, so I was planning to take private lessons.

Yuri was impressed that I had accomplished so much in the three days I'd been in Moscow, so I had to tell him about Marie, "my partner whom you met at the first investor meeting in Paris," I said. I explained that she "is also helping me get established, since she speaks Russian, having spent her early youth in Belarus before emigrating with her family to Israel and later to France." I could tell that Yuri was interested in learning more about Marie, but I got off the topic as soon as possible. I left him believing this was a romantic entanglement.

Yuri said he was delighted to be involved with my biopharma venture and pleased that I had agreed to come to Russia to start the business. "When the Toilette management told me about you and Pharmascent, I sent the information to the Russian Ministry of Science and Technology as well as the Commerce Ministry. Both responded that it would be interesting to have this work pursued in Russia, especially with an international group headed by an American scientist."

"In fact," said Yuri, "I was advised that there could be government funds made available. This suggests that some government officials would have an interest in partaking in the investment, and I was encouraged to bring this opportunity here. Importantly, I was instructed to provide them with all of the information on the business and on you personally, so I surmise there has been some work done to determine who you are and what prospects the research has from both your business and other potential uses."

"Are you suggesting that there may be government or even commercial or military interests?" I asked, trying to act naively.

"I can only say that it only took a few days for me to get a strong encouragement from the Ministry of Science and Technology to pursue this in the best interests of the Motherland," Yuri said. "So how can I help you, and what plans can you share with me?"

I found this most revealing because I surmised this science and technology ministry would be involved in some way with the research institute in Oryol and possibly also the Russian secret police agency, the FSB. I wasn't sure how much I could share with Yuri, especially since I hadn't been briefed by my CIA contacts yet. I wondered if Yuri was close to the Russian military and espionage communities, since, as a professed Jew, he might otherwise be of some mistrust in this government and business world. Yet, he seemed to be well-connected and very successful financially. I decided to stick to generalities and see how much I could delay sharing with him at this time.

"Well," I said, "after setting up the business office and getting our board functioning, I need to take the first prototype odor pharmaceuticals and produce them for further testing in human volunteers. My first odor drug is one that's used for jetlag and to improve sleeping, and once I show that this can be used via the sense of smell, I will turn to other classes of drugs that could have effects on the brain and nervous system."

Yuri responded enthusiastically. "Then you need to be introduced to some of our scientists and clinicians who may have an interest and who could help you in conducting these studies. I suspect that clinical studies can be done in Russia faster than in the USA, especially if it is for a science or business that is of interest to the Ministry of Science and Technology. I will talk with key people who can make introductions for you. In fact, I will get you an invitation to attend a reception I will be at to honor the incoming President of the Russian Academy of Sciences in about ten days. This will allow you to mingle and be introduced to leaders of Russian science."

"Thank you, Yuri," I said. "I would be delighted to attend, although my Russian is still very primitive."

"No matter — they will enjoy using their English on you. Now, I need to tell you something else. You must be careful at the Jewish Community Center, since many Russian government officials do not trust their loyalty, and I expect there will be considerable surveillance of their activities by various police agencies."

I was surprised that Yuri was so forthright, but I guessed that he wanted to protect me in this environment of intrigue that he presumed was unfamiliar to me. I didn't get any vibes of his suspecting any relationship to the CIA, much less the French and Israeli spy agencies.

I did ask him where he learned English so well. "My parents suffered much during the Stalinist era. My mother was a teacher who lost her position, and my father was a businessman who was successful in the import/export business until he had to reduce his work to a bare minimum. They are both dead.

"My parents had relatives in London," he continued, "so I was able to go to London University after graduating Moscow University and earned a master's in economics after two years in London, with the support of an aunt and uncle from my mother's side."

Yuri shared his views about the current climate for Jews in Russia, especially businessmen. He complimented President Putin as being supportive and having a number of Jewish business partners, despite some public controversies with others who were either jailed or had to emigrate elsewhere. His support of Putin was a surprise to me, but then I knew that this would be expected given his own success as a Jewish businessman in the Russian Federation.

We then went upstairs to have a cup of coffee in his library, which I had to admire because of the cherry wood bookshelves, especially the second story that also had stained glass windows alongside the bookcases. Yuri seemed to have an interest in world history, based on the book titles I read, with many in English and also Russian, German, and French.

49.

"HOW WAS YOUR visit?" asked Marie when I got back to the hotel in midafternoon.

"Really nice. He was educated also in England, with an economics degree from the University of London, has a beautiful home in a very affluent suburb, and a sophisticated and attractive wife, whom I only greeted briefly before she left for some expensive shopping."

"What about Pharmascent?"

"He is very well-connected, especially with the Ministry of Science and Technology, and wants to introduce me to some scientists from labs with whom I could collaborate. He also plans to have me invited to a special reception of the Russian Academy of Sciences next week sometime. This could be important for me to meet top scientists and politicians involved in science in Russia. His relationships are not yet clear to me, but he does speak favorably of President Putin." I said that without concern that my words might be recorded, since it was favorable to all parties and seemed quite natural for us to be discussing.

I'm sure that Marie understands my answer and motives.

"Do you want to rest or go out?" she asked.

"Let's stay here until about six or so," I said. "And how was your day?"

Marie wasn't inclined to give a detailed answer. "I dropped by the French Embassy, visited two companies that buy our reagents, and then our Moscow office. Unfortunately, the principals in one were absent, but the second visit was productive. The Toilette office staff seemed ambivalent about my visit and had nothing important to say."

I spent some time making a list of topics I needed guidance on from the resident Moscow CIA officer, whom I expected to meet tomorrow. I made this on a piece of paper, not my computer, in my own shorthand. I needed to rehearse, in my mind, how I could get my

CIA contacts up to date and what I needed from them going forward. I was also curious if they were going to discuss Marie with me during our meeting.

*

I WONDERED IF Marie had heard from her Mossad colleagues, but we couldn't discuss such things in our rooms.

"How about we take a walk and then pick up a pizza to bring back for a light dinner?" I asked.

"A walk sounds perfect," she said. "And I think there's a restaurant with take-out about three or four streets from here."

We left and started walking toward the area of the restaurants Marie knew about.

"I will meet with the CIA head and others at the Embassy tomorrow," I said. "Do you know if the Mossad contact here will also be there?"

"I heard the Mossad head in Moscow, Mordechai Abromowitz, may be contacting you, either during your visit at the embassy or possibly when you visit the JCC. Everyone believes the JCC is a reasonable place to have clandestine meetings, since you will be going there to learn Russian and to participate with the community."

"Well, I don't know," I said. "Yuri told me that the JCC was under suspicion and surveillance by the Russian police or counterintelligence. I'm going to report that to the CIA when I'm at the Embassy tomorrow."

Marie looked concerned. "Maybe we underestimated the Russian counterespionage group and their surveillance of members of the Jewish community," she said. "This information from Yuri is very valuable."

Did I say too much?

Yuri warning me of secret Russian police activity could compromise him if Marie were, in fact, a double agent. I dismissed this thought quickly, although Brad had indicated some concern.

I tried to smooth it over. "This was a general comment from Yuri that the Russian authorities still have mistrust for Jews, especially JCCs that have members from different Eastern European countries and where many have been emigrating despite having better conditions and freedom to practice their religion under the current regime."

Did that throw her off the track?

I made a mental note to discuss that with the CIA handlers I would be meeting with tomorrow.

"Nevertheless," said Marie, "it is a good reminder to be cautious, especially if you are not yet under any suspicion. By the way, I heard from my Mossad handlers that if I can get you settled in the apartment this week and can identify an office manager who has a good command of English, then I should return to Tel Aviv for instructions. I told them I felt sure I could accomplish that before the weekend, so I'm planning on going to Tel Aviv on Sunday."

"When will you be back? I thought you were trying to delay this."

"It is all very sudden and suspicious, Milt, as if I were being recalled because of some concerns. But maybe I am paranoid, and they will only redirect some of my activities to support the Scenturion project."

We picked up a large pizza and some beers and returned to the hotel to eat, watch the news, and go to bed early. I watched Marie carefully during the evening to see if I could notice any change in her demeanor or attitude toward me.

I detect nothing different, just her usual warm and uninhibited self.

*

THE NEXT MORNING, I walked to the closest Metro station to take a train to the U.S. Embassy, following directions from Marie. Marie said she was sure that we were safe in Moscow, but I should nevertheless watch if I were being followed.

I'm sure I won't be good at this.

Marie said she would spend the morning preparing for our move to the apartment by getting the rental papers to be signed and determining if there were any furniture we still needed. I was relieved that she was handling all that, and I asked if she could also get the contract for renting the office space on Tverskaya Street.

How would I have managed all this without her?

It was an easy Metro ride to the station closest to the U.S. Embassy, which was a white stone building standing auspiciously with tall stone walls and guarded gates. I showed my passport to the Marine guards, who then directed me to the main entrance used by the public. At the reception desk, I was given a number and told to watch the screen in the waiting room for it to be called.

I estimated by the current number posted and my number that it could take some time, maybe even an hour, for me to be called. However, much to my surprise, a staff member came to me before the number appeared, confirmed my number, and asked me to follow him through one of the doors off the waiting area. I was taken down a corridor through another door marked 'No Public Entry' and then led to a small conference room.

A tall blond-haired man who was probably younger than forty was sitting at the table and greeted me. "I'm James Bradshaw, vice-consul," he said. "I understand you came to register with the embassy and that you're here for an extended stay to develop a business."

"Thank you for seeing me so promptly," I said. "Yes, I just arrived and am trying to set up the Moscow office of my new company,

Pharmascent Sciences, which has its headquarters in France but is also registered to do business in the U.S., and now Russia."

"Very interesting," Bradshaw said. "This will be of much interest to our commercial officer, who is always seeking ways to build business ties between the U.S. and the resident country. I'll need to arrange that you meet her, Catherine Smothers, who stems from Boston. What brought you to want to develop this business in Russia?"

My perennial question.

"I searched for venture capital, and, through other contacts, I was introduced to Yuri Grobstein, a Russian oligarch whose firm invested in various business enterprises. After reviewing our plans, he agreed to help fund the project and to join the board of directors if we would also build the business in Russia."

"We don't have much time, since I'm to take you to some of my embassy colleagues," said Bradshaw. "You only have a little more than an hour to complete what should be considered a routine visit to the embassy as a newly arrived U.S. citizen."

He then took me down another hall to a back elevator marked "Restricted to Embassy Officers." We descended what seemed like a few floors, then exited on a low basement floor. I was then taken down a secure corridor that could be entered only after clicking in a code and doing an eye scan. My visitor's identification card was also scanned before the door opened.

Bradshaw then led me down another corridor to a room at the end that again had a secure entry process, but instead of the door opening, a phone on the wall rang, and Bradshaw identified himself, also looking into the overhead camera. He then shook my hand and departed.

After he was out of this secure corridor, the door to the room I was to enter opened remotely. All of my movements from the time I entered the first office with Bradshaw were followed by wall and ceiling cameras, so I guessed the door opened after I was videoed, and my face apparently identified.

Is my face also on other spy networks?

After entering, a woman introduced herself as Marcia Dubrovnik and showed me her CIA identification, clarifying that she was head of protocol at the embassy, but I remembered being told that, in fact, she headed CIA operations in Russia. The man seated at the table rose and shook my hand, saying he was John Caruthers, responsible for protocol; he was also another CIA officer in Russia.

Marcia was a short, stocky woman with dark hair cut in a short, masculine style, probably in her fifties, and spoke with authority. John was much younger, probably not more than forty, with a crew cut. He reminded me of a marine in his appearance.

Ms. Dubrovnik thanked me for my willingness to cooperate with them.

"Our mole at the Oryol research facility has confirmed the olfaction military research," she said. "*Aleksai* believes there is collaboration with other communist nations and that they are in the testing stages. We know there is a lot going on, but we lack details and, of course, don't know how much progress has been made in any area, such as influencing the mind for interrogation or even having odors that can have longer-term effects."

"Do you really think that my coming here to set up an olfaction therapy business won't arouse suspicions by the Russian FSB?" I asked.

"That's what we need to determine. If you're suspected and allowed to proceed with your activities, it would mean they want you to be fed with certain misleading information, which, nevertheless, could be useful to us."

"What do you know about Yuri Grobstein?" I asked. "And why is the CIA apparently concerned about Marie Chalfont? I understand she's being recalled to Tel Aviv for further instructions, and she expressed concerns to me about this, asking if I knew anything."

Marcia Dubrovnik paused for a moment and looked at Caruthers, then said, "We're not sure about Yuri Grobstein. He seems to be open about his Judaism and a relationship with the Jewish Community Center in his town. He's a successful businessman in this society, which means he's well-connected. In fact, we think he does have an acquaintanceship with President Putin. Perhaps they have business ties. The fact that he was introduced to you by Simon Fass of Toilette, the company Marie Chalfont works for, suggests that he may be sympathetic to the West, but this is still speculation and not an official position. As you may know, we think that Simon Fass is or was connected to the Mossad and, in this way, recruited Marie Chalfont into the Mossad."

"But Brad Williams, in his last conversation with me prior to my leaving New York, cautioned me about Marie," I said. "But if Marie is a Russian agent, does this not compromise the Scenturion project — and me?"

"Yes and no," said John Caruthers. "She could be truthful and loyal to us, but then again, she could be the liaison by which the FSB provides you with fictitious, misleading information. Or she may be placed to gain information from you. She wouldn't be the first undercover agent to have multiple loyalties."

"Yes, I'm familiar with the litany of double-spies who sold secrets to Russia, during the second world war and also during the cold war. I guess this is expected."

I continued then: "I think I may have compromised Yuri when I admitted to Marie yesterday that Yuri cautioned me that the Russian authorities were watching the members of the Natasha Roscha Synagogue and Jewish Community Center as potential subversives. If

Marie tells this to the FSB, it could threaten Yuri and put him under suspicion."

"Interesting," said Marcia. "We will increase our surveillance of Yuri and see if he is tailed, interrogated, or otherwise treated with suspicion by Russian secret police, which could then be traced back to Marie Chalfont. Of course, his mentioning his view about the JCC being watched may be mere speculation on his part. In that case, he may not come under scrutiny, and we would not be able to determine if Marie Chalfont is a double agent…"

She stopped and studied my face for half a moment. "In any case, your Marie will be given a new assignment by the Mossad to take on another project, to visit with you as she travels to the east visiting clients, but certainly less frequently than you both expected. We think her constant presence with you can be a deterrent to expanding your relationships and learning more about the Russian secret olfaction program, and it could make you a target for the Hezbollah, who have been searching for Marie for about two years, after two of their top agents were assassinated in France. They want to avenge this."

"I'm not sure I can play this role without Marie, who has become quite close to me," I said.

"Yes, we know," said Dubrovnik. "This is her talent and why she has been so successful as a Mossad agent. Although the Mossad professes not to require their female agents to use sex to advance their mission, they also do not interfere when this is apparent. Everyone knows of the relationship between Ms. Chalfont and you, and it has not raised concerns until now."

"And now," said Caruthers, "we need to find a logical way to extract her from Scenturion without raising suspicion by her and any others if she is indeed a double agent or places you at risk because of her past fieldwork for the DGSE or the Mossad. We'll leave it to the

Mossad to investigate this further. She is also an agent of the DGSE, which we all believe has a mole disloyal to France."

Ms. Dubrovnik said she would now excuse herself and give me some time with John to learn how we should contact each other and how I should use any drop-offs if absolutely necessary.

After she left, John gave me a number to call with my cell phone, which would be innocuous and not connect but would signal them that I needed to get into contact urgently. He also explained that since my apartment building and the building of the planned office for Pharmascent have basement garages connected by elevators, and I have a reserved car spot at each, this would be a good place for any emergency meeting, since they could have a secure car parked there and I could simply take the elevator or stairs down to the garage.

"However, if the garage had a camera surveillance system, this wouldn't work" he remarked. John also explained how he could have an agent visit the JCC if I were going to a religious service or to attend a function. He said that at least two contacts were Russian nationals who were Jewish but didn't openly practice the religion — although they were familiar with and visited the JCC.

John also explained that we should have a code to arrange for meetings in the garage. I should use the calendar in my cell phone, putting a time in to specify when we should meet, indicating whether it should be in the garage of my apartment building or the garage of the office building. "You should put in an evening hour for a meeting on the following day in the apartment garage and an early afternoon hour for a meeting on the following day in the office building. You should record in your calendar that the appointment is to remind you to contact your laboratory or another party in New York," he instructed.

I was told that I should definitely visit the JCC once or twice a week so as to establish a pattern. This should include taking Russian language once or more a week with Miriam Keslov, who, John emphasized, could be trusted to transmit information to them via the Mossad.

He also suggested that I attend Saturday services when the son of the chemist from Oryol was visiting. I could learn this from the Bar Mitzvah teacher or possibly from the email correspondence of the sister of Dr. Breslau, Katarina, and who usually picked up her nephew Daniel at the railway station late Friday afternoon, returning him there for the train back home to Oryol on Sunday afternoon. "We will follow Mrs. Breslau, Daniel's mother, when she visits the family in Moscow, and any other activities in Moscow," he explained. "We also plan to monitor Katarina Breslau's nephew."

John said that I needed to meet Katarina and exchange email addresses with her, so that they could hack her emails regularly and thereby learn of Dr. Breslau's personal email address. But I needed to be discreet, John cautioned. Once they had these emails, they would try to follow all correspondence as long as possible, but they appreciated that the Russians would be changing their protective walls to block hacking.

John explained that if Dr. Breslau texted or emailed anyone at the research facility, this could give them access to their computer at Oryol, possibly gaining the information we seek by hacking the system. "But I'm sure," he emphasized again, "they have a secure Cybernet defense system."

He also told me that if they could get a key to my apartment and office, they would sweep them regularly for bugs or video devices, and I could also leave something for them if pre-arranged. Finally, he said they were working out a plan to be able to pick me up with a town travel service, like Uber, which I could call via my cell phone to arrange for travel instead of a taxi, at least a day in advance, so the car and driver would be CIA.

He said they could have someone contact the local Russian car service, 'Yandex,' to see how they could intercede when I made an advance pickup reservation. John said this was a fallback if other meeting arrangements were less feasible.

I'm anxious about all of this intrigue, but glad my handlers are taking such precautions.

50.

"HOW WAS YOUR visit to the Embassy?" Marie asked back at the hotel.

"I waited around a lot before I met the Vice Consul and told him about my business plans in Moscow. He seemed pleased that an American scientist would come here to begin such a project and thought it would be useful for U.S.-Russian business relations, which were at a pretty low ebb, he said."

"Did you meet any CIA officers?"

"I'm not sure, since the other person I met was introduced as a protocol officer, but I didn't ask what that meant. In any case, they encouraged my expanding my business activities and keeping up an active relationship with Yuri, who they said could help connect me with scientists interested in olfaction."

I didn't look at Marie while telling this half-lie, though I figured she was observant enough to notice that I wasn't fully truthful anyhow.

"Did you ever attend a performance of the Bolshoi Ballet?" she asked, changing the subject.

"No. I would love to. When is it?"

"There's one tonight. I'll try to get tickets," she said.

Could she really get these so soon before the performance?

While Marie went to sit at the only table in the room, I sat on the sofa and checked my email and text messages.

Tania had written to ask how I was faring in Moscow and to tell me she was enjoying her part-time work as a medical technologist.

"Nothing has changed with regard to my separation," she wrote, "but I contacted a divorce lawyer in Moscow via the Internet, and he advised he can do this for me. If my husband opposes it, the attorney said it could take years, especially if he continues to support me. I am very anxious about this, since I want to be free of him and divorced. I miss you, Milt."

I didn't respond to that because I didn't know what to say. Instead, I simply ended by assuring her that I would be in touch.

I then texted my lab staff that I would try to call them tomorrow at 10:00 a.m. New York time to discuss the forms they needed to fill out to enable publication of our article.

Seemingly in no time, Marie interrupted me to say that she got tickets and we should leave soon to get an early dinner before the Bolshoi performance. I couldn't imagine how she was able do this almost in any city but decided not to ask.

Does she really have such connections in Moscow?

She emphasized that the dress was very casual, so I decided to wear my tan slacks with the blue blazer and a cream turtleneck sweater. Marie wore her hair combed out over her shoulders, probably made up of some hair attachments, and a black blouse with ruffles and tight-fitting black slacks, as well as black short-length boots. Again, this was a new appearance for her, with almost all-black hair now.

The Metro wasn't crowded, even though it was now late afternoon. After stopping for a quick bite to eat, we took a train to Teatralnaya, the underground Metro station on the Zamoskvoretskaya line named for the nearby Teatralnaya Square, the location of the Bolshoi Ballet and Opera Theatre.

The building was an impressive structure, having Greek columns as a portico in front, with a bronze quadriga above the portico. Inside, as with many theatres and opera houses, there was an abundance of classic heavy dark red drapes and chandeliers, with elegant carvings on the balconies and a lot of gold leaf artistry.

True to her usual role of tour guide whenever we were out together, Marie explained that "the Bolshoi was one of the leading ballets and opera companies in the world and a source of much pride to the

Russians." Marie was excited as she told me that this evening at the Bolshoi, especially with the production of Tchaikovsky's *The Nutcracker*, "will be one of our most sublime pleasures."

Having never heard such a prediction from Marie before, I anticipated a unique evening. I had seen this ballet in New York City a couple of times, usually around Christmas or New Year, and remembered enjoying the dancing and fairytale story. So, I was very curious about how different it would be performed by the Bolshoi.

Marie picked up our tickets for seats in the second row, off to the far right, of the parterre, where we had a reasonable view of the stage. We arrived early, so we had time to walk around the ground floor and see the grand theatre with the 'small stage,' which wasn't small at all, but seemingly used for ballet performances.

I was surprised to see that all seats were occupied on a Tuesday evening. The audience was generally well-dressed, including some in black tie and formal gowns, but most in casual clothes. Some even wore colorful country costumes.

The curtain rose for Act One and the scene of guests gathering for a Christmas party at the Stahlbaum home, including Drosselmeyer, godfather to Marie and Fritz, Stahlbaums' children. He brought them a funny Nutcracker as a Christmas present. Drosselmeyer fills another role as a wizard who can transform anything, even having the toys come alive and growing together around the tree.

Thus, the traditional fairytale story developed with exquisite dancing accompanying majestic scenery.

After the intermission, when we enjoyed a glass of champagne, Act Two began with Marie and the Nutcracker Prince sailing in their magic boat through the Christmas tree kingdom, as the dream continued. After several rounds of applause by the standing audience, we left for our hotel.

"So, was it as good as I said?" Marie asked as we began walking toward the exit.

"I'm still spellbound," I said, and I was.

This helps me to forget my treacherous role in Russia, at least for a couple of hours. But what are her connections to get seats for us on such short notice?

*

WE AWOKE REFRESHED the next morning, and after a nice breakfast downstairs, Marie and I went our separate ways. It took me about twenty minutes by Metro to get to the station near the JCC, and I noticed I was feeling more and more comfortable traveling on the Metro by myself.

When I arrived at the JCC, the building was buzzing with activity. I told the receptionist who I was and that I could find my way to Rabbi Gordon's office. His door was closed, so I knocked and waited. He said something in Russian, which I understood to mean, 'Come in.'

"Delighted to see you, Doctor," he said, rising to shake my hand. "Come and sit on my only free chair. Can I get you anything?"

"No, thank you, Rabbi. I thought I would come by to meet the Russian language teacher."

"Absolutely," he said. "Oh, have you heard from Katarina Breslau yet?"

"No," I said, surprised. "Is she going to contact me?"

"I called her and told her about you and said I had promised to introduce you both, since you have common interests in pharmacology. I thought she would've called by now. I didn't feel comfortable giving out her private email before asking her."

"I understand," I said. "But could I have the contact information for the two Jewish doctors?"

"Of course," said the Rabbi. "I'll write down this information for you, and then we can go visit the language tutor, Miriam Keslov. On second thought, let me try to reach Katarina Breslau on her cell right now." He dialed a number, spoke a few words, and then handed the cell phone to me.

I said hello in Russian, not knowing what to expect.

She responded in very Slavic-accented English. "I am so sorry for not contacting you after Rabbi Gordon wrote to me," said Katarina, "but I did not have your cell phone number, and I am awkward at writing in English. I am delighted to meet you, Dr. Davidson. I understand you are a recent arrival from America and will be starting a new pharmaceutical company."

"Yes," I said, "and I'm interested in making contacts in pharmacy and pharmacology, as well as in neurology. I understand that a neurologist is a member of the Jewish community here."

"Yes, of course, we can arrange for you to meet Professor Sergeii Koussevitzky, who works at the European Medical Centre in Moscow, where I also work as a pharmacist. He is a prominent researcher and neurologist here, and I am sure he would be honored to meet an American professor. Rabbi Gordon or I can send him an email with your contact information."

"Thank you," I said. "That would be great."

"And if you have time," said Katarina, "I will be at the JCC on Saturday for services and then on Sunday, accompanying my nephew who is being prepared for his Bar Mitzvah."

This is exactly what I had hoped to achieve, to get to know the sister of one of the principal chemists in Oryol.

"Yes, I can come on Sunday," I said. "Is nine-thirty in the morning convenient?" Katarina said she would meet me in the snack area, where drinks and light food are offered, so our meeting was arranged.

After hanging up with Katarina, Rabbi Gordon asked if I were 'settled in' yet.

"I'll be moving into an apartment this week and have also found office space."

"Wonderful," he said. "Please give me all the information for our registry, so we can list your latest information. I assume that you'll be joining us, yes?"

"Yes, I plan to join, though I confess that I'm not very religious in terms of attending services. What are the membership requirements and dues?"

"I think it's based on what the congregant and family can afford and whether there are children attending school, and so on," he said. "I'm not sure, but I'll have one of the office staff contact you with all of the information. Or you can drop by the office while you're here."

He then wrote down the contact information for the two physicians and handed it to me.

We then walked to the staircase, went down one flight, and found the small office of Miriam Keslov, the Russian language tutor. Her door was open, and she was busy reading at her small desk. She jumped up and greeted us both heartily, offering her hand to me as the Rabbi introduced us. Miriam said she had heard about me and that I was seeking lessons in Russian.

"Yes," I said. "I hope it will be possible for me to learn enough to be conversant."

"I do this all the time, since we have people here from many countries," she said. "It's my pleasure to be of service."

Miriam was a stout woman of about fifty, I guessed, with dark black hair combed up, a round face with rosy cheeks, sparkling large brown eyes, and otherwise plain-looking and dressed in a white blouse and a long black, wide skirt. She had a very friendly smile and gracious manner, which put me immediately at ease.

"Do you speak any other languages, especially a Slavic language?"

"Only a little German, some Yiddish and Hebrew words, and I can understand some French. But no Slavic language, I'm afraid."

"No matter," said Miriam. "Russian is difficult to read in Cyrillic for those with Latin-derived languages, but you should be able to learn how to speak in about three months if you can devote twice a week for lessons with me."

"I will try my best to arrange this if we can have a flexible schedule," I said. "I'm starting a business here and may not be able to come for lessons on a regular schedule."

"Then we'll do our best," said Miriam. "Here's my card in English and Russian, so just let me know your availability for the next two weeks, and I'll adjust my schedule." I was really impressed with her almost perfect English.

51.

THE METRO WASN'T crowded at this time of day, so it was easy for me to get back to my hotel, where I called my lab in New York in the late afternoon. Jhanella answered and was eager to talk with me.

"We were expecting your call, so let me get Mike to join us," she said. In a few seconds, he was on the line also. "Hi, Dr. Davidson, how are you, and how is Moscow?"

"Well," I said, "this is certainly a different world for me. The younger and educated generations of Russians can speak English much better than I can converse in Russian, or any other foreign language for that matter, and it's difficult for me reading signs and getting around in general. I do have help and have made a lot of progress. I found an apartment and also an office."

"You've been busy over these few days," said Jhanella.

"We hope you don't settle in too well," Mike said.

Once again, I felt guilty. "I just hope we can communicate frequently enough so that our research doesn't suffer," I said, but I knew none of us believed that that was going to be the case. "What's happening now?" I asked.

Jhanella summarized recent work. Evidently, some of the additional human tumors derived from patient surgical specimens and grafted to mice recapitulated what we observed already in the colon cancer transplant.

Jhanella and Mike had found that, like before, the more malignant, spheroid-like cells had an increased number of chromosomes and that many didn't resemble typical mouse chromosomes but instead had biarmed features, looking like 'Xs,' more typical of human chromosomes.

Mike said he was even able to show by special chromosome staining that some of these biarmed chromosomes were indeed human, but many also had extra pieces that could be from murine chromosomes, which would mean that the human tumor cells grown in the mice gained genetic features from the mouse. "We're working with Dr. Bogner to define the makeup of different malignant cells, compared to the parental human tumor cells, to try to define any repeated or key chromosome segments," Jhanella added.

"This could point to a commonality of genes from the human tumors that could be transforming the mouse cells adjacent to the human cancer cells," I said, "possibly by gene transfer or simply the fusion of tumor and mouse host cells, just as we reported in our article.

*

I FELT SOME nostalgia after signing off. I missed being there to review the results directly and, of course, to interact with them in person.

My cell phone pinged, a text from Marie. She was waiting for some papers from the office building's real estate office. I really hoped we could wrap all this up tomorrow and move out of the hotel by Friday. That would give us until Sunday, when Marie left for Tel Aviv, to get comfortable in our own apartment.

Probably not "our" apartment now — just my apartment.

I took a beer out of the small fridge and tasted the strong, dark, Russian brew. It relaxed me. Marie finally arrived and put her briefcase with all of the papers on the coffee table before sitting down next to me and giving me a hug and kiss. I pulled her close and rubbed her neck and back while planting kisses on her cheeks and forehead.

"I gather you had a nice morning and quiet afternoon," she said.

"Yes, the JCC people are friendly and very helpful. They have a busy social as well as religious program, trying to keep as many congregants active and involved as possible."

"Well, I don't want you too involved," she said. "You're an attractive target — an unmarried American doctor and professor building a pharmaceutical company in Russia. I can imagine that all the unattached young Russian women — and maybe even the attached ones — are setting their sights on you."

"Believe me, I have my hands full with you and with my duties here, so there's no need — or time — for any other affairs."

Her smirk let me know she was hardly convinced. "Well," she said, as she leaned over to get the leasing documents from her briefcase, "maybe my absence will make you fonder of me, as the saying goes."

The two lease agreements were in Russian, so Marie had to give me a synopsis. I understood most of the terms but wasn't comfortable signing Russian lease contracts without attorney review, so I asked her to try to get Jolanda Terofskia, our Russian attorney, to look over the papers before I signed.

"I'll leave her a message to ask if she's available to review this tomorrow morning," Marie advised.

"If we split up tomorrow, it would give me time to visit with Dr. Koussevitzky at the European Medical Centre," I said. "And maybe even time to meet the pathologist, Dr. Alexander Kandinsky."

Marie was okay with that, so I called Koussevitzky's number, although it was almost 6 p.m., and was able to tell the woman who answered who I was and that I wished to speak with Professor Koussevitzky. As I suspected, knowing the hours in European clinics were longer than in America, because they usually took a longer break for lunch, he soon came to the phone. I explained, "I have a clinical research project that I want to discuss with you."

We agreed that I could come to his office on the second floor at about 11:00 a.m. I said I would also like to meet Dr. Kandinsky if he were available, and Koussevitzky said he would try to arrange it.

"This worked out perfectly," I said to Marie. "You can go see the attorney while I'm talking with the neurologist. We could meet at the apartment building to sign the version approved by our attorney and then go to the office building. But I don't think I can get there before one-thirty, so you may have to handle the discussion until then. Or I could sign now on a separate page, and you can have the necessary changes made in the contracts. This way, the contract could be consummated even if I'm late."

"Good idea, Milt," she said.

Marie was successful in arranging to meet with the attorney on short notice, at 9:00 a.m., anticipating that she would be able to leave no later than 11:00 a.m., so she called the two real estate offices and arranged for finalizing the leases at noon and 2:30 p.m., respectively.

I can't imagine how I would've gotten all of this done without Marie.

52.

THE NEXT MORNING, Marie left first, since her appointment with the attorney was much earlier than mine at the EMC. With a little time to spare, I googled the EMC to see what I could find out about it. It was established in 1989 as a private multidisciplinary medical center in Moscow, partnered with a French company, and specialized in treating international patients, managing about 250,000 patients annually. Over time, it had evolved to four multidisciplinary hospitals in Moscow, and it was the first in Moscow to open a specialized cancer clinic. The EMC used American and European protocols for treatment.

I'm impressed.

This meant that they were experienced in performing research trials with the required ethics committee and research support staff. The website also indicated that the staff spoke English, French, and German, in addition to Russian, and had interpreters available for many other languages.

Suddenly, I received an email from Yuri Grobstein, telling me that he had arranged for me to be invited to the reception the following Monday evening at the Federal Agency for Scientific Organizations (FASO Russia), which was the governmental parent organization to the Russian Academy of Sciences. "The reception will honor the new President of the Russian Academy of Medical Sciences, Professor Aleksey Bolotkin." Yuri encouraged me to attend so he could introduce me to eminent Russian scientists and physicians, as well as officials of the Ministry of Science and Higher Education, which now governs all of the academies and state universities.

"I am sorry this is of short notice," he wrote, "but I did not know you would be here in Moscow at the time of this reception. I think it is very important for you to attend, especially since I convinced a high official of the Ministry to include you as a foreign guest. But remember to bring your passport, so you can be identified on the list of attendees."

He said, further: "There will be high security, since members of the Russian State Duma, or lower parliament, as well as many ministers, even President Putin, are expected to attend."

I immediately sent an email thanking him and accepting the invitation. "I am impressed at how quickly you could get me invited to this prestigious gathering, especially as a recently arrived American scientist not yet involved with any Russian organization or scientific group," I complimented him.

But do Yuri and the Russians have an ulterior motive?

I decided to text this information immediately to Brad.

*

THE METRO RIDE to the EMC station was short, and I had no problem following the GPS walking directions on my cell phone to the hospital center. The reception hall was modern, with a large cubist painting on the wall — probably a Braque or a copy of one, I thought. The receptionist telephoned Prof. Koussevitzky's office to announce me, and in short order, a woman with gray hair, rosy cheeks, and a nice smile introduced herself as Prof. Koussevitzky's secretary and asked me to follow her.

The professor, who was gaunt with thin grayish-brown hair and a wide and long gray mustache, hurried over to greet me with a firm handshake. I estimated that he was in his early fifties. He had a friendly smile and sparkling grayish-blue eyes.

"Welcome to Moscow and to the EMC, Dr. Davidson," he said. "Or better Milton if you would call me Sergeii."

"My pleasure, Sergeii. Just call me Milt."

"I'm curious as to what brings you to Moscow," he said, and I spent a few minutes filling him in. He was surprised to learn that I had formed a biopharmaceutical company with venture capital support from Russia, which provided the opportunity to establish a business subsidiary in Moscow.

"I thought that as a neurologist, you might be interested in assisting me in performing a proof-of-principle clinical trial to determine if delivering a therapeutic agent known to be active by giving pills or injections is feasible as an odor," I said. "Since the agent of interest, melatonin, is given to improve sleep problems and may also have other functions as an antioxidant, perhaps a small study in volunteers or patients could be of interest to you and the EMC, especially since I learned that you have a sleep clinic here."

"Ah, yes," said the professor, "this might be of interest, but it depends on the study objectives and whether we can do this here. We're involved in many protocols, but usually to treat patients with diseases and not volunteers where pharmacological studies are conducted."

He spoke very good English. "I'd have to share your protocol with my colleagues to see if there's an interest and the capability and, if so, it would have to be approved by our ethics committee."

"Thank you," I said. "I can email you a brief summary of the proposed clinical study. I would appreciate your comments and sharing it with your colleagues, but they need to agree to keep this confidential."

"Of course," he said. "If you have time, let me take you upstairs to meet the head of our medical center, Professor Andrey Krivoshapkin. He's a medical oncologist."

We took the elevator to the seventh floor and went to the director's administrative suite. When the director came out to greet us, Sergeii gave him — in Russian — a short introduction to me and explained my interest in doing a study with melatonin given by olfaction to confirm its action to improve sleep cycles.

So much for confidentiality.

In strongly accented English, the director said, "We are pleased to have you visit with us, and perhaps we can collaborate in your study." Then: "Which Russian businessman invested in your company?" He said the last part in Russian, which Professor Koussevitzky translated.

I felt put on the spot, since Yuri hadn't told me if I should keep his involvement confidential. Then again, he had arranged for me to attend the very public reception of the Russian Academy of Sciences.

"Yuri Grobstein is one of our investors," I said. "He had the interest to bring this business to Russia, which is why I'm here. The company, Pharmascent Sciences, is also registered in the USA and in France, but the first activities will be here in Moscow."

Professor Koussevitzky translated this too.

Professor Krivoshapkin then commented, again translated by Koussevitzky: "I have heard of him as a politically well-connected oligarch. This will help you in dealing with the Kremlin, I am sure."

After leaving the director, Sergeii took me to the basement to meet Dr. Alexander Kandinsky in the pathology department. We found him in the sign-out room, where the staff reviews the slides of tissue specimens prepared from various cases for diagnosis. He was sitting at a dual-headed microscope, evidently reviewing the slides with one of his junior staff members or students.

Sergeii walked over and spoke with him while I waited at the entrance. Dr. Kandinsky then looked at me and waved me over while he finished the interpretation of the slide he was viewing with the student.

"Welcome, Dr. Davidson," he said. "I heard you were coming to see me, and I'm delighted to meet you." He also spoke very good English.

"It's my pleasure," I said. "I also practice anatomic pathology at Empire State University in New York and conduct cancer research."

"Please come to my office so we can speak. Sergeii, do join us unless you are pressed for time; I can host our guest."

"I do have to return to my office," Sergeii said, "so I will say goodbye to Professor Davidson now. I will review the protocol summary and respond to you in the next couple of days. Don't hesitate to call me if I can be of any further help."

Dr. Kandinsky reminded me very much of a former pathology teacher I'd had, with dark-rimmed glasses, a high forehead, and heavy, long black hair, which he wore with long sideburns.

"We have a fully equipped pathology department here," he said, "with the latest microscopes, including an electron microscopy laboratory. I focus on tumor pathology, mostly from a clinical perspective. But we have so many patients and pathology specimens that I can hardly find time to undertake any research."

"I understand," I said. "I'm fortunate to be able to split my time with teaching medical students for a few months per year, rotating on the anatomic pathology or slide review responsibility, and then having about half of my time devoted to laboratory research under a grant from the government."

"What luxury!" Alex said. "Tell me about your research."

I explained, briefly, the studies in cancer genetics involving how cancers progress to advanced states of metastasis. Alex wanted to hear more details, so I explained the content of our impending article and promised to send him a copy when it was published.

Alex told me that he'd grown up in the Ukraine and that his family had suffered under the Soviet regime, but that he was able to attend medical school and then come to Moscow to work in this hospital. He was married to an architect's drafting assistant, he said, and they have two teenage children, a boy and a girl. They all participate in the educational program and religious services of the JCC.

"I would like to invite you to my home for a Friday night dinner, welcoming the Sabbath," he said.

"Thank you, but I really need a little more time to get settled before starting any social activities. I will certainly let you know when I have my life better organized," I said.

*

AS I MADE my way back to the Metro station, Marie texted me, saying she was already at the apartment building and gave me directions for getting there.

I arrived at the Smolenska Str. apartment building about thirty-five minutes later and met Marie in the management office's waiting room on the ground floor. Since we were the only people in the room, she brought me up-to-date.

The attorney did want some additional language defining the landlord's obligations to keep the premises and apartment in proper working condition. We also rented a car space in the garage, as recommended by my CIA handlers.

"We are finished here, since you already signed the last page on three copies; I'll return two to the management clerk," she said. "The apartment will be ready Friday, but we need to buy sheets, pillows, blankets, and some kitchen utensils and dishware before moving in."

After that, we went to the office building, where I signed the lease for Pharmascent. Marie introduced me to the building manager, Olga Katsyv, an elderly woman with gray hair tied back. Olga was fairly conversant in English, which made it easy for me to convey my office needs. Olga explained that getting telephone exchanges in Moscow, while easier for businesses, still took at least two weeks, usually quite more, but that she would make the order today.

The next need was to recruit an administrative assistant fluent in English and with some accounting or bookkeeping experience. Olga said they had a list of candidates, but that it may take some time unless I was especially lucky with the available candidates, some of whom might no longer be available. We agreed that she would check her list to determine active candidates and then send the resumés attached to an email to me.

How can I evaluate them from an espionage perspective? It would be easy to insert a mole into my operation, but then the manager, Olga, was unprepared for us to lease the office space until just these past couple of days.

I expressed my concern to Marie, who thought I was getting overly paranoid.

With that underway, Marie dragged me to a department store, TSUM, one of the largest and best-known stores in Russia. In fact, it was larger even than some of the biggest in New York and was a sightseeing wonder in and of itself. Marie appeared to know her way around, so she guided me quickly to the home furnishings departments, where we bought linens, towels, and even soaps and shampoos, and then onto kitchenware, where we found basic pots and pans, silverware, a toaster, and some other kitchen essentials.

A taxi got us and our packages back to our hotel quickly. After such a busy day, we wanted to stay in our rooms and have wine and take-out food. Marie dashed out to a local delicatessen-like store and soon surprised me with a bottle of red wine from Belarus, her birthplace — she reminded me — a loaf of thin white bread, Gervais and blue cheeses, and pot roast with cooked carrots and white beans. It was all delicious. I guess I was very hungry after the busy day.

We discussed our plans for Thursday, our last day before moving to the apartment, and I said I wanted to go to the JCC and set up a tutoring schedule. Marie needed to do some personal shopping before returning to Israel, and I didn't question it.

The less said about that, the better.

I did tell her about my invitation to attend the reception of the Russian Academy of Sciences with Yuri. Marie was surprised and impressed; she said that it's unusual for a foreign scientist visiting Moscow, especially an American, to partake in such events.

53.

WHEN I KNOCKED on Miriam Keslov's open door, she waved me in and stood to shake my hand.

"Dr. Davidson, welcome! I have been looking forward to getting started! Do you speak any Russian?"

"Almost none," I said, "though I tried practicing in a book on *Russian for Dummies*."

Miriam thought for a moment. "Russian can be difficult if we focus on grammar," she said, "but I think you are more interested in conversational language, correct?"

"I would like to study it properly, but I agree I would be satisfied if I could get by in conversing in Russian."

"Well," she said, "I will need to know your availability, so I can plan an instruction program and give you an estimate of costs for private tutoring." She spoke in a soft but nicely pitched voice. She then offered me a soft-covered manual that she wanted me to use and asked if I wanted to get started today so that she could gauge where I was and how she should organize my tutoring.

"Sure," I said.

"We can talk in the coffee shop if you like."

We found a quiet table in the corner after I got strong coffee and Miriam tea with lemon.

"So, tell me why you are here and your background, Dr. Davidson," she said.

It was apparently so strange that an American professor would come to Russia to start a biotechnology company that everyone had asked me the same probing questions. Having explained it so much already, I was able to cover the highlights in few minutes.

"I don't understand the science, of course," said Miriam, "but is not America more advanced than Europe, particularly Russia, in pioneering new areas of medicine, science, and industry?"

"In most ways, I suppose you're right," I said. "But in my case, I was starting a biopharmaceutical company that would be engaged in the U.S. and in Europe, and Russia provided an opportunity to get started quickly, since there were investment funds available, an ambition to get recognition in supporting commercialization of scientific and medical advances, and, in many ways, a less restrictive regulatory system to do clinical research. But I'll have to see if I'm correct in these assumptions. So, what about you?" I asked, turning the questions on Miriam. "Were you born here, or did you and your family emigrate?"

"I immigrated from Lithuania, where I grew up," she said. "My grandparents escaped the Stalin purges by living on a farm with a Christian family, where my parents also lived. When I was born, they decided to emigrate, and, at the time, the best prospect was coming to Russia. So, when I was five, I came to Moscow with my parents, and my father was able to get employment as an accountant in an import-export company.

"I fell in love with a university student when I was nineteen, and we eloped to get married, but this lasted only a few years, and there were no children. I then went back to school and studied at Moscow University, where I graduated with a degree in world literature. Although I was personally happy, it was difficult to find employment with this education, so I came to the JCC to work as a Russian tutor. I don't really need much because the JCC has many interesting programs, and cultural activities in Moscow are not expensive.

"But we need to be speaking in Russian," Miriam then said, "so that I can assess how to plan your tutoring."

We then began to simply talk as two people would after just greeting and asking how they are, what they are doing, where they are living, their work, and so on.

"You have some basic words," she said, now in English, "but really little knowledge of rudimentary sentences and grammar, so I will need to begin with some basics. Do you have time to come three times a week for an hour or so and opportunities to practice? Are you dealing only with Russians who speak English?"

"I think I can come Monday, Wednesday, and Friday mornings, especially if I can combine this with using the center's gymnasium and pool. Unless I'm traveling, I would like to start the day at seven-thirty or 8 a.m. exercising and swimming, then come to you for an hour of tutoring at about nine or so. Is this feasible for you?"

"I like it. In fact, it may be a good excuse for me to join you in the pool once or twice a week, since I have been too lazy to exercise as much as I should."

"That would be nice," I said. "Let's start next Monday, which will be my first day attending an official function in Russia."

"What is this event?"

"I am invited to a reception inducting the new President of the Russian Academy of Sciences, in a ballroom of the St. Regis Moscow Nikolskaya hotel," I said. "Do you know it?"

"Of course," she said. "This is perhaps the most famous hotel in the center of Moscow — only a few minutes' walk from Red Square and the Kremlin. It is a hotel where the government has many business and social functions. In fact, it is rumored that some members of the State Duma have financial interests in the hotel, possibly also Russia's president."

"I am honored that this invitation was extended to me so soon after my arrival, but I have to thank an oligarch who is one of our investors.

Coincidentally, he's Jewish and a member of a JCC outside of Moscow."

"Who is he?" Miriam asked.

"Yuri Grobstein."

"Yes, he is well known in the Jewish community because he does not hide his Jewishness, but he is, nevertheless, respected in the Russian business community and by senior government officials. It is rumored that he is an acquaintance or business associate of Vladimir Putin, but this is out of my expertise, of course."

Everyone has the same impression of him and his contact to the president.

"By the way," I said, "I have arranged to meet Katarina Breslau here on Sunday when her nephew Daniel is coming for Bar Mitzvah lessons. Will you be here?"

"Katarina? Is she going to be of assistance in your smell studies?"

So, Miriam has been advised about my need to get involved with the Breslaus.

"I would definitely like her to be. And I understand her brother is a chemist working for the government. It seems to be a project that prevents him from coming with his son to Moscow, correct?"

"You are clearly interested in this work," Miriam said. "Don't let it be so obvious," she said after confirming it is safe to talk. "Maybe I can see Katarina at services either Friday night or Saturday and casually mention that I have you as a new language student. I could then assess her interest. There is a rumor in the congregation that she and her mother are seeking to emigrate out of Russia, and, therefore, they may be very cautious speaking to strangers."

"Thank you," I said. "I would like to get to know the Breslau family, but I can't just begin a relationship so soon after moving here, especially if Dr. Breslau is doing some secret research for the military. But I'm sure you know that this is important."

She smiled at me and continued: "Mrs. Breslau also visits with Daniel occasionally, staying with him at the apartment that Katarina shares with her mother, or at their own apartment, which has been empty since their absence in Oryol. I see her, with Katarina, occasionally, but she rarely talks about their living in Oryol. But it is apparent that she is always delighted to visit Moscow, even if only for a couple of days occasionally."

Miriam didn't comment further but assigned me about six pages to study in the language manual, and we then parted with my thanking her for taking me on as a student.

*

I THEN WENT by the business office and signed up for the membership and tutoring, giving them a check covering six months. The office worker seemed pleased and surprised to get this done so fast, including payment for membership without having to send out a bill. I felt good about it because this affiliation served both my Scenturion Venture mission and my personal needs, especially getting back to exercising.

Leaving the business office, I proceeded to the pool, which was nearly empty except for a group of senior citizens having a class. In the locker room, I hung up my clothes and put on my bathing suit. It felt wonderful hitting the water and swimming a crawl across the long length in an empty lane and then taking a couple of laps in an underwater crawl. I felt revitalized after the last hectic days, and after about thirty minutes, I got out and relaxed in a lounge chair. I felt comfortable in this nostalgic surrounding away from home.

54.

BACK AT THE hotel, I took out my suitcase and started packing. After that, I began expanding the protocol for studying olfactory melatonin in patient volunteers. I emailed the Argus staff back in Maryland, telling them we would need more compound made under the FDA's Current Good Manufacturing Principles (cGMP) because of my plans to test this clinically, and I wanted our clinical data to be acceptable for review by the FDA.

After discussing the clinical trial with Sergeii, we concluded that we would likely be able to avoid doing preclinical, animal studies with the olfactory melatonin being prepared, as would normally be required before human testing of a new chemical entity. We all agreed that since melatonin is used so commonly without a doctor's prescription, we had a good chance of not being required to show safety in animals before testing in our human subjects. However, I knew this probably would not be permitted by the FDA, especially since there is no prior experience with melatonin in an odor form, so this could be another advantage to doing this clinical study in Russia, and then use it afterwards with other regulatory agencies.

Just after sending that note, my cell phone pinged with a text message. Jhanella was telling me to check my emails because our article in *Cancer Advances* was just published online. I stopped everything and scrolled down to find the communication from the journal that our article was now available publicly. I scanned the journal's website, found the pdf of our article, and read through it quickly to assure myself that it was published correctly.

It really looked great in print, and I just had to stare at the first page listing the title, authors, affiliation, and the abstract. This is always the rewarding part, when a high-impact, quality journal publishes your work for all of your peers to read and for your findings to become part of medical history.

I hoped Marie would arrive soon so I could share this news with her. I responded to Jhanella, telling her how good it looked in print and how grateful I was to my coauthors for their contributions. I also sent a copy of the article to my chairman, John Bickers, with a couple of sentences saying I was doing well and thought this paper would be of interest to him. I also sent it to Brad Williams and Dr. Kandinsky.

Marie arrived at about two o'clock with two croissants with tuna fish and soft drinks for a late lunch. She also had a few packages from the department store, which she said were small gifts for relatives in Israel, as well as some shoes and clothes for herself. I was surprised that Moscow might have shoes or clothing that were unavailable in Israel, much less in Paris.

I had learned long ago not to question a woman on a shopping mission.

I couldn't wait to show Marie the published article, and she congratulated me with a kiss.

"You waited long enough to get this published," she said, "so you deserve the excitement you feel at seeing it in print." I was a little embarrassed at that, since this wasn't my first publication, by far. But the excitement didn't decline with each subsequent one.

Marie said that we should go out for dinner to celebrate the publication and because we were finally moving to the apartment tomorrow. She said she would find a restaurant for a late dinner while I continued to work on the protocol and an agenda for Friday's Pharmascent board meeting.

Marie shares my bias for dining.

We changed for dinner at 7:00 p.m., and it was a short Metro ride to Tverskaya. And from there, we walked to Tverskoy Boulevard, with

Marie regularly checking the street behind and across from us. I then recognized the sign saying, *Café Pouchkine*.

"What a surprise, Marie," I said. "This is one of the best-known restaurants in Russia, but also very expensive."

"Yes," she said, "but it is really not expensive when you consider the quality of the food and the ambiance." We entered into a self-contained world of opulence and were immediately shown to our table, the formally dressed waiters wearing red vests hovering over us with menus, a breadbasket with butter and an olive dip. We ordered French champagne and Beluga caviar while we studied the extensive menu.

We toasted the publication of my article and to future articles. Marie also toasted to establishing Pharmascent Sciences in Moscow and to my soon starting a clinical trial, which reminded me how risky this was, especially using a medical system that was strange to me. This toasting got us to finish the entire bottle of champagne.

Then she admitted, in her less-guarded state, her anxiety at being called back to Tel Aviv, fearing that she may be reassigned and no longer together with me. "Maybe it has been concluded that I am a risk for the mission here, or I've been located by the Hezbollah who are also close to the Russian GRU," she said. "Or perhaps my loyalty is, for some reason, doubted. I am afraid of losing you, Milt, although perhaps I am making more out of our relationship than is the case."

"Don't jump to conclusions," I said. "They and my handlers know how much you helped me to get this project started here and all your help when I was in Paris. You know you have become special to me. Let's enjoy the evening."

"How did you ever get a reservation here on such short notice?" I asked to change the subject.

"A friend of mine at the French consulate knows the chef, so I imposed upon him to get us here tonight, and fortunately, it worked."

"Well, those are good contacts to have. Did you visit the French consulate today?"

"Yes, I did drop by to see a few friends, but only stayed a little while."

"You're certainly a busy woman, going shopping, visiting the consulate, what else?" I hoped she would see this as a friendly challenge.

"Oh, nothing important," she said.

What does she mean by "nothing important"?

We both savored our entrees, trout stuffed with fish mousse and baked under crayfish dressing, with champignons, shrimp and asparagus and parmesan for Marie, and arctic surgeon with stewed potatoes and tartar sauce for me.

We agreed to share an apple pie with vanilla ice cream serving and double espresso coffees, to end this wonderful experience.

It was about 10:30 p.m., merry from wine and the music, and glad that we'd had such a nice but fast week together in Moscow, when we finally left.

Back in the hotel, I finished almost all of my packing, telling Marie that I planned to go to the JCC very early in order to work out and swim before we moved to the new apartment. She said she would use that time to get our stuff organized.

"I also plan to go to the office building later in the day to interview two candidates for office manager," she said. "I've received two resumés from the building's support office, and one of them looks very interesting."

"That's very efficient of you, trying to identify an office assistant for me before you leave. You're not going to choose someone who's utterly unattractive, I hope."

"Of course," she responded. "I have to protect my interests," she said with a smile. "Since I have basic knowledge of Russian and experience in interrogation, both the Mossad and your agency thought I should help you find a suitable and safe assistant," she added.

What are your flight plans?" I asked.

"I am on an Air France flight from SVO airport to Charles de Gaulle in Paris, leaving here at 8:45 a.m. and arriving at 10:05. Then I connect to El Al, departing CDG at 2:45 p.m. arriving at Ben-Gurion airport at 8 p.m. It will be a long day. I decided not to fly directly from Moscow to Tel Aviv, so as not to arouse any suspicion with Russian intelligence, since my trip to Moscow originated in Paris. I also wanted to keep my disguise on until I am in the El Al plane en route to Tel Aviv."

"That's smart," I said. "You know I won't be able to go to the airport with you, since I have to be at the JCC early on Sunday, where I agreed to meet with my tutor." I didn't want to say that it was really the pharmacist whose brother was a chemist at the secret chemistry laboratory in Oryol. My handlers didn't want me to discuss any of that with Marie.

I'm always unsure what I can and cannot share with her.

"That's fine," she said. "I can manage on my own to the airport, but I will miss you nevertheless during this absence."

55.

WHEN I ARRIVED at the JCC at about 8 a.m., it was busy with students in the hallways and adults mingling and talking in different corridors.

I then went to the gym, where I changed and spent the next thirty minutes on the cardio equipment. Afterwards, I swam laps in the pool, for a half hour. I felt winded, so clearly out of condition, as I climbed out of the pool. And who was standing there holding my towel for me but Miriam.

"It looks like you had a busy morning here," she said, handing me my towel.

"Yes, but I'm also out of shape. I need to exercise more regularly."

"Will you come to services tonight?"

"No, and tomorrow is a busy day for me, but I plan to be here on Sunday. Are the Breslau boy and his aunt going to be here too?"

"They usually attend on the Sabbath of the weekend Daniel comes for Bar Mitzvah lessons and will certainly be here Sunday morning."

"Good. As you know, I want to meet with Katarina, since I need some advice from a pharmacist."

"Well, as I said the other day, if I see her first — maybe tonight — I'll mention you and let her know you will be looking for her."

I figured Miriam would let my handlers know of my plans through her Mossad contact, although I wasn't sure about her precise role and contacts — only that she was someone I could confide in and who could get information to the CIA officers at the U.S. Embassy through her Mossad contacts. I knew she wasn't directly involved with the CIA; instead, she was probably a *Sayan*, a non-Israeli Jew used by the Mossad to support their efforts in foreign countries, in this case, Russia. The Mossad had a network of Sayanim serving as contacts and resources abroad. Brad certainly knew this.

*

MARIE WAS WORKING on her laptop when I came in, completed her typing, and quickly closed her laptop as I said hello.

"How was your workout?" she asked, looking up with a big smile.

"Oh, fine," I said. "But I'm clearly out of shape, with only two workouts in more than a week and all those rich meals that you insist I enjoy."

"You look fine to me," she said. "In fact, I sometimes worry that I don't have your stamina." That line was delivered with her perfect coquettish smile. "We're almost ready to check out — how much time do you need?"

"I just have to change and pack some papers and my computer, which should take me all of thirty minutes. I'm excited to move into my new apartment in Moscow!" I added, noticing a sudden frown on her face.

We crammed everything into a taxi and, in about fifteen minutes, were at the apartment building. With assistance from the building superintendent, we soon got our bags and carry-ons upstairs and into the flat. We were pleasantly surprised to find how clean everything was. There was even some furniture that hadn't been there when we first toured the apartment, such as night tables in the bedroom, a couple of extra sofa chairs in the living room, and a desk and chair in the second bedroom.

Marie first took time to check that the rooms were secure from bugs or video devices. Then she went to make the bed and distribute the towels and bathroom contents before we left for the office to interview the candidates for office manager, so I walked around and tested everything out, including the TV in the living room. It wasn't as new as the one we'd had in the hotel, but it would suffice for me, since I only watched a couple of channels.

While Marie was busy in the bedroom, I called out to see if she had a pen that I could use, since I had misplaced mine.

"Check my handbag on the kitchen table!" she said.

I looked inside but couldn't find a pen among all the stuff women typically carry around. Then I went to the closet, where I had seen Marie place another handbag and took it out. I was surprised to see a small revolver in the side pocket, as well as a pen. I took them both out and walked into the bedroom.

"I found a pen in your other handbag, but what's this surprise?" I held up the gun. "How did you get this here in Moscow?"

"You shouldn't have opened my other purse!" she answered.

"When and why did you get this?"

"I got it during my visit to the Israeli embassy. I am in Moscow, and I know the GRU plays rough. After leaving the Israeli embassy, I was being followed. So now I realize this wasn't a good move going there.

"I didn't notice any surveillance on our walks," I said, "but I did see that you were often checking the rear."

"Yes. I am afraid that I am a risk to the Scenturion Venture, as we experienced in Paris, and this is maybe why I have been recalled to The Office."

"You really think you won't be allowed to return?"

"It is a likely explanation for the abrupt order to return to Tel Aviv, since I expected to remain here for at least another month."

"And what will you do with the gun?"

"I was planning to get rid of it safely, probably in the Moscow River. It is not something you should have seen. If discovered, it would destroy your role as an American scientist developing a business here. Are we ready to go to the office?"

"Yes," I said, and we just picked up our briefcases, locked the door, and left. "So, you made sure the new apartment was free of bugs?"

"Yes," said Marie, "but you will need to provide a key to your CIA handler, so they can do routine comprehensive searches."

I'm not telling her that that's already been arranged.

When we got to the building, Marie directed me to the administrative office. They had a conference room for use by the residents, and she left me there while she went to talk with Olga Katsyv, who had arranged the meetings.

We decided to interview each candidate separately, since both were here and waiting. This worked well, since of the two, I decided on thirty-six-year-old Julia Daskalov, who had a ten-year-old son with her husband, Pyotr. Julia had had diverse office experience, even working in a startup publishing company, and her English was very good. I found her personable, well-dressed, and well-versed in all office procedures, especially computer skills. Julia could work in the office only from 9:00 a.m. until 1:00 p.m., Monday through Friday, which was exactly the coverage I needed at first; otherwise, the building also provided receptionist services.

After conferring with Marie, who agreed with my assessment, we made Julia an offer, and she accepted immediately, saying she could start on Monday. I then made a list of some additional office equipment and a couple of chairs that I needed, and Marie made the arrangements with the resident management to have these provided.

We returned to the apartment, since I had the Pharmascent board of directors call at 5 p.m. local time, and I needed to do a little preparation. I also had to text Sergeii Koussevitzky at the EMC to find out if my summary of the protocol was acceptable to him and his colleagues.

Marie used this time to go shopping because she wanted to cook a meal for our first evening in the new apartment. Before she left, I took her in my arms and gave her a long kiss, which she understood was my way of thanking her for her devotion to me in so many ways.

*

SERGEII RESPONDED THAT he felt confident they could execute my protocol to study melatonin as an odor in normal volunteers, but he was concerned that their toxicology lab couldn't do the assays to measure melatonin and its metabolic products in urine and blood. We needed this information in order to assess how much of the odor that entered the nose was delivered to the blood circulation by the nasal capillaries, which would deliver melatonin independently of really smelling. He said he would inquire and possibly find another laboratory that could do it. We agreed to meet at his office on Tuesday afternoon. He also asked if he could have me to his home for dinner.

"I would love to meet your family," I said. "I can book a Yandex car to take me back to my apartment, so you won't be inconvenienced." I knew the CIA would want to know how my attendance at the Russian Academy of Sciences reception with Yuri Grobstein had gone, and the Yandex was a convenient cover. I told Sergeii that I would send him the latest version of the full protocol by Sunday.

At 5 p.m., I called into the international conference number arranged for our board meeting. I called the meeting to order and thanked everyone for making the time available, and began by specifying that I was chairing the meeting, which had been called earlier in the week, that we had all directors present, thereby fulfilling a quorum, and that our new New York business attorney, Bart Orlove, also on the call, would serve as secretary and prepare the minutes.

I began by summarizing the legal filings to do business in Russia, U.S., and France. I reported that I had leased an apartment as well as office space in downtown Moscow, these leases committing me for up to one year but with clauses allowing earlier termination with the loss of one month's rent. I said that I was negotiating with the European Medical Centre to do our first dosing trial of melatonin given as an odor in a small group of normal volunteers. I explained that this was a proof-of-concept study and not necessarily a first product, although there would be commercial opportunities for an odorous melatonin if we could prove effective delivery by this route.

Yuri offered to be of assistance if I experienced any delays or bureaucracy getting the trial started, saying he thought Russian ethics committees were usually more flexible than those in many Western countries. I agreed and said that so far, there was interest and that I would soon be submitting a protocol to the neurologist whom I hope to have as principal investigator.

The second order of business was to define my spending authority, which Simon Fass suggested should be $150,000 per matter. This was moved and seconded and then adopted unanimously.

The next order of business was to appoint committees of the board. We decided to have an Executive Committee, consisting of Robert Selden, Yuri Grobstein, and myself, to act for the entire board when the latter could not be assembled in a timely fashion. The Audit Committee would be constituted by Otto Pinedo and Rene Marseult; the Compensation Committee by Simon Fass, Robert Selden, and Otto Pinedo; and the Governance and Nominating Committee by Robert Selden, Simon Fass, and Rene Marseult. This was approved unanimously.

Robert Selden asked how long I thought we would be operating in Moscow. This was a sensitive question, since Yuri had his priorities, and I was expected to build the business first in Russia. Of course, they had no idea that the Scenturion Venture was the critical aspect defining my activities in Moscow.

I responded, "If the clinical trial went smoothly, it would make sense to continue here so long as the quality met FDA and European regulatory standards." I said that "advancing the business in the U.S. was, of course, a priority, but I could do this only after finding a manager for the Russian operation, should I return to the U.S., which was my goal." Apparently, this was acceptable, since there were no further comments made.

Simon asked, "Is Marie still assisting you?"

I responded that she was leaving Moscow soon and probably would be returning to Paris. Her travels to Israel were, of course, a secret, since other than Simon, she wasn't known to be associated with the Mossad. As her employer, Simon was, of course, concerned about if and when he could expect her back at Toilette.

I advised the directors that Yuri had been very helpful and, in fact, "had arranged for me to be invited to a ceremony to install the new President of the Russian Academy of Sciences, which would occur on Monday evening."

Yuri then explained: "This will give Milt an opportunity to meet many of the Russian leaders in science, government, and industry." He also added that he would accompany me.

The last order of business was to make two board officer appointments. I nominated Yuri to be Chairman and Simon Fass as Secretary/Treasurer, as well as myself as CEO and President, as well as a board member, which were approved unanimously. We were finished with this organizational meeting in about forty-five minutes, which seemed to please everyone, and agreed to have a second telephonic board meeting within a couple of months or so unless needed sooner.

56.

BY THE TIME Marie returned, balancing several packages, I had made very good progress on the clinical research protocol that I wanted to send to Sergeii by Sunday.

"I see you had no problem shopping," I said, as Marie plopped her packages down on the kitchen counter.

"I went to a supermarket in the neighborhood, a butcher shop, and also a bakery," she said, "so I think we should have enough ingredients for my cooking tonight and maybe even tomorrow night. But I am out of practice, so I did not plan anything elaborate."

"Well, after eating out continuously over the past week, I look forward to some home cooking and relaxing in our own apartment."

"You mean *your* apartment," she said, "but I appreciate the thought. How did your board call go?"

"Really well. Short and to the point, but I do need to develop a budget and plan for the company very soon. I don't feel ready for that yet."

"Oh, you'll get it done, I am sure. But I know it will be difficult in a foreign country and with as yet little support, although I think your clinical contacts and Yuri Grobstein will be very important."

"I worked on the clinical protocol, which I hope to send to the EMC by Sunday," I said. "Then I'll visit Sergeii on Tuesday and maybe get it revised for submission to their hospital ethics committee a week or so later."

"That is very aggressive and optimistic," Marie said, "but I don't underestimate you."

"Did you run into any problems?" I asked.

"No, but you know the feeling you sometimes get of being watched? I had this all the time while shopping but could not identify anyone following me."

"You're experienced enough to rely on your instincts, but maybe they were from the CIA, DGSE, or even the Mossad?"

"Yes, maybe. But it also means I am here too long, and I need to return to Israel, where I don't have to look over my shoulder all of the time."

Over the next half-hour, I heard a lot of movement and noise from the kitchen, so I finally called out to ask what she was cooking.

"Don't expect much, chérie," she said, laughing. "I hardly have time to be a cook, but I am doing my best to offer a modest and tasty dinner."

About an hour later, the table was set, and I was impressed to see a fresh loaf of bread cut so we could remove slices evidently warmed and covered with garlic, a bowl of salad containing cucumber, carrot, and tomato slices on a bed of lettuce, with vinegar and olive oil bottles for the dressing, and a bowl of spaghetti, a bowl of meatballs, and parmesan cheese. We also had a bottle of Italian Chianti.

"Wow, I didn't realize you were going to make all of this," I said. "It's very impressive."

"*Merci beaucoup*," she said. "I also filled the kitchen pantry and refrigerator so you can operate for a few days before having to shop again. I also bought some fish for dinner tomorrow night if you survive tonight's meal."

"You are really something," I said. "I'm going to miss—"

But she cut me off. "Let's just eat and not talk so much," she said.

I savored the food and asked how the meatballs were made — they were unusually good.

"I combined beef, veal, and pork ground meat and sautéed it in a frying pan with melted butter, if you must know the chef's tricks."

"Not exactly kosher, with pork," I remarked.

"Did you expect me to be Jewish and also kosher?"

I decided not to respond.

The wine was very nice and not heavy, and it went well with this.

"And what do we have for dessert?" I ventured to ask.

"Pie a la mode, with apple pie from an excellent bakery that I found a few streets away."

After coffee, we ended the evening by sharing the bathtub, where we relaxed in each other's arms for almost an hour before crawling into bed. This was an amorous evening with a woman I had come to admire and possibly even love. I guess Marie had similar feelings, because she began whispering her concerns about our uncertain future.

"I fear that I will not be returning to Moscow and that we will not see each other again. Do you feel this also?"

"It has crossed my mind," I said, "but we're so involved together in the Scenturion Venture and my new company that it's hard for me to imagine that you'll simply disappear."

"What would you say if I wanted to leave the service and just move in here and be with you until you return to the U.S., and we could decide then whether we wanted to live together?"

"I would say you would be a little hasty in making such a decision, and we really need to determine if this is the life we want. We work closely together and are intimate, but is this a real-life or a pressured situation? After returning from your trip, which I'm sure you will, I think everything will be clearer."

Marie was then still, and we repositioned ourselves and remained quiet. I wasn't sure if she were asleep, but I certainly wasn't. All I could think about was the conversation we'd just had, which confused me. It must've been an hour or more before I finally dozed off, only to think about it all in a semiconscious state.

*

IN THE MORNING, Marie rolled over and kissed me as if nothing of consequence had happened the night before. She was all smiles, anxious to get up and plan our last day before she left for Israel.

"I think we should just relax and take a long walk in Gorky Park," Marie said.

"I like that," I said.

We were at the park within the hour, and soon we found a remote bench away from the walking path. We sat close together so we could speak softly, and Marie even pulled up the neck of her turtleneck sweater above her mouth so as to prevent any telescopic viewing of her talking. I covered my mouth with my hand as often as I could remember.

"I think I am distrusted by the Mossad," Marie whispered, "and maybe also the French secret service, and, for this reason, I am being recalled and will undergo an interrogation."

I didn't say anything, knowing this was still on her mind, and just waited for her to continue.

"I haven't been totally honest with you, Milt," she said. "We came to France from Israel because of my father being recruited as a DGSE agent by the French. This was, of course, after we had emigrated from Belarus to Israel. But my father, who was an engineer, had also been pressured by the Russian military spy agency to be an undercover spy for them in France, and because he had a brother and family in the former Soviet Union that was still under Russian control, he felt that he couldn't refuse. So, he became one of their agents who was employed by the French DGSE on technical issues involving Russia.

"Eventually, he was exposed and convicted of treason and sentenced to prison in France. This left my mother and me destitute. So, as I grew up, I became dependent on support from France, which actually helped me get an education and eventually an advanced degree from the Sorbonne. My mother and I separated when she went to live with a cousin on a farm in northeastern France, and I would see her very infrequently, but we keep in contact by phone and by an occasional letter.

"She is doing well but resents that I am involved with the very spy agency that took her husband and my father away. My father died in prison about two years ago, a broken man whom we visited maybe twice a year.

"Because I had chemistry courses at the Sorbonne, and because France had given me an education despite my father being convicted of espionage, I felt an obligation to France. So, when the DGSE recruited me, I accepted. The DGSE even supported my being trained by the Mossad and becoming a joint asset. I did not know that such a thing was possible, but my Zionist feelings made me happy with this arrangement, which led to my employment with Toilette, evidently a company established in France by former Mossad agents. Eventually, I came to believe that both countries were collaborating over concerns that Russia was developing olfactory weaponry.

"Then you came into the picture, and I was told to make your acquaintance to learn what the CIA was doing. Clearly, the Mossad knew of your association with the CIA, and although cooperating with them, they wanted a direct contact by their own agent, in this case, me."

"So, your meeting and affair with me were destined by the Mossad?"

"Yes, to meeting you, but the Mossad frowns on women agents using their sex and getting emotionally entangled in their work. My handlers actually disapproved because they thought this would make me vulnerable, which, I guess, was correct. I was vulnerable, and you just overwhelmed me and, I guess I could not stay objective and uninvolved. This is where the Mossad, the DGSE, and probably also your CIA began distrusting me, and I myself felt dishonest to you, with whom I was falling in love.

"I know that you have not shared all of your activities with me, Milt, and this is good, since I feel vulnerable and probably will undergo intense interrogation from my Mossad bosses, which is understandable. But I must assure you that I have been loyal to both the DGSE and the Mossad, and, of course, I have not intentionally compromised you."

What a story! What an admission!

"Do you think you can straighten this all out with the Mossad?" I asked.

"I don't know. They are clearly suspicious, and I don't know what role, if any, the CIA may have in this."

I was now concerned that she was probing, so I simply didn't respond.

"Do you want me to do anything to help?" I asked.

"I think anything you say will not be useful," said Marie. "They consider you an involved lover."

"If we can get answers to what Russia is doing in olfaction for military purposes, maybe we could defuse the mistrust. Do you think?"

"I am not sure if this alone would be enough," said Marie, "but certainly it could be helpful, since the DGSE, Mossad, and CIA will have completed their joint mission successfully. But I do not believe it is that simple. In any case, I return to Tel Aviv tomorrow night and will be in Mossad hands until they can give me a clean clearance. Otherwise, I fear we will not see each other again."

I put my arm around her shoulder and squeezed her close to me, trying to comfort her, though we both knew the future was very unpredictable.

She clearly has concerns about her future welfare.

*

THAT NIGHT WAS the most difficult we ever spent together. We did have a snack in the early evening, more out of custom than hunger. Marie spent a little time finishing her packing because she'd ordered a car to pick her up at six-thirty. I busied myself on my computer, working to complete the clinical research protocol. It was in pretty good shape, but I didn't want to leave much to be completed on Sunday because of my meeting with Katarina Breslau. I wasn't sure how much time I would have with her; I didn't want to limit it if she were available beyond just our meeting.

Marie and I went to bed early, setting the alarm for 5:30 a.m. Marie was very affectionate, kissing and embracing me as if this would be our last contact, at least for a good while. I reciprocated, realizing that she did mean much more to me than I had realized until today, when she'd confided so much to me. She seemed truly fearful of what lay ahead, and I wanted to give her as much support and comfort as I could — although I certainly didn't know what the spy agencies were deciding about her.

Or about me too.

Oh my God, had it made any sense for me to take this sabbatical to become a spy while exploring my interest in olfaction therapy? Had it made any sense for me to have left so much important cancer research to my colleagues back in New York?

This reduced commitment was no way to pursue a science project seriously — I knew that. But I had become trapped in this Scenturion Venture because of my ego. I had become convinced of my own importance in helping protect my country from its enemies, especially Russia, and romanticized about being another Bourne or Bond, although I didn't have their physique or abilities.

And now, I was so deeply involved that there was no way to extricate myself. At this point, my only exit strategy would be to learn what the Russians had cooked up in Oryol and to get Pharmascent Sciences in such good shape in Moscow that I could hire a scientifically oriented manager to take over, allowing me to return to New York. But I knew I wouldn't be able to do that until the clinical trial was either completed or very far along.

I am stuck here.

In the morning, I helped Marie to her Yandex car, and we only kissed quickly as a farewell, since we'd said all that we had to say the night before. We were tired, too, having just gotten a couple hours of sleep. Marie did turn her head as the car drove off, waving to me from the rear window.

I was depressed as I returned to the apartment, which already felt cold and empty without her.

57.

THE JCC SEEMED very crowded and noisy this Sunday morning. Classes were in full swing, and adults were busy with their different meetings.

I peeked into Miriam's office and saw her sitting with a young boy with long blonde hair and full, rosy cheeks. He was a little pudgy, typical for a twelve-year-old. Miriam stopped when she saw me and introduced Daniel Breslau. She then said that Katarina was expecting me in the library, where she usually reads as she waits for Daniel. Daniel was with Miriam until his Bar Mitzvah teacher was available.

I hurried over to the library and immediately recognized Katarina. She looked like someone related to Daniel, also having blonde hair and a somewhat short, stocky body, and a friendly smile as I approached her. We greeted each other and kept our voices low, since others were reading or browsing in the library. I invited Katarina to the coffee shop so we could talk and fortunately found a table in the corner away from most of the others there.

"I've heard a lot about you," she said in her heavily-accented English, "and understand you may need a pharmacist for your project. Is it Doctor or Professor Davidson?"

"It's Milt," I said. "In the U.S., it's Doctor, but in Europe, it's Professor, since Europeans are more formal about academic titles. It's nice of you to help your nephew with his Bar Mitzvah training. Does your brother, I believe his name is Joshua, ever visit? I understand he is a chemist. I'm curious as to what chemistry he practices and if you have a specialization in pharmacy."

"Yes, Joshua is a chemist, but rarely comes to Moscow. I'm a very general pharmacist, working here in Moscow and support the needs of the physicians and patients," she said. "I also participate in providing the drugs and placebos used in our clinical trials. I'm sure you know that the EMC conducts a lot of international clinical trials, since we have an international roster of physicians and patients, especially oncologists and cancer patients."

"Yes, I do know that. My own field of research in New York is also cancer, although I'm a pathologist and not a medical oncologist. Still, I do interact with the oncology team in our multidisciplinary conferences before a course of therapy is chosen. I'm discussing a new protocol with your Dr. Koussevitzky but involving the sense of smell.'

"You mean Professor Sergeii Koussevitzky?"

"Yes, of course. I'm trying to evaluate an agent that can affect sleep disorders, but which will be given as an odor."

"An odor?"

"Yes, the olfactory receptors can deliver signals directly into the brain. This has been a totally neglected area of drug delivery, and I'm trying to develop 'olfactory pharmacology' in a new company I've founded."

"Fascinating," said Katarina. "I had no idea that this could be done, but how do you determine which chemicals will bind to the smell receptors and stimulate the brain?"

"That's the challenge," I said, "and since olfaction is perhaps the most neglected of our five senses, in terms of knowledge and research, we need to proceed by trial-and-error, starting with categories of drugs that we believe are perceived by our sense of smell and affect our body."

"And I suppose you need a pharmacist to help make or deliver the odor in some quantified manner?"

"Exactly," I said. "You understand this well, and I would like to solicit your assistance. If you agree, I could include you as one of the participating investigators. Of course, the company will pay the EMC for the appropriate amount of time devoted by each of its staff."

"I am interested, but of course, I will need to review the trial design and what my contribution is before I can agree. I will also need to get the permission of the chief pharmacist."

"Good," I said, and then returned to my question about her brother. "And is your brother involved in pharmaceutical research or in some pure chemistry research?"

"I am not really sure what Joshua does," said Katarina. "He occasionally mentions that he synthesizes compounds that affect moods and have pharmaceutical potential, but as with most government pharmaceutical research, it is kept secret."

"Unfortunately, this is common in the pharmaceutical industry," I said, "but I thought most of the major pharma labs were in the big cities, like Moscow and St. Petersburg."

"Joshua is in a small city south of Moscow, Oryol, and I frankly do not know which drug laboratory it is. In Russia, we don't ask too much more than we are told, as I am sure you can imagine."

"I didn't want to pry, but for a Jewish chemist to work in a small rural area and send his son back to the big city for religious training, especially Judaism, which hasn't fared well in Russia in the decades since the Second World War, is quite exceptional."

"I agree," said Katarina, "but he seems happy, and Daniel also enjoys his trips here and staying with his aunt and grandmother for one weekend or more a month. It gives him a different perspective about Russia than his schoolmates in Oryol. Sometimes, his mother also visits with him, and I get time with her, since we like to shop together."

This was very interesting and suggested that although Dr. Breslau was under tight control in Oryol, his wife had some travel freedom. This could be important, I thought, and needed to be communicated to my CIA handlers.

But I bet they know this already.

I concluded that that was as far as I could go without arousing Katarina's suspicion, so I changed the subject, asking about her family and how they managed during the years that Jews were discriminated against under Stalin and some of the later presidents. Katarina was quite talkative, saying they had been fortunate because her grandfather was a prominent psychiatrist who treated high-level government ministers, and her grandmother came from a family that was well-respected and educated, even by the communists who were quite anti-intellectual.

We had a second cup of coffee as we waited for Daniel to finish his lessons with the Bar Mitzvah rabbi. At about eleven-thirty, Rabbi Barenholtz came into the café with Daniel, proceeding to our table.

"Are you hungry for lunch, Daniel?" Katarina asked.

Before he could respond, I said, "Please, let's all get a table together for lunch. Are you available, Rabbi?"

Rabbi Barenholtz smiled but shook his head, explaining that he had another lesson to teach. So, Katarina, Daniel, and I all went to the dining room together. Soon Miriam came in and joined us at the buffet line.

The conversation was just general small talk, with some focus on Daniel and how he liked living and attending school in Oryol. He told us, in reasonably good English, that he was the only known Jewish student in the school, and sometimes the other kids either made fun of him or bullied him, but the teachers were polite and treated him well.

I thanked Katarina for her time and wished Daniel well in his studies. Before heading back to my apartment, I told Katarina that if she would give me her email address, I would send my protocol for her review, but to please keep it confidential. I explained that Professor Koussevitzky completed an NDA which covered her institution, which would include her, so we could dispense upon doing this again.

When I was ready to leave, I returned to Miriam downstairs and informed her that I couldn't come to our first lesson on Monday, since I would be moving into my new offices with a new hire as office manager.

"I'll see you on Wednesday," I said.

Miriam was very understanding but encouraged me to try to read the first chapter of the language manual she'd given me so I would have some familiarity with the Russian Cyrillic alphabet. I knew this would be a challenge, but I didn't want to appear unwilling.

I also reminded her that I would be at the Russian Academy of Sciences affair that night, thus putting some time pressure on me for Monday. I also mentioned that I planned to have dinner at Dr. Koussevitzky's home on Tuesday evening, mentioning that it would be my first ride with the Yanex car service. I hoped she would pass that on, since I had not received confirmation that the CIA would have a substitute car for our clandestine meeting.

*

I ARRIVED BACK at my apartment before 2:00 p.m., and after a short break to relax, I returned to my protocol draft, which I completed in a couple of hours and sent to Sergeii, with a copy to Katarina.

I hadn't heard from Marie about her arrival in Paris, so after I finished eating, I texted her.

She responded immediately: "Arrived about an hour late because of a delayed departure, but all is fine. I love you and miss you!"

I was relieved to hear from her, since I had felt a kind of low-level concern about her all morning, especially after the time she was supposed to have landed. I was surprised that I felt this way about someone.

Then, I turned my attention to overdue correspondence, including to Tania Kudnoska, who'd sent me an email a few days earlier. I told her I was very busy during this first week or so in Moscow and that I had linked up with the JCC that she'd told me so much about. I said I was taking Russian lessons with Miriam Keslov and was hoping to begin a clinical trial of my first test odor at the European Medical Centre.

Surprisingly, despite the early hour in New York, Tania replied immediately, thanking me for this information and asking if I had a personal Russian guide for my sightseeing and restaurant experience. I wrote back that I did have a business associate who'd grown up in the Soviet Union and who had just left to return to Israel. I didn't mention anything more about her, but I knew I shouldn't underestimate Tania's ability to read between the lines.

What really surprised me was her mentioning that she might have to return to Moscow for a short while to resolve her marriage dissolution. I said that I was excited at the prospect of seeing her again. In actuality, I became concerned that her visiting me in Moscow could complicate everything, with Pharmascent, with my collaboration, and, more importantly, with the CIA.

Why do I get into these imbroglios so easily?

When it was approaching the time that I expected Marie to land at Ben-Gurion airport, I just put on the TV while I waited for her text message or call. I started getting worried at about 8 p.m., since that would've been about the time Marie should have been collecting her luggage from baggage claim. At 9 p.m., I texted her. With no response, I called her cell phone at about 10 p.m., and there was no response at all, not even a recorded message.

I couldn't fall asleep, having not heard from her. I checked El Al on the Internet, where the arrival of her scheduled flight was confirmed. I even called El Al but, of course, they wouldn't provide information on a specific passenger's itinerary or arrival.

I decided to wait until the morning before I made any other inquiries or efforts to locate her, but I hardly slept, keeping my cell phone at the bedside.

I was wide awake at 6 a.m. and still no message from Marie, so I was now very concerned. I decided to text Simon Fass at Toilette in Paris, asking if he'd heard from her. At 8 a.m., Simon responded that she hadn't contacted him but that he would inquire with her relatives in Tel Aviv, which was his way of signaling that he would contact the Mossad.

I was dressed by 7 a.m. but had nowhere to go. I just felt like I had to be prepared to leave; I was very upset. I sent a message about Marie's silence to Brad Williams in Washington, D.C., but it was in the middle of the night there, and I wouldn't be hearing from him anytime soon.

I made a pot of coffee and waited a little longer before finally having to leave for the office, to be there when my new assistant arrived.

58.

JULIA ARRIVED IN a long, warm gray coat and a wide-brimmed hat. She smiled hello and moved quickly to remove her coat and hat, and to push her hair back with her left hand. Evidently, she was exposed to the wind on her way here. She looked very well dressed, with a long black dress falling well below her knees and a black belt emphasizing her narrow waist.

She was surprised and embarrassed when I handed her a cup of coffee, as if I might have done it to remind her that this was her job. I assured Julia that I enjoyed making coffee, especially if I were the first to arrive. She responded with a gaping smile and nodded her head to express her understanding.

I told her I appreciated her good knowledge of English and that it would take quite some time for me to be able to speak Russian.

After looking around, Julia said we needed a phone system, which I assured her we had ordered already from the building manager, as well as some basic office equipment. She was also going to find out from the building's support services what we could use and when the company name would be displayed on the building directory and outside our door.

The rest of the morning was devoted to our discussing the filing system, my forwarding important documents from my computer to the company computer temporarily provided by the building management, a copy of my protocol draft, and the names and addresses of our board, attorneys, and other business contacts.

Julia learned very quickly, and in fact, had more experience than I at these office matters, so I just delegated it all to her. She said very politely that when my time permitted, she would like to learn as much about the business and our plans as possible, which I took as a very good sign of her interest and ambition to advance. I didn't suspect any spying, but I knew that I needed to be cautious here in Russia.

Julia seemed to get a lot done for the first day, and before we knew it, it was 1:00 p.m., and she was ready to leave. I didn't want to leave yet, although I did need to get home by about five p.m. to dress for the reception. I remembered there was a cafeteria on the second floor of the office building, so I decided to go down for lunch and socialize with my co-tenants.

The cafeteria was reasonably large and very well lit. It had trays and a food line, including some warm dishes, salads, soup, and desserts. I chose my usual tuna fish sandwich with chips and grapefruit juice and took my tray to a table with two occupants, a man and a woman.

I said hello (*zdravstvujtye*) in my accented Russian, to which they responded in Russian and then asked, in English, if I were British or American. So much for my Russian pronunciation, where one word identified me as a foreigner with English as my mother language.

I learned they were both with different companies in the building, the woman with a film contracting group and the man with an engineering company that consulted on product manufacturing. They were very interested in learning about Pharmascent, even from the little I shared.

I excused myself after finishing the meal and returned to my office, where I cleaned off my desk, looked around with some pride of my first business venture, and then called the receptionist to announce that I was leaving and wanted our calls taken by her. I also gave her my cell phone number in case there was an urgent call for me, which, of course, I had no reason to expect. I was pleased that this communication had taken place with my rough Russian combined with some English. I turned off the lights, locked up, and took the elevator down.

*

YURI'S LIMOUSINE WAS punctual, waiting for me as I exited my apartment building at 6:45 p.m. I had on a dark blue suit, white shirt with light blue tie, and black shoes, whereas Yuri was dressed in black-tie and all the formal accessories. He said that the Russian Academy of Sciences' event was being held was a short distance away, but we had a lot to discuss before getting there, so he told his driver to take his time driving around.

"I need to inform you that I had an unexpected visit by two FSB agents late in the previous week. They had said they wanted to learn more about me and my involvement with Pharmascent, but they also wanted to know of my involvement, if any, with the JCC that you were visiting," he advised.

I immediately expressed my concern to him that his statement to me about the FSB being interested in the JCC may have been conveyed to them by Marie, who has departed from Moscow. This may have compromised him with the FSB. I told him that my acquaintance, Marie, may have said something, since I had mentioned his statement about the JCC being a focus of interest for the FSB to her.

"I am not concerned," Yuri then said. "Everyone knows it is expected of them to closely watch Jewish Groups with Zionist interests, and this JCC certainly qualifies for that. But if your acquaintance may be a link to them, this means you need to be very, very cautious."

Of course, I couldn't explain that my CIA contacts were waiting to see if my mentioning that remark by Yuri would result in the FSB becoming involved, which would then implicate Marie. Now, suddenly, with her disappearance before reporting to her supervisors at the Mossad in Tel Aviv, the suspicion that she might be a mole for the Russians was especially worrisome.

I know this will be the main topic of my meeting tomorrow night with my CIA handlers.

Having already alerted them to Marie's disappearance, I was anticipating that they would have more information about her whereabouts. If she had truly arrived in Paris, where did she go afterward?

Was she still in Paris or even in Europe? What caused her abrupt disappearance?

I needed answers and could hardly wait until they were forthcoming. Could I have been so wrong about Marie? Could she have used me and my contacts for the benefit of the Russians?

Yuri interrupted my thoughts by raising the subject of tonight's affair.

"Before I tell you about the Russian Academy of Sciences, let me forewarn you that this is a controversial issue. The government, under the leadership of President Putin, is trying to put the Academy, with all of its components and members who constitute the heart of Russian science, under more government control. The State Duma, one of the two chambers of the Russian parliament, is attempting to pass a law that gives Putin the decision on the election of the Academy's president. Three candidates would then need to be approved by the government, and the candidate who gets more than fifty percent of the members' vote would be the newly elected academy president — if approved by the Russian president.

"This has been controversial," he continued as we just drove around, "with candidates refusing to stand for election and the acting president resigning precipitously. So, the installation of a new president tonight has political implications. This is also because the academy will lose its independence, becoming part of the Federal Agency for Scientific Organizations, which will also manage the two other academies, the Russian Academy of Medical Sciences and the

Russian Academy of Agricultural Sciences. Putin has said that this would result in the academies working more efficiently."

"Is this now resolved, or does the controversy continue?" I asked.

"There is still opposition to these changes by an informal union of regular and corresponding members of the Russian Academy of Sciences, even opposing its merger with the medical and agricultural academies. But the State Duma has not yet acted finally, so we are not sure what the election tonight means. But no one dares to ignore or oppose it."

"Sounds like I'll be a witness to the making of new history in Russia," I said. "At least with regard to these academies. Is this a prologue to opposition to Putin?"

"Definitely," said Yuri. "The reform was supposedly authored by Mikhail Kovalchuk, brother of Yury Kovalchuk, who is known as the personal banker of Vladimir Putin."

He went on to explain that the Russian Academy of Sciences dated back to 1724 when it was founded by Peter the Great in St. Petersburg. "For centuries it was the most prestigious organization of Soviet science. Its members came from virtually all areas of science."

"How many members are there?" I asked.

"I think there are more than fifteen hundred," he said, "comprising about five hundred academicians, eight hundred corresponding members and, I think, two hundred foreign members. During the Second World War, the Academy contributed to the development of modern weapons, including the Soviet atomic bomb. As I am sure you know, the Soviet space program was one of its major achievements, with the first satellite launching in 1957. Yury Gagarin was the first astronaut in space in 1961, and in 1971 the first space station, *Salyut 1,* began operating. This was an important era for Soviet science."

"Do you know the incoming president, Professor Bolotkin?"

"Not personally," said Yuri. "But he is a distinguished mathematician and economist, who, some say, is a very close advisor to President Putin."

*

OUR CAR ARRIVED at the hotel, an impressively large building surrounded by a lot of security controlling the traffic and the long line of cars waiting to enter. Finally, after about 15 minutes, Yuri and I were dropped off, entering together and proceeding to the registration desk. Name cards were made for each attendee and we had to show our identification. In my case, I showed my U.S. passport, which seemed to raise some curiosity, but an entry card was waiting for me.

Yuri then directed me to an adjoining parlor, with elegant chandeliers and mirrors, just as one would expect in a large ballroom or banquet hall. There were waiters carrying champagne and other drinks for the guests, and a small string quartet in a corner played Liszt as well as classical Russian music.

The atmosphere was subdued, and Yuri and I just moved about, waiting for the program to begin. By now, I estimated that about 200 people, mostly in black-tie, were gathered. Perhaps about twenty-five of the guests were women, most dressed very formally in long dresses, a lot of jewelry, and low-cut necklines.

Yuri seemed comfortable with this crowd, introducing me to a number of State Duma ministers, some businessmen, and three or four women who seemed to recognize me as not the usual guest and curious as to who I was. I was probably the only one not having a black-tie suit. I learned that one of the younger women, maybe in her late thirties, was a deputy minister in the Federal Agency for Scientific Organizations, which was established in 2013 as a managing organization for the RAS.

She gave me her card: "Dr. Natasha Petrushkin, Deputy Minister, Federal Agency for Scientific Organizations, Moscow, Russian Federation," with telephone, fax, and email information, as Yuri translated it for me. Dr. Petrushkin appeared very self-confident, both from her position and also from being clearly the tallest and most attractive woman in the room. She was obviously popular as well — many of the attendees wandered over to greet her, no matter whom she was talking with.

Dr. Petrushkin spoke English quite well, and I noticed she spoke authoritatively as if she represented Russia.

"We are delighted to have you as a guest and collaborating with Russian science, Professor Davidson," she said as she shook my hand firmly.

It was my impression that she knew of me even before Yuri introduced us. He and Natasha seemed to be acquainted, kissing each other on both cheeks. But she didn't stay long with Yuri and me, instead wandering around the room greeting as many attendees as possible. I also tried memorizing the names of people I met, but I knew my recollection of all the strange names would be poor, so I asked Yuri to help me out with a list afterwards, saying "I want to make sure I know whom I met."

Then a gong rang, and the ceremony was beginning, so we took seats in the middle of the audience.

The outgoing president greeted everyone in Russian, so I could hardly understand more than an occasional word. Yuri did lean over and give me the essence of his welcome, thanking everyone for coming and sharing the induction of the new president, Professor Aleksey Bolotkin. But before Bolotkin could be introduced, everything grew silent, and the string quartet began playing the traditional entry song for the President of Russia, Vladimir Putin, who was making his typical self-confident strut to the front alongside a file of ministers and bodyguards in black suits. I was surprised on how short he was, maybe 5 feet, 7 inches or so. But he walked with his chest out, clearly exhibiting his station and dominance. He wore a slim dark blue suit with a black tie.

Putin walked to the lectern and immediately took charge of the proceedings. I, of course, could not follow his speech, but again Yuri whispered the gist of it to me. Putin said this was an important event, since it installed a new president under the reforms being passed by the State Duma, making the Russian Academy of Sciences more integrated within the government's structure and with more federal support for its facilities and programs, especially as they support government initiatives in science and defense. Getting his choice for president elected and the reform of the Academy was Putin's mission, and he meant to make this clear with his presence and the evening's event.

Then he shocked Yuri and, in turn, me, when he said towards the end of his talk that thanks to the efforts of one of the nation's most successful businessmen, Yuri Grobstein, an American scientist and entrepreneur has chosen to form a new biopharmaceutical company here in Russia, which will be a partnership with the United States and France, setting a good example of international cooperation in advancing medical science.

This was, of course in Russian, so I had to wait until Yuri translated it for me while heads turned toward us. Putin said he hoped this would lead to other future partnerships, since medical science was a goal that should engender partnerships among all nations, especially those at the leading edge of technology and for the benefit of all mankind.

A true politician.

Then he said, in Russian and then in English, that "Professor Davidson is among us tonight, and we welcome him to our country and wish him success in his endeavors and collaboration with our distinguished Russian doctors." His English was quite good, I thought.

This was unexpected, even by Yuri, who leaned over to translate when Russian was spoken — but also added that now that he had been given credit for my coming, he hoped I wouldn't embarrass him in any way. It, of course, made me known to everyone, which I wasn't sure that my CIA colleagues would relish.

I imagined that Yuri was both complimented and maybe concerned, because he risked his reputation by being my mentor and a Board director, in fact Board Chairman, of Pharmascent. He was very vulnerable should I be discovered to be more than an entrepreneurial scientist.

I have the distinct impression that Yuri knows much more about me than he lets on.

President Putin then introduced the new RAS president, who bowed in respect and evidently thanked everyone for their attendance and support. After he spoke, Putin walked toward the exit with his entourage but broke away briefly to come over to Yuri and then shake our hands, addressing me in good English: "Welcome to Moscow, and good luck in your research and helping our countries cooperate."

All eyes focused on me, and I was embarrassed at this unexpected and, frankly, undesired attention. Several of the attendees then proceeded to join Yuri and me, introducing themselves and giving me their business cards, all of course in Russian. I noticed that Yuri also seemed somewhat embarrassed at this attention, yet proud, especially because of being recognized by the President of Russia in the presence of many government ministers, politicians, and businessmen/oligarchs.

"Let's hurry into the dining room for dinner," he whispered as he took my arm and escorted me out. Before we reached the dining room doors, Natasha Petrushkin was at our side and walking with us to a table, which filled up quickly because of the attention President Putin had given to Yuri and me.

The string quartet had already relocated to the dining room and played Rachmaninoff as everyone took seats. Nevertheless, the room became very noisy, and it was hard to hear even conversations at our table, although it didn't matter much to me when everything was in Russian. Occasionally, someone would say something to me in English, mostly platitudes, to be polite and conversant.

Natasha, who sat on my right side opposite Yuri on my left, dominated my attention and was as personable and charming as possible. She insisted on knowing my personal information (married or not), professional responsibilities and stature at ESU, and what my immediate plans were now that I was in Moscow. I was as diffuse and noncommittal as possible, since I was a little apprehensive about her and her intentions, and I noted that Yuri, even when he talked with others, paid attention to our conversation and occasionally looked at me with an expression of caution.

I was surprised that Natasha spoke in a voice at a lower octave than expected for a woman, which could be explained by her having a more prominent Adam's apple than usual in women. I was wondering what her testosterone level could be. But I had no concerns about her gender inclination, since she was clearly trying to be coquettish while also business-like with me.

I learned during dinner from Natasha that she is employed with the Federal Agency for Scientific Organizations, supervising programs at certain government-supported medical centers, including biological programs at various universities, like Moscow State University, where she had earned her advanced degree in biological sciences.

"After graduating, I spent a year at Cambridge University taking courses in medical genetics. Thereafter, I returned to Moscow to work in the genetics department of Moscow State University and then was recruited to various government jobs before being appointed to the Federal Agency, where I am now Deputy Minister."

I told her I was surprised she had accomplished so much at such a young age, which caused her to blush. But she was trying to impress me.

"I am lucky to be the youngest Deputy Minister in the Duma," she said, "and with considerable autonomy in the management of various science programs."

"Congratulations," I said. "I'm sure you can be helpful to our program as well."

The dining room atmosphere grew loud with people trying to talk over the music, and of course, much wine and vodka were flowing while the waiters brought out cold borscht, a fish entree with vegetables, and then a cheesecake dessert with coffee or tea.

I noted how much the guests enjoyed eating and drinking and would have stayed for many more hours had not the new RAS president stood up to thank them for the noteworthy evening and wishing everyone a safe journey home.

This was the signal it was over, so everyone began to rise and take leave of their neighbors as they went to get to their transportation. Natasha kissed my cheeks as she said goodbye, and I didn't know how to react. She made a point of saying that she looked forward to hearing from me. Yuri kissed her cheeks also and said it was nice being together again.

When we got into Yuri's car, he complimented me on a very successful evening and that I should keep the business cards given to me but to copy them and email them to him. He also said I should respond to Natasha after a few days, since it was obvious that she wanted to get to know me better.

"But be cautious," he said, "since she is a very clever and ambitious person who is a rising star in the Putin regime." He explained that she came from a well-known family of bureaucrats; her father had been a high-level department head in the Post-Stalin regime.

Yuri also said, "Now that you have the attention of President Putin, you need to be ultra-cautious in any dealings here since, as a former KGB officer, he will likely have you under some form of surveillance."

"In fact," said Yuri, "my chauffeur had noticed that our car was being followed from the time I picked you up, including now."

I don't want to tell him that they could be CIA agents tailing us.

But his warning that I'm probably a focus of interest by the Russian intelligence was disturbing news, especially since I was to meet my CIA contacts tomorrow evening. Now I was doubly concerned that I would be in big trouble if my spy activities were discovered.

59.

THE NEXT MORNING, I arrived at the Jewish Community Center before 8:00 a.m. and proceeded to the locker room to change for swimming. When I came into the pool, there were already about a dozen people there, including, surprisingly, Miriam Keslov, my Russian teacher, in a one-piece, black bathing suit that nevertheless showed some of her flab, certainly not the torso of Tania that I admired. She was all smiles as she greeted me, saying she'd decided that she also needed to work out more seriously, and we could also use this time to converse in Russian. So, I guess I had a positive influence on her.

She was gentle with me, speaking in simple phrases and starting with questions about my prior evening. I could not respond well in Russian, so I switched back into English to give her a summary of the evening's events, including my being noted by President Putin and meeting many of the government officials.

When I mentioned Natasha Petrushkin, the deputy minister for science, Miriam's face turned serious. She warned me to be careful of this woman "who regularly devours testicles." I was shocked at Miriam's off-color remark, which was clearly her translation of a typical Russian phrase.

"This woman is known inside and outside of government as a very ambitious rising bureaucrat, who is loyal only to those in clear power and control."

Miriam was adamant that I couldn't trust Natasha.

"She is clearly interested in learning why you are in Russia," she said, "and if there is anything that she could expose, that would advance her own agenda."

Since Miriam is connected with the Mossad, thus indirectly also to the CIA, I took her comment seriously, thinking she knows a lot more about Natasha than she is sharing with me.

We swam in different lanes for about thirty minutes, Miriam showing she was struggling, then got out of the pool to change. After that, we met in the coffee shop to pick up coffee and pastries to take back to her office.

So much for her slimming down.

With the language pamphlet in hand, she began by reviewing the Cyrillic alphabet with me and proceeded to helping me construct simple sentences of daily conversation.

I told Miriam I would be with Professor Koussevitzky in the afternoon and then a guest in his home for dinner. As my handlers had advised, I kept Miriam fully informed of my whereabouts and activities as part of our 'innocent' conversation. But I now knew that Miriam was also in danger so long as the Russian authorities were concerned about the loyalty of JCC staff and members, as Yuri had shared with me and that I, stupidly, had mentioned to Marie.

Even during my lesson with Miriam, my thoughts often turned to Marie. I was still thinking about her as I took the Metro to my office, and on the way, I again texted Simon in Paris to see if he'd had any news about Marie. He answered quickly, saying he didn't know her whereabouts but knew that Interpol was working to trace her since her arrival in Paris.

*

JULIA DASKALOV, MY office manager, greeted me with a big smile as I came in, and I said hello, along with a few words in Russian, drawing her surprise and a compliment. She said I had only one message, from Professor Koussevitzky, confirming our meeting this afternoon and dinner tonight. That reminded me that I needed to pick up a bottle of wine, so I asked Julia if she could do it for me. She was delighted, she said.

I checked my emails and saw that I received a draft of the board minutes from our New York attorney, requesting a review from me before he distributed it to the entire board. It was fine, and I said he should go ahead and send it out.

Julia brought back an excellent bottle of red Beaujolais, which she then wrapped nicely after I approved it. I later realized it wasn't kosher, so perhaps it wasn't the proper gift for the Koussevitzky's. But I decided to take it along anyhow.

When I visited with Sergeii, after shaking his hand I saw the protocol laid out on the conference table, where he obviously had read and worked on it.

"This is quite detailed," he said, "and I had some difficulty understanding all of the English. We will have to translate this into Russian once we have a final draft."

We also needed to start building a budget, which would involve paying the subjects for their time and effort. Since I didn't anticipate needing more than a dozen subjects to determine the proper dose, safety, and possible effects, this wouldn't be expensive.

When we began discussing a pharmacist to compound the melatonin into the smell device that I would make available, I suggested Katarina Breslau.

"I met her at the JCC," I said, "and she seems both interested and well qualified." Sergeii agreed, saying he would speak with Katarina and her boss, the chief pharmacist at the hospital, about her participation.

It was already 5:30 p.m., so Sergeii packed his briefcase and said he would take the protocol home with him and try to work on it later tonight, but that we should now get on the road to his apartment, which was in a northeastern suburb of Moscow, about forty minutes away.

Sergeii's building was a high-rise of about twenty stories, he said, and one of about ten in the development. He explained that they had waited three years to be able to rent their small apartment with three bedrooms, one of which he now used as an office, since his oldest son, Mikhail, was away at university in St. Petersburg.

"He is completing his studies in art history," Sergeii said. He explained that his wife, Lada, worked at a local rehabilitation facility for the aged and that they still had a sixteen-year-old daughter, Nina, at home and attending the local high school.

"But with our son away, the apartment is quite spacious, compared to when the children were younger."

The complex reminded me of a tenement in New York City or one of the boroughs, built decades earlier and somewhat run down. There were playgrounds and small park areas with grass and benches, making it a family-friendly community, I thought. But the fact that the chief neurologist at a major Moscow hospital lived here and couldn't afford better for his family, or maybe couldn't get a suitable apartment because of a shortage, was striking.

They had slippers waiting for me to use when I entered, in good Russian tradition, with Lada at the door welcoming us. She was about five-feet, five-inches tall, not thin but also not fat, with a round face and large brown eyes, and her hair combed up in a bun. She wore a plain dress with a blue and white apron and greeted me with a wide smile, showing large teeth, mostly somewhat yellow.

Nina also came out to say hello. She was a little taller than her mother, looking slim in jeans and a sweater, and almost the image of her father. They thanked me for the wine and invited me to sit on their couch in the living room, where glasses and a decanter were already prepared.

Whereas Nina was pretty good at conversational English, her mother was embarrassed at not being able to join our conversation. I apologized to her that my Russian was still poor, although I was trying to take lessons. Nina said that English was her main foreign language since her early school years, and she enjoyed it when she could converse in English with Americans. She told me that, at times, she and her father restricted their conversation to English, so they could practice.

The apartment was furnished nicely, with many family pictures, some local artwork and sculptures, a TV console in the living room, a large kitchen with a dining area that would seat six, and then three bedrooms and one full bath and another half bathroom off the kitchen. The apartment was well heated, almost too much for my comfort, but I was sure that was an important factor for the cold winters here. They were obviously proud to give me a quick tour.

After we had a glass of heavy Romanian wine, kosher I noted, Lada invited us to the table where she had laid out plates of salad, herring, tomatoes, potatoes, carrots, pot roast, and dark bread. There was also carbonated water on the table. Everything looked and tasted delicious. I hadn't had good, pickled herring in a long time, so I accepted a second portion. So good and authentic was this home-cooked meal that I ate as if I hadn't eaten for days, even though I had feasted the night before. Plus, the warm family atmosphere was so conducive to enjoying Lada's specialties, which I, of course, praised to her delight.

After clearing the table, Lada brought out a honey cake she had baked, and I said I didn't know how I could eat another piece of food. But it smelled so good that I agreed to a small piece, which then led to a second — along with black tea and a small glass of cognac that Sergeii insisted I have.

It was already 9:00 p.m., and I knew my ride would be downstairs for me at nine-thirty, so I joined Sergeii in the living room while Lada attended to the kitchen, and Nina said goodbye and returned to her room to do homework. Sergeii and I discussed a little about his hospital, about his reception as a Jewish doctor by the medical community, and the few trips he had taken abroad, mostly alone, to medical conferences.

The wine and cognac I had dampened my attention, but I was able to keep an acknowledging smile on my face. I remember Sergeii telling me that although his hospital was very international, they restricted travels abroad by their busy staff, partly because of budget considerations and partly because the Russian government kept tight controls on foreign travel by their professionals, even if not employed by the government.

*

I INSISTED TO Sergeii that I would find my own way downstairs, since I didn't want him there when I was picked up by a large black limousine with two occupants, but I was not all that steady on my feet. Fortunately, when I got outside, I noticed the car waiting for me. I immediately recognized Marcia Dubrovnik, the head of the CIA assigned to the embassy, sitting next to the driver, John Caruthers, after getting into the back seat.

When we drove away, John explained that he wanted to get on a road where he had good visibility of the cars traveling behind us. Both he and Marcia wore heavy black coats, and John also had on a wide-brimmed black hat.

"How was your evening with Professor Koussevitzky and his family?" Marcia asked.

"I was pleasantly surprised with the warmth and hospitality, even living in modest circumstances," I said. "And the home-cooked meal was great."

"It looks like you also enjoyed some good drinks," Marcia remarked with a smile on her face. I guess it was easy to recognize my jovial mood.

John said that Professor Koussevitzky had a good reputation in the medical community, seemed to be apolitical and devoted to his patients and his hospital, and the family lived comfortably within their means.

"Full-time hospital doctors don't earn much," John explained, "but they do garner a lot of respect in the community, especially when they've earned professorships at a university in Moscow."

Marcia then got down to business, saying they needed to return me to my apartment within an hour, and there was a lot of information to cover.

"First," she said, "we've lost all contact with Marie Chalfont, at least after she landed in Paris. Interpol could trace her to a flight from Paris to Rio de Janeiro —"

"Rio de Janeiro!" I interrupted. "What on earth?"

"But she disappeared afterward," said Marcia, "and they aren't sure she's even in Brazil. She hasn't communicated with the Mossad, with her employer at Toilette, or anyone else they know of. We've alerted all of our agents, as has also the Mossad and France's DGSE."

"My God," I said. "I can't believe this. Do you think it's related to her learning that the FSB interviewed Yuri Grobstein about his statement regarding the JCC — the source of which had to be Marie?"

"That's the current theory," said Marcia. "But Marie is an enigma, and all the Western agencies are now concerned about her loyalty and possible ties to the Russians."

"I just don't believe she's been a traitor or using me," I said. "Do you think she's in danger and didn't disappear of her own free will?"

"All the agencies and Interpol are looking for her," said John, "and we'll eventually learn the truth. In the meantime, we need to proceed hastily yet cautiously."

"Is there any possibility she has been kidnapped?" I asked.

"We are also considering this, since she is 'wanted' by the Hezbollah because of being identified with the assassination squad that attacked their agents in France a couple of years ago," John said.

"Did Katarina Breslau's email address lead to anything?" I asked.

"We hit the jackpot there, Milt," said Marcia. "Katarina Breslau told her brother about you — that you're in Moscow to conduct research for a biopharmaceutical company developing therapeutics via olfaction, and that you'd received investment from Russian business interests and possibly even the government. Joshua Breslau cautioned her to be careful, so the group he's working with doesn't start thinking he and his sister are violating any secrecy, since his project is to develop mood-controlling olfactory drugs.

"Joshua later reported this contact to the security staff at his facility in Oryol, and during the various emails, it became clear in information we got from his email history that they're working on psychedelic drugs being delivered as odors."

"The fact that the Russians are doing this research doesn't surprise me," I said, "but I need to know which compounds are of current interest to them. Do you think we can get that info?"

Marcia said she thought Dr. Breslau or his sister might reveal it if I played my part right, but they couldn't get this from his emails or computer documents, at least those in his personal use.

"Maybe you can suggest to his sister that Pharmascent Sciences should investigate some of these psychedelics as olfactory agents," Marcia said. "Maybe you can even suggest a specific compound and see how she responds. There has been some research done on specific psychedelics as treatments for depression, PTSD, and end-of-life fears."

"Yes, if I can. But I really don't think she is privileged to this information," I volunteered.

I then gave them a summary of my protocol development and implementation plans with Professor Koussevitzky at the European Medical Centre, hoping to use this effort as a way of legitimizing my research in Moscow and allowing me to interact with Katarina Breslau.

"We notice you have admirers in both President Putin and Dr. Natasha Petrushkin," said John.

"You people work fast," I said. "I was at the Russian Academy of Sciences reception and dinner just last night."

"We try to keep you under protective surveillance," John said, "and we were quite impressed with the attention you received. But this is both good and bad. Good from the perspective of opening doors and contacts, but potentially risky if higher government officials want to learn more about you and become suspicious."

"How do I manage Dr. Petrushkin?" I asked.

"She's known to us," said Marcia, "but she's still an enigma and unpredictable. She's ambitious and well connected, but also operates on her own agenda. She could be quite helpful to you and to us, but she could also be very dangerous because she has good instincts, knows the inside politics of the Kremlin, and may want to be the one to either promote you or expose you, depending on its value for her. Of all of your acquaintances here, she is, in my view, the most dangerous until we learn more, so be extremely cautious, Milt."

"Got it," I said. "But I want to go back to the subject of Marie. I'm really worried about her, since she knew my mission, has disappeared, and could put me in grave danger. I also worry about her own well-being. I need you to assure me that nothing bad will happen to her at your hands."

"We want to talk to her, too," said Marcia, "so we're applying considerable resources to finding her and bringing her in safely for debriefing."

We agreed to start having at least weekly meetings unless we needed to set something up sooner. It was nearly ten-thirty when they dropped me off in front of my apartment building, and, once inside, all I could think about was that disturbing conversation with my handlers.

*

I SLEPT A little later the next morning, so I texted Miriam that I wouldn't be coming to the JCC but would try to meet up with her tomorrow or Friday. Miriam wrote back that she understood and congratulated me on being introduced to the Russian science community by the Russian President himself on Monday evening. I was surprised at how fast this news traveled. Maybe it was on the news programs, and I didn't know.

When I arrived at the office, Julia told me I had a call from Dr. Petrushkin, who asked that I call her back. Julia then connected us.

"Hello, Dr. Petrushkin," I said, "nice hearing from you."

"I hope we can be on a first-name basis, Milton or Milt?"

"Milt is just fine, Natasha. How are you?"

"Fine, but this is not a social call. I believe your prominence will get you a visit from some government officials, so do let me know how it goes and if I can be of any assistance. You have my office number and now take down my private cell phone number," which she proceeded to give to me. I thanked her and said I would be in touch.

60.

WHY WOULD NATASHA give me this warning on an open phone line, especially if I'm a subject of interest to the Russian FSB? Maybe this was all part of the inquiry to see how I reacted and if I made any phone calls to others about this. I had no intention of doing anything that crazy.

After having a quick salad and drink in the cafeteria, I returned to the office at about one o'clock, Julia's usual leaving time. But I found her still there and very nervous, since two men were waiting for me. They introduced themselves and said they were from the local resident-registration office, showing official-looking identification, and needed to ask me some questions related to my visa and business. I escorted them into my office and asked Julia to bring us coffee.

They said in broken English that their visit was routine, and they needed to provide information in my visa file as to my activities since arriving in Russia and my immediate and long-term plans. I responded that I thought my presence was welcome because just on Monday night, at the Russian Academy of Sciences celebration, President Putin personally greeted me and wished me much success in building my company in Russia and with the cooperation of Russian medical doctors.

"Are you concerned that President Putin may be meddling by encouraging me to work here and advance my company to have better relations between our two countries?" I asked sarcastically.

This, of course, was unproductive and made them very uncomfortable, possibly even resentful. They ignored this and moved on to their list of questions, which I responded to as briefly as possible, mostly innocuously, about my activities since arriving, whom I am working with, other plans, etc.

They then asked me which Russians I knew before coming here. I responded, "Of course, Yuri Grobstein, who sponsored my visa application and is the Chairman of the Board of Directors of Pharmascent. That's the only specific relationship I had.

"Oh, Dr. Davidson, don't you have a companion, Marie Chalfont, registered as an employee of the French company, Toilette, who has been here with you?"

"I do," I said, "but she returned to Paris last Sunday."

"Is she not also Russian or with some Soviet background?" he asked to my surprise.

"I'm not sure. It could be that she grew up in a Soviet republic and emigrated during her youth, but I'm not sure. She does have knowledge of Russian, as well as some other languages, I know."

I'm not going to mention Tania or Vladimir Borofskov.

Then, to my surprise, the younger one asked, "Do you not know Dr. Vladimir Borofskov?"

I paused, suggesting I was thinking, and then responded, "Yes, of course. He introduced himself to me in Vienna a few months ago, before I decided to move here. We both attended a conference there, but I haven't seen him since."

This suggests that the FSB is in contact with Borofskov.

Before they could ask anything more, I ushered them out the door and said goodbye in Russian (*dasvidaniya*) and then returned to my desk. I decided not to contact Natasha to summarize this meeting, expecting that she would either call again or wait for me to follow up.

I spent the remainder of the day making edits to the protocol and confirming with Dr. Haber of Argus Laboratories that they could test blood and urine samples for the presence and quantity of melatonin and its immediate breakdown product, and I also asked when they would be able to deliver the melatonin prepared for olfaction to me as a sterile product.

It was early, about 5 p.m., when I got home, planning to relax. But at five-thirty, my bell rang, indicating that I had a visitor in the lobby for the first time. I answered in Russian, and the visitor replied in English.

"This is Natasha. Can you come down and take a drive with me?"

I didn't know how to respond, but I certainly didn't want to offend her. "Of course," I said. "Can you wait five minutes?"

"Yes."

I put on my warm jacket and was down to the lobby in a few minutes but didn't see her at the entrance. There was a car with the motor running at the curb, so I walked out and carefully looked at the driver, whom I immediately recognized as Dr. Petrushkin. She motioned me to get in and then sped away. She had driven a few blocks before saying a word.

"You must be shocked, but I was worried about your visit with the FSB agents, and I needed to talk with you privately. Can we drive for a while and then find a quiet restaurant to have dinner together?"

"Sure," I said. "It will be my pleasure, but I am very casually dressed." I had gone down to meet her in my jeans, flannel shirt, and a wool-lined jacket.

While driving, she told me that she was "a loyal Russian citizen" and would like to be of assistance to me, but this had put her in a conflict because she had some doubts about me and my mission.

"Nevertheless," she said, "I have an interest in your work. I want you to know that I can help you and even protect you and your work if you let me. Perhaps you can find a way to enlist my collaboration, of course, on a very confidential basis."

This all caught me by surprise, but I remembered the caution that several people had given me about her.

"I do appreciate your concern and interest, Natasha. Although your background in science, genetics I believe, is a little distant from olfaction, I'm sure you could be helpful to me in your administrative, government role."

"All right," she said. "Let's just have dinner and get to know each other. Tell me about your visit today by the Russian secret service?"

"They presented themselves as officials of the resident-registration office, checking on foreigners with visas, wanting to get information on my activities and plans. I told them of President Putin's remarks on Monday night, and that seemed to cut their visit short."

"They were, of course, FSB investigators," she said again, "and it concerns me that they decided to make this visit and interrogate you."

I'm not going to give her more details before I checked with my handlers.

We drove for another fifteen minutes or so, then turned into a quiet side street where Natasha parked across from a small restaurant. We went in, and I saw there were only ten tables, of which two had guests. She told me the menu was only in Russian, and she would take the liberty and order for us both.

Natasha was dressed quite differently than when she'd attended the RAS celebration. Now she wore a gray wool turtleneck sweater and long, tight, woolen trousers, and mid-size black heels. Her hair hung over her shoulders, and she wore much less makeup than when I'd first met her. But her large eyes were as staring and inquisitive as I remembered from her sitting next to me at the Academy dinner.

The sole waiter brought out a carafe of red wine; lettuce, tomatoes, and cucumbers as a salad; and then roast chicken with kasha (buckwheat) and carrots. The plates were very generous, and we ate and drank quietly while looking up at each other often.

Natasha is a very attractive woman, self-confident, but now a little awkward because I had rejected her overture of further involvement. My interpretation was that she was offering her services to my associates and me, and if she believed I was a spy, then she had seemed surprisingly direct in offering to be — what for us? A mole? Or maybe she worked for the FSB. I didn't know how to interpret this. But what I did know was that it could be very dangerous for me if I didn't handle it correctly.

Natasha watched me carefully, then smiled and gripped my hand. *She feels very warm.*

"I am afraid I have been too forward with you, Milt, making you uncomfortable. Do you think we can get to know each other better, or do you already have an important female acquaintance who may object?"

She doesn't waste any time.

"As I mentioned to you at the Academy dinner, I'm not engaged or seeing anyone regularly, if that's your question. And I'm, of course, complimented by your interest, but let's get to know each other a little more before such personal matters are raised, okay?"

Are all European women this aggressive?

I believed my answer was honest, since I wasn't sure I still had any relationship with Marie, and we both discussed that we would probably be apart in the future. Her disappearance did not diminish my feelings for her, but I was not, literally, her steady companion.

Natasha looked embarrassed. "I am so sorry," she said, "but you have intrigued me since we first were introduced, and I assumed that you were in need of friends in this new country and society."

She feels rejected.

I didn't continue this conversation, but she decided not to give up on this when we ordered coffee, saying: "Would it be too forward of me to ask you about yourself, what you like to do — and if we can meet again?"

"I would like that very much," I said. "Are you free Saturday evening?"

I'm surprised I said that.

"Yes," she said. "But because of our different positions, I think we should not be seen too soon in public unless it is at a scientific or government function. Here is my home address. Can you come over for dinner Friday night instead? I will try to make sure it's secure and private."

I took her card and said that I would be there at 6 p.m.

But we need to slow this down.

I knew I wouldn't refuse jumping into bed with her if that were her intention, but I needed to consult with my CIA handlers before things went any further. This seemed like a dangerous trap.

And here I am, in my forties, waiting for permission from my handlers before I share myself with a solicitous and beautiful woman!

Natasha drove me back to my building and let me out about a half-block away. Before I left, she leaned over and kissed my cheek, which I accepted as a simple, friendly, Russian gesture.

But it feels good.

*

AFTER RETURNING TO my apartment, I sent a coded message to Brad Williams, expecting that he would forward it to John or Marcia in Moscow, so they could arrange to meet with me before Friday. I preferred this over the complicated messaging system John had given me.

The next morning, I received a text that a car would pick me up in front of the JCC at 10 a.m. and drop me off at my office building. I then hurried to meet with Miriam at the JCC after taking my swim, and we worked on my Russian conversation and grammar for about an hour. I told her I had a pickup at 10 a.m., so she would know that I had to leave by then.

The black limousine was in front of the JCC when I came out, and I got in as a passenger in the back. John Caruthers was driving and alone and immediately asked why the emergency meeting. I explained the FSB visit, and the pickup and dinner with Natasha last night.

"This is almost too strange to be a setup," John said. "I think you should be friendly with her, but, of course, don't reveal your relationship to us and any confidences with Yuri Grobstein. We can't even follow up and test if she wants to work for us, since this would obviously link back to you."

My advice," he continued, "is to be friendly and behave as you would with someone you're attracted to. Otherwise, she'll suspect that you have other motives related to her offer to collaborate with you. We need to learn more what she means by that. We'll try to hack her computer, since you have provided her email information, but her ministry probably has a secure, cyber-protected computer network."

"I'm not sure I can handle this, John. She's certainly a beautiful woman, but I'm not schooled in developing this relationship as a spy. Anyhow, I'm still thinking about Marie. I'm very worried about her."

He turned and smiled as he pulled to a stop at my office building. "There are worse things we do in the service of our country."

Then: "To be clear, Milt, I'm not telling you to get romantically involved with Natasha, but I'm also not advising you to reject her outright. I'll leave this to your discretion. But be very careful and try to act as if you were a visiting professor starting a business and not a CIA agent."

This advice was shocking to hear. But what else could he say?

Finally, I got to the visit by the so-called immigration officers.

"They were clearly from the FSB or another such police agency," I explained, "and focused on what Russians I knew before coming here. I only mentioned Yuri, but they knew of Marie and even Borofskov, so I'm clearly being monitored. I had little to say about each, emphasizing that I haven't seen Borofskov since moving here, and I avoided mentioning his wife, since they only asked about him."

"We have to assume that Borofskov made a report of meeting you, suggesting that he is involved with their intelligence, probably the FSB. I wonder how much Natasha is implicated," John commented.

Julia had no messages for me when I arrived in my office, but I did have a text message from Katarina Breslau, saying she'd read the protocol and had some questions for me. I texted her back asking if she wanted to meet at the JCC for lunch tomorrow, which was Friday, or preferred my coming to the EMC. She answered that it would be better to meet at the JCC, so I suggested an early lunch at 11 a.m.

61.

MIRIAM THOUGHT I was making good progress with Russian, but I said she was being kind, that I still felt totally lost, especially reading Cyrillic letters. She smiled and encouraged me to be a little more patient. "You have only been in Moscow a couple of weeks," she said.

That, too, is shocking. So much has happened.

At 11 a.m., Katarina was waiting for me at the entrance to the cafeteria, and I escorted her to a table at the far end of the room. Staking out that spot with coats and a bag, we then went to the buffet line to get our food and beverage. Soon we were seated and eating. It was early, so the dining room was nearly empty.

"I read through your protocol, although I cannot say that I understood all parts of it," she said. "But I did get the idea, and I think I understand the goals and procedures. I will need to discuss it with my chief further, but I am sure that Professor Koussevitzky being involved and conferring with my chairman will enable me to participate. I am wondering why you chose melatonin."

I was glad she'd raised that — it gave me an opening to discuss using olfaction to affect the brain and moods, which I hoped would lead to a discussion of her brother's research.

"Melatonin has functions beyond sleep," I said. "It may be useful in controlling certain symptoms of neurodegenerative diseases, such as dysphoric and euphoric moods. It's a good model for my understanding how to develop olfactory drugs, since so much research has been done on melatonin in sleep disorders when prescribed as a pill."

"I guess these other applications would make this a valuable drug," said Katarina. "Is that your point?"

"Yes, but there are many other mood-altering drugs that have been studied over the years, such as psychedelic drugs like LSD for depression and PTSD, which I think may also be worthy of reexamination." I watched Katarina's eyes and expression carefully.

No evidence of surprise or another reaction.

"Do you think these can be given by using smell?" she asked.

"I'm not sure, but it may be worth examining. What do you think?"

"This is not my expertise," she said, "but it seems logical that if their oral use had such effects, maybe the smell or generally the intranasal route would also work."

I thought this was an important statement, suggesting that she might have some other knowledge of this, possibly from her brother.

"While I'm here in Moscow, I'll discuss these other possibilities with my Russian colleagues," I said, just to see her reaction.

"Yes," she said, "there may be a lot of interest in this area, especially from a military perspective."

That's as close to an admission as I could extract from her.

But I already planned to see if any of my neurological colleagues, like Sergeii, had any information about research on psychedelics for espionage or military uses.

Before Katarina and I said good-bye, I asked if I could meet her brother sometime in the future, since he was also doing chemistry research.

"Joshua rarely comes to Moscow," she said, "even to see his mother and me. He's so busy at work that I have to manage his son's Bar Mitzvah lessons. But I will certainly keep you in mind if he plans a trip here. I will, of course, mention to my sister-in-law that you inquired about him when she visits here next time."

I suspected that Joshua was being kept at Oryol because of security due to his very sensitive work. I hoped the CIA could learn more by monitoring the computer exchanges they'd intercepted at the facility after hacking Dr. Breslau's computers at home and work. But Miriam mentioning Mrs. Breslau's visiting Moscow occasionally, confirmed by Katarina, seemed to me that this was an intended message.

*

I GOT TO my office a little before 1:00 p.m. Before Julia left, I asked her to again buy a bottle of the same Beaujolais that she got for me on Tuesday, since I had another dinner engagement. Later, on the way home, I stopped at a florist and bought a small bouquet of flowers to take to Natasha.

Back at my apartment, I called for a Yandex car to pick me up at five-thirty in front of my building and drive me to Natasha's place. Then I texted Yuri to tell him about the visit I'd had from the resident-registration office, but no specifics, since I wasn't sure about our telephone connection being safe. He thanked me for the information and said he wasn't familiar with this kind of inquiry but would look into it. I didn't mention my interactions with Natasha or our planned dinner tonight. I knew he wouldn't be pleased, and we were perhaps on an unprotected line.

The car arrived at five-thirty sharp and headed toward Natasha's apartment in a southeastern area of the city. The driver didn't speak any English, so I merely showed him her address, and he nodded that he understood.

Natasha's apartment complex looked to have been built more recently than the one that Sergeii and his family lived in, with fewer floors and generally better landscaping. The building had a nice lobby, a receptionist's desk, and a comfortable seating area, but no one was there. I then went back to the entrance and rang Natasha's bell, and she answered: "Take the elevator to the fifth floor, apartment 5R."

Her door was ajar, so I knocked and walked in. Natasha called from someplace within, saying she'd left slippers for me at the door and that I should come to the kitchen, which was down the hallway off to the right.

She greeted me by kissing both cheeks and then thanked me for the wine and flowers. She was dressed very casually, wearing very tight designer jeans and a denim shirt with buttons down the front, but which was open halfway to the top, emphasizing her cleavage. Her hair was again combed down over her shoulders, and her face lacked much makeup — just pink lipstick and eyelids colored blue, accentuating her large, gray eyes. She looked better each time I saw her, and I knew it was going to be a struggle to keep this relationship platonic.

After putting the flowers in a vase on the dining table, she invited me to sit while she finished preparing dinner. I poured the wine into our glasses and proposed a toast to good health and good times in my new country with my new friends.

Natasha was quite agile and in command of her kitchen, having several frying pans cooking with fish and vegetables and with a bowl of salad.

"Dinner will be ready in a few minutes," she said. "Tell me about your day."

"Not much to tell," I said. "I started the day working out and swimming at the Jewish Community Center downtown, then had a lesson in Russian. After that, I had lunch with a pharmacist from the European Medical Centre to discuss my clinical research protocol."

"I know I should try to use more Russian with you," she said, "but I am too impatient to talk with you and learn more about you. Why did you meet with the pharmacist at the JCC?"

"Katarina Breslau is Jewish and is a member, caring for her nephew who's preparing for his Bar Mitzvah by coming to Moscow's JCC. So, we find it convenient to meet there unless I'm already at the EMC."

This question worries me, especially if she knows about Dr. Breslau's secret work in Oryol.

"Where does her nephew live?"

"His family is living in a town about three hours from Moscow, where his father is a chemist at a government laboratory."

"Yes," said Natasha, "I know that the government has many research laboratories dispersed throughout Russia and the former Soviet Union. In my role as Deputy Minister responsible for a number of medical and biological research laboratories, I, of course, learn of different programs."

She then wrote a note on a pad and handed the slip of paper to me: "Let's only talk of business or what may be sensitive when we go out on the balcony. I will turn up the music."

We then discussed how the weather was turning very cold and that I would soon experience my first frigid winter in Moscow. We sat down and enjoyed the dinner, which consisted of a delicious white fish that Natasha said came from the Black Sea. The French Chardonnay wine she served really enhanced the taste of the fish and was almost empty by the time we finished eating.

Natasha suggested that I go out on the balcony to see the view of the countryside while she put everything in the sink for soaking. Evidently, she didn't have a dishwasher.

The air was quite cold but refreshing, and the music in her apartment was also transmitted via a speaker on the balcony, so I continued to enjoy hearing a Mozart concerto. Soon, Natasha joined me, bringing out glasses of port for us to drink.

She spoke in a low voice to me, easily drowned by the music.

"I am always concerned about listening devices, despite my doing routine searches. It is the worst part of living here, always worrying who is listening in or videorecording you. It is this paranoia that most of us despise, and I am sure you have not experienced in America."

"I guess your time in England was an enjoyable change," I said.

She laughed. "At first, I was not able to adapt, always wondering who was watching or listening — until British friends gave me confidence that this was not the case and that I could relax. I then thrived, going out to different events, attending parties, learning how happy one could be in an open society. But I still loved my Motherland and did not want to abandon it."

"And now, are you having second thoughts?"

"Sometimes, when I recognize that government decisions and the actions of bureaucrats can be so counterproductive to the needs of our people, our institutions, and our potential. I am hoping to make a difference as a member of the new generation, but attending the gala of the RAS on Monday brought me to a more sober realization. It was then that I thought maybe I could contribute more by becoming involved in an enterprise advancing medical science, especially one with international ties, like your Pharmascent."

"This is very trusting of you," I said, "since you really don't know me and don't know much about the business or science we're pursuing."

"This is why I have been asking you questions and wanted to be alone with you," she said. "I want to learn more and determine if this is for me and if you may have an interest. I also know about Katarina Breslau and her brother's work in Oryol, since that facility falls under my jurisdiction — although I am not privileged to know secret research, especially for the military. Once you mentioned Katarina Breslau, I concluded that this association most likely is related to her brother's secret military research in olfaction, since your Pharmascent is developing olfactory drugs. Correct?"

This caught me off guard. But then, she knew so much already that I decided to just plunge into this discussion.

But can I trust her line of fishing with me?

"I am interested in Breslau's research in olfaction but from an entrepreneurial perspective and not from any strategic or military perspective," I said. "But their using mind-altering drugs delivered as odors intrigues me, so I did discuss this with Katarina, but she of course didn't know specifics about her brother's research."

Natasha looked into my eyes for a few seconds. Then she said, "Evidently, Dr. Breslau and his small group of chemists are very important to this research, since they are not permitted to leave the laboratories to travel anywhere, even to see their relatives in Moscow. As an administrator reviewing their personnel budgets, I am surprised that this important mission has so few chemists and so many more internet and computer specialists."

"Really? Why do you think this is so?" I asked.

This surprises me, and I need to learn more without being obvious.

"I have no idea, but obviously, the internet is an important part of their research."

"I don't know what to say," I answered, "other than my work at Pharmascent is very important to me and evidently also to the other scientists and physicians whom I'm attracting at the EMC. Yet, I'm curious about psychedelic olfaction, independent of any Russian military project if that is, in fact, a focus.

I need to test the water.

"But even if the exploitation of psychedelic olfactory substances isn't a major focus here, I still think more work needs to be done in that area. This was the subject of intensive research in the U.S. from about the 1950s to the 1970s, and revived in 2006 with the research of Roland Griffith and later research at Johns Hopkins, UCLA, and New York University. I may want to return to this project after my studies with melatonin, which interests me as a therapeutic for certain neurological diseases beyond sleep disorders."

"Interesting," Natasha said. I wasn't sure how she meant it.

"But if Breslau and the other chemists at Oryol are not alone in the olfaction project but have collaborating cyberspace specialists, the project must be of a somewhat different nature," I speculated, hoping she would offer more information.

"Now you are talking like a spy, Milt, asking me so much about a secret project."

"Not really. I was only commenting about olfaction, and we became involved in discussing Oryol when I mentioned Katarina Breslau."

She's testing me.

"I do not know enough to compromise anyone or the program," she said. "I only know that it is top secret. But maybe I should not even mention this. I really do not know more, only that their team has more computer programmers than chemists."

"Maybe you should come with me to my next protocol meeting with the doctors at the EMC," I suggested as we prepared to go back to the living room. "You can get more involved in the science at Pharmascent, and we can both assess if there's a potential role for you."

"Just what I was hoping you would suggest," Natasha said with a smile. "You go relax in the living room while I make some coffee. I have a surprise dessert."

I wandered and looked around her apartment, especially at family pictures, although there were noticeably few. Natasha soon brought out a tray with coffee, cups, plates, silverware, and a honey cake.

"You also bake?" I asked.

"Only when I have a male guest whom I want to impress or seduce," she said.

"I have to admit you've been successful at impressing me — I find you radiant and charming, but seduction?" I asked.

That line was clearly a mistake, since Natasha put down the cake knife, wrapped her arms around my neck, and in a swift motion had her mouth against mine and her tongue probing. She tasted wonderful, and I lost all resistance as she continued to kiss me. Finally, I did break away sufficiently to say, "Natasha, I'm not sure we're ready for a romantic relationship. I was with someone until very recently, and I still have strong feelings for her."

She pulled back. "I have been curious about the companion you brought with you to Moscow," she said, returning to her cake cutting after calming down somewhat.

"She left Moscow last Sunday and probably won't return," I said. "But she's still on my mind."

"Maybe, as you say, any romantic involvement may be too soon, so I will be patient. Do you think she is not returning?"

"I'm not sure, but let's not discuss it," I said. "I've had a wonderful evening with you and welcome our continuing relationship. But let's keep it professional and related to Pharmascent if that's your true interest."

"Definitely," she said, but she looked dejected. "I will join you at the EMC when you invite me."

I then ordered a car to return me to my apartment, which only took about fifteen minutes to arrive. Natasha walked me to the door and started to kiss my cheeks, but I interrupted and kissed her lips, probably longer than I should have. She smiled and again hugged me good night.

In the car going home, I reflected on how much I had enjoyed Natasha's company, despite moments of concern about her real intentions and forwardness — not helped by my own weakness, I had to admit. But beyond her personal attractions, her information about the composition of the research group in Oryol interested me, and I couldn't wait to discuss it with my CIA handlers.

When I got to my apartment, I sent a coded email to Brad in Washington, telling him I needed a meeting as soon as possible, then suggesting that we talk tomorrow, Saturday afternoon. Since I had an ongoing correspondence with "my friend Brad" back in the U.S., we believed no one monitoring my emails would be suspicious, even if the encryption was not effective.

About an hour later, I received a pickup confirmation at 5 p.m. downtown, which really meant 1:00 p.m. tomorrow at the JCC. I could innocently attend Sabbath services and then take a ride with Caruthers and/or Dubrovnik.

62.

I ARRIVED AT the JCC at 9:30 a.m. when the service had already begun. I noticed the social events leader, Laya Springer, sitting in a row by herself, so I went to join her, since I also saw men and women sitting together, contrary to an orthodox service.

Laya was surprised and greeted me with a "Guten Shabbos," which meant good Sabbath in Yiddish. We shook hands, and I checked the page she was on in the prayer book, which was in Hebrew. Fortunately, I remembered enough Hebrew to be able to follow the prayers, although I was clearly not as fluent as the others. When I asked her about the seating of men and women together, she explained that they make this exception, upon request, for certain celebration services, such as Bar Mitzvahs, and with two synagogues, they use one for orthodox services and the other for more liberal prayer events. I had no idea that this could be done, but who was I, a twice-yearly synagogue attendee, to question this?

My presence at the service was noted; the rabbi conducting the service calling me up by my English name, Milton Davidson, to say a prayer for reading from the Torah, or Pentateuch. I gave him my Hebrew name, *Michel ben Levi*, just before I chanted the prayer. I knew this was an honor, and I was congratulated by handshakes, even from strangers, as I returned to my seat. Laya was all smiles, also congratulating me with a "Mazel Tov."

After the service, the congregation retired to the adjoining room to say a prayer for the ceremonial bread (*challah*) and wine. There was a table laid out with cakes, herring, vegetables, and small stuffed cabbage pieces, as well as sliced fruits. I filled my plate but didn't get a chance to eat because many of the congregants came over to introduce themselves. It was a mixed group, with a large number of senior citizens, a few teenagers and very few smaller kids, as well as many adults, mostly men, of all ages. I had estimated some sixty congregants at the service, and now almost all were mingling in this reception room. Even the rabbi and cantor came over to welcome me, speaking English quite well, saying they'd heard of my attendance at the JCC and that they hoped I enjoyed the service. These interactions were helped along by Laya standing next to me and prompting me whenever — which is to say, often — when I had a language problem.

Finally, I had to break away and go outside to meet my handlers. At first, I didn't see the usual black limousine because it wasn't in front of the JCC, but instead was parked down the street, on the opposite side.

I took a seat in the back, next to Marcia, while John Caruthers drove. I immediately told them about my dinner conversation with Natasha the night before, saying that she had offered to help me with Pharmascent, to which I hadn't committed, although I had offered to have her join me in my protocol discussions at the EMC. I recounted our discussion regarding Katarina and how Natasha had immediately recognized that I was interested in Katarina's brother at Oryol, whose research facility was administratively one of Natasha's lab programs, although she claimed not to know anything about their actual research, beyond it involving odors.

"But she did reveal that their research staff has more computer and internet techs than chemists," I said. "She didn't offer any explanation for that, and in fact, would only talk about such matters on her balcony, with music playing in her apartment and piped outside."

"That's very interesting," said Marcia. "Our inside information tells us they're conducting olfaction research for military purposes at Oryol. If that's true, how do the internet techs fit in?"

"That's why I asked for this meeting," I said. "Something's not right, unless —"

"Unless what?" asked John.

"I couldn't sleep when I returned home last night, since I remembered reading about a project in Japan and France involving sending chemical compositions via the internet — these people were using special receivers at the remote sites to create odors from these formulas. I wonder if this is related in some way. There's research involving the development of electronic noses for smell, using artificial intelligence. Maybe the Russian scientists in Oryol are advancing the messaging of smells via the internet, so that odors can be sent to a recipient who has a compatible computer for electronic smell receptors?"

"But why would this be critical for the Russians to develop?" Marcia asked.

"We know that there are lethal odors and mind-controlling odors, and I'm working on pharmaceutical odors," I said. "Imagine if you could deliver these remotely to an expecting or, more importantly, an unsuspecting recipient — or even to a group that you want to target, such as leaders of government or industry."

"You mean," said John, "they could poison someone remotely by sending a chemical via the internet?"

"Sounds like science fiction," I said, "but it does make sense. Odors are nothing more than chemicals sensed by our olfactory receptors and also transmitted to the brain and probably also other organs via the capillaries in the nose. So, if we can transmit a chemical that can become volatile and sensed by the olfactory or chemical receptors, it would constitute remote or digital olfaction. I need to do an internet search for the *Digital Olfaction Society*, which I learned was formed in about 2012 and has annual meetings. Maybe I can learn something from their presentations."

"Well, this would explain why our computer scientists are perplexed by the messages they're detecting from the Oryol computers," Marcia said. "They can't interpret them and thought protective walls were in place against our hacking. Maybe they were detecting the odor messaging being sent?"

"This certainly needs exploring," I said. "Just imagine if you wanted to control someone's thoughts or get information from them remotely — or if there was an assassination planned that could be done remotely and be undetectable. Imagine if you can interfere or take this over by hacking remotely!" I exclaimed.

"This would explain why we learned about their psychedelic olfaction efforts," said Marcia. "They distracted us from the real mission of developing digital olfaction transmission. We need to report this back to Langley right away."

"And what about Natasha, Milt?" asked John. "What are your plans for her? Do you trust her, or is she a Russian agent trying to discover or mislead your mission?"

"She is a puzzle to me," I said. "I want to believe her, but is it my vanity making me think she's coming on to me, or does she really want to join my research? I feel I need more time with her — because of Natasha, we've learned a lot about what's probably going on at Oryol. I guess your mole there — Aleksei, correct? — knew about the olfactory research as part of a military effort, but isn't a scientist and, therefore, was probably unaware of any details of their ultimate mission."

Marcia agreed that I should foster my relationship with Natasha, who possibly could play a role with Pharmascent and even become a CIA double agent if she truly has concerns about Russia and her allegiances.

"But tread cautiously," Marcia said. "She could be an agent of the FSB while also serving as a Deputy Minister of the Federal Agency for Scientific Organizations. This position gives her access to virtually all medical and biological research organizations and laboratories in Russia, which could be of great value to us."

After a pause, she said: "At a minimum, she might be turned as an asset."

"If this digital olfaction project is real, Milt, and if you've concluded that from your discussion with Dr. Natasha Petrushkin, both of you may be in danger," John added.

I got out of the limo about two blocks from my apartment building and made it back home without being noticed, I thought. It was 3:30 p.m., and I planned to stay in for the rest of the day. I wanted to use that time to search the internet for any other articles on digital olfaction.

63.

I WAS WIDE awake at 6 a.m. the next morning, no doubt because I'd been obsessing about Marie, Natasha, the work at Oryol, the secrecy about Mrs. Breslau, and how long I would need to stay in Moscow if my suspicions about the digital olfaction research were correct.

Once we confirm this, my role in Moscow really ends.

Then I remembered I had both an interest in and a commitment to completing the clinical study with melatonin.

But it's not a big study and probably can be completed in a couple of months.

It was obvious that I missed being in New York and doing my own laboratory cancer research at ESU, despite the excitement of becoming adjusted to living in Russia. Although I feared some of the intrigue, it was arousing, certainly stimulating my adrenalin. And then there was Natasha — could I really resist her romantic overtures?

Thinking about Natasha made me think about Marie. Where is she? What happened to her? Suddenly an idea came to me: Marie spent her early childhood in the Soviet Union, specifically Belarus, before her family emigrated to Israel. Maybe there's a file on her and her family in Belarus or elsewhere in the former Soviet Union, and if there is, maybe it would give me a sense of the Russian perspective on Marie. This was a long shot, but I wondered if Natasha could help find such a file. I decided I would use this as a test to see how much she could — and wanted — to help me.

I texted Natasha and asked if she would like to meet in the late afternoon or early evening. She wrote back quickly: "How nice of you to ask. Why don't we meet at 5 p.m. and then have an early dinner? Where shall we meet?"

"Let's meet in front of the Bolshoi Theatre," I suggested. "It's easy for us both to travel to the Metro station there, and it would be nice to walk around the square and then have dinner there."

I'm hoping to keep her on neutral ground for both our sakes.

This worked out well, since it gave me time to get additional work done on improving the protocol. I also reread it and decided, after making some redactions, to send the latest draft to Natasha, indicating that this was still in development and should be kept confidential. She responded that she was glad that I'd shared this with her and promised to read it before our 5 p.m. date.

Am I really seriously asking a Deputy Minister in the Russian Duma to keep my protocol confidential?

*

IT WAS DARK at five o'clock, and the Bolshoi lights made the square look festive. Natasha was dressed for an evening date, wearing a long, tight red dress under her Persian lamb fur coat and with her hair in a ponytail with a gold clasp. She wore a matching lamb fur hat, mid-size red heels, and black sheer stockings. I actually miscalculated, since I didn't dress up for the evening, thinking we would simply find a nice small restaurant somewhere.

Natasha threw her arms around my neck and kissed me on the cheeks and then on my lips. I was surprised, since she'd said we needed to keep our relationship private. Kissing in front of the Bolshoi Theatre, on a square with hundreds of sightseers, was arguably the exact opposite.

"I was so happy to hear from you today," she said, slipping her arm in mine as we began walking. "So glad you wanted to meet me today."

"Well, you've been on my mind since our dinner together, and I wanted to clarify some things," I said. "But first things first — do you have any questions on the protocol I sent you?"

"I must admit it is above me — I was just glad to be able to read it," she said. "But I am curious about what you plan to do with melatonin if, in fact, you find its olfactory form is effective in changing behavior."

"I think there could be other medical indications for this agent, such as treating neurodegenerative diseases, but probably in combination with other proven drugs. My initial focus is Parkinson's disease, where a rapid-working agent may be needed between conventional doses of standard therapy. But it all depends on my proving that the olfactory compound is rapidly absorbed and has direct effects on the brain, which is the goal of this first protocol."

"It sounds reasonable to me, but what do Professor Koussevitzky and his colleagues think?"

"So far, they're interested and willing to collaborate, but I do need to meet with the doctors running the sleep clinic at the EMC. I hope to visit with them this week."

"Thank you for including me," she said. "I would love to learn more and be of help. Now, what's on your mind?"

"I'm confused and need to ask for your understanding. I am very excited about getting to know you. I'm, of course, attracted to you physically as well as emotionally, and I'm sure I'm not the first man to express this. But I believe I am in love with the woman who came to Moscow with me, and she has now disappeared after returning to her home in Paris. I need to bring this to some resolution before our relationship gets more serious. Do you understand?"

Natasha stopped walking and turned to face me. "What, Milt, do you want me to do?"

"Maybe you can help me learn more about her or why she disappeared. She was born in the Soviet Union, in Belarus, but emigrated as a Jewish refugee with her family to Israel more than twenty years ago. I'm thinking that maybe the Russian immigration office or even some security agency may have access to a file on her and her family, or maybe even more recent information, since she has come here from France on business trips. There must be a file related to her Russian business visa."

It's a risk that if any file shows her to be a foreign agent, I'll be implicated.

"What is her name?" Natasha asked.

"Marie Chalfont, which doesn't seem like a Russian name, so I don't know if the family took on a French name when they emigrated later from Israel to France. Marie is employed by the Parisian perfume company, Toilette, and travels frequently for work throughout eastern Europe because of her knowledge of Slavic languages."

"I really do not know if I can be of help," said Natasha, "and it is, of course, risky for me to make inquiries about foreign nationals, however discreet, unless I have a clear reason related to my work. But I will try to see if there is any file on her. I guess she received a visa to visit Russia on business. Whether I can get any information from Belarus is doubtful."

"Thank you so much, Natasha, but don't take any risks. I could have been wrong about her, and she may have had to disappear for reasons I don't understand. Maybe she was in some way involved with illicit activities and not perfumes. Maybe drug trading. I just don't know."

"Give me a few days," said Natasha. "I will confer with some friends in the visa office and maybe even someone I know in the FSB."

When I heard FSB, I was both pleased and worried — pleased that Natasha might, in fact, have good government police contacts, yet worried that this inquiry could get out of control and lead to my being incriminated through a relationship with Marie. But I thought it was better than waiting to hear something from the CIA or the French intelligence agency, or from Interpol. Marie had been missing a week already, and I didn't even know if she were dead or alive.

And I got no help from the Mossad.

We were getting cold after walking for about a half-hour, so we found a café on the main street and went in to look at the menu. It had both Russian and Italian food, so we decided on pizza with Chianti wine. It was just the right amount of food and a welcome change from the heavy Russian meals I'd been eating. I could tell Natasha enjoyed it too.

"Do you want to come home with me?" she asked as we were finishing our pizza.

"Not tonight," I said, "but I would like to have what we call a 'rain check' — another invitation when my mind isn't so consumed with problems."

Natasha said she understood, and we walked back to the Metro station together, kissed each other goodbye, and then took our different trains home. On the way, I checked my messages and saw that Yuri wanted to meet with me sometime next week.

Wonder what that's about.

*

THE NEXT MORNING, I went to the JCC for my regular workout and Russian lesson. Miriam seemed a little nervous when I got there, but the lesson went well, but she signaled it was safe to talk. I asked her if everything was alright.

"You are very observant," she said. "A good friend of mine has been diagnosed with prostate cancer, which is a shock to him and me. He has to go through much testing before a therapy is chosen, and I am, of course, very worried."

"I'm sorry to hear about your friend," I said, "but this is usually a manageable cancer. If it hasn't spread elsewhere, there's a very good prognosis. So, wait to see what the diagnostic tests show in terms of extent of the disease, whether it is restricted to the prostate. And, Miriam, please don't hesitate to ask me if you have any questions."

"Thank you so much," she said. "I will come back to you once we know more. Everything in life seems in order and manageable, and then, all of a sudden, something happens that we cannot control."

Exactly the dilemma I'm in about Marie.

I was able to get to my office a little after 11 a.m. and was glad to see Julia and her usual good cheer. There were a few messages, though no urgent matters. I did, however, receive an extended email from my pathology chairman at ESU, Dr. John Bickers:

> Milt, I hope all is well with you. I am sorry we have not communicated earlier, but I am delighted with your provocative publication in *Cancer Advances*. But over the past few weeks, it seems that there is a growing mutiny in the department among some of the faculty, evidently unhappy with my leadership and claiming that the department does not get its fair share in support and positions from the medical school.
>
> I feel this is a challenge that needs to be addressed by either the disgruntled staff coming to an understanding or leaving, or by my stepping down as chairman. After serving as chairman for twelve years, with an additional three due in my term, I am willing to resume a role as a full-time professor without this administration if this is best for the department, but I am not convinced that the criticisms are justified or that a new chairman is the solution.
>
> My writing is to ask if you may be able to return for a few days so you can participate at the faculty meeting that I am planning to hold.

Although I knew there was dissatisfaction by some in the department, I had no idea it had risen to this level. I felt a loyalty to Dr. Bickers, who had recruited me and who supported me and my research from day one. I immediately wrote back: "I'm sorry to hear this, John, but of course I will return when you need me. When do you think this should be? Returning this week is a problem, since I am trying to get a project started, but I can try to return in a week or two. Please advise."

John responded that the following week or later would suffice. I should just let him know my plans, and he would schedule a meeting of the entire pathology faculty accordingly. "In the meantime," he said, "I am going to discuss this with one of the associate deans of the medical school."

Now, it became quite serious.

I was pleased at the prospect of returning to New York soon, not only because I needed a little break from Moscow and spying, but also because I wanted to reassess my activities and plans. I could also meet with Brad Williams and possibly also the Argus Laboratories staff, as well as Dr. Calhoun and his associates at the CIA's olfaction laboratory. Now that this digital olfaction issue had arisen, I knew that the Langley group would want an intensive face-to-face meeting and discussion.

I texted Brad that I would likely be returning to New York in the next couple of weeks, giving me a chance to discuss some recent developments with him and his associates. Marcia and John at the embassy had probably already informed him about the possible digital olfaction program being pursued by the Russian military.

Yuri also responded to my earlier email that he could pick me up at noon on Wednesday, preferably at my office building, so we could go out for lunch. I agreed and put it on my calendar.

I then confirmed with Sergeii that I would join him on Tuesday at 1:00 p.m. at the EMC if he could arrange for us a meeting with the physicians running the sleep center. I also said that there was a possibility, if he didn't object, that Dr. Natasha Petrushkin, Deputy

Minister of the Federal Agency for Scientific Organizations, would join us.

Sergeii responded he would make the arrangements and that he knew of Dr. Petrushkin. "It is impressive that you have garnered her interest," he said, "since she very much influences budgets for most medical programs affiliated with the Russian Academy of Sciences, including the Russian Academy of Medicine, with which the EMC is affiliated."

I then asked Julia to check flights back to JFK airport next week, preferably on Monday and Tuesday, with a U.S. carrier. I felt safer than being on Aeroflot. Julia asked when I planned to return. I said I didn't know yet, but probably a week or so later.

Before the day ended, Natasha sent me a text asking how I was doing. I said it was a busy day, but I did confirm our meeting at the EMC tomorrow at one o'clock and that she was expected to participate.

"Thank you so much, Milt," she wrote back. "I will clear my calendar for tomorrow afternoon and will meet you there, in Professor Koussevitzky's office."

She also said: "I am working on that special request you made and hopefully can update you somewhat tomorrow. Should I keep dinner free?"

She certainly was persistent, which pleased my ego. I agreed that we should go out for dinner, but she insisted that we eat at her place — "If you will be satisfied with a simple meal."

I was pleased to accept and said we could also bring in food, so she didn't have to bother in the kitchen. She refused and said she wanted me to feel indebted for her feeding me, so I just said thanks and added a smiley-face emoji.

It's amazing how a charming woman showing an interest in you can have such an effect on your mood.

64.

WHEN I EMPTIED my mailbox after arriving at my apartment building, I was surprised to see, among the usual Russian ads and promotions, a postcard having the picture of a beach indicated as Saint Martin in the Dutch West Indies. It looked very attractive, in front of a small hotel with many balconies. The postcard was addressed to me as 'Dr. Milt Davidson,' and the handwriting almost doubled my heart beats – clearly Marie's penmanship, certainly intended for me by a confident, since it addressed me as Milt and not Milton. But nothing else was written except the hotel's advertisement and toll-free number, promoting discount rates for renting rooms during the next month.

Clearly, this was Marie's way of contacting, since no foreign promotions would likely have my personal address in Moscow or know me as 'Milt.'

She's alive and wants me to know where to find her, but she is being very cautious in sending just a postcard, which would unlikely raise suspicion unless the reader knew her writing.

But what do I do; how can I drop everything and fly to St. Martin?

Since I was to travel to New York in the next week or so, I could fly directly from New York, returning through Paris and then back to Moscow. But making a visit to Simon Fass, Marie's employer in Paris, would also enable me to make a short, secret trip to St. Martin, if I can rely on him keeping this confidential.

Yes, I'll revise my travel plans to visit Marie in St. Martin, but I have to give more thought to how I can do this without my CEA handler or the Mossad being aware. Maybe the Mossad was involved in Marie's disappearance?

ACKNOWLEDGMENTS

AT THE END of a challenging and rewarding career in academic medicine as a physician-scientist researching various aspects of cancer, including serving on the faculties of five medical schools, founding two cancer centers and two biopharmaceutical companies, what made me embark on writing a novel on science and espionage? And can I define it as my own different, literary genre?

The science I relate is mostly from my own research or work of current interest by others. The plot of becoming an entrepreneur is based on my own experience founding Immunomedics, Inc., and making it a publicly-traded company until it was acquired after developing a new therapeutic for a very aggressive breast cancer, and potentially many other very malignant cancers.

But the espionage and romance stories are my alter-ego fantasies. I hope my grandchildren are not too embarrassed with the romance scenes. With these confessions, I also have to admit that my credentials in spying are, fortunately, not first-hand. I am grateful to Wikipedia as a research source.

Whereas everything contained in my story is fictional, even with the inclusion of living politicians, I tried making it as realistic as possible. Olfaction is the most neglected of our five senses, yet it is governed by the most genes, and has been a very prominent, primordial sense from an evolutionary standpoint. It became the subject of my Sc.D.-thesis in natural sciences, where I owe a great debt to my late thesis advisor, Professor Walter Neuhaus, Ph.D. Olfaction is historically the dominant sense of vertebrates and mammals as they adjust to their environment and species. I envision that defined odors will gain a role in medicine, particularly influencing neural functions, and certainly should go beyond their current uses in our daily pleasures by affecting conscious and unconscious behavior.

This is my debut work of fiction, inspiring me to let my protagonist, Milton Davidson, M.D., Ph.D., continue his adventures in science and espionage in other sequels of the Milt Davidson series related to the *Scenturion Venture*. But I appreciate that the first impression is the most critical, so I hope that this book building the story of Milt and his plots will serve as the basis of what will be a continuing relationship for the reader with him and with me.

Although many friends and relatives have helped and encouraged me, none can be held responsible for any errors. In fact, I was usually elated when I could find someone, even one of my children, to read it and some of the sequels, from beginning to end. In this regard, a special thanks to my firstborn, Eva, who was my strongest supporter, impatient to get to the next part of the story and the next book in the series, while she did considerable proofreading. She introduced me to Israel and David Ben-Gurion's kibbutz, Sde Boker, in the Negev, where I visited with her during her Hadassah year-course in 1979, after announcing to her parents that she found her 'love' there. But we did get her home to commence her studies at the University of Chicago, my *alma mater*.

My writing time was protected by my other daughter, Deborah, and her husband Brett, who are my personal advisors as I retired from leading a biopharmaceutical company that I established already in 1982, while I continued my academic activities. My other children, Denis, Neil, and Lee, also provided me with their encouragement and support. In addition, Denis found additional edits needed after we thought the text was final, while Neil contributed his writing skills to editing the back cover. I am pleased that this was truly a family enterprise.

The original draft of this book was much too long, reflecting my inexperience as a new writer of fiction. Fortunately, I had the assistance of gifted editors, James Morgan, Eric Muhr, Carolyn Roark, and Wayne Purdin, who helped me condense and improve the text.

Angela Hoy and her efficient staff at BookLocker made it easy to publish this with minimal inconvenience. I especially appreciate Todd Engel's patience and talent in developing the book cover.

My sincere gratitude to my first wife, Hildegard, the mother of my six children, and to their spouses, and of course our 12 grandchildren (10 boys and 2 girls), who always bring us down to reality and give us much to appreciate and worry about. Hildegard was my partner in the critical years of my professional development.

Finally, my wife Cynthia, who was my partner at Immunomedics, is an avid reader of novels and was critical of my story. She undertook two final editorial reviews and proofreading. I am particularly grateful to her for contributing two children, Jill and Steven, and their spouses and children, as a second family for me to nurture and enjoy. Cindy tolerated my mood swings and erratic sleep, since it was in this less-conscious state that I enjoyed weaving much of the plot and characters. She has been my closest friend and love.

Ingram Content Group UK Ltd.
Milton Keynes UK
UKHW011935170523
421912UK00002B/147